UNDER PRESSURE

ABIGAIL REED

FORGE®

A TOM DOHERTY ASSOCIATES BOOK
NEW YORK

This is a work of fiction. All the characters and events portrayed in this book are either products of the author's imagination or are used fictitiously.

UNDER PRESSURE

Copyright © 2000 by Abigail Reed

A Forge Book
Published by Tom Doherty Associates, LLC
175 Fifth Avenue
New York, NY 10010

www.tor.com

Forge® is a registered trademark of Tom Doherty Associates, LLC.

ISBN: 0-812-53928-1

First edition: July 2000

Printed in the United States of America

0 9 8 7 6 5 4 3 2 1

ACKNOWLEDGMENTS

I WOULD LIKE TO THANK MY EDITOR, MELISSA ANN Singer, for her cogent ideas and input, which helped to make this book so much better. My literary agent, Cherry Weiner, also gave feedback and encouragement when most needed—thanks, Cherry! Also deserving of my grateful thanks are the courageous women who told me about their own on-the-job experiences. They will remain anonymous, but their input is nonetheless appreciated deeply. Thanks also to Beth de Baptiste of the Oakland County Prosecuting Attorney's office for her legal advice.

In researching this book, I consulted an excellent book, *Sexual Harassment on the Job: What It Is and How to Stop It*, by attorneys William Petrocelli and Barbara Kate Repa. It is published by Nolo Press. This book takes the reader through the entire spectrum of sexual harassment, from background, causes and effects, to workplace policies and filing a lawsuit. It is "must" reading for any woman who thinks she's being sexually harassed on the job. Another very helpful book is *Back Off! How to Confront and Stop*

Sexual Harassment and Harassers, published by Simon & Schuster, which tells women how to halt sexual harassment both on and off the job.

The characters in this book—and the department store called Cybelle—are fictional and are not intended to depict any real-life corporation or individuals. Legal cases mentioned in the book are actual cases filed in a court of law, but names have been omitted to protect the privacy of individuals involved.

ONE

By the time Karyn Cristophe stepped out of the shower, the bathroom was clouded with steam, water droplets running down the vanity mirror. She could see herself grinning happily as she picked up a washcloth and wiped circles in the steam.

In less than forty minutes she'd be sitting at a computer terminal, starting her new job. A fresh beginning with everything lying ahead of her, and this time there was no way that Mack, her erratic ex-husband, could show up at her place of employment and spoil things.

Her stomach churning with pleasurable excitement, Karyn combed out her damp blond hair, reaching for the blow-dryer and brush. The job, at the international headquarters of the upscale Cybelle department store chain, was only temp-to-perm right now, but there was every chance it would work out.

Oh, it had to work out! She'd finally taken control of her life, pulling up stakes and moving nine hundred miles from Atlanta on the promise of this job, which her Aunt Connie, who owned two employment agencies in the Detroit area, had snagged for her.

"Mom . . . Mom . . ." She could hear her eight-year-old daughter, Amber, banging on the other side of the bathroom door.

"What is it, cupcake? I'm running late."

"Can I wear my Pocahontas T-shirt?"

"Of course you can. Don't you always pick out your own clothes?" Karyn poked her head around the corner of the bathroom door, gazing at her daughter, whose mop of blond hair just about dwarfed her thin, intense face.

"I can't find it," wailed Amber. "It's probably still in one of those boxes."

"It wasn't in your suitcase?"

"I think I threw it in a box. I don't know," said Amber, crestfallen. "It was in the dirty clothes, I think. Back in Atlanta."

"Oh, honey." Karyn sighed in frustration. "Well, maybe you'd better find another shirt to wear and we'll look for it tonight when I get home. You're staying at the Caribaldis', remember?"

She'd registered Amber for school the previous Wednesday, the day they arrived from Atlanta, and Amber had already attended for two days. Thank God for the Caribaldis, who lived upstairs. Jinny Caribaldi, who was divorced and worked nights as a cardiac care nurse, had agreed to "latchkey" Amber after school until five-thirty. Even better, Jinny had a daughter, Caitlin, who was exactly Amber's age, a stroke of fortune Karyn hadn't counted on.

"Are we really staying here?" queried Amber now. "I mean *here*. Forever?"

"Maybe not forever, but for a long time," replied Karyn with enthusiasm. "Honey lamb, it's been amazing luck, Aunt Connie getting me this job. You're going to have new friends at school . . . maybe we can even get a cat."

"A kitty cat? Oh, Mom!"

"If it works out—and now I really have to fly." Karyn hurried into her bedroom and began cutting off the tags from the new suit she'd bought at Cybelle during the Labor Day weekend sale. It was a Gemi suit, leaf green and cut narrow at the waist, with a long, sexy back slit, and it had cost her $450 from the cash stash she'd borrowed from her dad for their freedom money. But Karyn figured she had to impress them on her first day.

She stepped into the skirt, shrugged into the little matching silk shell, and quickly buttoned the jacket.

In the mirror, she inspected herself. *Nice.*

Her last act was to slip a pair of small pearl stud earrings into her ears. She'd been wearing them two years ago when she'd won $1,544 in the lottery, and she hoped they would lend their glow of good luck today as well.

When she emerged into the apartment's small dining room, Karyn found her daughter hunched over a bowl of cereal, a full glass of orange juice at her elbow.

"Come on, Amber, drink up, we have to get ourselves in gear."

Languidly, Amber picked up the glass. "Will you type at a computer all day?"

"Probably. And I'm going to love it."

"You'll be too busy to call," Amber pouted.

"Oh, no, I won't. I'll program a reminder right in my computer—'Call Amber Sweetpea Cristophe right away.' Finish your juice, baby," she added.

"I hate plain orange. Can't we get the kind with banana in it?"

"If you'll drink it." Karyn paced impatiently, suddenly anxious to get started—to get those first few hours on the job over with. "Down the hatch," she told her daughter. "Jinny's taking you and Caitlin to school in exactly two minutes. We both have busy days ahead of us."

Karyn gulped at a container of 7-Eleven coffee, trying not to spill anything on her new suit jacket as she maneuvered her 1994 Ford Tempo into the long double line of cars waiting to turn right into the Cybelle International Headquarters parking lot. Aunt Connie had warned Karyn that if she didn't arrive at least ten minutes early all the parking spaces would be taken, and now Karyn could see that the warning had been no exaggeration. In fact, where *were* all the cars going to be slotted?

In the morning sun haze, the huge office complex glowed, its acres of tinted windows catching the yellow light. Made mostly of glass, it covered an entire city block. Connie had told her that five thousand people toiled there, bee workers tending to the corporate business of thirteen hundred department stores spread from Bar Harbor, Maine, to Honolulu, Hawaii. Cybelle was often compared to Lord & Taylor or Nordstrom's, and to most American women it meant accessible glamour.

The lot was a sea of cars, the biggest parking lot she had ever seen, bisected by yellow-painted pedestrian walkways. Hundreds of workers on foot streamed toward the building. As a group of women walked past her front bumper, Karyn began to study how they were dressed: skirts, slacks, dressy pants outfits she'd seen in Cybelle's Casual Career Shop. Many of the women wore tennis shoes and lugged canvas tote bags, which presumably contained their office shoes.

About thirty yards away a man was cutting across the lot, not bothering to stay on the pedestrian walk. He was built like Mack, all knees and stride and angles, and had the same black hair that fell loosely across his forehead. Karyn's eyes focused on him, angry heat pouring up from her stomach.

Her ex-husband's humiliating appearances and barrages of unwanted phone calls at her job at a computer leasing firm in Atlanta had resulted in several reprimands, and finally the company had installed a new security system—on account of her. Eventually her boss had let her know he'd really prefer it if she quit. A company couldn't be too careful about security risks. . . .

Then Karyn saw that the man was two decades older than Mack and thirty pounds heavier. An involuntary sigh of relief puffed out of her. Although the divorce decree specified that Mack had to stay at least four hundred yards away from her and Amber or he'd be in contempt of court, Karyn still worried he might somehow show up and start causing trouble again.

She finally found a parking space in the next-to-last row, pulling in beside a van sporting a bumper sticker that said

My Child Is on the Honor Roll at Beaconsfield Elementary.

Even in the few seconds since she'd switched off the ignition, the Tempo was warming up in the early September heat. Karyn gave herself a quick inspection in the visor mirror, deciding that the blow-dry and curl she'd done on her chin-length, honey-blond hair was good enough to pass muster. Several people had told Karyn she should model, but of course she was already twenty-nine, much too old for that now. Not that she'd ever want that kind of lifestyle. Karyn knew she wasn't sophisticated, and she had little desire to be.

Karyn got out of the car, joining the throngs of workers streaming toward the building. Seen up close the sprawling building was even huger-looking, its windows molten under the onslaught of morning sun.

Exhilaration spurted through Karyn, and she began to walk faster, swinging her arms. Her high heels made clacking noises on the pavement. Her first day of work. And the beginning of their new life.

Lou Hechter had noticed the blonde in the Ford Tempo right away; she had to be new because he would certainly have remembered those high cheekbones and that full, curvy mouth. And he knew damn well *she'd* noticed *him.* Even from yards away he had felt her eyes riveted on him. It was as if she couldn't look away.

Lou continued toward the headquarters building, straightening his shoulders and pulling in his stomach. He looked pretty damn good for fifty-one, all the women told him so. And not "distinguished," either, that kiss-of-death word that Lou had always loathed—along with the damning phrase "silver fox."

His black hair had only a few threads of gray in it, artfully left there by Dori, his stylist, so it wouldn't look like he dyed his hair. She even trimmed Lou's eyebrows, which, left to their own devices, would look like Einstein's. Lou paid Dori big bucks to keep him looking ten, fifteen years younger than his age.

And why shouldn't he? He was Lou Hechter, a vice president and company maverick who had been written up in the *Detroit News* and *Detroit Free Press,* plus all the trades, for the creative, innovative ideas he'd brought to Cybelle.

But this new lady, whoever she was, interested him. Even though the company had several thousand female employees, Lou knew a surprising number by sight, especially the good-looking ones. Was there a possibility this one was the new secretary in his own department, Fashion? Cilla had told him she hired someone from an employment agency, a woman who could type over one hundred words a minute.

He decided that if the new secretary was the blonde he'd send her a rose in a bud vase.

Reaching the entrance door marked "#2," Lou bounded lightly up the eight cement steps, pausing at the row of newspaper boxes positioned just inside the entrance to buy himself a copy of the *Detroit Free Press. Women's Wear Daily* and the *Wall Street Journal* were hand-delivered to his desk every day. Automatically he glanced at the chalkboard on the wall. Cybelle stock on the NYSE had closed three quarters of a point higher, which was great for Lou's portfolio. He and his wife, Marty, owned over twelve thousand shares of Cybelle blue-chip stocks, accumulated in the company's stock option program. As long as you owned Cybelle, you couldn't go wrong.

"Good morning, Mr. Hechter," said Cherise Souza, an African-American security guard, who stood in the doorway, glancing perfunctorily at the incoming workers' blue employee cards. During her first week of work she'd made the mistake of actually asking to look at Lou's card. He'd set her straight, though.

"Hi, Cherise, hon," said Lou, favoring her with one of his big smiles.

He walked on past, feeling his usual jolt of adrenaline as
he entered the big office complex that seemed like a hive
to him, jumping and humming with life. His kingdom—
yeah, Lou would rather be here than anyplace else on earth.

In Human Resources, Karyn filled out a series of papers—
an IRS form for her payroll deductions, another employment
application form, a form stating her next of kin in case there
was an accident.

She wrote down her father's name, Ed Cristophe, and her
parents' address in Norwalk, Connecticut. She could have
moved to Connecticut, she knew; in fact, her parents had
begged her to do so, assuring her there were good jobs in
the area. Or she could even commute into New York City
on the train.

She hadn't wanted to do that. In the first place, Mack
knew where her parents lived, and what if he decided to get
in his car and drive to Connecticut, resume his harassment
of her? Not that he'd ever been dangerous. It was more like
obsessive, phoning her eighteen to forty-five times a day on
the job, leaving dozens of voice-mail messages, driving past
her office building over and over again, for hours.

Mack needed psychological help, and she'd finally convinced him to see a therapist, but she didn't dare trust him
yet—not when it was *her* job at stake. Which was why she'd
decided to move far out of Mack's orbit, plus getting a restraining order against him.

She concentrated on the last paper, which was a form
stating that her job was "temp-to-perm," that she would be
paid through People Resources, her aunt's agency, that Cybelle *could* but was not obligated to hire her after her ninety-
day probation was up.

"But this temp-to-perm business is only a formality,"
Connie had assured Karyn. "Honey, your skills are top-
drawer, you're great at Microsoft Word, and you've got
heavy experience in Power Point. And if you type a hundred

words per minute, well, you can do the work of a secretary and a half. Temping is the only way you can get in most big companies nowadays. They want to try out the merchandise before they buy."

"Are you finished, dear?" asked an older woman, coming into the room now.

Karyn nodded and handed her the papers. The HR assistant shuffled through them. "Good . . . good. Well, I'll call Cilla Westheim's office and tell them you're on your way over. Oh, is that a Gemi suit you're wearing?"

Karyn smiled. "Yes, I bought it on sale."

"Well, here's a map. You're going to get lost a lot at first, everyone does, but eventually you'll get the hang of things. Oh, yes, and here's an employee booklet. It gives all the information on the dress code, company regulations, sexual harassment and so forth."

Leaving the Human Resources office, Karyn glanced down at the photocopied map of the building. It *was* confusing, a honeycomb maze of squares intersected by crisscrossing corridors on three levels, except for the five-story Executive Tower.

Karyn had loved to window-shop at the Cybelle store near Peachtree Street and Ponce de Leon Avenue in Atlanta, coveting the designer clothes and designer knockoffs that were always so tempting. She'd blown a few paychecks on special dresses that she still treasured.

Now she was at the company headquarters. The building seemed glamorous to her, its gray marble floors elegantly veined with pink. There were displays of framed fashion sketches that dated back to the 1950s, when a Frenchman named Roland LaRivière had opened the first store in Chicago, naming it after his wife, Cybelle. The Chanel suits and evening gowns by Patou, Yves St. Laurent and the house of Dior were still eye-catching.

Hallways forked, then forked again. Karyn wandered past offices, hundreds of them lining every outside wall of the building. Some had views of inner courtyards with fountains and landscaping; others looked out onto the street. Huge center areas were filled with shoulder-high work cubicles. Secretaries, she noticed, usually seemed to have their desks set inside alcoves in the hallways.

At last she came upon a brass sign with the words FASH-ION DEPARTMENT etched in script lettering. Two hallway desks were positioned in paneled alcoves, one of them empty, the other one occupied by a woman with tawny skin and impish, dark eyes. A sign on her desk said RAQUEL ESTRADA.

"Is this the Fashion Department?"

"Yes—you must be Karyn, right?" When Raquel stood up, she was only about five feet tall, and this was in three-inch heels. "So how many times did you get lost finding this place? I keep telling HR that their map sucks, but nobody ever does anything about it. Well, you picked a great day to start here. Lou—he's my boss and your ultimate boss—has four meetings. Plus we have a big buyers' meeting coming up and we have about fifty phone calls to make on that. Oh, and Cilla is late again. She's the one you work for."

"Cilla Westheim?"

"Yeah, she's never in before eight forty-five so she always has to park in the back forty. So she rushes in here . . . well, you'll see. But, hey, she's nice. She expects a lot, but if you can deliver . . . well, Cilla will like you. Oh, by the way, welcome to Cybelle."

Cilla Westheim wasn't in a mood to like anyone right now. Damn, she couldn't believe she'd overslept again. It was getting to be a very inconvenient habit.

Now her oversleeping had cut off all her chances for getting a decent parking space. She didn't even bother to cruise the main lot; she knew from experience that it had been full since before 8:00 A.M. Instead she drove around in back to the new annex lot that had been laid down the previous spring on some land that had previously belonged to a neighboring church. The only spaces left were on the grass.

Oh, lovely, Cilla thought grumpily, pulling her three-year-old Mercury Cougar onto the rutted, weedy surface. Her new, strappy Maud Frizon shoes were going to look like crap after she'd trudged over grass and dust. Why the hell didn't she remember to bring tennis shoes, like most of the other women employees?

Cilla's dream last night had put her in a strangely edgy mood. It was the same dream she'd had off and on since high school, herself frantically running across a huge shopping mall while security people chased her. She ran and ran, her heart pounding out of her chest as she clutched her shopping bag, into which she'd stuffed a Chanel silk scarf.

Even today, thirty-one years later, the nightmare had the power to cause Cilla to wake up sweating. Not that she'd ever shoplifted since then; it had only happened that one, humiliating time. She'd paid back every penny by modeling clothes in the junior department at Jacobson's, a job that had started her on her retailing career.

Whoa, Cilla thought, relegating the dream back to where it belonged. She gathered up her purse and started the ten-minute trek toward the building, her mind clicking to an idea she'd had on the drive in. Cilla had heard a song on the radio by Jazzy Kulture, that new, sixteen-year-old rock star who was getting to be even bigger than the Spice Girls used to be before Ginger Spice quit.

Even the name was so perfect. They'd call the line "Jazzy." All they needed was the star's endorsement, and Cilla felt sure they could get that.

Walking fast, Cilla encountered a few stragglers who'd also been forced to park in the limbo of the "back forty." They smiled and waved to each other, caught in the camaraderie of tardiness.

As she approached the #2 door, Cilla began mentally organizing the first half hour of her day. Oh, today was the day that new secretary, Karyn, reported in.

She'd been told that Karyn was "very sharp" and was a superior typist, with a lot of software expertise, including Word 7, Excel and Power Point, plus Harvard Graphics. She had experience making travel arrangements, could schedule meetings, and had done mail merges of up to eight thousand data records. She sounded ideal for the job.

Let this Karyn like us, Cilla found herself thinking. Please, don't let her quit like those others. Please, let Lou treat her decently.

Yes, especially that.

Raquel Estrada got the new secretary, Karyn, settled at her desk and showed her the company's E-mail and voice mail system. "I'll fill you in on more of the details later, but right now there's a ton of phone calls for you to make, and I've gotta finish this spreadsheet for Lou. Hope you don't mind plunging right in."

"I can't wait," said Karyn, smiling.

"That Gemi suit looks great on you," remarked Raquel, eyeing Karyn's tall, model-thin figure enviously. "Really sexy. I was here when they first showed the sample to the buyers. Everyone loved it. I wish they made it in petite, though," she added.

"It must be so much fun to see the clothes before anyone else does."

Raquel grinned. "It has its moments. Look, I'll take you down to the cafeteria today for lunch. It's a bit intimidating to go down there by yourself on your first day."

"Thanks!"

"I go about eleven forty-five to beat the rush."

Karyn again smiled, looking grateful, and Raquel decided that she was going to like her despite Karyn's high cheekbones and knockout figure. The secretary before Karyn had been another blonde, a snooty type who had her own clique of friends—everyone Anglo, naturally—and ignored Raquel except when she needed something.

Raquel went back to her own alcove, which she'd decorated with Dilbert cartoons and snapshots of Brett DiMaio, her fiancé. There were Brett and Raquel on the dunes at Lake Michigan, all dressed up at someone's wedding, sitting together on a snowmobile, and so forth. On top of her computer she'd arranged five or six Beanie Babies, which had been very popular in Michigan for a while. Brett had given Raquel all of hers.

For a moment she studied the glittering diamond ring she wore on her left hand, then she started entering sales figures into the spreadsheet. However, almost immediately her phone interrupted.

"You and Brett are coming to the party at Aunt Adelina's, aren't you?" said her mother. "They haven't seen Brett in months, and they're starting to ask me why you're staying away from family, Raquel. They call you a stranger."

"I'm not staying away from family." Raquel sighed.

"You never stop by the house anymore, and you never bring your fiancé around the way you should. You're twenty-eight, Raquel. Back in Mexico you would have been married by now with three or four children, but here . . . here you don't care, you just do as you please, family is nothing for you."

Just then several men in shirts and ties walked past, probably on their way to a meeting.

"Mama! Please!" Raquel uttered a whisper of anguish. "I'm sitting at my desk—people can walk by and hear."

"Well, all right, but just bring him to Adelina's then," insisted Modesta Estrada.

As her mother talked on about her aunt's party, Raquel started typing more numbers into the Excel chart. She hadn't dared tell her family that Brett had broken the engagement— her mother would freak. Modesta would blame her for "giving everything to a man before marriage," claiming that was what had caused the breakup.

"I can't bring him to Adelina's, Mama, because he's got family obligations himself. His uncle is very sick with prostate cancer, and all the family is in town and they—well, Brett is spending a lot of time with family."

What a lie. Raquel felt her skin turn hot from shame, but what else was she supposed to say? If she could get Brett back, maybe by the end of this week, her mother would never have to know.

Finally she said good-bye and replaced the phone, feeling sweaty and irritable.

Her fingers hovered over the phone's speed-dial list, where she'd programmed in Brett's office number. When their romance was going strong, that had been one of their pleasant morning rituals—their phone calls and the many E-mails they sent back and forth to each other. Now he'd asked her not to call or E-mail him anymore.

But he couldn't have meant it, not deep down.

She pushed Brett's extension, waiting impatiently for him to pick up.

She just had to hear his voice—even if only for a few seconds.

In a few minutes Cilla Westheim arrived, striding down the hall, a attractive, slim woman who could have been anywhere between forty and fifty, clad in an aubergine-colored suit with a loose jacket that seemed to fly out behind her. She had an oval face with beautiful coloring, a few delicate, fine lines fanning at her eyes and the corners of her mouth. Her chestnut hair glinted with red. She exuded charisma.

"Hi, Karyn—I'll be with you in a sec—just let me get into my office and get my computer switched on."

A minute later, Cilla buzzed Karyn on the intercom, and Karyn ventured into her new boss's office. The room had two big windows overlooking an inner courtyard and reflecting pond. A clothes rack loaded with beaded evening dresses was pushed against one wall, and file folders were stacked on the floor. Another wall was hung with photos of Cilla Westheim taken with various celebrities. The one that caught Karyn's eye was that of Cilla and Gemi Adams. Gemi had been nominated for an Academy Award this year. It was "her" suit that Karyn was wearing.

Cilla was still on the speakerphone, having a discussion about a deadline for a shipment of sequin-sprinkled halter tops. Karyn listened eagerly, wondering who the designer was and if she'd recognize the name.

"Well," said Cilla, finally hanging up. Her smile transformed her face, making it seem warm, almost beautiful. "I want to tell you how glad I am to have you here. I've been begging for a new secretary for two weeks. Your predecessor left us a bit in the lurch. I'm afraid the work has begun to back up badly."

"I can handle it," said Karyn confidently.

"Good. And you type a hundred words a minute? That's really incredible."

"Actually, it's more like a hundred and four or five when I'm relaxed and not being tested."

"And your Power Point experience is impressive, too. I'll give you plenty of chances to use it. I promise we'll keep you busy and, I hope, happy."

Cilla went on to explain some of the workings of the department, and Karyn took notes on a steno pad she'd brought in with her.

"The Fashion Department is really the heart of Cybelle," Cilla explained. "All of our celebrity lines originated here, and you may even encounter a celebrity or two yourself. . . . They occasionally stop by here for meetings. In fact, Gemi Adams has been here twice for stockholder meetings."

"Really?"

"But mostly it's their business managers who pay us a visit," Cilla admitted. "Still, it's exciting here, Karyn. One day you might be sorting through color samples, the next you could be picking up a model at the main door and escorting him or her to the department. Or even helping to select that model. How would you like to do that?"

Karyn couldn't help laughing with pleasure. "It sounds great here—I'm sure I'm going to love it."

"By the way, have you met Lou Hechter yet?"

"No, I haven't."

"Well, he's my boss, and he'll be giving you work, too, from time to time, especially when Raquel gets overwhelmed. We'll keep you busy, no question about that."

"That would be great," Karyn said.

"Now, I assume Raquel has given you a long list of things to do," said Cilla, making it plain the meeting was at an end.

Karyn zipped down the list of phone calls, priding herself on sounding both friendly and efficient. Several of the staff members seemed very cordial when she gave them the meeting reminder. She wanted to belong there so badly.

A couple of women were pushing a big metal rack crammed with luscious-looking silk suits down the hallway, struggling to get its swaying bulk into a conference room. Karyn couldn't help staring at the odd sight, not exactly what she'd expected to see in an office setting.

"That's a rolling rack," explained Raquel. "And those are samples on it. This place is just bulging with samples. Up in Buying that's all you see, stuff hanging on hangers. And they're always trying to steal our steam iron. We have to hide our ironing board or it'll disappear."

"You *iron* here?" Karyn asked, beginning to laugh.

"Yeah, we all do, even Cilla sometimes. We have this grotty room at the back, it's full of clothes and junk. We keep our iron and ironing board in there. You're gonna get your turn at it, too. It's just part of the job."

Raquel took Karyn around the department, introducing

her to about thirty people. There were merchandisers, graphic artists, designers, clerks, and two student interns from the University of Michigan.

"Lou Hechter is the big cheese, though," Raquel went on. "He's my boss. He's a vice president and he heads this department and Buying. Come on, you have to meet him."

Raquel ushered Karyn into a corner office, twice as large as Cilla's but with a similar view of the same courtyard and pond. This office was much neater than Cilla's, crammed with expensive furniture. A credenza held several Degas dancer statuettes and a beautiful, foreign-looking clock. There was a collection of stunning fashion sketches by Givenchy, Scaasi, Valentino and others.

A middle-aged man with dark hair looked up from his computer monitor.

"Lou, this is Karyn, Cilla's new secretary."

"Ah, yes, our new secretary who types a hundred words a minute," drawled Lou, looking up from his computer screen.

Karyn blurted out a reply, realizing that he was the man she'd seen in the parking lot.

But now she could see that Lou resembled Mack only very superficially. For starters, he was twenty-five years older. His hair was shoe polish black except for a few threads of silver, and his jet-black eyebrows seemed somehow too small for the rest of his face. His features were strong-looking, his complexion so ruddy brown that he either lay in a tanning bed for several hours a week or regularly sunbathed.

She'd bet it was a tanning bed. He wore an expensive-looking shirt and an Italian silk tie, and his watch glimmered in a shaft of sunlight; to her, it looked like a Rolex. Of course, she'd seldom seen any real Rolexes other than in advertisements in magazines like *Town and Country*.

Lou began asking Karyn perfunctory questions about her previous job experience, his eyes studying her closely, his scrutiny giving her a brief feeling of discomfort.

"Pardon me for looking, but it's your suit," explained Lou, smiling. "Gemi fall line, size eight. Am I right on the size?"

Karyn flushed. "Yes."

"You see, I always notice what a woman is wearing." Lou's teeth were big and square, slightly yellowed. "It's my job. I've been in fashion for, well, more years than I'd like to confess, and the day I can't tell you whose clothes you're wearing and what size they are is the day I'd better just hang up my hat."

Karyn nodded. This explanation made sense to her.

"Did you get your rose?" inquired Lou.

"Rose?"

He grinned. "If it isn't at your desk yet, it will be soon. I believe in flowers for the ladies in my department. You'll soon discover that."

Lou's phone rang and he terminated their interview to take the call. Walking back to her alcove, Karyn discovered a crystal bud vase on her desk with a long-stemmed pink rose in it, arranged with some baby's breath.

"Welcome to Cybelle, Karen," read a neatly lettered card. Her name had been misspelled.

Cilla Westheim began playing back her voice-mail messages that had accumulated since Friday night. They were the usual stuff. Two or three had been tagged "urgent" but weren't. One was the weekly multiple-recipient message from Randy Caravaglio, the corporate comptroller, giving the week's numbers on how women's fashions, juniors, men's, children's and housewares had done.

Cilla frowned. Women's was down a half point from the previous week. And it had been flat for three weeks before that. Was this starting to form a trend? Christ, she hoped not. Despite the current rosy economic climate, competition was fierce among retailers, and even a one percent drop couldn't be tolerated.

She pushed 1 to play the next message.

"Shane Gancer, from Legal," said an unfamiliar baritone voice. "We met at that breakfast meeting last week with Dom Carrara. Extension 3567. I'll be around until eleven."

Cilla's mind raced down her mental Rolodex, trying to place Shane Gancer. Then suddenly she recalled him. Tall, blond, about twenty-five or twenty-six years old, he was a new hire who had come to Cybelle from one of the many automotive suppliers in the area, ITT Automotive.

She dialed his extension, getting through immediately.

"I thought I'd touch base with you about that meeting," Shane began. They discussed it for about ten minutes, while Cilla wondered why he had singled her out for the call. "And I wanted to maybe see if you wanted to talk further," he finished.

"Further?"

"Over dinner on Friday night."

Cilla caught her breath. *Good God,* she thought.

"I really . . ." she began, but the words came out with a nervous laugh. Maybe he didn't realize she was fifty years old.

"Maybe over to the St. Clair Inn if you'd be interested in being on the water for a while. Even if it is on the sunrise side, the lake is beautiful at sunset."

Oh, shit, Cilla thought. And double shit. When Shane had been in diapers, she'd been already working at her first job at Jacobson's. When he graduated from high school, she'd been a working mother with a twelve-year-old daughter. He probably listened to the same rock stars Mindy did, she thought in dismay.

"Well, I've been super busy at work," she said, framing a polite refusal. "And I really don't date within the company."

"Just a casual dinner," he insisted. "No strings, just a

pleasant evening. We can talk business if that'll make you feel better."

She couldn't help laughing, hanging on to the phone and watching through the half-open door as her new secretary, Karyn, came back from the copy room. Karyn was very pretty, Cilla again noticed. That hair, blunt cut and shiny. She had an appealing, fresh look that came with being in the late twenties—a look that Cilla had to re-create with makeup these days.

"Cilla?" Shane was saying.

Jolted back to her phone call, she repeated, "I'm sorry, Shane . . ."

"Is it because I'm younger? Because it's not at all a problem with me."

"It's not just younger, it's a lot younger," she said, compelled to be honest.

"If two people are compatible, then age is just a random number, Cilla."

Age wasn't a random number to her. Her fiftieth birthday blues had stretched on for over two months. Age was the damned hot flashes. It was realizing she could never wear a two-piece bathing suit again unless she chose the high-waisted kind. Age was giving away the sleeveless dresses in her closet and doing those harrowing mirror inspections when you stretched out your face with your fingers and wondered if you should get plastic surgery. Age was being embarrassed because she was no longer very lubricated "down there." And noticing that the bottom curves of her butt now contained three lines, instead of the former one.

God, now she was blushing. "I really can't, Shane."

"Just one dinner," he pleaded. "And afterward I'll charter a boat and we can go out on the lake for a while. The wind in your hair . . . the sunset . . . and I promise I won't talk at all about Gen X."

"Oh, such a relief," Cilla said, laughing.

"Then will you? It's only one night," he insisted. "If you don't like me, I'm history."

How could she argue with that? Since Mindy had gone back to Albion College, Cilla usually ate a microwave dinner standing at the sink. A real meal sounded good to her. "And I promise I won't mention baby boomers, deal?"

"Deal," said Shane. "What time shall I pick you up?"

"Seven, I'll meet you at the restaurant," Cilla said hastily. "I've been there before and I know where it is."

After she hung up, she just sat there, not knowing whether to start laughing or take two Advils. Would the waiter think she was Shane's mother? Probably! Of course, Cilla assured herself, most people didn't take her for fifty. She'd been told over and over that she looked around forty-five, or even forty. Since her age wasn't listed in any company publications, Cilla realized that Shane probably thought forty-five was her real age, not fifty.

Still, it was only one dinner, and they could talk business, as he'd suggested, if they found they had nothing in common. And the food certainly would be better than nuking herself a box of chicken marsala.

By the time 11:45 A.M. arrived, Karyn was ready to take a break.

"Ready for lunch?" asked Raquel, showing up at her alcove, an expectant smile on her face.

"Hungry as a bear."

"Good. We'd better hurry, though. It can be a mob scene over there."

They started out on the long walk to the cafeteria, threading their way through the corridors to the main, marble-floored artery, as crowded with passersby as a sidewalk in downtown Atlanta. Dozens of people smiled or said "Hi" to Raquel.

"I love my rose that Lou sent," Karyn commented. "It's the first time I ever got flowers on my first day of work.

Does he usually do that with new people here?"

Raquel nodded. "Women, anyway. You should see the arrangements he sends on Secretaries' Day. They're huge. Mine was so big I didn't even have room for it on my desk. Of course a raise would have been a lot better. I didn't get that."

"Really? And does he always . . . well, tell you what brand of clothes you're wearing?"

"Well, sure, Lou's got a very sharp eye. If he ever catches you in Kmart clothes, he'll put a rusty safety pin on your desk."

Karyn giggled. "A rusty safety pin?"

"Yeah. Lou is sorta the company maverick. He has strong ideas about stuff sometimes."

The cafeteria was big enough to seat fifteen hundred people at once, a huge space dominated by a big bank of windows that overlooked another of the beautiful reflecting ponds that had a geyser splashing up in the middle of it. The room reverberated loudly with voices, the clink of cutlery, and music being played over a PA system. The food area was jammed, everyone acting impatient. Karyn stopped short, feeling intimidated by the mobs of workers.

"Today is Greek salad day!" exclaimed Raquel, elbowing her way toward the salad bar. "Come on!" she called to Karyn. "Every day they serve a different ethnic food. On Fridays they have Mexican pizza." She made a little face. "On a tortilla, with cheese and pepperoni. If my mother could taste it, she'd freak."

Karyn got in line behind Raquel, balancing her tray and her shoulder bag, relieved that she wasn't going to be forced to sit alone among all these hundreds of strangers.

The line of people split in half, streaming on either side of the long salad bar, helping themselves to feta cheese, beets, tomatoes and other items. Karyn ended up separated from Raquel. As she served herself, she heard a loud, rattling clatter. Her salad plate had somehow slipped off the tray, catapulting bits of lettuce, beets and other salad fixings all over the floor.

"Ah!" she cried, jumping back.

Looking down, Karyn saw that a slice of beet had adhered to the top of her right shoe, and something damp had streaked the skirt of her expensive Gemi suit. However, the line of people merely streamed around Karyn, everyone continuing to load their plates.

She was near tears as she bent down and attempted to pick off the beet from her shoe and gather up the bits of lettuce before someone stepped on them.

"You don't have to pick that up," said a male voice above her. "Look—don't grub down on the floor like that. I'll tell the cashier and she'll phone for someone to clean this up."

Flustered, Karyn straightened up and saw a stocky, sandy-haired man just a few inches taller than she was, with a ginger-colored mustache and pleasant laugh lines around his brown eyes. "I guess I really goofed," she began.

"Not seriously. I'll get you another plate," he said, moving away. In a moment he had returned, carrying one of the crockery plates that bore the Cybelle logo, an elaborate script *C*. "By the way, I'm Roger Canton," he told her, handing her the plate, still warm from the dishwasher. "I'm head buyer for Women's Fashions. It's your first day here, isn't it? I can tell."

"Does everyone spill lettuce and beets on the floor on their first day?" Karyn queried, laughing nervously.

"No, sometimes they spill a ten-ounce glass of Pepsi all over the cashier, like I did. She still mentions it when I go through the line."

A young man in a white apron came hurrying over with a mop. Embarrassed, Karyn began restocking her plate. Oh, lord, was her new suit ruined? It was dry-cleanable only. And her shoe, would the beet juice stain it? She'd already gotten the impression that you were expected to look stylish and fashionable here at Cybelle, and it was going to strain her budget. Of course, if she was a permanent employee she'd get clothing discounts. . . .

"Come on," urged Roger Canton. "You don't have to sit alone on your first day, you can sit at our table if you want. It's over there in the corner by the big planter." He waved toward the sea of tables.

"I'm—with Raquel."

"Oh, Raquel Estrada? You must be in Fashion, then. Well, tell Raquel to come and join us, too. Remember—by the planter. And try some of the dessert today. The cherry tarts taste like Grandma Cybelle whipped them up in her kitchen."

Roger Canton smiled at her, his eyes sparkling with interest.

"Maybe I will try them."

Roger veered off, joining the line for the soft drinks. Karyn wandered over to the counter where a cheerful woman in a white apron was handing out small, beautiful tarts with attractively crimped edges, each dolloped with whipped cream.

"Want one, honey?"

"Well . . ."

"Go on, it's calorie-free," urged the zaftig cafeteria worker. "Especially if you eat it standing up."

Karyn laughed. "In that case, I'll have one. Light on the whipped cream."

"Well," said Raquel, coming up beside her with her loaded tray. "I see you attracted Roger's attention."

"I—he just helped me when I spilled my salad. He said we could sit at his table. But I'm not sure I want to. I haven't been divorced very long. I don't want to get involved with anyone right now."

"Oh, yeah? Listen, Roger's okay. He's one of the good guys around here. But we can sit with some of the women from the department. I usually sit with—" Raquel stopped, her eyes darting around the cafeteria. "Annie and Jan and a couple of others," she finished.

Carrying her tray, Karyn followed Raquel into the vast, noisy room.

They sat down and Raquel suddenly narrowed her eyes, again staring across the crowded cafeteria. "See him?" she said. "That's my honey."

Looking, Karyn saw a good-looking young man—nearly six feet tall—with olive skin and a full head of curly, dark hair. He wore shirtsleeves and a tie, and was carrying his tray toward the far end of the room near the door. He was either unaware of Raquel's scrutiny or else he was ignoring her.

"Your boyfriend?" said Karyn.

"My fiancé. He's a programmer. Well, we've been having some troubles recently, but it's just a matter of time," said Raquel vaguely, her gaze still focused on the man. "His name is Brett. We were going to get married . . . are going to get married," she amended hastily.

Karyn felt a flash of pity for Raquel. "I suppose it's tough, having a boyfriend or girlfriend who works at the same company," she remarked, not wanting to pry.

Raquel gave a brilliant smile. "It's okay. Well, it could be tough if you were in the same department, but we're not."

A group of people from the department arrived with their trays, and Raquel joined in the repartee, introducing Karyn to several she hadn't met earlier in the morning.

Karyn ate her lunch and tried to participate in the conversation. One of the buyers was telling about a meal she'd eaten in Paris . . . it sounded incredibly exotic to Karyn.

The fashion designers and merchandisers were dressed differently from some of the other women in the company, she noticed. No pantsuits or slacks for them. All wore suits or dresses, most with above-the-knee or mid-thigh hemlines. Several wore opaque tights with these outfits.

Mentally she began going through her own wardrobe, trying to see it with new eyes. Thank God she owned a lot of separates. But she might need a few new skirts.

At 3:30 P.M., Karyn took a minute to call Amber.

"Hi, Mom," came the high, piping voice of her eight-year-old daughter. In the background, Karyn could hear a TV set playing an afternoon soap.

"Hi, sweetums. How was school?"

"Great. We did cursive writing. The teacher said I write really pretty."

"Fantastic. You having a good time at Caitlin's?"

"Yeah, cool. We're washing out her Barbie doll dresses."

Karyn pictured her blond daughter, small for her age, skinny and intense, splattering water all over Jinny Caribaldi's bathroom. "Oh? I hope you aren't making a mess."

"No, it's in the bathroom sink. And we're using lots of towels to get everything up. Mom? Can we go out and get pizza tonight? Pretty, pretty please? With candy and sugar and Cool Whip on it?"

Karyn smiled. "I thought you were sick of pizza."

"No *way*. The only stuff on pizza I don't like is meat. Oh, can we?"

"Sure, honey. Just clean up your Barbie doll mess in the bathroom, okay, so Mrs. Caribaldi won't have to do a lot of extra work. And then hang up the towels on the rack so they'll dry."

"Okay. How's the, you know, your new boss?"

"She's very nice."

"Caitlin's mom has a real mean head nurse who yells at everybody. She says it gives her indigestion. And that other stuff, st—"

"Stress?"

"Yeah. Stress. She says someday she's just going to tell her job to go screw."

Karyn bit her lip, thinking how fast little girls grew up.

"Honey, my boss is named Cilla and she's great. She's very nice and cheerful."

"Good," said Amber. "And you're not going to get fired? Daddy's not going to come by and wreck your job?"

"No, honey. No, he's not."

"Because I want to stay here for a long, long while and I want to be Caitlin's best friend and I want to have a *ton* of Barbies and I want them all to have beautiful clothes, really fashionable with ribbons and beads and stuff," Amber finished breathlessly. "And I want a kitty cat."

"Well, we'll start saving up some money then," promised Karyn, feeling such a powerful surge of love and commitment that her fingers clenched the phone.

"I want to *stay here*," repeated Amber. "I don't want to move again, okay?"

"We won't. We're here for the long haul, Amber."

"Promise?" said her daughter.

"Promise."

Karyn was forced to hang up. Lou Hechter was walking past her desk. He smiled warmly at her and she smiled back.

"How's your first day working out?" he asked.

"Fine, just fine."

"If you have any problems at all, you just let me know."

"I will," she responded.

A date with a younger man. Cilla Westheim struggled to concentrate on her work, assuring herself that the December–May coupling wasn't so unusual these days. She had several women friends who'd dated men as much as ten years younger than themselves. One was living with her partner and kept telling everyone how much he worshipped her and how happy she was. Of course, Diann had gotten a face-lift and liposuction, too.

Cilla was beginning to feel a lift of excitement, coupled with flattered pleasure.

She only had to see him once, that wasn't much of a

commitment, and after that they probably would naturally drift apart.

Cilla worked through lunch, pausing to pick at a pasta salad she'd had delivered from the main cafeteria. The company also had a small "mini" cafeteria that served fast food and yogurt by the pound, but Cilla only went there for the yogurt. Small coffee vending rooms in each area also dispensed vending snacks in case employees needed a quick caffeine or sugar fix. Their own department also kept a coffeemaker, which people usually let run empty.

"I want an overview report of all the celebrity lines pushed by the big chains," Lou told her, popping his head in. "You know the stores I mean. By tomorrow morning."

She looked at the man who was her boss, and who daily made her aware that she was his subordinate. "Tomorrow? But Lou—"

"I don't care how you do it."

"Fine, Lou," she agreed crisply.

He gave her some of the specifics he wanted, which included merchandise samples from each line and their pricing. Cilla's mind flew over the logistics; she'd have to dispatch her merchandisers immediately to shop all the department store chains in the tri-county area. Later, everything would have to be returned. Ten years ago, Cybelle had simply eaten the prices of the hundreds of garments it purchased, but recent austerity campaigns meant merchandisers now had to trudge back to the stores with their sales slips just like any shopper.

"That's my girl," he said in a familiar way.

She sighed. "I'm not a girl, Lou, and I haven't been one since high school."

"Oh, you know what I mean."

After Lou left, Cilla sat with her eyes shut for thirty seconds, calming herself down. Lou was Lou. She was stuck with him if she wanted to keep her job here. Finally she recovered herself and printed out a list of the chains Lou

wanted covered and distributed them to the six merchandisers she could spare.

When she handed them the list, several groaned.

"A nice afternoon of shopping? Now, what more could
you want?" Cilla said, smiling to take away the sting.

Her phone rang again, and automatically she reached to
pick it up.

"Dress casual," said a male voice.

"What?"

"For Friday night, I mean. In case we go on the boat."

Cilla laughed. She had no idea why; she just did.

"What's so funny?"

"I don't know." She suddenly felt so good, so free, and
slightly wicked.

"You're too funny, Cilla. I'm looking forward to getting
to know you better."

Cilla smiled, and smiled again. She couldn't even remember the last time she had done something this crazy, and she
was beginning to believe she would enjoy it.

" 'Night, Raquel," called Cherise, the friendly security
guard, as Raquel trotted past on her way out the #2 door.
"Have a good one, hear?"

"You, too, Cherise." Raquel waved cheerfully.

She joined the crowds streaming to their cars.

A familiar figure in a Gemi suit was walking only about
twenty feet ahead of her. Raquel recognized Karyn Cristophe gazing around her with that puzzled look new people
got when they were trying to spot their cars after the first
day of work. She hurried her steps to catch up.

"Karyn! Karyn! Hi!"

Karyn turned, surprised, and then gave Raquel a rueful
smile. "I lost my car. I thought I parked down that aisle
there—" She pointed. "But I don't see my car. And with
the sun shining on everything, it makes the colors of the
cars look different."

Raquel grimaced. "I can't believe they don't have aisle markers here, but they don't. Look. I used to lose my car all the time when I first came here, and it pissed me off something awful. What you do is you park in the same place every time if you can. Then you always know where to start looking. I try to park as close to an aisle as I can get, and I use those landmarks over there to orient myself."

Raquel pointed to a row of distant trees and a small strip mall.

"Ooohkay," said Karyn.

"Hey, why don't you get in my car and I'll drive you around until we find it?"

"So how did your first day go—I mean really," said Raquel as they slowly drove around the lot.

"Great. I think I'm going to really love it here."

"Good. I mostly like my job," confided Raquel. "If it wasn't for Lou . . ."

"Lou?"

"He's . . . crabby sometimes." Raquel closed her mouth. "Look, Karyn, just a little hint between you and me. You're a great-looking woman, very sexy. And that suit you have on today is sensational. Maybe you ought to tone it down a little, you know? Leave off the makeup and dress a little plainer."

She could see the surprise cross the face of the other woman.

"That doesn't bother you, does it? That I said that?"

"No," said Karyn with relief. "Actually, my working wardrobe is not this fancy—I only bought the Gemi suit to impress everyone. I was starting to worry that I'd have to spend all my paycheck on clothes."

"Skirts, though, you have to wear skirts," Raquel warned. "Lou doesn't like pants, so none of us get to wear them."

Karyn nodded. "Look—over there. I think that's my car."

Raquel dropped Karyn off at her Ford Tempo, which was beginning to show a few spots of rust along the fenders.

"See you tomorrow," she said cheerfully.

"Sure. And—thanks."

Karyn waved at her, and Raquel drove off down the aisle, which had begun to clear of cars. She exited onto the main road, turning in the opposite direction from her own apartment in Troy. All she was going to do was drive past Brett's house. If she saw his car in the driveway, maybe she'd stop by, just for a couple of minutes.

Brett DiMaio lived in a modest, three-bedroom brick ranch in a subdivision full of similar homes. He had a flower basket hung on a hook from his porch ceiling, a basket Raquel had bought him at Bordine's the previous May.

Possessively, she eyed it as she slowed her sporty-looking Pontiac Grand Am to a crawl. The magenta-colored petunias and pink impatiens were at their late-summer best. Brett must be watering, because the plants looked healthy. Also, he hadn't thrown the basket out—which Raquel took as a positive sign. If he really and truly didn't want her around anymore, she reasoned, he would have thrown out everything she had given him. The fact that he had not gave her hope.

Unfortunately, his Jeep Cherokee wasn't in the driveway, where he usually parked.

She made two more quick turns around the block, slowing up each time as she passed Brett's home, but he still wasn't there. She circled the block four or five more times, then drove past a restaurant he frequented. His Cherokee was not in the lot. She cruised past his health club, making the circuit of the big parking lot. Then back to his house. Frustrated, she gave up, turning toward her apartment.

As she drove, Raquel fiddled with the car radio until she found a country station playing a sad song that fit her mood. She'd had sex with Brett on their fifth date—a big mistake, she now realized. In fact, maybe a fatal one. Raquel's older sister, Ana, had saved herself for her husband and look at what happened! Ana got married. Her man had *begged* her to stand in front of the priest with him. Now Ana was set for the rest of her life.

Raquel gripped the steering wheel, fighting to maintain her optimism.

A wedding still had to be in her future. If she could just talk to him and they could hash out their differences, she felt sure she could get Brett back.

Karyn dug her keys out of her purse and let herself into the apartment building. She felt exhilarated from the long work-day, dreams already tumbling through her mind of all the things she might do once she became a permanent employee. She would sign up for the 401k plan and . . . oh, a hundred things! Aunt Connie had told Karyn that top secretaries and administrative assistants could make anywhere from $27,000 up to $50,000, and a few, in big corporations, earned over $60,000.

To Karyn this sounded like a fortune.

Karyn hurried up the stairs and knocked on the Caribaldis' door to pick up her daughter.

"Mom—Mom!" cried Amber, running to the door.

"How was school, cupcake?"

"It was great. We had tacos for lunch and did stuff on the computer."

"That's wonderful."

"Mom, we washed *all* of Caitlin's Barbie stuff and we even ironed!"

"You ironed?" Dismayed, Karyn thought about steam puffing out of vents and boiling hot water.

"I made them keep the iron set on wool," said Jinny Caribaldi, a pencil-slim blond with a plain face who had been divorced a year longer than Karyn and had been left with a pile of credit card debts and no child support. "And I stood right there with them."

"I hope Amber wasn't any trouble," fretted Karyn.

"Oh, no, no. I had them down in the basement washing towels, and then I let them wash and blow-dry Barbie's hair."

Karyn scooped up Amber for a hug. Karyn could feel her daughter's skinny shoulder blades and smell coconut-scented shampoo. "Hey, honeybear, you blow-dried Barbie?"

Amber's blue eyes were sparkling. "Yeah, and she ended up beautiful."

Karyn laughed, remembering Barbie dolls from her own childhood with big wads of hair incredibly frizzed from non-stop combing.

"Mom, are we getting pizza tonight?" Amber went on. "Can we go to Chuck E. Cheese? It's where Caitlin always goes, and she says the cheese pizza is great there."

"Sure, honeylamb," said Karyn. "I promised, didn't I?"

"And can Caitlin come with us?" the child inquired eagerly.

"If her mother says it's okay."

"Actually, it would be more than okay," said Jinny Caribaldi. "I have to run out to the drugstore and pick up a few things before my mother gets here to baby-sit Caitlin."

Karyn and Jinny had already worked out an arrangement that Karyn would take care of Caitlin at night if Jinny's mother became sick or couldn't sit. It was going to work out well for both of them. Another huge stroke of luck, Karyn thought. She couldn't believe how well her life was working out here.

Karyn collected her daughter and Caitlin, a round-cheeked child wearing a Walt Disney World T-shirt, and they were in the car again, on their way to the pizzeria, located in a shopping mall about three miles away.

Giggles erupted at the pizza place as the girls discussed TV shows and Barbie dolls. Families filled most of the tables, the standard nuclear type, and Karyn couldn't help glancing a bit enviously at fathers who cradled babies and helped toddlers wipe their faces. She saw that Amber had noticed them, too, and felt a stabbing pang. Mack had either ignored his daughter or spoken to her cuttingly, criticizing everything she did.

Later, when their pizza arrived, Amber gazed at Karyn over the top of a huge, cheese-dripping slice. "We're gonna like it here, right, Mom?"

"Right," said Karyn. "We're going to love it here."

"And we're gonna stay here a long time, aren't we?"

"A very, *very* long time," Karyn promised for the third time.

"Forever?"

"Maybe even that long."

"And Daddy?" asked Amber.

"He—he won't be with us. He caused so many problems, baby."

"I know," said Amber sadly.

Karyn's bedroom was still only partially unpacked. She spent the evening putting stuff in drawers and on shelves, locating Amber's favorite T-shirt, which had been packed with Karyn's clothes. Then she pressed some blouses for work and put together several skirt outfits she could wear.

She tucked Amber in bed, smoothing up the sheets under her daughter's narrow chin. "Was the pizza good tonight, cupcake?"

"Yeah!"

"And you like Caitlin?"

"We're best friends."

"That's so wonderful, Amber." Karyn reached down and scooped her child into her arms. "You're my most special, sweet and wonderful little girl—the best girl in the whole world."

Amber snuggled up to her trustingly.

"Mom?"

"Yeah, honey?"

"Can we have a kitty?"

"As soon as things settle down."

"I want a kitty with blue eyes."

"Will green eyes do? Or maybe yellow? I'm not sure there are that many kitties with blue eyes."

"Maybe we can find one." Amber sighed, already drifting off. "Or I'll take green."

Karyn switched on the night-light and kissed Amber again, feeling her chest go tight. What had it done to Amber to see her parents battling as she and Mack had done? They'd had plenty of yelling matches when Mack kept bothering her at her job. All she wanted to do right now was smooth away those ugly memories and replace them with new, better ones.

Aunt Connie phoned just as Karyn sat down to watch a little TV.

"How'd the first day go?" Connie Hilverda wanted to know.

"Oh, just great!" Karyn began telling Connie all about it. "I can't tell you how grateful I am to you, Aunt Connie, for getting me in. Raquel told me that it isn't exactly easy to get hired at Cybelle—everyone wants to work there."

"Now, you don't have to thank me. No way. Just bring that beautiful little girl of yours over here for dinner some night, that'll be payment enough for me." Connie hesitated. "You haven't heard from Mack, have you?"

"No. He doesn't know where I am."

"Good," said Connie. "Just in case, get an unlisted phone number and don't use your credit cards. Do you need money?"

"My dad loaned me enough money to get started here, but thanks, Aunt Connie. I love you."

"I love you, too, Karyn."

At 11:00 Karyn put on a faded Paula Abdul T-shirt she

and Mack had gotten at a concert years ago, and a pair of pink flowered cotton panties.

She switched off the lamp and crawled into her double bed, plumping up the other pillow so that it would take up more space and make the bed not seem so empty. Whatever the flaws of their marriage, her sex life with Mack had been good, and she deeply missed cuddling up in the mornings before the clock radio went off.

That man she'd met in the cafeteria, Roger, she tried to recall his face but all she could remember was his brown eyes sparkling with interest.

He'd been attractive. . . .

Restlessly, Karyn tossed and turned, the adrenaline in her body still not dissipated yet. In her mind she was back at Cybelle, hurrying through the maze of corridors and offices. Cilla wanted her to deliver some papers but she couldn't find the right office. The maze stretched everywhere, doors leading to more doors. She kept asking but no one knew where the office was. She walked faster, getting more anxious, and then Lou Hechter appeared.

"If you have any problems at all, you just let me know," he said, smiling.

Tonight, Raquel's roommate, Heather, was out. Still frustrated from her fruitless driving around, Raquel turned on HBO and watched a rerun of *GI Jane*, where Demi Moore shaved her own head and was nearly drowned and tortured by her instructor while trying to become a navy commando. Raquel frowned at the screen image of the hard-bodied, bald star.

Estrada women prided themselves on their long, glossy hair, and believed it was unfeminine to work out or get too many muscles. Raquel's sister, Ana, who now had three children, was becoming heavy. She still was pretty, Raquel thought loyally, but Ana didn't believe in health clubs. She said she didn't want some man to see her with her legs spread apart at some exercise machine. Ana, too, nagged at Raquel about getting married.

"You just don't know what you are missing," she kept saying.

Raquel had picked up a tuna sub on the way home from Brett's neighborhood after her final pass by his house. Listlessly, she peeled off the paper wrapper and ate the sandwich. Then she went to the refrigerator and grazed until she found some low-fat ice cream.

The telephone, hung on the wall near the dinette table, seemed to mock her with its silent presence. Raquel had hooked up an answering machine to it, and its red message button remained stubbornly dark.

Brett hadn't called.

He never called—not anymore. And where was he tonight, what was he doing? Did he already have another girlfriend? Even thinking it was painful. During their horrible breakup fight, he had mentioned that he "wanted to date other women," words that had burned into Raquel's heart like the steam iron they used at Cybelle to press samples.

Raquel scraped the rest of her ice cream into the sink. Then she moved toward the telephone, punching in the speed-dial for Brett's number.

Let him be home now, she willed the phone.

But after the fifth ring, Brett's answering machine picked up. Raquel listened to the familiar message spoken in her lover's somewhat flat voice: *Hey, this is Brett. At the beep, start talking. This better be good.*

"I love you, Brett," she said onto the tape. "I always have and I always will. I drove by your house but you weren't home. Call me. Tonight. Please." She drew in her breath, about to continue but then the end-of-message beep cut her off. Brett had reset his machine so it would take only a twenty-second message.

Raquel replaced the phone, dialed again, listened to the message again, and continued speaking. "We *have* to talk,

Brett. This is ridiculous, us going on like this. We love each other, we're a couple. I've still got our ring on. We have so much together, we can't let it go just like that. . . ."

She talked faster, this time managing to get in quite a bit before the machine cut her off.

Four times she repeated the procedure, each time adding to her words of love.

Finally she hung up for the last time, feeling peaceful for the first time in hours. Brett would come back, play his messages, hear her voice, and—hopefully—feel a stirring of the same sort of feelings she felt for him.

Cilla brought her laptop home and nuked herself a Weight Watchers lasagna meal, preparing a big salad with fresh mushrooms and diet Italian dressing. Twenty years ago, Cilla had been able to eat just about anything she pleased, but since she had passed forty that was no longer the case. She now had to monitor her appetite like Oprah's personal chef, being ready to weather the slightest changes in her cravings or energy level.

Not only that, the fat deposits in her body had subtly changed. Her waistline was trying to thicken, while her legs and butt tried to become skinnier. She fought these changes, exercising to a video four times a week. She was in the fashion business; she *had* to look good. And now a younger man had asked her out, which put even more pressure on her to be thin.

She ate in her den with the laptop opened in front of her, trying to get a jump on the celebrity lines analysis that Lou demanded by tomorrow.

However, she found that her concentration kept slipping, and by 11:30 she finally gave up, shutting off the computer and taking out a stack of bills she'd been meaning to pay for a week.

She opened envelope after envelope, noting the recent purchases. God, were her Maud Frizon shoes really $380?

And that age-defying cream she'd bought last week; it was going to take her a decade just to pay for it. Oh, and her account with Chase Advantage was just about maxed. How could a credit limit of $15,000 get sucked up so fast? Cilla wondered. But it had. And another tuition check was coming due.

She wrote two or three checks, then became impatient, tossing the rest of the bills back into the hand-painted wicker basket she kept them in. She wasn't exactly poor, Cilla told herself. She made $110,000 a year, much more than most women made. Her salary, in fact, put her in the top 1 percent for women.

Disgusted with herself for her spending habits, Cilla padded into the kitchen, where she prepared herself a glass of iced tea—sugarless, of course.

The ringing of the phone startled her as she was adding ice to the tall glass. Cilla stiffened, wondering if the caller was Lou. Lou slept poorly, and frequently worked at home until 2:30 or 3:00 A.M. He thought nothing of phoning his employees in the middle of the night to pick their brains or order them to do something. *The asshole,* Cilla thought, knowing her anger toward Lou was due to a lot more than just inconvenient phone calls.

The phone rang again, insistently. Cilla sighed, picking up.

"Hi, Mom," said her twenty-year-old daughter. "What's up?"

Dorm noises sounded in the background: the pound of music, the shrill of female voices. Albion was a small Methodist-affiliated college situated between Jackson and Battle Creek along I-94, on a jewel-like campus studded with historic buildings and multimillion-dollar new buildings. A private college, it was one of the most expensive in the state. Even with Mindy's Cybelle employees' scholarship it cost more than $15,000 a year to keep her daughter there, but Cilla thought the expense well worth it. The place was a relatively safe haven from the binge drinking, student riots and drugging that contaminated state-supported campuses.

"Oh, not much," said Cilla, pouring ice tea into a glass. "The usual, you know."

Mindy giggled. "Weight Watchers microwave dinners, huh? If they took away your microwave, Mom, you'd probably starve to death."

"Now, I cooked chicken this week."

"Really? Who made it, Stouffer's?"

"I got out the wok," said Cilla proudly. "Every bit of it was skinless, that's sixty percent lower in fat than chicken with the skin on."

Mindy seemed in a very good mood as she gave Cilla a long, detailed rundown on the classes she'd enrolled in and her new boyfriend, a junior named Dylan who came from Midland, a city about an hour and a half north of Detroit. Dylan had taken Mindy to a movie in nearby Jackson.

"Well, this Dylan sounds nice," said Cilla warmly.

"He is," said Mindy, giggling. "*And* he has a new Blazer that his parents let him drive. It's so cool."

"I hope he's a good driver," said Cilla, remembering certain incidents from her own college days at Michigan State.

They talked some more about Dylan, and then Mindy said, "So, who are you dating right now, Mom? Any more geeks like that one blind date you had? The one who let the waitress slip him her phone number?"

"A real charmer. I hope they're very happy."

They shared a laugh.

"Come on, Mom . . .'fess up," insisted Mindy.

"I did get a phone call from a lawyer who works in Legal," Cilla finally admitted.

"Is he cute?"

"He's attractive enough," Cilla said, thinking of Shane's square jaw and deep blue eyes, the two dimples that scored his cheeks. Also his wide shoulders and firm buns, intriguingly obvious even in the regulation business clothes he wore to work.

"Attractive *enough?*" Again Mindy giggled. "And what's that supposed to mean?"

"It means that he doesn't have a big beer gut and he hasn't got any really ugly facial moles. He still has most of his hair and his socks both match." This was the truth, certainly. She was just leaving out most of it.

"And where is he taking you?"

"To the St. Clair Inn, and then we're going out on Lake St. Clair, if the weather's good."

"Romantic."

"Not really."

"Does he like you, Mom?"

"I suppose, or he wouldn't have asked me to dinner."

"What's his name?"

"Shane Gancer," said Cilla, suddenly afraid that her daughter's next question was going to be Shane's age. "Look, Mindy, it's late and I'm still working on a report for Lou."

"Stupid Lou," said Mindy a bit sullenly. She had met Lou at a party Cilla had given last year and had not liked him.

"Yes, well, do you need any money?"

"Yeah, my checking balance is getting kinda low. And can I buy a new dress for the Delt fall mixer? And some shoes to go with it? My other shoes have a broken strap."

"They don't have a shoe repair place in Albion?" Cilla heard a sharpness in her voice and realized that something about this conversation had set her nerves on edge.

"Mom, when was the last time you got shoe repair? I *need* stuff. I can't keep wearing the same two dresses all of the time."

Cilla could sense an argument brewing, and she was too tired for it. She completed the financial arrangements, told Mindy to try to get something on sale, and hung up, feeling her heartbeat pounding irrationally fast.

She sat down at the table to sip her tea. She still felt edgy.

Finally she admitted to herself that the way Mindy had quizzed her about Shane had gotten on her nerves. Shane was twenty-four years younger than she was, and Cilla knew her daughter well enough to know that Mindy would be shocked, even angry at the age difference.

Cilla got up and rinsed out her iced tea glass, telling herself that she was worrying for nothing. In the first place, nothing permanent could possibly work out between her and Shane Gancer. Twenty-six-year-old men did not remain interested in fifty-year-old women . . . not for more than one or two dates at the max.

So Mindy would never find out how old he was.

Cilla expelled her breath, feeling a sudden push of sadness.

By Wednesday, Karyn was settled into her new job. She had taken Raquel's advice about parking and had not lost her car again. She'd learned the shortcuts around the huge building, could now make her way down "Marble Walk," as the employees called the main, marble-floored hallway, as well as anyone. She explored the tiny, cluttered "ironing board room," with its ashtrays for clandestine smokes and handy back-door exit in case Lou ever came exploring. She'd already tried the ATM and visited the employee store where Cybelle workers could purchase clothing and houseware samples at incredibly low prices.

"Been doing a little shopping?" Raquel teased as Karyn walked back from the store lugging two huge sacks.

"I can't believe the bargains. I got this cute dress for Amber for only seven dollars."

"There *are* advantages to working here," declared Raquel smugly. Today, Raquel had swept her dark hair to one side of her face, securing it dramatically with a tortoiseshell comb. She wore a black-and-white dress that skimmed her petite, exquisite figure.

"This place is like a small town," marveled Karyn.

"Yeah—wait until you see the print shop. We do all our own printing. And there's a travel agency right here in the building. And a post office. They sort more mail here than some real towns. Oh, and HR has a computer over in their area. You can look up company job openings on it and see if you want to apply."

"I think I'll stay right here for now."

"Good, because I hated that other girl, Angela, who was here before you. She never sat with us for lunch, and she spent half the day on the phone making dates with guys."

"Why did she leave?" asked Karyn curiously.

"Oh, I don't know." Raquel looked away. "She was just a snot-face, that's all. And I don't think she liked us Hispanics too well, either. She was afraid some salsa might rub off on her or something," added Raquel, lifting her chin.

Cilla had set Karyn to doing a presentation in Power Point. Karyn enjoyed using the colorful software program, and experimented with several of the preset styles, pulling in graphics she had found on her computer's hard drive. She printed everything on the color printer. Karyn felt a surge of pride as she took the charts in and laid them on Cilla's desk.

"Why, these are gorgeous," Cilla exclaimed, pleased.

"Thank you." Karyn glowed. "I put in a few fly-in titles and a couple of other animations. You could look at them on my computer and see if you want to keep them for your presentation."

"Unfortunately, I'm not going to lug a computer to my meeting, but I'll be putting the presentation on overheads. Still, keep the animations in mind. I will want to use them sometime. Is everything going all right for you here, Karyn?" Cilla asked it almost anxiously, as if she thought Karyn might tell her it wasn't.

"Just great."

"No problems of any kind?"

"No, everything is fine. More than fine. I love it here."

Cilla seemed relieved. "Well, I don't have to worry about you then, do I? Look, Karyn, I've got about fourteen faxes I need you to send. If you have any trouble with the international codes, just ask Raquel to help you. International faxes can be tricky."

Standing in the fax room, Karyn was thrilled to discover that the faxes were to go to Paris, London and Tel Aviv, as well as Taiwan. These destinations seemed incredibly exotic to her.

Following Raquel's instructions about the international code, country and city codes, she began feeding papers into the machine.

Suddenly she heard footsteps, and before she could turn, someone had bumped into her back, colliding with her in such a way that their bodies touched. The other person's front hit against her right side, making nearly full-body contact.

"Oh!" Karyn jumped away, startled and annoyed at this too-personal contact. She had felt soft body parts. . . .

"Sorry I ran into you. Are you almost done?"

Karyn looked up to see Lou Hechter standing there with a sheaf of papers in his hand. He was smiling at her, as if the collision had been totally unplanned but not all that unwelcome. "Hey, pardon my clumsiness. I get preoccupied when I'm in a hurry."

"It's all right," she said, wondering why he hadn't stopped to look before hurrying into the room like that.

"Since you're here, would you mind sending this for me? It's fifteen pages to London," said Lou. He handed her the papers, and Karyn had no choice but to take them. He was looking at the outfit she wore today, a dark blue twill skirt worn with a white shell and a melon-colored linen jacket.

"This is, let's see, J. C. Penney's, am I right?"

"Why, yes," she responded in surprise.

Lou's smile was triumphant. "See? I always can tell. Karyn, you're going to have to try to upgrade your clothes to the level of Cybelle," he went on firmly. "I know Penney's and Kmart are a lot cheaper, but they aren't what we are about. We have to set a fashion example here in our department."

"I'm afraid I have to buy the clothes I can afford."

"You look good in the Gemi line," he told her. "That's the line for you."

The expensive, sexy line, Karyn thought.

Lou left the room, and Karyn fumed as she bent over the fax machine, not feeling adventurous about it at all now. Was Lou going to put a rusty safety pin on her desk, the way Raquel had told her? She'd never received a comment at any of her other jobs about her attire being unacceptable and she resented it now.

To make matters worse, the number Lou had provided on his fax was incorrect. She kept getting some recorded message from a London operator. She was going to have to go back to him and ask him for the correct number, which she did not want to do right now while she was still simmering. She didn't want him to start thinking that she had an attitude.

She finished sending the rest of Cilla's faxes, then tried Lou's two more times, each time getting the same recorded message. Finally, Karyn walked down to Lou's office to ask him about the number.

"You just dialed it wrong," he told her brusquely.

"I keep getting a recorded message."

"If you'd followed my instructions, the fax would have gone through by now," Lou told her. He began waving her away as if she were an insect buzzing around his head. "Go—go—ask Raquel about it. She has the list of all my vendors. She'll check the number for you. It should have arrived fifteen minutes ago."

* * *

Karyn backed out of Lou's office feeling angry and humiliated. He was the one who'd given her the incorrect number, but now he was acting as if it were her fault.

She walked up to Raquel's desk and asked her to recheck the fax number.

Raquel grinned as she gave Karyn the correct number. "Lou always reads off the phone number, not the fax. Or he transposes the numbers. I think he's dyslexic. I keep a list of all the designers and companies Lou does business with, so if he gives you a fax number, just come to me, okay?"

Karyn smiled back, feeling a little better. "And my clothes," she added, pointing to the outfit she was wearing today.

"What's wrong with your clothes? That outfit's pretty."

"It's—Lou said—"

"Oh, don't pay any attention to Lou," said Raquel. "He's supposed to go upstairs for his weekly 'Up to Speed' meeting with Dom Carrara today. All the vice presidents have to go. But Lou hates it, he used to be a big buddy of Vic Rondelli when he was CEO, and he doesn't like Dom."

"Hmm?" said Karyn, hoping to draw Raquel out.

"Oh, yeah, he and Dom are real rivals. But you know Lou wants to be the company president. Oh, yes," Raquel added as Karyn looked surprised. "Can you believe that? Sometimes I think, What if he really does it, what if he really makes it? Then I'll be the secretary of the company president." Raquel got up and began mincing around her alcove, putting on la-de-da airs. "Would you like some Oolong English tea, madam? Veddy good. And some, what are those things, crumpets?" She made her voice haughty. "Oh, I'm veddy sorry, but Mr. Hechter is in a meeting and won't be out for a year."

Karyn giggled. "You're funny, Raquel."

"I'd really like to be like Sondra Zapernick, though," the petite woman went on. "She's Dom Carrara's personal secretary. He brought her from New York when he came here; she's been with him for years. He doesn't rule this place, she does."

Karyn lingered at Raquel's desk, talking for a few minutes. There was something about Raquel's feisty good humor that made Karyn feel good.

Karyn was beginning to work on revisions of a letter for Cilla when Lou Hechter strode past her desk, heading in the direction of the main lobby. Lou no longer looked confident and smiling the way he had when he "bumped" into Karyn in the fax room. He now had a preoccupied expression on his face and was walking so fast that his tie flapped in the breeze.

Karyn couldn't help grinning to herself. Yeah, Lou looked edgy, all right. She guessed even vice presidents could receive pressure from above.

She wished she could be there to overhear his meeting with Dom Carrara.

Lou Hechter walked down the main corridor toward the lobby, where the executive elevator gave access to the fifth floor of the Executive Tower. Lou reached for a keypad and punched the elevator access code; the keypads had been installed last year when a deranged stockroom worker, employed in one of the department stores, had entered the building armed with a .45 revolver.

No longer could the president of a company like Cybelle peacefully go about his business. Instead, he was a potential target for crazies and disgruntled employees. However, Lou felt he could take all this in stride once he was settled in Dom's job. When Lou took over the reins, he would tighten security restrictions even further, and he certainly wouldn't keep that old bag, Sondra Zapernick, around. Dom Carrara's secretary had to be at least fifty-five, one of those old war-horses who had been around forever. She didn't even color her hair. Christ, even looking at her made Lou feel old.

In a few seconds the elevator had whispered up to the fifth floor, and the door slid open. Lou walked out and found himself facing a huge marble desk presided over by a pretty woman with silver hair attractively coifed in a modified wedge.

"Good morning, Sondra," Lou said, giving her a power smile. "I'm right on time, I assume."

"Yes, you are, but he's running a few minutes late," said Sondra. She was dressed in a dove-gray suit that brought out highlights in her short hair. "Would you mind taking a seat for a few minutes, Mr. Hechter? And would you like a cup of coffee while you're waiting? Or would you prefer tea?"

Lou glanced pointedly at his watch but finally sank into a leather-upholstered chair. "Black," he ordered grumpily. "Coffee."

In a few minutes Sondra Zapernick had returned with a mug of steaming coffee. Lou didn't bother to thank her as he took it. She was a bitch, and he'd had run-ins with her before when she had tried to tell him that Dom Carrara was in a meeting when Lou knew damn well he wasn't.

Lou had nearly finished his coffee when a discreet buzzer rang at Sondra's desk, and she nodded at Lou, giving him a cool smile. "There. He can see you now, Mr. Hechter. Just go right in."

Lou left his cup on the coffee table, bounded up, and strode into Dom Carrara's office.

"Well, Lou," said Dom, who was sitting with a stack of reports, copies of the *Wall Street Journal, USA Today, Women's Wear Daily, W,* and other industry publications piled in front of him. "How are you this morning? Have a seat."

Lou sank into another leather chair, looking around him covetously. Hanging over Dom's credenza was a big oil painting of the original Cybelle department store. On another wall were dozens of eight-by-ten photographs showing

Carrara with a whole roster of fashion designers, supermodels and politicians. Amber Valetta had her arm around Dom and was smiling into his eyes.

Shit, Lou thought. *How did the guy do it?* Everyone liked him. Several times a week Dom Carrara walked into the company cafeteria and sat at a table with the regular employees, talking with them as if they were equals.

Now Dom put aside a thickly bound report and looked straight at Lou. "Well, we have lots to talk about this week, don't we?" he said in a manner that Lou found faintly ominous.

"I'll say we do," began Lou. "I've got a new ad agency, Ruhnau Bravo, and I'm looking into a whole new advertising campaign. The theme is going to be 'Cybelle for the Glamour of It.' Doesn't that have a great ring? We're going to start running it around the holidays, and I'm betting it'll send holiday dresses through the roof. I'm very excited about this."

"Good. I want everything run past me first before any final decisions are made."

Lou didn't like being second-guessed.

"My campaign is going to go through the roof," Lou insisted. "Trust me on that. Too many people around here are dinosaurs," he added. "Afraid to think creatively, afraid to disturb the status quo. You know that's what happened to Kmart. They got a lot of old fogies in there, people who couldn't cut the mustard and didn't even want to try. They're still trying to struggle out from under."

Dom raised a silver eyebrow, smiling crookedly. "I think Kmart has successfully turned around its numbers. And 'cut the mustard,' Lou?"

Lou felt the color surge to his face as he realized he'd used an outdated phrase. "You know what I'm talking about," he forged on. "In this business if you're not leading the pack, you're running at the back with your nose up someone's asshole."

"Interesting analogy," said Carrara. He gazed at Lou with steely eyes. "All right, let's get to this sales report, let's talk about the numbers. And then we'll talk about that ad campaign of yours."

Forty minutes later Lou was in the elevator again, descending to the lobby. He'd been able to support all the figures, of course, and Carrara had approved the basic concept of the ad campaign.

Which was good. He was still cutting it around here, and then some. They'd better not discount Lou Hechter, not yet.

Raquel gave Karyn interesting tidbits of company gossip, including the fact that Roger Canton was divorced, with a ten-year-old daughter he seldom saw because she lived in California with her mother. "Lonely guy," hinted Raquel, giggling. "Ripe for the picking."

Karyn was beginning to realize that Cybelle was actually a hotbed of intrigue. Annie Fiacci, a designer, had also befriended Karyn, filling her in on some of the gossip about Raquel.

"She's a terrific secretary and she puts up with Lou, which ought to earn her double hazard pay. But ... well . . ." Annie shrugged. "She's one of those women who won't take no for an answer. With men anyway."

"Oh?"

"Yeah, she has this ex-fiancé. Brett DiMaio. He dumped her last month but she refuses to admit it. She calls him about sixteen times a day on his voice mail. Leaves these love messages. And she goes up to his department all the time, at least she did until he told her to back off."

Karyn felt guilty for talking about Raquel this way. "Maybe they'll get back together."

"Dream on. I heard she was all over him, he couldn't even breathe. She's got this real hard-core Catholic family, you know? I mean, they're in church all the time. They push her to get married and start having babies. That's the way those people are."

"What people?"

"Well, you know." Annie had the grace to look uncomfortable at her ethnic slur.

Karyn changed the subject, feeling disloyal to her new friend. No wonder Raquel had looked so sad in the cafeteria on that first day when she'd spotted her ex-fiancé across the room. But why was she still wearing an engagement ring if they'd broken it off?

"Don't forget we have a birthday party this afternoon," said Raquel around 11:00 A.M. "Annie. She's thirty-three. I'm running out on my lunch hour to buy the cake—do you want to come with me?"

Karyn felt a twinge of anger that Annie had called Raquel "those people" when Raquel was nice enough to collect money for and buy her a birthday cake.

Karyn and Raquel left the building and walked across the huge lot to Raquel's car, which was parked the closest. "Only one thing wrong with going out at noon," explained Raquel. "When you come back you really have to hike because you lose your parking space."

They drove to Sanford's Deli, which had an attached bakery with a glass window where customers could watch cakes being decorated. They had to stand in line for ten minutes before they could get the cake, and during that time Raquel began telling Karyn about her life. "My mother raised five of us girls waiting tables, usually working two jobs. Lots of times it was three jobs. My dad—he was gone by the time I was six. I learned to fight for what I wanted, though. I had to with four older sisters, and sometimes we didn't have enough food."

"Is your family still living in the area?" Karyn asked.

Raquel nodded. "Mama lives down in Ferndale in a little two-bedroom house that my sisters and I bought for her two years ago. Prices are low down there and it was all we could afford. Ana's my only sister who still lives around Detroit, though. Constanza and Neva are in L.A. now, and Mercedes is living in New York. She designs jewelry and I think she's gay and I *know* she doesn't go to mass. If Mama ever found out she would surely kill her."

"Are your other sisters married?"

"Yeah, big-time," said Raquel, grinning. "And trying to make me get that way, too. Well, I might just surprise them. When the time comes," she added, holding up the modest engagement ring that glittered on her left hand.

At 2:00 that afternoon, people were in the hallway conference room standing around a half-sheet cake with HAPPY BIRTHDAY, ANNIE written on it in green frosting. Work in the department had slowed to a standstill, and almost everyone was packed into the room, with the exception of Lou Hechter and Cilla Westheim.

"That guy in Printing was a jerk again today," declared Raquel, scraping up a dollop of frosting with a plastic knife and putting it in her mouth. "You know, that guy who holds up the sheet of cardboard with the number on it when you walk past?"

"And what number did he give you, Raquel?" someone asked, laughing.

Raquel shrugged. "No number today. He was just making these licking sounds, you know, slurping with his tongue. Gross! Especially since he's got a tongue coated with white fur."

All the women laughed, a little hysterically.

"Everyone laughs, nobody reports the asshole," exclaimed Annie crossly.

"You first," Jenny said. "I don't want it in my employee folder. They'll think I'm a troublemaker."

The women began trading stories about on-the-job sexual shenanigans by men.

"At the job I had before this, I opened a supply closet door once and there was this salesman standing there with his pants down," said Renee Bugossi. "I shut it again on him and locked it. People had gone home for Good Friday and he didn't get out of there for three hours, when a security guard finally came by."

Howls of laughter.

There was a discreet knock on the conference room door. "I hope this is all business, people," said Cilla, looking in. She looked fantastic today in a long yellow skirt with a side slit, and a fitted yellow plaid jacket, coupled with high-heeled, strappy shoes. "Because you are having entirely too much fun for this to be legal."

The laughter died a little but didn't entirely stop. "Can I cut you a piece of cake, Cilla?" Karyn offered.

Cilla gazed at the cake with a mixed expression of longing and disgust.

"No, no, thanks. That butter cream frosting doesn't even reach my stomach; it goes directly to my hips. But I do need you to run down to the Travel Department and pick up my itinerary for that New York trip, Karyn. When you've finished your cake, of course."

As Karyn walked back into the department forty minutes later she could hear Lou's raised voice.

Suddenly, Raquel burst out of his office, her chin held defiantly high. The petite woman marched over to her alcove and sat down at her computer, staring at it with a grim expression. Her glossy, black hair seemed to quiver with indignation.

"Are you all right?" asked Karyn, going over to her.

"I'm just peachy fine. Just peachy. Mr. Vice President is on the rampage, that's all. He kills secretaries and eats them raw. But he's going to choke on me."

They could still hear Lou, speaking loudly now to someone else on the speakerphone.

Raquel grabbed her mouse, clicked on the Excel icon, and then, when the spreadsheet appeared on the screen, glared at it as if it were a dead snake. The chart, Karyn couldn't help noticing, had been named *Loucrap.xls*.

"*Loucrap*. It has a nice ring to it," Karyn dared to say. "Rather . . . emphatic."

Raquel glanced at her, startled, and then started to giggle. Karyn laughed, too, and then they were both doubled over, laughing and gasping. They tried to stifle their screams of merriment, and that only made them laugh harder. In a minute, Lou himself was going to hear them.

"*Loucrap*," gasped Karyn, dissolving in mirth again.

"Too funny," Raquel gasped. "Too, too funny. Oh, Karyn, I'm so glad you came to work here."

Cilla had closed her office door but she could still hear Lou shouting at Raquel, with the secretary giving back as good as she got. Lou should be damn grateful for her, Cilla thought in irritation, instead of badgering her. Raquel practically ran the department, and on more than one occasion the tiny, 4'9" woman had saved Lou's ass, stopping him from making a costly error.

There was a sudden silence in Lou's office, and she realized he'd ended his phone conversation. When her own phone started to ring, Cilla felt her gut squeeze.

The phone shrilled again, and Cilla's hand reluctantly moved to pick up the receiver.

"Cilla," said a familiar deep whisper. "Meet me."

"Lou, I have two meetings this afternoon," she responded stiffly.

"Cancel them."

"These aren't cancellable."

"Who do you think you are, Edsel Ford II? Any meeting is cancellable. Just get your butt out of here and meet me in our regular place. I'll join you in about twenty minutes."

He hung up on her.

Cilla's gorge rose, and she sat very still at her desk, fighting a sudden urge to throw up. Desperately her eyes darted around her office. Oh, Jesus . . . she really *was* going to toss her cookies. How had this nightmare started? And how was she going to get out of it?

She swallowed, feeling perspiration cover her skin in a heavy sheen. But finally the urge to vomit passed, and she again reached for the phone, telling Karyn to cancel her two meetings.

When this was taken care of, Cilla gathered up her purse and walked down to the ladies' room, where she washed her face with a dampened paper towel. Oh, shit. Oh, hell. It was happening again, the nightmare. Each time Cilla thought it would be the last time, only it never was.

She walked briskly out of the building, nodding at Cherise, the security guard at the #2 door, as she went past.

"Great suit," commented Cherise, cheerful as always. Cilla had never seen Cherise in a bad mood.

"Thanks. It's one of our samples."

"Wish they had samples in a size twenty," lamented the black woman.

Then Cilla was descending the steps toward the pedestrian walkway, walking into a blindingly sunny September afternoon. Gentle, moist breezes tugged at Cilla's auburn hair, ruffling her bangs. The sun was like a kiss on her face.

Grimly she walked toward the back forty, where she had left her car. Somehow the wonderful fall day only made it all worse. Had she remembered to put a couple of latex condoms in her purse? She'd learned from hard experience always to carry one, along with a diaphragm. Although her periods were now irregular, it was still possible for her to turn up pregnant.

Lou, she thought in despair. *You bastard. Why do you do this to me? What are you trying to prove?*

* * *

The Auburn Hilton was a luxe high rise located about six miles away in Auburn Hills, serving the massive Daimler-Chrysler Corporation Headquarters as well as other Fortune 500 companies located in the burgeoning area. The hotel had a number of meeting rooms as well as several bars and restaurants. If Cilla and Lou were seen there, they could always say they had a business meeting. Fortunately, the facility was seldom used by people from Cybelle, who preferred a hotel only a block away from the headquarters building.

Cilla walked up to the desk and gave Lou's name, registering herself as Mrs. Lou Hechter. As always, the deception turned her stomach. But his wife would never see the bill. It went on Lou's personal American Express card.

The room this time was on the fifth floor.

She took the elevator up and began walking down the carpeted, impersonal hallway lined with doors. Someone had left a room service tray sitting on the floor. Sometimes, Cilla dreamed about this corridor, or one like it, and woke up covered with hot flash sweat.

The first time this had happened was three years ago, when Lou had insisted she join him here in the bar for a drink. It was right in the middle of Cilla's painful divorce, her husband leaving her for a much younger woman who dressed and looked like a *Playboy* bunny. A very tough blow for a woman who was then forty-seven years old. Cilla had suffered a tremendous blow to her self-confidence.

In fact, she'd been depressed as hell. However, Lou had been upbeat and jovial, complimenting her, talking shop with her, buying her drinks, telling her she was better-looking than Candice Bergen. Telling her she had legs like Tina Turner. That's why he insisted the women in the department wear skirts all the time, he admitted. He was a leg man.

Recklessly she'd drunk three Manhattans, two more than her usual limit. And when Lou had suggested they go upstairs to a room . . . well, he had hit Cilla at a very weak point.

The truth was she'd just wanted to prove that she, too, could still get a partner. And Lou wasn't repulsive; in fact he was attractive—for a man in his fifties.

The sex was unmemorable—or maybe it was just that Cilla'd been too drunk to remember much of it.

However, driving home that night, she'd started sobering up, fast. What had she been doing? She didn't even like Lou very much, and here she'd given her body to him. She had vowed that she would never let it happen again.

What a major, big-time mistake, Cilla thought now, pacing the well-appointed hotel room like a lioness in a cage at the zoo. From the first, Lou had assumed that their relationship was going to be a continuing thing. When she tried to tell him it wasn't, he'd gotten tough on her, telling her that her job was in his hands.

And, of course, at that time Cybelle had been going through a reorganization under Vic Rondelli, and heads *were* rolling. Over five hundred people had been early-retired or let go. High-salaried managers on Cilla's level were the main targets. Fire someone who made $95,000, hire someone else who would work for $45,000. Or just not bother to fill the position at all.

She'd seen people walking down the hall carrying boxes and crying. Plus, Lou himself liked nothing better than to ax a few heads, most on the spur of the moment without even bothering to go through Human Resources except to announce to them what he had done. She knew he would do it to her. . . .

She heard a sound at the door. As usual, her heart squeezed sharply inside her chest. Then Lou let himself into the room.

"Well," he said impatiently. "Didn't you order something from room service?"

"Sorry, I just got here," said Cilla, stretching her lips in what might pass for a smile. "What do you want, Lou?"

"Forget it," he snapped. "We'll send for drinks later. Why are you wearing that damn long skirt? Haven't I told you a hundred times that I like you in above-the-knee skirts?"

"Hemlines change."

"Bullshit," said Lou, his tone aggressive. "You just don't want to please me, that's all. You never did, Cilla."

Cilla stood with her hands fisted at her sides, trying to shut Lou's hectoring voice out of her ears.

Suddenly, Lou was standing close to her, and she saw something silvery flash in front of her. Startled, she glanced down and saw that Lou was waving a pair of gold sewing scissors.

"Lou!" she exclaimed, jumping back.

"Don't get in an uproar, it's just the scissors out of my desk drawer. Trust me, I'm not going to hurt you."

"But . . . *scissors*, Lou?"

He snapped the scissors in the air a few times, *snip-snip-snip.* "I just want to pretend a little, that's all. Fantasize. So humor me."

"Lou, what are you talking about?"

"Just stand there, Cilla. Yeah . . . don't move. Look like a beautiful statue for a couple of minutes, yeah, I know you can manage that. . . ."

Lou bent over.

He was cutting away the bottom half of her skirt.

"Lou! Lou!" She uttered a horrified little scream, jumping back.

"Stand still, Cilla, will you? This is just my little game, my little fantasy," Lou murmured, moving in on her again. "I started wondering what it would be like to have a woman standing there while I cut her clothes off her . . . every stitch she's wearing. *Every stitch,* Cilla," Lou whispered.

He had gone psycho on her, that had to be it. Or else he'd read some porno magazine and now wanted to play out the fantasy with her. The scissors' blades made a metallic, snipping sound. He was now slicing through the side seam of her expensive skirt, peeling her as if she were a banana.

"No," she groaned. "My clothes. Lou . . . no, Lou, please . . . oh, God, don't do this. . . ."

"Stand still, stand still, oh, Jesus," he muttered, continuing to cut. Scraps of yellow dropped to the floor. Cilla's skirt fell. Lou slid off her jacket, then began cutting away at the silk shell she wore. He snipped off her lacy Olga bra. The blades slid under the waistband of her panty hose, next to her skin.

"Lou—Lou—"

"I'm not going to hurt you, Cilla. Trust me."

Standing there naked and vulnerable, she struggled not to cry.

"Lou . . . Lou . . . Lou . . ." she kept whispering. "My clothes . . . How will I go back to work?"

"They have a shop down in the lobby. Get on the bed, Cilla."

She could feel herself beginning to move into her robot-like mode as she obediently moved to the bed.

She wouldn't participate anymore; she wouldn't feel, or hear, or see.

She would be very far away, lying in the surf at Big Sur, and what happened would not be happening to her but to her body, which wasn't Cilla at all but a plastic sex doll.

"How was that, huh, baby? Was that good?" Lou asked after a frenzied two minutes, during which Cilla held on and thought about all the bills she had to pay, making a mental list of them and then pretending she was writing out checks. "God, this was the best it's ever been. The supreme, the total supreme."

She drew in a long, quivering breath. Her relief that it was over was intense. She pulled away from him and sat up, wrapping a sheet around her. Her genitals burned from lack of foreplay and the unwanted penetration. Sometimes they stung for hours afterward. She had never told her gynecologist about this and she never would.

"I'm going to call down to the shop in the lobby and have some clothes sent up," she told Lou. "And I'm going to charge it to the room, Lou."

"Go ahead," he said, zipping his pants shut. He hadn't even bothered to undress. "Meanwhile, I'm going down to the bar, get myself something. I'll see you back at the office—and don't be too late."

Cilla felt a sudden, wild spurt of rage at the way he was treating her, like she was his private prostitute. She'd had enough . . . more than enough. She didn't know who she hated more, herself or him.

"I've seen you looking at that new secretary, Karyn," she blurted recklessly. "Lou, you're starting it again, aren't you, that thing you do with certain assistants."

"What 'thing' is that?" said Lou.

"You *know* what," Cilla dared to say. "It's going to keep on escalating, isn't it? Until she's forced to quit like your other victims. Well, I'm not going to tolerate it this time. I like Karyn. I need a good secretary, and I'm going to keep her—"

Lou's face reddened. Suddenly he pounced on her, throwing Cilla back onto the bed. He had tough, stringy muscles, and his fingers were like claws, pressing into her forearms.

"Shut up, Cilla, don't you know when not to talk?"

"Lou—Lou—you're hurting me."

"You are mine. *I* made you, Cilla. *I* made you what you are. Is the price you pay all that bad?"

"Lou . . ."

"*Is it?*"

"Let me up. How dare you manhandle me like this."

"Don't I give you a good fuck? Isn't that what all you women want, a good fuck?" With every word, Lou pinched Cilla's arms for emphasis. "Well, let me tell you this, sweetheart. You are going to keep your mouth shut about anything we do, and if I find out you've said even one word, well, *you're going to be packing your desk in sixty seconds flat.*"

Lou sprang off the bed, adjusted his clothes, examined himself in the dresser mirror and combed his hair, then left the room, slamming the door behind him.

Cilla lay trembling, rubbing her upper arms, which were going to have finger bruises. Tears burned out of her eyes. Then slowly she sat up, beginning to take control of her life again.

She picked up the scraps of her clothes and dumped them in a wastebasket. The jacket was still wearable. Everything else had been trashed. She phoned down to the lobby dress shop, requesting that the clerk bring her up a skirt and shell in her size, plus some hosiery. She used the credit card to charge the garments, adding on a generous tip, and told the clerk just to leave them inside her door. That way she'd avoid the shame of having the woman see that Lou had cut her clothes off.

The incident with Lou was over, finished for now. And it might not happen again for a month or more, depending on Lou's mood. By then she would have worked up her courage to stop him.

This time, she vowed, she'd manage it.

Karyn spent an enjoyable hour in the ironing room, pressing some beautiful, lace-trimmed cotton blouses, made by one of the smaller New York design houses, that would retail for over $200 apiece. They were all in her size and she wished she could try them on. She wondered if these would actually end up in Cybelle's department stores or if she would see them later in the employees' store, sold as samples.

Back at her desk, she was checking out her E-mail when she glanced up to see Cilla Westheim returning from wherever she had been. Karyn gazed at her supervisor in surprise. Cilla was wearing a different skirt than the one she'd had on this morning. The skirt was beige, not very flattering, and it looked like hell with the jonquil plaid jacket. Also, Cilla had added a beige silk shell, instead of the pale lemon one she'd had on before. The total effect was drab instead of striking.

Karyn drew in her breath. Had her supervisor had some sort of accident? But of course she would never dare ask Cilla why she had on a different outfit; it would be incredibly rude.

"Hold all of my calls, Karyn," Cilla said to her in a muffled voice. "I've got to crash on a couple of things. And you don't have to stay late, just go home at your regular time."

Karyn watched her boss go into her office and close the door.

Thoughtfully she returned to the E-mail program. Karyn had worked only a few more minutes when her phone rang.

"I managed to get your extension from Raquel. They don't have it in the directory yet." The voice was male and warm-sounding, vaguely familiar.

"Who is this?"

"Roger Canton. I was the guy who helped you scoop your lunch up off the floor on Tuesday. I hope it didn't do any lasting damage to your clothes."

Karyn's heart started racing nervously.

"No, I managed to wash everything off," she told him.

"I've been looking for you in the lunchroom," said Roger.

"Have you? Well, I've been going at different times. Lots of times we go early. And I have to work my lunches around Cilla."

"Maybe you could work one around me."

"What?" Karyn gripped the phone. He was asking her to lunch! And all she could do was say "What?" like a fool.

"There's a very nice Mexican restaurant right across the street from the company; we can walk over there. They make great fajitas and you can get served in forty minutes. Want to try it on Monday?"

"I . . ." Karyn started to stammer, then clamped her mouth shut and started over again. "I don't know if I'm ready to date yet," she told Roger. "I mean, I've only been divorced for a few months."

"My divorce has been final for a year. Look, Karyn, this isn't really a date, it's just lunch. Lots of people from Cybelle go over to Hernando's all the time; the cafeteria gets pretty boring after a while and a change feels good. We can meet in the lobby if you want, at eleven forty-five and walk across."

Maybe she needed a little fun, Karyn told herself. And Roger was right, cafeteria lunches got to be "been there, done that" very fast.

"All right," she agreed.

"Good. I'll meet you by the fountain in the front lobby. Monday, now don't forget."

Karyn hung up.

A date. No, not a date. Lunch. How long ago was it since she'd done that? Years and years ago, when she and Mack first started dating, he'd taken her to lunch a couple of times. She couldn't even remember.

"Well?" said Raquel at quitting time. It was Friday afternoon, and not much work had been accomplished in the department as the younger, single employees were busy planning their weekends. "I don't suppose you have time to go somewhere and have a drink with me?"

Karyn was in the process of exiting from the Windows 97 program. She glanced at Raquel, surprised. "I'd love to, only I can't stay too long. I have to cook supper for Amber."

"No big plans?"

"Just watching a video on the VCR."

"I know a place just around the corner," said Raquel. Her dark eyes sparkled. "And right next door is this great roasted chicken place, so on the way out you can buy dinner. All kids love chicken, right?"

Karyn laughed. "Yeah. . . . Well, I guess I can. And I'll bring some back for Jinny Caribaldi so she won't be mad at me because I was late."

Karyn made a phone call to her sitter, who was delighted at the prospect of not having to cook dinner, and then she and Raquel walked out of the building together, joining the thousands of employees exiting the Cybelle complex.

It took them nearly twenty minutes to make it to the little bar called Klancy's, and by the time they got there the place was filled with wall-to-wall bodies, most of them Cybelle employees.

There was no place to sit, but tiny Raquel managed to shoulder her way to the bar and return with two glasses of beer, and then a couple of men vacated a small, high bar table, so the two women grabbed it for themselves.

"Did you catch Cilla's change of outfit today?" Raquel inquired.

"Yeah . . ."

"You think she spilled her lunch or what?"

"Maybe," said Karyn loyally. "You know how yellow shows everything."

"Right," muttered Raquel.

They talked for a while, Raquel gossiping about various people at Cybelle.

Finally, Raquel began talking about her "fiancé," telling Karyn about how she had become engaged. "I had to keep dropping hints," she confessed. "Like, I'm a good Catholic girl and I can't live with a guy, it's against my religion. Finally we went out to dinner at Mountain Jack's. He gave me my ring in a glass of ice water, isn't that cute?"

"Yeah."

"I nearly drank it all down before I saw the ring and then I just screamed. I cried so hard that a waitress had to bring me Kleenex."

Karyn shifted uncomfortably, remembering what Annie had told her about Raquel and Brett breaking up. She couldn't help staring at the ring on Raquel's finger, wondering if Annie had been wrong. Maybe they were back together now, and Annie just hadn't heard.

She told Raquel that Mack had asked her to marry him in the car one night after they'd been making out. "Not very romantic, I guess. But Mack wasn't big on romance. I was pregnant six weeks after we got married."

Raquel nodded. "Yeah ... the pregnancy thing. That scares me so much. I use three kinds of birth control when I'm with Brett. The pill, the condom and foam. And even then I worry. In my family, you're supposed to be a virgin when you marry, see? And birth control is a sin. So I'm really a sinner, huh? My sister Ana thinks I'm awful."

Finally, Karyn excused herself, saying she had to stop and buy the chicken, then go home.

"Hey, it's been great," said Raquel. "But I gotta go now, too—I've got to call my honey, see what he's up to."

Raquel was smiling brilliantly, every inch the happy, engaged bride-to-be.

Most of the department's employees had gone home over an hour ago. The PA system had stopped playing its usual elevator music, and Cilla could hear the roaring of a vacuum cleaner and floor polisher coming from somewhere down the hall. Several of the maintenance workers were laughing and joking.

She sat in her office, still trying to regain her composure after her nightmare afternoon with Lou Hechter.

Please, God, she prayed. *Don't let it be repeated.*

What was she going to do with this awful beige skirt and shell she'd purchased at the hotel shop? She hated beige. She would throw it out, she decided. After all, it was Lou's dollar, not hers.

Cilla forced herself to start reading a big stack of reports, and had gotten halfway through a mall-intercept survey when her phone rang.

"Well, Cilla, are you ready for our date tonight?"

"Tonight?" she squeaked. "Oh, lord."

"Don't tell me you forgot," said Shane Gancer, sounding crestfallen.

"No," said Cilla, breathing fast. "I didn't forget, I was just crunching at work. A million projects. I have to go home and change, shower, and then I'll drive over there to the lake."

Cripes, she was thinking. Lake St. Clair was an hour-and-a-half drive away. In rush hour traffic, with M-59 slowed by more construction, it could easily take her closer to two hours. Why had he suggested a place so far off? Right now she'd settle for something within ten minutes' drive of her condo. In fact, she'd be perfectly happy if she'd never even had the foolish impulse to say yes to his dinner invitation. She must have been totally out of her mind to agree to going out with a man so much younger than herself.

"I could pick you up," he suggested. "It would be much more fun if the two of us rode over there together; we could sort of talk along the way."

What she should really do was postpone this whole fiasco, Cilla thought. She was tired, and the ugly session with Lou that afternoon had drained her. She no longer felt like being adventuresome with a younger man.

"Or we can go somewhere closer to where you live," suggested Shane. "Then we wouldn't have to battle major gridlock. I know a little nightclub that just opened on Rochester Road. They've got a really great band. Top forty stuff," he added. "Not industrial or anything like that."

Cilla stifled a groan. Dance? But at least it wouldn't take them two hours to get there.

"All right, let's try it," she heard herself say.

"Great!" The enthusiasm in his voice speared her. *He* didn't sound tired at all. In fact, he sounded almost obnoxiously bubbly and "up" as if he'd just been the forty-ninth caller on a rock radio station. But, hell, he was twenty-six, Cilla told herself wearily. Twenty-six-year-olds had enthusiasm for everything. They never got tired. It was nothing for them to work all day and dance all night.

She hadn't planned on going to a club. She'd heard Mindy talking about some music called "industrial" but had no idea what it was. Oh, he'd said they didn't have it. Still, what was she going to wear?

"I'm really looking forward to seeing you," said Shane Gancer, sounding eager.

"So," said Raquel's older sister, Ana, later that night. Ana had stopped by Raquel's apartment with a basket of homemade tortillas and some brownie squares. With her she'd brought her youngest child, Tonio, a chubby, adorable six month-old, who sat in his baby carrier seat bubbling spit out of his mouth and cooing.

"So how you been doing, sister? We never see you. Guess you don't want to be around your family anymore."

"It isn't that," said Raquel, flushing. If Ana only knew.

"Mama's been making remarks—well, you know how she gets. She says she bets you don't even go to church anymore, either. You missing mass, Raquel?"

"A couple of times," admitted Raquel sullenly.

Her sister went on. "What's the matter, you stay out too late to get up in the morning? Why don't you and Brett just go to the Saturday night services like we do? Then you can sleep in all you want."

"Ana—"

"Missing mass is a sin," insisted her sister, pressing her full lips together. "If Mama and I don't remind you, who will? Living in this apartment like this . . . where's your roommate?"

"She's at her boyfriend's," responded Raquel tightly.

"And I can imagine what she's doing, huh? When you

give it to a man before marriage then why should he stick around and stand in front of the priest with you, huh, Raquel?" Ana shook her head. "You'd be better off, come back and live with Mama down in Ferndale. The house, it isn't much, but at least you wouldn't be tempted to sin." Ana paused significantly. "By the way, where *is* Brett?"

Raquel stared hotly at her older sister. "Why do you ask, Ana? Don't you know that they're asking the same thing about your husband, Fred? Where's Fred on Friday nights? Is he over at the lodge playing pool? Is he—"

Ana reached down and picked up the baby boy, who began to squirm in her arms, wailing as he sensed the changed mood of the two women. "You don't know nothing about Fred. You think life is all sweetness and pleasure, you can do what you want when you want. Well, that's not the way it is. There are rules to follow, God's rules. I follow them. So does my husband. We have a happy marriage under God. And you should be looking to have that, too. Where *is* Brett, Raquel? Mama heard them talking at church. They said they saw him with another girl."

"They did not!" Raquel cried in horror.

"Jeanetta Barclay and Maria Fernandez, they were having lunch at Chi Chi's and they saw him with her. It wasn't no business lunch, Raquel. They were sitting real close and they kissed," said her sister in a loud voice.

Raquel slumped in her chair. Waves of hot and cold traveled through her body, and her stomach twisted so violently she thought she might vomit.

"You're still wearing his ring," said Ana after a long moment.

"Yeah—I am." Raquel quickly recovered herself. "And we're still engaged, Ana . . . we're still getting married. We just had a fight, that's all."

"You'd better get that man back again, Raquel. Before it's too late." Ana looked at Raquel with moist eyes. "I know I come down hard on you, but Mama sent me here and I had to say it. You gotta get him back. We all love you, Raquel. Really. We just want what's best for you."

Raquel felt sick after Ana left, almost too ill to move. She stumbled to the living room couch and threw herself down on it, listening to the heavy, panicked thump of her heart.

Cilla was an expert at putting Lou out of her mind. She wasn't sure how she did it, she just knew that she could shove him into a tiny compartment of her brain, chaining him in with heavy chains and locking two or three padlocks. When she had finished locking him up, he no longer existed for her. That was the way it had to be.

By the time Cilla stood under a shower for the third time that day—once in the morning, once in the hotel room, and now, getting ready for her date—she started to feel better.

She hadn't danced in—when? A year? The last time a date had taken her dancing, he'd been so out of condition that he was puffing and panting after two fast songs and kept begging her to return to their table and rest. Yes, and he'd been fifty-eight years old.

She wondered how long Shane Gancer could dance. She'd bet it was an entire set without stopping.

Cilla stepped out of the shower and began rubbing body lotion over herself to soften her skin, which tended to be dry. Of course, he probably wanted to get her in bed, Cilla thought, her mood dropping a notch.

But she caught it before it descended too far. She certainly didn't have to sleep with Shane; in fact, she had absolutely no intention of doing so.

Sex was very low on Cilla's list of priorities right now. Not that it had ever been that high.

The bathroom was steamed up, and even the face of her little Cartier watch was befogged, but when Cilla picked it up and glanced at it, she was first galvanized, then panic stricken. Christ, it was already 7:50. Shane was going to be there in ten minutes and she was totally naked, her hair dripping.

"You look beautiful," said Shane Gancer, gazing deeply at Cilla across the dinner table. He wore a black silk shirt and light tie, with pleated black trousers, his hair combed straight back from his face. He looked wonderful. He added, "I mean, you are gorgeous, you remind me of Sharon Stone."

Sharon Stone? Cilla had met Sharon personally and knew there was absolutely no resemblance.

"Thank you," she said demurely, stifling a laugh. Fortunately, he'd been twenty minutes late, giving her time to mousse and dry her hair, and climb into a slim black silk jumpsuit she'd found at Nordstrom's last week. It had a sexy, low neckline and a little half-attached vest covered with silver soutache embroidery. With it she wore a pair of Mindy's shoes that her daughter had forgotten to take back to college with her. High heels, clunky and saucy.

In fact, she'd better get the good out of the jumpsuit now, because as soon as Mindy spied it, it would probably end up in a suitcase on the way back to Albion.

The nightclub was getting crowded, every table filled. Most of the people, Cilla couldn't help noticing, were twenty-somethings. Cilla found herself searching the restaurant, looking for couples who might be around her own age. She felt a stab of relief when she finally spotted a couple on the other side of the room who looked to be in their late thirties. God, was Cilla the oldest person in the room?

She wrenched her mind away from the idea.

They looked over the menus. Cilla had been afraid that Shane would start talking about rock groups, but instead he began making conversation about the latest congressional scandal. She began to relax a little; at least she wouldn't be forced to admit that she got all of her information about current rock groups from her twenty-year-old daughter.

Their meals came, shrimp-and-vegetable stir-fry for her, and grilled ahi tuna for Shane. Shane started telling her about some of the Thai dishes he had learned to prepare from a law school roommate who had come from Bangkok.

"You cook?" Cilla had just assumed that men of Shane's age lived on pizza, tacos and fast food. Lord, she was making all sorts of assumptions about him that weren't even true.

"Love it. And I've been jumping since I was seventeen."

"Jumping?"

"Sky diving."

Cilla laughed, gazing at Shane and totally reassessing him. "You sky dive? Really?"

"Cilla, there is a moment when you have just jumped and you're freefalling through space and the plane has moved far away from you. The sky overhead is this incredible, deep blue. Everything around you suddenly becomes awesomely quiet. I call it the blue silence. It's something you just have to experience."

"Blue silence. That's a wonderful phrase."

"It's a wonderful experience. You'll have to jump with me sometime, Cilla."

"Whoa," she said. "Me?"

Shane's face lit up. "You would love it. It's awesome."

"Oh, I couldn't."

"Yes, you could. Everyone is terrified their first time, but then that moment happens, and it's all worth it."

Cilla nodded, picturing herself crouched at the lip of some open hatch at the edge of the sky, screaming and begging to be taken back to earth. Probably wetting her pants as she swung from a harness four thousand feet up. She couldn't afford to be that crazy; she had a daughter to support, a job to do. Did Shane really want her to risk her life for some "awesome" experience? Did all of his girlfriends jump with him? But, of course, she wasn't going to be his girlfriend.

*   *   *

The band turned out to be an all-girl rock band who had opened for Salt 'N Peppa. They were curvaceous black women dressed in spandex and glitter, and they did two entire sets without one slow song.

The dance floor was jammed with dancers, everyone elbow to elbow, butt to butt. Cilla was astonished to see what an easy, fluid dancer Shane was, and also how tireless he was. And sexy. Oh, that, too.

By the end of the second set, Cilla thought she would be tired, but her adrenaline had kicked in, and she felt as fresh and energetic as all of the other women who were boogying. Her sessions with the aerobic videos had paid off. She was here with a good-looking man; she was keeping up with him, having a wonderful time.

"You are something," remarked Shane as he walked her back to their table while the band took a break. "Every man on that floor was looking at you."

Cilla could hardly believe this; some of the women had been only a year or two older than Mindy.

"The music is great," she responded, deflecting the compliment.

"*You're* great. I mean that. So classy-looking. You just look like class, Cilla."

"Shane—"

"Oh, I know, I'm coming on way too strong, but it's the way I am. We resonate together; I feel it, don't you? On that dance floor we are dynamite." The way he said it, Cilla knew Shane was implying they'd also be dynamite somewhere else.

Whoa, she thought. But wasn't she also enjoying this a great deal?

They spent the band break talking about themselves. Or rather, Cilla kept the conversation on Shane. She wasn't ready to tell him that she had a twenty-year-old daughter and had been already thirty when she gave birth.

Shane had two young nephews whose father had died in

a plane crash at Selfridge Air National Guard Base during practice maneuvers. The boys lived in Chicago now. He regularly visited. He liked children, Cilla realized, feeling a small pang.

"I suppose you plan to have a family of your own some-day," she began.

He looked at her. "Why do you say it like that, Cilla? I haven't got a mad urge to have a dozen children, no, if that's what you're thinking. I have a feeling I'll never have children, but it doesn't really bother me as long as I have Jeffie and Kurt. They're my children, really."

She looked down at the table top, feeling another surge of the same discomfort she'd felt when he first asked her out. Good heavens, she was at the end of child-bearing age. Yes, a few women of fifty-five or sixty had borne children, but they'd had to be pumped full of hormones—and didn't they use some other woman's eggs?

Suddenly her feeling of vibrancy about the evening evaporated. She was having a great time dancing, sure, but she was just fooling herself if she thought it could ever be more than that.

On the way home, Shane chatted cheerfully about the band, who he said had played in Ann Arbor when he'd been a student.

Gradually, Cilla became quieter and quieter. Yes, she'd kept up with younger women, and she supposed she was "classy," as he said, but . . .

"I had a really superlative time," said Shane, pulling his Ford Explorer onto the driveway apron of Cilla's condo. He leaned across the gearshift and gave her a soft, searching kiss. His breath tasted as sweet as a slice of watermelon.

"I . . . I really should get inside," Cilla mumbled, terrified he would want to come in with her.

"I know; I've got to get up early tomorrow and catch a flight to O'Hare," he told her. "I'm visiting my two nephews this weekend."

Cilla started; after all that sexiness on the dance floor she'd expected him to try to put the make on her, not to inform her he had to fly to Chicago. Every time she made an assumption about him, he surprised her.

"Good night," she whispered, opening the passenger door and stepping down out of the vehicle. Men she knew didn't generally drive sport utility vehicles.

Shane got out and walked her to the door. He didn't touch her again. "I'll call you."

Cilla looked at him, nodding, and then she fumbled in her purse for her house keys, in her nervousness dropping them on the pavement.

Grinning, Shane bent over and picked them up, handing them to her.

"For you, my lady."

She found herself looking into his eyes, seeing the kind, good humor there. And suddenly she was smiling back.

"My daughter is twenty," she blurted. "And I was thirty when I had her. Which makes me fifty, Shane."

His smile gentled. "You were born in, when, 1949?"

"Yes."

"A very good year, 1949. A vintage year for women."

He waved to her and was gone.

For Raquel, the weekend stretched on forever, endless chunks of time she was unable to fill satisfactorily. Her roommate, Heather, was staying most of the time at her boyfriend's now, and they were talking about living together, which meant Heather would be moving out soon and Raquel would have to find someone else to share the rent.

Raquel spent Saturday morning sleeping, her head hunched into the pillow as she tried to forget that Brett wouldn't return her phone messages and wasn't home anymore, was probably with a woman.

They'd seen him with her, seen them kissing. . . .

Was it serious? Was he falling in love with this other

person? Maybe it was just a casual thing, Raquel tried to tell herself. Maybe even a one-night stand. Although Raquel didn't believe in promiscuity, for once she hoped that's all it was.

At 1:30 P.M. she finally dragged herself out of bed and phoned Brett at home, but of course, all she got was the machine again. Raquel left several messages, but her voice faltered. She really needed to see him in person.

She went shopping at Somerset, buying herself a clingy silk sweater, which she put on to wear on the drive over to Brett's house, just in case she'd find him home. Wrong. He wasn't there, and the plant hanging on the porch was beginning to droop slightly from lack of water, a sign Raquel didn't like at all.

She pulled into the neighbor's driveway and told a middle-aged woman that she was Brett's fiancée and was worried about him because he hadn't been home in several days. Had the neighbor seen his car in the driveway? Would she tell Brett that Raquel had been asking about him?

"Honey, I don't keep track of my neighbors' comings and goings," the woman told her kindly but firmly. "Call and leave a message on his answering tape, why don't you, and I'm sure he'll call you back when he can."

Raquel left, disconsolate. When she'd been seeing Brett their weekends had always been packed with activities. The comedy clubs down in Royal Oak, dance clubs, concerts, going to the Mongolian Barbecue, the movies, taking in the Auto Show at Cobo Hall, or doing things with his or her family.

Now what was she supposed to do?

She ended up going to her health club, working out on the exercise bike, then taking an aerobics class. Then she bought herself a sandwich at a restaurant the two of them had frequented, hoping she'd see him. She did this both Saturday and Sunday.

She had never felt so lonely and abandoned in her life.

* * *

"Morning.... Good morning.... Jim.... Good morning. ... Hey, Raquel.... Good morning...." Cherise, the security guard, was glancing at employee cards, greeting the hundreds of people who thronged past her on their way in to begin another Monday at Cybelle.

Raquel waved at her friend, then continued on down the marble walk, heading toward the center tower of the building instead of to the Fashion Department. Lou had a meeting this morning and wouldn't even notice she was late, and she just had to try to see Brett, even for two minutes.

Raquel boarded an elevator with a surge of arriving workers, riding up to the third floor, where she turned right, left, right again, progressing through a maze of cubicles, and rooms opening into other rooms. Around seventy women sat elbow-to-elbow at rows of computer monitors punching in data. Raquel always felt guilty when she walked past them. In Data Entry you were judged by how many characters you could enter in a minute, and supervisors were strict. The women couldn't even use the bathroom except on designated breaks.

Brett and the other programmers were located at the far end of the wing, and she made her way there, finding her ex-fiancé's cube empty, his computer turned off. He usually got to work about five or ten minutes late, Raquel knew.

There was an extra chair, so she sat down in it and began looking possessively around Brett's office space. He had a mouse pad printed with the logo of Amazon.com, the online bookstore. He had pinned several Detroit Redwings posters on his wall, along with a big map of Maui, Hawaii, where Brett had spent a summer working at a restaurant in Lahaina. They'd planned on going to Maui for their honeymoon.

Raquel blinked back hot tears. All the pictures of her were gone. But at least there wasn't a picture of any other woman.

... not yet. She sat there miserably, wanting him to arrive yet somehow dreading his arrival as well.

"Raquel." Brett came around the corner and stopped abruptly at the sight of her. He was wearing a new, blue-striped business shirt she hadn't seen before, and looked freshly showered, clean and handsome, his damp hair curling at his temples. She could smell his deodorant and cologne, the familiar scents hitting her like a punch to the gut.

"Hi," she said hoarsely.

"What are you doing here?" he demanded.

"I . . . we . . . we have to talk."

"Please. I asked you not to come up here. Raquel, I've got a ton of work to do this morning."

"Two minutes."

"Which you'll turn into a hundred," he said bitterly. "Raquel, please, why can't you accept the fact that we're not together anymore?"

"I can't . . . I can't accept it."

"We broke up. It's over."

"No, no, it's not!" She jumped to her feet, starting toward him, intending to fling her arms around him, but Brett stepped away, leaving her clutching at air. His face was creased with embarrassment and distress.

"Raquel, I know it's rough on you, but you've got to stop doing this to yourself. All those messages on my answering machine . . . I don't even listen to them, I just erase them. You drive past my house all the time. And you're still wearing the ring I gave you. I'd like to have it back."

Raquel snatched her left hand behind her back. "No, please . . . Please. I can't give it back."

"Why not?"

"Because we—we could work this out if we tried. Brett, you know we always were able to talk; you said I was too possessive but I can change, I can be more what you want me to be."

Another programmer, heading toward his cube, turned to

stare curiously, and Raquel lowered her voice, shamed. "I need you," she whispered. "Please, Brett. Please let me keep the ring and we can work this out. Let's meet after work tonight and we'll have dinner, and then we'll go to your place and we'll—"

Brett looked miserable. "No, Raquel. I don't want to hurt you, but . . . no."

"Brettie . . . why? Why are you treating me like this?"

"Because I can't spend the rest of my life with you, Raquel. You suck a man dry." Brett rubbed his temples as if his head was aching. "Shit, Raquel. Please. Keep the ring if you want, if it means that much to you. It's yours. Just promise me that you'll go on with your life, okay? It'll be worth it to me if you'll just go away, Raquel. Don't call me. Don't bother me anymore."

She lifted her reddened eyes, stunned by the angry weariness in Brett's tone of voice.

"Brett," she whispered. She could barely force his name out past the hurtful lump in her esophagus.

He moved toward her, pulling her up by both hands and gently pushing her out of his cubicle. "I've got to turn on my tube and get to work, Raquel. Don't come up to this department again, okay? I mean it. Or I'll report you to Human Resources."

Raquel stumbled toward the elevator, forced to stand and wait while it picked up arriving employees on the main floor. All the horrible things that Brett had said were reverberating through her brain at once, like a racquetball bouncing around a court. She heard all of them and none of them; they pounded at her skull until she thought she'd scream.

Still, he'd let her keep the ring.

She clung to this precarious hope. He wouldn't have let her keep it if there wasn't a tiny chance for them to still be together.

*   *   *

Back at the Fashion Department, Karyn Cristophe was just arriving, hanging up her jacket in the departmental coat closet.

"Hi," said Raquel, giving her coworker a fake, too-brilliant smile.

Karyn looked at her. "You okay, Raquel? You look like you're coming down with something."

Raquel gave a little for-show cough. "Maybe just a cold. I stayed up late over the weekend," she volunteered. "It's bringing down my immune system."

"Well, I brought in some doughnuts from Dunkin' Donuts, that should help your immune system," said Karyn, holding up two colorful boxes imprinted with the chain's logo. "It always helps mine."

"Doughnuts! Great!" cried Raquel, reaching out greedily. "Any chocolate covered?"

"About a half dozen. You can grab one first if you want."

They walked to Karyn's alcove, where she opened both boxes and set them on the top ledge for people to take as they walked past. Raquel poked among the offerings, selecting her choice, then moved into Karyn's space, sinking into the extra chair. Delicately she took a nibble from the pastry.

"Men," she muttered. "I mean really. Men!"

Karyn looked up. "I know just what you mean."

"I don't understand what they do, why they are the way they are."

"They don't understand us, either, I guess," Karyn offered.

"They don't even try!" Raquel munched silently for several minutes. "My fiancé, Brett, doesn't want to talk about anything."

Karyn laughed a little bitterly. "My ex-husband wanted to talk too much. He wouldn't leave me alone even after it was over. I lost my job because he kept calling me at work."

Raquel did not want to hear this. "So why did you get divorced anyway?"

"A lot of things. We got along great in bed, but we argued all the time as soon as we got out of bed, and once Mack got an idea in his head . . . well, he just wouldn't change, no matter what I said or how much I begged. He had some funny habits, too. Like a shopping neurosis."

"Shopping neurosis?"

"Yeah. He'd go to the department store and buy a blue jacket that he liked, and later he'd sneak back and buy it in eight other colors and hide the other ones away. I'd find them months later in the basement or in the back of his closet. It cost us a lot of money."

"That's weird," commented Raquel.

"One time Amber wanted a certain doll, and Mack went out and bought her thirty of them."

"Thirty!"

"But he only gave her two, the rest he stuffed in a box in the garage. The store took them back, thank God. . . . Our bills were terrible, Raquel. He'd cry and tell me he wouldn't do it again, and then he would. I dreaded getting our charge card bills. Fortunately the cards were in his name, that was really lucky, because we were late making payments quite a bit."

"I'm sorry."

"He didn't hit me, but he . . . threw things, like a VCR, and once some spaghetti. It got to be scary. When he threw the spaghetti in front of Amber, that's when I decided to see an attorney."

Raquel continued to eat her doughnut, wiping her fingers on a tissue she found in a box on Karyn's desk.

"So, are you glad you got your divorce?"

"Yes, I am." Karyn said it firmly. "Raquel, I know it sounds awful, but I couldn't love a man who did all those things. Every time I looked at those two dolls of Amber's,

I hated him. I just didn't want to be near him anymore. Even if he gets better, I'll never want him back."

Neither Patrick nor Carrie, the two University of Michigan interns, were in today, so a bunch of their work fell on Karyn. She sent more than fifty two-page faxes to a group of people in Cilla's merchandising association, very time-consuming, especially when a number of the machines were busy and had to be redialed.

Lou Hechter had flown to New York early this morning and would be there for the remainder of the week. He also kept the machines jumping with faxes he was sending to Cilla.

In between sending her own faxes, Karyn trotted back and forth delivering Lou's faxes to Cilla.

"Thanks, Karyn—you're a godsend," said Cilla, accepting one of them. There were blue shadows under her eyes this morning and she kept yawning. "When the interns are here they'll do most of the faxing."

"It's no problem," insisted Karyn, smiling.

Returning to the fax room, she discovered the machine rolling out another six-page fax from Lou, this one addressed to her. It was a nearly illegible list of names, phone numbers and E-mail addresses, and Lou instructed her to give the list to Raquel so she could add it to his Lotus Notebook program.

It was the note at the bottom of the last page that startled Karyn, causing her to look twice. It said, "Thanks, luscious Karyn."

Karyn lifted up the fax and reread the note, wondering if she'd interpreted it correctly. Surely it couldn't say what it looked like.

But what other word was similar to *luscious*? *Delicious*? That wasn't much better. Well, it was probably just a mistake, she assured herself. Lou's handwriting was dreadful, and maybe he had been jet-lagged when he wrote it.

Anyway she didn't have time to wonder about it now.

It was time to go comb her hair and get ready to meet Roger for lunch.

At exactly 11:45, Karyn crossed the big Cybelle main lobby, a beautiful space that soared three stories high, domed over by a huge skylight. She'd heard that Dom Carrara frequently utilized the dramatic setting to hold press conferences right here.

A computerized water fountain splashed, played on by blue, pink and green lights. Seated on the edge of the fountain, looking just as nervous as Karyn felt, was Roger Canton.

He rose, starting toward her. "You're right on time," he remarked.

"I'm usually pretty prompt."

They smiled awkwardly. Sunlight fell down from the skylight onto Roger's head, revealing reddish highlights in his short brown hair. He had a smooth, ruddy face, just slightly padded, but on him the few extra pounds of weight looked good. He looked like a man who regularly watered his front lawn and spent Saturday afternoons washing his car. Cozy, comfortable, ordinary.

They walked out past the security desk. "You do have your employee ID with you, right?" asked Roger. "I mean, to get back in again."

"I always carry it," responded Karyn.

Traffic was three lanes in each direction in front of the complex, cars whizzing back and forth. They had to walk about one hundred yards down the street to the light, where knots of other Cybelle employees were also waiting to cross. Karyn recognized several familiar faces, including Dennis Gabriel, a menswear merchandiser from her own department.

"Hi, Karyn . . . Roger," he said, looking at them both.

"Hey, Dennis," said Roger, managing to say it in such a

way that Dennis wasn't encouraged to join them.

They walked across with the light, then strolled a half block west to the Mexican restaurant, Roger telling her all about how a woman from Cybelle had jaywalked last year and ended up getting hit by a car.

"Pretty stiff price to pay for a couple of tacos," he said, smiling.

"I hope she's all right."

"Yeah, you see her every day. It's Cherise, the guard at the number-two gate. She broke her leg and over two hundred people signed her cast."

Karyn smiled back, ordering herself to relax.

The lunchtime crowd was gathering, the restaurant lobby jammed, but Roger had made reservations and they were escorted directly to a booth.

Roger recommended the fajitas, so Karyn ordered the chicken and he ordered beef. Tortilla chips and salsa arrived, something for them to do with their hands while they tried to get a conversation going.

She asked Roger how long he had been working at Cybelle.

"Over ten years, can you believe it?" he told her. "I started out in the Vic Rondelli regime. I've seen a lot, believe me. I've seen them come and go."

Roger began telling Cybelle stories. Then he got started on what it was like to attend the ready-to-wear shows in Paris. Actually, it was more like a lecture on the fashion industry. Somewhere in the middle of it their food came, and Karyn attempted to load up her fajita and eat it without dripping. She saw that Roger had spilled a dab of fried onion on his tie.

And all the while Roger continued to talk. About work. And the fashion shows. Then more Cybelle stories. She tried to be interested but felt her eyes begin to glaze. Karyn felt relieved when the lunch was finally over and the waitress deposited their check tactfully in the middle of the table.

"This has been fun," she lied as Roger put several bills in the folded leather case for the waitress to pick up.

"Hasn't it? We'll have to do it again."

They walked back across the street, caught in another crowd of returning Cybelle employees, while Karyn fought her sudden, deep disappointment. Roger had seemed so nice. But he didn't know what to talk about, and he didn't even know enough to ask her about herself. Face it, he was a dud.

They entered the lobby, both of them showing their employee cards to the guard behind the big main desk. Roger suddenly turned to Karyn and said, "Oh, hell, I really blew that one, didn't I?"

"Blew it?" But she knew what he meant.

"I acted like a total jerk, pounding your ears off with those boring stories. Karyn, I promise you, I'm not really like that. You intimidated me, I guess. I don't usually have diarrhea of the mouth like that. Honest I don't. Sometimes I even ask penetrating questions."

She couldn't help it; she laughed. "Roger, we were both nervous. I kept eating that fajita and wondering how much I was spilling."

"I did spill." Grimacing, Roger pointed to his tie.

"Am I really intimidating?" Karyn asked in a low voice.

"Yes. To me. Karyn, you may not be aware of this but you have the beauty of a fashion model. You're tall and you're a classic size eight. If you lived in New York, you could get a job on a runway. I know you could."

"A runway model?" Karyn giggled. "Not with the way I stumble all over my feet."

"Well, you'd have to have a training program, I guess."

"A very comprehensive training program."

They were both smiling now. "I'm glad you're not a model," said Roger. "I'm glad you're here at Cybelle. Do you suppose you might consent to try it again with me? Lunch, I mean, or even dinner. I promise not to talk like a company brochure."

Karyn hesitated, then reached in her purse for a pen and a scrap of paper. "This is my home number," she said. "But don't call after nine, that's when my daughter, Amber, goes to bed, and I don't want the phone to wake her."

Roger gave her a long, searching look. "You have a daughter? How old is she?"

"Eight."

Belatedly, Karyn remembered that Raquel had told her about Roger's divorce, his ten-year-old daughter now living with her mother in California. She could see the pain in his eyes.

"Well . . ." she said awkwardly. "I have to stop at Travel on my way back to the office to pick up some E-tickets. I really enjoyed lunch."

"You didn't. But I promise you'll enjoy it a lot more in the future. I'll call you, Karyn."

The week passed quickly, and so did the following weekend, which Karyn spent hanging wallpaper borders in her small kitchen and picking out some curtains at Sears for the dining room window. She also took Amber and Caitlin to the movies and bought them McDonald's afterward, allowing Caitlin to sleep over.

Her parents called on Sunday night, and Karyn raved about her job, telling them how much she was enjoying it.

"Cybelle is just so big, there's always something interesting going on, and I love seeing all the new fashions. One day at lunch this week they had a fashion show in the cafeteria with employees modeling all the styles. That was a lot of fun. Raquel said I should sign up to model next time."

"Are you financially all right?" asked her father.

"I'm doing fine, Dad. The money you loaned me has been just a lifesaver. I'll start paying you back as soon as I'm on permanently."

"Now, we told you it was a gift, not a loan."

"I can't take your money, Dad. You and Mom need it for retirement."

It was heartwarming to talk to her parents, and she repeated all the fashion news for her mother when she came on the line, describing the styles that women would be wearing nearly a year from now. "Everything is getting more ladylike, but sexier, and you should see the tube tops and camisoles they're buying!"

Shortly afterward, Roger Canton called her. Again, Karyn received the impression that Roger was a kind, caring, ordinary man—but ordinary in a good sense.

He told her that his hobbies were skeet shooting, working on the two cars he owned—one an antique DeSoto—and reading. "Nothing fancy. Just the Tom Clancys, the John Grishams, and I like Dean Koontz, too."

"I should read more," Karyn admitted. "I watch TV too much. I'm trying to break myself of it. Sometimes I tape the afternoon talk shows on the VCR and watch them after Amber's gone to bed. Oprah's my favorite, though. I thought I might get some books from her book club."

"What's your favorite book of all time?" he asked her.

Just a pleasant conversation. She remembered his brown eyes and the sparkling interest in them. They arranged to have dinner.

They ate at Scallops, a seafood restaurant in Rochester, then strolled along the sidewalks of downtown, window-shopping and looking at the fashions displayed in the windows of Mitzelfeld's, the local department store, which catered to a slightly older crowd than Cybelle.

They capped off their evening by buying ice cream cones at the Baskin-Robbins across the street. Mocha almond chocolate for her, plain chocolate for him, both in waffle cones.

"I haven't walked along eating an ice cream cone in years," confided Roger.

"Me either."

"My ex-wife stopped wanting to do things with me. This is really great, Karyn. I can't tell you."

When they finished their cones, Roger found a trash receptacle for their napkins, and then he took Karyn's hand in his. They walked holding hands like high school kids, their shoulders occasionally brushing. They were almost the same height, and Karyn enjoyed being able to look straight at him, instead of up.

Finally, Roger drove Karyn home.

"Thank you for making my evening," Roger told her at the door of her apartment building. He gazed at her, smiling, attractive wrinkles fanning out from his eyes. A moment hung between them—would he kiss her, should he, did she want him to?

Karyn solved the problem by leaning forward and kissing him lightly on the lips. His mustache was faintly tickly. His lips were soft, and he smelled of a vanilla-scented aftershave and clean soap. Roger allowed the kiss to be light and didn't grab her or try to make it more than it was. Right then she realized how nice he was, and it almost scared her a little.

"I had a great time," she whispered.

"Me, too, Karyn."

The following Wednesday, Amber was in a talent show at school, and Cilla gave Karyn the afternoon off so she could go and see her daughter perform. Amber was going to be singing "Tomorrow," the song made famous in *Annie,* and had been practicing it all week at home.

Sitting in the audience, Karyn found her mind drifting back to the evening with Roger. If he'd tried to come on too strong, she knew, she would have backed off from him and ended their relationship.

There was enthusiastic applause for a young magician. The teacher who was serving as the emcee came out and announced that the next act would be Amber Cristophe singing her version of "Tomorrow." "Everybody give a big round of applause for Amber."

Karyn pounded her palms together until they hurt, pride swelling her chest as Amber walked up to the mike, her hair a cloud of gold, brushed until it shone. She was wearing a new red dress that Karyn had brought home from the sample store at Cybelle, adding a white collar. In it she looked like a real stage Annie.

The petite girl took the mike off its stand, waited for the background tape to start playing, then began belting out "Tomorrow" in a voice that—to Karyn—sounded professional enough to go on Broadway.

As her daughter sang, Karyn felt tears prick her eyelids. Just in time, she remembered to pull out her flash camera and take several pictures.

Amber received more applause than any of the other kids, accepting it with a radiant smile, waving over the top of the microphone at Karyn and blowing her mother repeated kisses. "Isn't she talented?" some woman in the row behind Karyn said. Karyn snapped more photos.

When it was all over, the parents were invited on the stage with their children for cookies and Hawaiian Punch. Amber ran up to Karyn and threw her arms around her mother. "Did I sing good?"

"You sang perfect! Amber, you were wonderful. And I'm not just saying that. You really, really were."

"I like singing," said the child complacently. "I like everything here. We aren't going to move again, are we?"

"No," said Karyn, feeling a choke in her throat. How many times had her daughter asked her that? "We're staying right where we are, cupcake. Michigan is our home now— for good."

The next morning, Roger called Karyn at her desk. "There's a chili fest going on Sunday out in Saline. They're going to have clowns and an egg-drop contest, and plenty of chili to taste. Would you and Amber like to go?"

Karyn felt her skin go red as she remembered that sweet, light, on-the-lips kiss.

"I'd like to go," she agreed cautiously. "But Amber's having a busy weekend. I'll need to see if I can find a sitter for her."

"Oh? She'd have a lot of fun and a lot of other kids will be there."

"It's maybe a little too soon, Roger. It'll confuse her . . ."

"Oh. I understand. Don't wear good clothes," he advised. "This is going to be kind of a messy day. You'll see what I mean."

When she arrived home that night, Karyn asked Jinny if she'd mind taking Amber on the following Sunday afternoon.

"If you'll take Caitlin on Thursday night and have her sleep over at your place." Jinny blushed. "An old friend of mine is going to be in town and, well, we haven't seen each other in a while."

Karyn stared at her, not realizing at first what her neighbor meant, but then she did and felt her mouth go dry. Jinny was going to have a man over, of course. Karyn felt the fiery blood throb through her skin. Sex with a man . . . how long had it been for her? Well over a year.

Did she feel . . . that way . . . about Roger Canton? Could she?

Later, she sat down at the kitchen table with Amber and began going over math flash cards with her daughter, barely able to concentrate.

"Mom, ten times eight is eighty, not forty!" cried Amber, interrupting Karyn's thoughts. "I gave you the wrong answer on purpose and you didn't even hear me."

"Sorry, cupcake. Let's go over the stack of cards again."

* * *

Another busy day at Cybelle. Antwan Jones, the mail clerk, had just rolled his cart through the department, dropping off a pile of letters, periodicals, junk mail, FedEx and DHL packages, interoffice envelopes and memos accompanied by "buck" slips. A nursing student at nearby Oakland Community College, his skin so dark that it had bluish tinges, he greeted Karyn cheerfully. "Your usual humongous stack of mail and five DHL packages, isn't that nice? They're keeping you busy, I see."

"Well," said Lou, looking up from his desk as Karyn walked in to give him the internationally sent DHL packages. "Aren't we looking spiffy today."

Karyn flushed. It was a sunny, Indian summer day, and the sun streamed in through the windows, heating up the hallway, so she'd taken her jacket off. Underneath she was wearing a cotton blouse open at the throat.

She said quickly, "Antwan left three or four more packages for you, and a binder. I'll go get them." She turned and started to leave, but he stopped her.

"Wait. All those packages . . . would you like to see what this firm in Amsterdam sent me yesterday?"

Reluctantly, Karyn paused.

"Come, come, come," said Lou impatiently, waving her behind his desk as he bent to take a manila envelope out of a drawer in his credenza. "I just want to show you some of the stuff we reject. It'll really educate you about the fashion business."

He opened up the clasp and shook out a pile of crudely printed brochures. One was a lingerie catalog, the garments garishly cheap, modeled by big-breasted blond women wearing "big hair" wigs and heavy makeup. And the poses . . . Karyn stared, shocked, at a photo of one woman in a black lace teddy squatting down and toying with her own crotch.

"Really," she began, backing away in discomfort.

"Amazing, isn't it, what some of these foreigners will try

to sell us," Lou remarked, laughing jovially. "Looks like the models are a bunch of the pros that sit in the windows in Amsterdam trying to get customers."

Why was he showing her this stuff? He was acting like it was perfectly normal to show an employee suggestive pictures. Maybe for Lou it was. The male way of thinking . . . Maybe Lou did not realize how distasteful she found it, Karyn tried to tell herself.

"I need to get you your packages because Cilla wants me to go down to Travel and pick up some airline tickets," blurted Karyn. She heard Lou laugh as she darted out of the office. She hurried back in with the remaining DHL shipments, anxious to get the chore over with and depart.

When she returned Lou had already put the brochures back in their envelope and was peering at a spreadsheet on his computer monitor. The incident might never have happened.

"Oh," he told her in an offhand manner. "Put those on the floor by my credenza."

Karyn did as she was told, then left, anger spurting through her. She strode fast down the hall, reaching her alcove, where she immediately put on her jacket again, despite the fact that the air hadn't gotten any cooler.

"You're wearing a jacket? It's so hot in here," remarked Raquel, coming into Karyn's alcove. "I called down to Building Systems; I think the air-conditioning is on the fritz."

"I just—I just would feel better with my jacket on."

Raquel cocked her head to one side. "Anything wrong?"

"No . . . I guess not." Karyn felt hot and flustered. "It's just that Lou showed me these pictures . . . I mean, they were a little, well, awful."

"Underwear catalogs, you mean?"

"Yeah."

"He does that with new women, thinks he's going to impress them or something. If he does it again, you tell him it's against your religion and make the sign of the cross."

Karyn couldn't help laughing a little as she gazed at the petite, intense Raquel, who did, at this moment, have a small gold cross hanging on a chain around her neck. "It worked for you?"

"I called my priest, Father O'Meara. He came down here and had a short talk with Mr. Hechter."

"But what did the priest say?" Karyn wondered.

"I don't know. But Lou backed off all right. Ever since then it's been all business, no funny stuff—if you don't count the yelling. I hate him, he hates me, but I think he's afraid to fire me . . . afraid the Catholic Church will roast him in hell or something."

Karyn nodded, the smile leaving her face. "Seriously. Why would Lou do that? Doesn't he know I'd find it offensive? Those pictures were . . . more like porn than a real catalog."

"He didn't even do it," said Raquel bitterly. "That's the thing you have to realize about guys like Lou. If you react the wrong way he just gives you an excuse and puts a different spin on it, and suddenly you're the one who's acting out of line, not him, and the whole thing never happened."

A group of women from the buyers' floor were trooping down the hallway and began calling out. "Raquel . . . Karyn . . . we're going down to the mini cafeteria for yogurt and strawberries. Come on with us."

"Sure, why not—if it doesn't take too long," said Raquel. She grinned at Karyn, including her in the group. "Karyn here needs to cool off."

Walking down the hallway with the group of women, Karyn tried to put the incident with Lou Hechter out of her mind. This was a prestigious Fortune 50 company. Lou was one of the top-earning executives at Cybelle, and he was Karyn's boss's boss.

She didn't want to get on the wrong side of him. She couldn't afford to, not if she wanted to be hired on permanently. A company needed no excuses to end a temp's assignment—they could tell her on Friday afternoon at 4:45 P.M. that her assignment was over and that would be that.

On Saturday, Jinny Caribaldi's sister, Marie, and her husband were giving a picnic and had invited Karyn and Amber to come, along with Jinny and Caitlin.

Jinny's sister had a farm out near Ortonville. The place was enchantingly rural, with a falling-down red barn, a couple of horses, and a clutch of orange farm cats. In a field a crop of pumpkins in varying sizes awaited harvesting in a couple of weeks. Amber and Caitlin raced through the pumpkins, marveling at the biggest ones. Both girls were allowed to pick out small ones for themselves.

"One of the tabbies had kittens," said Jinny to Amber. "Do you want to see them?"

The kittens were eight-week-old, mewing balls of fur. Amber cradled first one, then another, oohing and aahing.

"Would you like to take one home?" offered Jinny. "If it's all right with your mother. Caitlin's going to get one, too."

Amber's face lit up. "Is it?" She rushed over to Karyn. "Oh, Mom, is it?"

They ended up taking home an adorable orange kitten that Amber named Missy, stopping at a pet store to stock up on cat food, cat treats, a cat pan, and kitty litter.

Amber begged Karyn to buy a little carpeted shelf they could hook up to their window for the cat to sun herself on.

"Honey . . . all this cat equipment is really adding up," said Karyn, thinking about her dwindling checking account balance.

"Please! Please!" Tired out from her long day, Amber seemed about ready to throw a tantrum in the pet store. "Missy needs a shelf! She needs this! You can't be cruel to her and not get it!"

"All right, then, you can pay for half of it out of your allowance," said Karyn finally.

At home, they settled the kitten into a cardboard box, which Amber planned to keep in her bedroom at night. "What will she do when I'm at school and you're at work?"

"She'll probably sit on the kitty shelf," remarked Karyn dryly. "She'd better, after all the money we paid for it. Scoot, Amber—go and take your shower and get ready for bed."

While Amber was in the shower, Roger Canton called.

"I tried calling you most of the day but you were out," he said. "I was just calling to say hi."

They talked for over forty-five minutes. About kittens and pumpkins, the chili fest he was taking her to tomorrow, his divorce and hers, and where they had both grown up.

"I was born in Norwalk, Connecticut," Karyn said, hearing the shower stop running. In a moment she saw Amber run past, wearing her sleep shirt. She motioned to her daughter to go to bed and that she'd be in in a minute.

"So that's why your accent isn't real thick Southern."

"I don't have an accent!" she cried indignantly.

"I think you picked up a *little* bit of an Atlanta drawl."

She laughed. "I don't drawl."

"If you say so," he teased.

The following morning, Roger picked Karyn up at 11:00 A.M. wearing a pair of well-worn jeans and a polo shirt that showed the effect of many dozens of washings. Karyn decided he looked much sexier in jeans than in work clothes.

Amber spoke politely to Roger when introduced, then immediately dragged him off to see the kitten in its box.

"Isn't she fuzzy?" Amber enthused.

"She's just about the fuzziest cat I ever saw."

"We bought a shelf so she can sit in the window and look out."

"She'll really enjoy that. We had one for our cat, Cleopatra, and she practically lived on the windowsill."

"Oh, you had a cat? Don't you have it anymore?"

"My daughter still has her." A cloud passed over Roger's face, and Karyn hastily intervened, saying she had to take Amber and the kitten upstairs to Jinny's.

"Mom," whispered Amber as they climbed the stairs. "Are you going on a date?"

"Yes."

"Is he gonna, you know, kiss you and all that sex stuff?"

Karyn grimaced. When she was eight she hadn't even known the word *sex* but now kids picked up amazingly adult things from talk shows and sitcoms.

"He's going to be very polite. And you are, too, today, you and Caitlin. Jinny tells me that she's taking you two to the movies."

"Yeah! We're gonna see that movie with the parrot. I saw him on TV. He's so *cuuuute*."

While Roger waited downstairs in the hall, Karyn brought Amber upstairs to Jinny's, digging into her billfold and producing enough movie money for all three, handing it to Jinny. Jinny refused, but Karyn pressed it into her hand. She wanted the latchkey arrangement to work out and did not want to take advantage of her upstairs neighbor.

"I'll probably be back around seven or eight," she told Jinny.

"I saw your date out the window when he drove up. He's cute."

Karyn flushed. "You could say that."

Returning to the first floor, Karyn excused herself to fetch a jacket. She decided to change to a pair of black running shoes that would not show dirt or mud. As she was lacing the shoes, her phone rang.

She picked it up, at first hearing only breathing on the other end of the line.

"Hello? Hello?"

"You're just a little tease," said a male voice, hoarse and

muffled, with a ring of familiarity to it. "But I know what you want."

Quickly she slammed down the phone. She hadn't heard the voice clearly but . . .

"You seem upset," Roger remarked as they got into his Ford minivan, its interior vacuumed spotlessly clean and smelling of leather upholstery.

"It's . . . that was a heavy-breather phone call."

"Oh?"

"Yes. I've had them before, but it's always a little scary. I usually just hang up fast."

"Maybe you should think about getting Caller ID."

"I'll wait and see," she finally said. "My budget is already so tight. Also, now I'll have cat food to buy, and I can already tell Amber's going to want nothing but the best."

The rutted field near Saline, on the outskirts of Ann Arbor, was already lined up with cars, vans and pickups, and dozens of parked motorcycles, more roaring in by the minute.

The long tent held a double row of tables presided over by about thirty local chefs who were already heating up their versions of chili, with names like "Super Red Hot Mama Chili" and "Road Kill Special." At 2:00 the chili would be ready for tasting, Roger told her, served in tiny paper cups. Crowds would pour into the tent, people carrying the little chili cups, and everyone would soon be bumping into everyone else, slopping chili.

"And then there's the egg-drop contest," Roger added, pointing outside to a huge cherry picker. "A guy's going to stand in the top of that thing and drop eggs for people to catch, and if you think the chili gets messy, wait until you see what a flying egg can do."

"Oh, I want to catch an egg!" cried Karyn, suddenly caught up in the gala mood of the afternoon.

Roger laughed. "Wait until you see a few other people catch them before you decide if you want to enter the contest, Karyn. Raw eggs can be mighty slippery."

Karyn quickly changed her mind when she saw the first contestant get splattered with yellow from hair to shoes. Roger and Karyn stood watching, standing at a safe distance from the yolk splatters.

"I have to admit, meeting your little girl made me feel a bit sad," remarked Roger. "She's younger than Annie but she looks something like her."

"Raquel told me you had some legal problems with visitation."

"I'm working them out."

A young, leather-clad biker was trying to catch an egg now, and after two tries managed to cup one in both hands without shattering it. The crowd whistled and applauded, and the loudspeaker blared that the kid had won two tickets to see Randy Travis.

"I'm not every woman's dream man," Roger admitted. "Renee told me I was boring. She said I didn't offer her enough excitement. But I feel that I'm exciting inside."

Karyn stood close to him, so that their shoulders brushed. "Maybe exciting isn't everything there is," she said. "Mack was exciting, but the downside of excitement is fear. I don't want to be afraid again. I don't want to worry about what's going to happen if a man gets mad. I don't want to scrape spaghetti off another wall, and I don't want to open another drawer and find nine identical windbreakers hidden in there, each one in a different color."

He grinned. "I only have three jackets, and one of them is eight years old, Karyn. And I cook spaghetti, not throw it."

There was another heavy-breather phone call on Sunday night, and again Karyn slammed down the phone. This time the muffled voice had sounded different—maybe it wasn't Lou. Still, she slept restlessly, waking several times during the night to go in and check on her daughter.

Thunder was rumbling on Monday morning when Karyn dragged herself out of bed, got Amber ready for school, and drove her and Caitlin to Simonton Elementary School. She watched her daughter and Caitlin run into the building, joining a group of other little girls.

At Cybelle, Karyn found her In basket filled with dictation tapes Cilla had done over the weekend at home. She put in the earpiece and began crashing on the work, typing letters and memos and a mail-merge letter to twelve recipients. In all, she created twenty-one letters. Karyn was proud of her fast typing and enjoyed having the opportunity to show it off.

By the time she looked up it was nearly noon, and she'd promised to meet Roger Canton in the cafeteria for a quick bite. But before she could gather up her purse, Lou Hechter suddenly appeared at her desk.

"Raquel left for lunch early and I need some faxes sent," he told her brusquely.

Karyn looked at him, wondering if he had been her unwanted phone caller.

"All right."

"Come into the fax room and I'll show you what has to be done."

This was the very last thing that Karyn wanted. But she felt she had little choice except to follow her employer into the fax room. Lou spent several minutes explaining that the same cover page was to go on all six faxes, then paused, staring at Karyn assessingly.

"How old are you?"

"What?"

Lou gave a quick, snorting laugh. "Not that you have to answer if you don't want to. With all these crazy new rules and laws, an employee could be eighty-two years old and no one would dare say a word."

Karyn shifted uncomfortably, remembering the "luscious Karyn" fax he had sent her a week or so ago. She decided to ignore the question and just concentrate on punching phone numbers into the machine.

"You're very pretty, you know," he remarked. "Were you always this pretty? Were you one of those high school prom queens?"

What was she supposed to say? In Norwalk there had been a clique of wealthy girls who were the prom queens, not girls like Karyn. She finished one fax, started the next one.

"I'll bet you were. All dressed up in a pink gown with a big corsage on your wrist," said Lou, smiling. "Did you ride to the prom in one of those white limousines all the kids use?"

"We didn't use a limo," Karyn finally said. "His parents drove us."

"So sweet and Southern. What is your ancestry, Karyn?"

"I'm an American," she said evenly.

"Those cheekbones and those eyes," mused Lou. "I keep wondering if you might be, you know, Eurasian or maybe French. You *know* what they say about Frenchwomen," he added in an insinuating undertone.

"No, I don't," Karyn snapped.

Lou seemed startled at her negative response. But before he could react, Dennis Gabriel walked into the room with a paper in his hand.

"Uh, oh," Dennis said. "A long line for the fax?"

"No, I'm finished," said Karyn, walking out of the room.

She took a short break, walking down to the coffee room at the end of the hall, where vending machines dispensed coffee, soft drinks and snacks, and there was a telephone employees could use for private calls.

The truth was, she just didn't like Lou.

She found his personality grating and his innuendos offensive.

One of her ancestors had come over to this country from France right after the Revolutionary War. Some of her ancestors had been mountain men and trappers, helping to open up the country to trade. She hated it that Lou had made this into a sniggering, off-color joke.

After lunch Karyn made some travel arrangements for two designers on the staff, typed up itineraries, dealt with a printer problem, helped Cilla fix a footer on one of her reports, and sent group E-mails to fifty people about a meeting.

"So you're dating Roger Canton," said Raquel that afternoon when she and Karyn walked down to the mini-cafeteria for a yogurt break. Only one man was getting a hamburger at the counter. The room seemed small, much more intimate than the huge regular cafeteria that served meals to thousands daily. Outside, it was drizzling gray rain. The good days of fall were disappearing.

They stood at the yogurt machine, mixing strawberry with vanilla into cardboard cups.

Karyn blushed. "How did you know?"

"Somebody saw you in Saline last weekend. They said you were holding hands."

Karyn felt a stab of annoyance. "Is there much that people don't know?"

Raquel giggled. "But, hey, this is one man you ought to grab. I mean it. He's a good catch, and there're tons of women who are after him."

"Oh," said Karyn, taken aback. Roger hadn't given her that impression somehow. In fact, he'd told her he'd dated very little, and she believed him.

"Do you like him?"

"Yes, but . . . I don't want it to move too fast."

They took their yogurts to a table. From the cafeteria window they had a view of a cement patio where fifteen or twenty employees were gathered for a smoke break. One of the men was flirting with a woman, pretending to pull her long hair, and she was laughing.

"Food," advised Raquel. "Food is the way to a guy's heart. I hope you have lots of really special dishes you can cook up for him. That's what I do for my Brett. I have a recipe for beer-battered chicken he's crazy about. And I make *chalupas* and soufléed green chile enchilada; that's very good, and it's cheap." She shrugged. "You know, south-of-the-border, burn-your-mouth stuff."

"I'm more the microwave type," admitted Karyn. "Well, I do cook a little pasta once in a while."

"Then maybe you should buy some sexy underwear from Victoria's Secret."

"I'm more the bargain panties from Penney's type."

"Girl!" cried Raquel. "Revise some of that thinking! This is a *man* we're talking about. You've got to be exciting. Keep him just a little off kilter, always keep him guessing. Meet him at the door wrapped in pink Saran Wrap."

Karyn laughed. "Get back. Did you ever do that, Raquel?"

"Well, once. It made me sweat. I felt like a piece of fried chicken."

"What did Brett think?"

Raquel looked proud. "Well, let's put it this way. I didn't wear it too long."

They walked slowly back to the Fashion Department, Raquel carrying a tray with five yogurt cups on it for others who'd begged for a treat but couldn't leave their desks.

As soon as Karyn got back to the department, Cilla asked her to walk up to Dom Carrara's office and hand-deliver a report.

"Don't forget you'll have to ask the security guard to punch in the tower elevator code for you. He'll have to call up there first. So maybe you'd better call and tell Sondra Zapernick you're coming."

A visit to Dom Carrara's office! Karyn felt a buzz of excitement as she walked to the special executive elevator near the main lobby and gave her name to the security guard. In the business world, Dom Carrara was a semicelebrity. Since he'd taken over as CEO of Cybelle, he'd been on the covers of *Fortune, Forbes,* and on CBS and NBC, plus CNN.

To her he seemed so down-to-earth, and she really liked his smile, which seemed genuine. It was hard to grasp that he was paid over $12 million a year in salary and bonuses and was a multimillionaire.

The elevator whispered up five floors in a matter of seconds. A beautifully groomed woman with silvery-gray hair was seated at a marble desk and talking on the telephone. In a moment Sondra Zapernick hung up and smiled at Karyn. "You must be Karyn from Fashion."

"Yes . . . Cilla Westheim has a report for Mr. Carrara," Karyn explained eagerly.

"I don't believe we have met before," said the corporation president, emerging from his office just as Karyn was handing the report to his secretary.

Karyn smiled with pleasure, beaming at the tall, handsome, gray-haired man who ultimately held the fate of her job in his hands.

"I'm Karyn Cristophe, I just started in Fashion. I'm Cilla Westheim's secretary." She didn't add that she was only temp to perm.

"I'm very glad to meet you, Karyn." Dom extended his hand and Karyn shook it. His handshake was pleasantly firm. "May all of your weeks be excellent here, Karyn. I know this is a big corporation, but I do try to keep in touch with our employees. If you have any problems or concerns, give my secretary a phone call or drop me a quick memo."

As Karyn nodded in surprise, he excused himself and went into one of the conference rooms on the floor.

Sondra Zapernick smiled kindly at Karyn. "I heard that Cilla had a new secretary who types over one hundred words a minute."

"Yes." Karyn blushed. "When I relax and I'm not thinking about my speed I can go even faster."

"I only type ninety," admitted Sondra. "But most of my job is being a gatekeeper anyway," she added. "I schedule just about everything Mr. Carrara does. And by the way, his offer to see you if you had a problem was genuine. He doesn't have a lot of time, but every week he sees two or three employees for about ten to twenty minutes each."

Karyn felt the urge to linger and talk to Sondra more, maybe ask her how she'd climbed the corporate ladder as she'd done, but she knew the woman was terribly busy.

"Thank you. It was great meeting you," she said.

"Good luck here, Karyn."

Riding back down in the executive elevator, Karyn's cheeks blazed pink. Not that she'd ever bother Dom Carrara with a memo or phone call. Still, she felt a sudden surge of pride that she was working at Cybelle, that she was a part of everything here. That he *would* talk to her if she really needed it.

After Karyn left to deliver the report to Dom Carrara, Cilla got up from her computer and went restlessly to the window, where she stared out at the reflecting pond, which was being dimpled right now by thousands of pelting raindrops.

She'd spent the weekend sitting by the phone, hoping for a phone call from Shane. Even though he was in Chicago, she'd hoped he might call her anyway. Finally she'd given up and gone shopping.

She'd found herself buying way too much, selecting clothing that was much younger and trendier than the garments she usually purchased for herself. Her chief extravagance was a Todd Oldham black sequin dress with spaghetti straps and naughty tassels at the neck and back-slitted hemline. Definitely not your average fifty-year-old's dress.

But turning in front of the three-way fitting room mirror, Cilla admitted to herself that she could still wear the young outfits. Her stomach was still flat. She *didn't* look her age. She looked great for fifty. Hey, she looked great for forty.

But as she changed back into her street clothes, a mood of depression swept over her.

Was she being a fool, picturing herself wearing that expensive Todd Oldham on another date with Shane? What was *he* doing this weekend while she was shopping and waiting? Were there other women he saw? A hunk like him, only twenty-six . . . he could have his choice of women.

"Mom," Mindy had said, calling late on Sunday night as Cilla was in her home office, dictating some letters. "I just got back from Dylan's house—I met his whole family— they have a cottage on Elk Lake. I had such an awesome time."

"Mindy," said Cilla. "I thought you were going to be working with freshman women. Didn't you tell me those were your plans?"

"Sure, but they got someone else to fill in, Mom. I'm not *tied down* to Albion College; I can go somewhere for the weekend if I want. Anyway, why are you so concerned? You have that new guy you're dating, right? That Shane guy?"

"Yes," Cilla heard herself say, not quite the truth.

"Well, then. Hey, does he have kids?"

"No."

"He doesn't? I thought most older guys had a couple of grown kids."

Now, Cilla thought, now was the time to tell her daughter that Shane was only twenty-six. But he hadn't even asked her out for the weekend and she might never see him again, so why was his age important?

"Shane doesn't have kids," she responded nervously. "And I'm really not seeing him—"

"Shane, that's a funny name, don't you think?" Mindy giggled. "Most guys in the baby boomer generation have these awful names like Alan and Barry and Bruce. Or even Hoooowaaard." She stretched the vowels out, making fun of it.

"That'll be enough, Mindy," said Cilla crisply. "Next time you go to spend a weekend at a boy's house, I want to know about it ahead of time or you don't go, is that understood?"

"Mom—"

"You are still not twenty-one yet, and I'm responsible for you, Mindy."

"Oh, you are such a *worryass*," cried Mindy. "Honestly! I guess I can spend a weekend at a guy's house without you making a federal case out of it. Anyway, I didn't sleep with him there because his mother put me in a room way down the hall. But I have slept with him at Albion."

"Melinda. Are you using protection?" Cilla managed to say.

"Mom—"

"I want to know if you're using a condom and if you're still getting your pills refilled every month."

"Of course I am, do you think I'm stupid? I don't want to get knocked up like Daddy's girlfriend. Oh, I forget, she's his *wife* now. Gotta go, Mom. 'Bye."

Cilla stared at the phone in her hand, finally replacing the receiver, filled with an acute sensation of frustration and loss. Mindy had been such a cute, precocious little girl. Her first word had been "Buh Buh," after her beloved teddy, Billy Bear, then had come "Daddy" and "Mama." When Mindy had spinal meningitis as a six-year-old, Cilla sat by a hospital bed holding her daughter's hand, even sleeping on a cot in the room. She would have given her own life to save Mindy's—and still would.

Now, Cilla admitted to herself that Mindy was basically out of control. The divorce between her and Bob had come at a time when her daughter was very vulnerable. Mindy had gone through a traumatic year, deciding to place all of the blame on Cilla for "driving Daddy away."

Never mind that Bob had selected a bimbette with pneumatic breasts and buns and a few spots of teenage acne still on her face, getting her pregnant like any stupid high school boy. Never mind that Bob had drained their savings accounts and cashed in an account earmarked for Mindy's college expenses. Sure, the judge had later made them divvy up what was left semi fairly, but Mindy was unable to see how selfish her father was, and she didn't want to see it.

The desk phone rang, jerking Cilla away from her unpleasant thoughts.

"I catch you at a bad time?" said Shane Gancer.

Cilla flushed. "Just catching up on some work."

"Hey, I've got a ton of things to tell you about. I went to Mt. Pleasant with the Sky Jumpers. We were practicing this incredible circle jump with seventy-five people all diving in a huge circle. It was awesome. Sorry I didn't call but somehow I left your number at home and you're unlisted. Well, anyway, I'm back and the Sky Jumpers are giving a party next weekend, want to come along with me?"

She thought about refusing, but the idea only lasted a nanosecond. "I guess I could."

"You won't be pressured into jumping, if that's what you're worried about. We have plenty of spouses and girlfriends who just participate in the social events. Anyway, I really want everyone to meet you. They're a great group—and I know you'd have a lot in common with them."

They talked a while longer, then Cilla said good-bye and hung up. Her heartbeat was surging, adrenaline dancing through her again.

He'd called. He wanted to see her again. Deep in her heart she had believed he would not. She sat in her swivel chair, laughing. This was so crazy. . . .

Maybe she would call her hair stylist and see if Bobbi could fit her in for a cut. Something a little different. A little younger.

The restaurant located in the top of a Troy high rise was crowded with businesspeople eating on expense accounts and enjoying a sweeping view that stretched for miles across

Oakland County, giving glimpses of Pontiac's white Silver-dome stadium and the Daimler-Chrysler Corporation Head-quarters complex in Auburn Hills.

Lou Hechter sat across a booth from Chuck Krantz, a gray-haired vice president of Legal Operations. Chuck was one of the company's veterans who had been around even longer than Lou. He and Chuck had climbed the ranks together. Together with Vic Rondelli, Ray Karmer and a few others, they now comprised a formidable bloc on the company's executive committee.

The executive committee was meeting tomorrow, and Lou and Chuck had a few matters they wanted to get straight.

"So how's it hanging, Lou?" Chuck wanted to know as a waitress brought them drinks.

"The usual. Gets to be boring after a while, the same-old, same-old," complained Lou. "Only bright light on the horizon is a new lady in my department, looks like Michelle Pfeiffer on Demi Moore's body."

"Hey, I'll have to swing by and take a look at her."

"She's sexy, all right. A natural-born flirt," said Lou.

"You know how to pick 'em," said Chuck, gazing at his crony admiringly. "Every woman in your department looks like she just stepped out of *Playboy*. Even Cilla. For an old lady, I sure wouldn't push her out of bed."

Both men grinned. They knew Lou hadn't. Chuck was one of the few people Lou'd told about Cilla, and as far as Lou knew, Chuck had kept totally quiet about Lou's relationship with his employee. Hey, Chuck couldn't afford to talk, either; he'd been banging his secretary for years, giving her raises way out of line with raises other women at her level were getting. Chuck had also bought the woman a summer home near Traverse City.

Lou had helped him out a few times with the suspicious wife thing, providing a cover when Chuck wanted to get away for a weekend.

"This new lady, you think you can get in her pants?" Chuck wanted to know.

"Does a beaver wear a fur coat? Of course I can get in her drawers. I always do, don't I?" Lou drained his Manhattan and waved at the waitress to bring him another one. "It'll just take some time to work on her, is all."

"Are you ready to order, gentlemen?" asked the waitress, a woman in her thirties.

"Yeah, sweetie, I think we are. Give us good service, pretty darling, and we'll give you a nice tip. And if your phone number comes with the check, the tip will be extra big."

The waitress tightened her lips, getting out her pad to take their orders.

Karyn was feeling more at home at Cybelle every day. Cilla sent her on many errands, and she now was friendly with five or six departmental secretaries, various travel agents, and other employees scattered over the huge headquarters building.

One morning she got a phone call from Cherise, at the #2 door. "A Russell Brandon is here at the guard desk to see Cilla Westheim. Can someone come and get him?"

"I'll be right down."

Karyn's heart skipped a beat as she got up from her desk. Russell Brandon was a male model sent by a local agency to appear in a resort season ad. He was here to meet Cilla and several of the merchandisers, who would talk to him about the shoot. Karyn had never met a male model before and was looking forward to the experience.

When Karyn reached the door, however, she saw no one standing at the guard desk except for two security guards.

"Is Mr. Brandon here?"

Cherise grinned. "He's in the men's room, primping. Said he'd be right back."

Ten minutes later, Karyn was still pacing around and

glancing at her watch. Cripes, she thought, he was taking more time than she did. But finally the model appeared, strolling down the hallway from the direction of the nearby rest rooms, attracting more than a few stares from passing employees.

Karyn, too, couldn't help staring.

Brandon was dressed as if he were already at the ad shoot, wearing tight jeans and a white leather vest hanging open to reveal a muscular, suntanned chest and a washboard stomach. Underneath the vest was nothing but skin. Hadn't he realized he was going to be entering a standard, shirt-and-tie office environment?

"Russell Brandon?" asked Karyn, feeling a strong urge to laugh.

"Yeah . . ."

"This way. It's kind of a long walk, and it's confusing around here, that's why I had to come and get you."

On the eight-minute walk back to the department, Karyn tried to make conversation, but Brandon answered mostly' in monosyllables. His walk was more of a strut. As they passed knots of Cybelle employees, people did double takes at the sight of the partially dressed model. Karyn felt as if she were leading around a Chippendale dancer.

When they reached the Fashion Department, Raquel was busily typing at her computer screen and barely looked up, even though she'd known the model was arriving this afternoon. Karyn wanted to giggle—was Raquel really that blasé? Then, just as the model passed, she observed Raquel taking a discreet peek.

Karyn knocked on Cilla's office door. Two of the merchandisers, Mary and Jenny, were already in her office. "Cilla, Russell Brandon is here."

"Oh, good," said Cilla. "Show him right in."

Karyn stepped aside to usher Brandon into the office, then was startled when the model suddenly ripped off his vest, exposing his bare, ripplingly muscular chest to the three women in the room.

"This is how I'll look in the ad," he told the three executives. "I just wanted to show you."

He turned and strutted and preened, naked from the waist up.

Neither Cilla nor the others showed a change of expression, keeping poker faces. Surely this couldn't be standard procedure, could it?

Karyn backed out of the room and went to her desk, sinking into her chair and giving way to waves of giggles. Only at Cybelle, she thought. And the way Cilla and the others had kept straight faces . . . It had been hilarious.

"Did you see him?" she whispered to Raquel when she passed her alcove to go to the color copier.

"Did I ever."

"He just—and they—" Karyn sank into Raquel's extra chair, still giggling. *They didn't even crack a smile.*

Raquel grinned impishly. "They're trying to keep it professional. After he leaves they'll get down and talk about his lats and his pecs and all that. I've heard them arguing about models before. Cilla hates it when they have moles. You wouldn't believe. Everybody wants to be in the Cybelle ads because they're so sexy and appear in the major women's magazines."

Ten minutes later, the model reappeared at Karyn's desk. "Okay, now how do I get out of this maze?"

She jumped to her feet. "I'll show you back to the door again. You'll have to sign out in the guest book."

He had his vest back on and was gazing at Karyn intently. "I really want the exposure here," he told her. "Put in a good word for me, will you?"

"I . . . I'm not sure my opinions have that much weight."

"But try," he pleaded.

Karyn felt flattered to realize that this man believed her opinions would be listened to. "I'll do what I can."

To her amazement, about half an hour later Cilla buzzed her on her private line. "So, what did you think of our would-be model, Karyn? Do you think women are going to go for him?"

Guiltily remembering her promise, Karyn thought a minute. She could tell this was a serious question. "To tell you the truth, I can't remember his face, I was so busy looking at his chest. His body did remind me of that romance cover model, Fabio. His body was great. But . . ."

"Go on," said Cilla. "I want your full, honest opinion."

"Okay. He seemed just too cocky. His smile was too hard—I can't explain it. When I'm looking at magazine ads, and there's a male model, the first thing I look at is his smile. I want him to look nice, not all full of himself. I don't care for those snotty, bad-boy type of ads."

"Thank you very much, Karyn. You've been a big help."

Cilla hung up, leaving Karyn bemused. She *had* mentioned the man's good points . . . but had she killed his chance at getting the job? She hoped not, but then maybe she had. So this was the fashion industry.

She loved it.

On Friday night, Shane invited Cilla out to dinner before the skydiving club party, taking her to a Thai restaurant in Rochester Hills.

It was obvious that he was a regular, for both the waitress and the restaurant owner seemed to know him, and Shane suggested that he order for both of them.

"I hope you don't think I'm being sexist," he apologized. "I just wanted to make sure that you got the house specialty, Cilla. If I was a condemned man, this is the place I'd choose to eat my last meal."

The dish was some type of spicy, stir-fried shrimp that was described on the menu as "Angry Young Shrimp." There were subtly flavored vegetables and transparent noodles, and it was delicious. However, Cilla pushed the food around on her plate, unable to do justice to it. Her stomach muscles were clenched tight with nerves.

Shane just looked so great tonight, in an eggplant-colored shirt and tie, his blond hair again slicked straight back from his face. Cilla had worn a pair of stovepipe black pants and a black surplice sweater by Jazz Sport with a hint of metallic weave in it. With this she wore a pair of high-heeled slides. The outfit was a success; Shane's eyes had widened when he first saw her in it, and now he was leaning across the table, his pupils dilated very large and black.

Dilated pupils were a sign, Cilla had read, of extreme sexual interest.

"The Sky Jumpers range in age from twenty to over sixty," he was saying. "About twenty percent of the active jumpers are women. One of them, Jill, is amazing; she is fifty-eight years old and she has over two hundred and fifty jumps to her credit. She's an instructor."

A couple was entering the restaurant, but totally caught up in Shane, Cilla paid them no attention until she heard her name being called.

"Cilla Westheim! Cilla, is that really you?"

A man and woman in their mid-fifties were headed in their direction, the woman dressed in a long, rather matronly beige jacket dress with a designer silk scarf pinned at the neck. The man wore a business suit.

"Aileen . . . Bill . . ." Cilla felt a surge of dismay. Aileen and Bill Hanran were members of a theater group that she and Bob had belonged to before their divorce. Aileen was on the boards of several charities, considering herself a "pillar of the community," and Bill was early-retired from an upper-management job at Daimler-Chrysler Corporation.

Politely, Shane rose to his feet, and Cilla was forced to introduce the Hanrans.

"Well, how nice to meet you, Shane," said Aileen, her eyes resting on Shane with curiosity and interest. In the dim restaurant light he looked incredibly young, Cilla realized in embarrassment. "What company do you work for, Shane?" Aileen inquired.

"I'm with Cybelle," responded Shane courteously. "In Legal."

"Legal? Oh . . . well, don't let us interrupt your meeting," said Aileen, saying a few more pleasantries and then taking her husband's arm as they followed the host to their own table on the opposite end of the room. As the host pulled out Aileen's chair, Cilla saw her dart one more curious glance in their direction.

Cilla sat rigidly, her cheeks stinging. She knew that if Shane had been fifty instead of twenty-six, Aileen would have assumed they were on a date, instead of having a business meeting. Why hadn't she spoken up, why had she allowed Aileen to make the incorrect assumption?

"Relax," Shane said.

"What?" Cilla jumped.

"You have a right to go out with any man you choose without being judged or made to feel uncomfortable."

"I know, but . . ." She faltered. "I couldn't believe she assumed we had to be having a *meeting*."

"My age," said Shane. "It really bothers you, doesn't it?"

She looked down at the covered serving dish that held their "angry" shrimp. "Well . . ."

Shane's smile was warm. "Cilla, I need to tell you that I like older woman, and I always have. I've dated plenty of women my own age, but I've usually found them to be too shallow, wanting to talk about rock concerts, TV shows, their roommate, their annoying job, or the bars they like to go to. I start cracking yawns after about an hour of being with them."

"Oh." She raised her eyes to his, searching his face to see if he was telling her the truth.

"Older women have so much more—of all the inner things," Shane explained. "They've had more years to learn how to love, and they are so much more interesting. Like you, Cilla. I love it that you're a beautiful, intelligent and powerful woman who has her life together and knows who she is and what she wants."

Was that how he saw her?

"And I also find you incredibly sexy," Shane added huskily. "You must have guessed that."

"Yes." She couldn't stop flushing. The hot flashes kept surging over her skin, overheating her body.

Shane's eyes were locked on hers. "I need to tell you this so that you'll understand me better. My first sexual experience happened when I was fifteen, with one of my mother's close friends. We were all staying at a condo on Daytona Beach. The others went out to the beach but I came back to get some money so I could buy myself a boogie board so I could body surf. Georgia was taking a shower. She came out with this towel wrapped around her . . . well, it was an amazing experience for me, just amazing. She told me that women were always going to love me, that I could have just about any woman I wanted, that I could have her anytime, all I had to do was call her."

"I see," said Cilla, stunned at the mind pictures Shane was conjuring up in her head. "How old was Georgia?"

"At the time she was forty. Nowadays they would probably have pressed charges against her, like they did that teacher who had an affair with her fourteen-year-old student, but we kept it a secret. We saw each other off and on for nearly three years. Then Georgia's husband got transferred and they moved away. She marked me for life, Cilla. After knowing her, high school girls seemed immature. They didn't know how to talk. They couldn't make love. All they thought about was themselves."

Cilla was silent, thinking that it was almost a cliché, *The Graduate* reenacted. And it had happened only eleven years ago.

"Does that story bother you, Cilla?"

"No, not really," she lied.

"I haven't had that many lovers," Shane went on. "There was one of my professors at Michigan. And a woman I met while I was in Cozumel one time."

Aileen Hanran was still staring, Cilla noticed. It irritated her. *I'm not a damn cradle robber,* she found herself thinking angrily. *I'm just out to enjoy a pleasant evening.*

She lifted her hand and finger-waved to the woman, and Aileen gave an uncertain smile and looked away.

"Please," Cilla said, hoping to stop Shane from making any more of these revelations about his sexual history. "I don't need to hear any more. I accept it that you like older women. Let's just take it one step at a time, all right?"

"Cilla, we are two adults, right? Adulthood covers a wide range, from about age twenty to ninety. We both fit in that range. Why do we have to worry about what small-minded people like your friends over there think?" He reached out and took her hand in his. His flesh felt warm, full of vitality. "I want you to promise me that you'll just enjoy being with me, and stop worrying."

The fall evening was crisp, a gala yellow harvest moon hanging overhead like part of the party decor.

The party was being held in a big, rambling house in Bloomfield Township, more than 150 people crowded around a bar and a buffet table loaded with a huge variety of hors d'oeuvres apparently brought by the club members.

Shane introduced her around, and everyone seemed to accept her as Shane's date.

"Are you going to jump?" asked Jill Brewton, a vibrant-looking woman with dark brown hair and fine wrinkles on her face. Jill must be the fifty-eight-year-old jumper that Shane had told her about earlier. Startled, Cilla realized that Jill was actually very beautiful. Had Shane dated her? Did his taste for older women extend to women thirty years older than himself?

"Oh, no, I don't think so," she responded.

"Jumping is a peak life experience," said Jill. "Even if you only do it once, you'll never forget it. If you ever decide to try, our club offers classes for beginners. You can take the class and jump all in the same day. Some people jump two or three times in that one day."

"Interesting."

Later, Shane and Cilla walked out on the lawn, where some of the guests were dancing to Top forty music in a large, Victorian-style gazebo equipped with stereo speakers.

"What did you think of Jill?" asked Shane, putting his arm around Cilla.

"She's very unusual."

Shane leaned closer. "I've never dated her, Cilla, if that's what you're wondering. Oh, I saw your face when you met her," he went on, smiling. "Jill has a live-in lover who is also a member of this club. He's sixty. She's a wonderful friend, but that's as far as it goes."

He'd been sensitive enough to read her mind on that one. Cilla relaxed a little. "Age, age, age," she said lightly. "How about if we forget it for the rest of the evening, okay? And maybe we could dance. I think they're just starting to play a slow one."

"My pleasure," said Shane, leading her toward the gazebo.

It was nearly 2:30 A.M. before Shane finally drove his Ford Explorer into Cilla's driveway. Outdoor floodlights lit up the condo complex, but otherwise nearly all of the windows were dark. Most of Cilla's neighbors were in their forties or older, and seldom stayed up much past midnight.

Shane shut off his motor and headlights, and they sat in the vehicle, enclosed by glass and steel. It was a privacy much more stringent than a hotel room.

The kiss began softly but within seconds became deep and seeking, and Cilla wrapped her arms around Shane, straining to get her body closer to his over the gearshift box. Her heartbeat was slamming.

"Cilla . . . ah, God, Cilla . . ." Shane pulled away briefly to mutter her name, then they were locked onto each other again, urgent need consuming them.

Cilla felt her vulva beginning to moisten, honeylike ripples of pleasure traveling through her pelvis. She felt panic rush over her. All she had to do was say one word and he'd be inside her condo and then her bedroom.

"You're so incredibly sexy," murmured Shane, sliding his hands up and down Cilla's sides in such a way that his palms brushed the bases of her breasts. His touch was unbearably tingling, and Cilla couldn't help thrusting herself toward him again, willing him to cup her breasts in his hands.

He had just the right touch, his fingers gently kneading her tautened nipples. Panting, Cilla lifted up the front of her sweater.

"Ah, God," husked Shane, sliding both hands inside to caress her curves through the barely-there lace bra she wore. "Ah, Jesus."

Caught up in the rapture, Cilla was totally focused on the physical sensations. It wasn't until a pair of headlights flared on the street that she realized she was sitting in a sport utility vehicle in her driveway, necking and half naked, in full sight of any of the condominium residents who might happen by.

"Let's go inside," whispered Shane, instantly catching her mood.

Cilla nodded, too excited to speak.

Within seconds she had punched her code into the security pad. Cilla had several lamps on timers, but only one of them was still on in the living room, casting a dim, pinkish glow. Shane slid her sweater up over her head, slipping off the bra, kissing her nipples greedily, his tongue sucking and licking until Cilla thought she would have an orgasm just from this.

"Clothes," she muttered.

They started stripping right there in her foyer, tearing the clothes off each other. Shane had an incredible body, deep-chested and muscular, with a mat of blond hair that began on his chest, wandered down in a thin line to his navel, then broadened again in a springy mass of curly hair. He was already erect, his penis so thick that Cilla wondered how her body could possibly take the breadth of him.

"Bedroom?" she whispered, but Shane was already lifting her up and carrying her to the middle of the living room, where he laid her down on the carpet, spreading her open as if she were an artichoke he intended to nibble bite by bite.

"Please!" she managed to gasp with the last shreds of her common sense. "What about—we need to use a condom. And . . . have you been tested?"

"Yes to both. I tested free of virus. And I put a couple of condoms in my billfold tonight; they're fresh and new."

"I was tested last year and I haven't had sex since then. I'm fine, too." She caught her breath. "A couple of them?"

"Well . . . actually I brought four. I had high aspirations."

She didn't know whether to laugh or to flush bright red the entire length of her body. She settled for both.

Cilla fought under a blaze of pleasure so intense that it burned her like a fire, while she gripped Shane's shoulders, digging her fingernails into his skin.

It was the second orgasm he had given her in two hours, even more piercing than the first one, which had lifted her to heights she hadn't believed possible. In fact, the heights hadn't *been* possible before. During her marriage to Bob, her climaxes had been few and mild. And, of course, with Lou there was no question of orgasm. Now, Cilla had been stunned to hear herself utter a muffled scream of ecstasy.

Just as Cilla came down, Shane began to climax, stiffening and grunting slightly, his head rocked backward, his mouth moving. Cilla opened her eyes, feeling like a voyeur as she watched him, but she couldn't stop herself. Caught out of control, Shane's face seemed beautified, almost angelic. And young. God, he only looked about fifteen, the same age he'd been when he'd had his first sexual experience.

In a moment his orgasm was over; it hadn't been nearly as intense as hers.

Cilla felt a wave of drugged satisfaction. She folded herself over, lying with her head cradled on Shane's chest. The carpeting was fuzzy and not really that comfortable, but she didn't have the energy to suggest that they move.

When was the last time she'd made love on the floor? Maybe when she first met Bob, she thought. And then he had complained about rug burn. Well, she'd bet that Shane had a hell of a case of rug burn tonight.

"You're like a fantasy come true," Shane murmured sleepily.

"And so are you, Shane, believe me."

"Good. I want to be your fantasy for a long, long time."

Shane folded both arms around her, his breathing becoming deep and regular. Perversely, Cilla wasn't sleepy. She tried to lie still, so as not to disturb him. Damn . . . carpeting was very prickly on bare, damp skin, wasn't it? She wanted to scratch herself but didn't dare. Finally she settled for wiggling her butt a little, but that didn't really take care of the itch all along her back.

Lying there, she became aware of ambient night sounds. A siren somewhere on the main road. The on-off humming of her refrigerator's motor. The crackle of ice inside the ice-maker. It occurred to her that they'd stained the carpet with their love juices. In the morning, she was going to have to use a carpet-cleaning solution.

In the morning. Oh, lord, was Shane planning to stay all night? Or even worse, did he plan to sleep on her carpeting all night?

Her mantel clock gave a little click that meant it was the hour, and by stretching a little, Cilla could see where the clock hands were positioned.

Five o'clock A.M.

Suddenly, Cilla remembered her maid, Kristi, a college student who came in twice a month to do a deep cleaning. Oh, lord, Kristi was due to arrive today at 7:30 A.M. If they didn't move, the young woman would walk right in and see both of them naked as jaybirds right in the middle of the living room floor.

Cilla sat up anxiously.

"Shane."

"Huh?"

"You have to get dressed now. I've got a maid coming at seven-thirty this morning—really, I'm not lying. You'd better go. I've got to straighten up a few things before she gets here."

Shane woke up quickly and easily. He sat up, the lamp-light flashing off his bare, beautiful body.

"Cilla, this was wonderful. I can't tell you how wonderful. I want to see you again and again. Can I call you later tomorrow? I mean, today."

"Yes, please do."

He leaned over and kissed her again, this time gently. "I think I'm going to become very addicted to you, Cilla Westheim."

Cilla put on a bathrobe to say good-bye to Shane, who repeated his promise to call her later in the day. It was still pitch-black as he backed out of her driveway.

As soon as Shane's Explorer turned the corner, Cilla rushed into her kitchen, where she rummaged under her countertop until she had found an aerosol container of carpet-cleaning solution.

She had to switch on all of the living room lights in order to see where the stain was. Crouched in the middle of her floor in the first light of dawn, Cilla could still smell the musky odors of their bodies, the delirious scent of sex.

Instead of spraying, she sank with a groan onto the living room couch.

What was happening to her?

Her life was spinning out of control. *She'd made love to a man twenty-four years her junior—on the floor.* And now he wanted to see her "again and again" and had declared that he intended to become "very addicted" to her.

And she wanted it to happen! She was glorying in it.

She breathed deeply. Maybe it could work for a while, she told herself. She deserved something good to happen to her. She'd worked hard for years, she'd been in a bad marriage all that time, and then there'd been the nightmare with Lou Hechter. The financial mess. Her problems with Mindy.

Please, God, she prayed. *Just a few months with him. It's all I ask. I deserve a little happiness.*

Saturday morning for Raquel meant depression. She lay in bed as long as she could, feeling too blue to get out of bed, and then finally awakened around 1:00, only to repeat her usual futile phone calls to Brett's answering machine. It was as if Brett never picked up his phone anymore. Or maybe he had thrown the answering machine onto a basement shelf, forgotten.

"Come on over to the house," said her sister, Ana, calling at around 2:00. "We got a new big-screen TV plus we got digital cable, and it's really fun. You've gotta come and see how great it is. It's like having a computer on your TV screen."

"I don't know. . . . Brett and I were going to do some stuff."

"Yeah?" said Ana, not believing.

"Yeah. I'm helping him wallpaper his bathroom," lied Raquel.

She made an excuse, ending the conversation, then took a shower, and dipped her engagement ring in a cleaning solution so it would sparkle as brightly as her love for Brett. She fussed with her hair, finally piling it high on her head and securing it with a clip. Defiantly she added a touch of lipstick and some plum-colored eye shadow.

Maybe she wouldn't drive by Brett's house today. He was never there anyway. Instead, decided Raquel, she would visit his health club. She'd gotten a cheap, three-days-a-week membership when she'd been going with him, and Saturday was one of the days she was allowed to use the club. Brett used to go there every Saturday afternoon. . . . Why hadn't she thought of this before?

Carefully, Raquel packed her gym bag with the sexiest workout clothes she owned.

The club was located on Telegraph Road. Raquel cruised the parking lot, not seeing Brett's Cherokee. She fought her disappointment, but then told herself that he could have bought or leased another vehicle just to throw her offtrack.

She walked into the lobby, which was crowded with StairMaster machines and rows of exercise bikes, most of them being used, swiveling her eyes to see if she could spot Brett. After showing her card at the desk, Raquel walked through the various free weight rooms, the jogging track, the aerobic room, and even looked through the steamy windows at the pool, where members were swimming laps or relaxing in the Jacuzzi.

No Brett.

Well, maybe he was in the locker room or hadn't arrived yet. She'd make her stay here last a long time, and she'd stick to the lobby machines. It would be tough, using nothing but the StairMaster or the bikes, but at least she'd be more likely to see him if he did appear.

She was on the computerized exercise bike, pedaling along steadily, constantly monitoring the lobby door while CNN played on the television set suspended over the bike area.

Suddenly the man on the bike next to hers spoke up.

"Do you come in here every Saturday at this time?"

Raquel jerked around, startled.

"Are you speaking to me?"

"Yeah." He was about thirty, a slim, compact man with dark hair slightly receding from his forehead. His smile was amused, friendly. "I've seen you here occasionally. Don't you do the aerobics classes?"

"Yeah. And sometimes I do the step classes."

"I've done those; that's really a workout."

They talked about the club for a while, then the topic branched out to personal trainers. "Ever use one?" he asked her.

Brett had been the closest Raquel got to a personal trainer; he had often supervised her on the free weights.

"No . . . I get enough nagging from my family," she quipped. "My mother and my sisters, they try to run my life enough as it is, I don't need a personal trainer to do it for me, too."

He grinned. "I know exactly what you mean. Well, look. I'm going onto the running track for a while, but I've enjoyed talking to you. Would you mind if I gave you my business card? Maybe you could call me sometime if you wanted to have lunch or a drink together."

Raquel wondered where on his workout outfit he could possibly put a business card.

He pulled one out of a pocket in his shorts, and handed it to her. "Hopefully it's not sweaty. I'm John Burgee, by the way. My office number and home number are written down. I'm not married and I'm not living with anyone. I'm heterosexual and I test clean. I don't smoke and I drink socially. I even go to church once in a while."

"I'm Raquel." By now she was laughing. "Do you really carry cards to the club, hoping to meet women?"

"In your case, I do. I saw you outside in the parking lot and I knew I wanted to meet you."

"You're too funny, John."

He inclined his head, giving her a cute, rakish look. "Thanks. Call."

He got up and left, and Raquel followed him with her eyes as he left the bike area and went down the corridor that led to the track. John was taller than Brett, and thinner, his arms and legs all wiry muscle. He had a nice, firm butt, she couldn't help noticing. But she'd bet anything he wasn't Catholic. Catholics didn't go to church "once in a while." They either went every Sunday or they never went.

She didn't know where to put the card he had given her, since her leotard did not have a pocket, so she slid it inside her sock.

He'd been cute, yes, but she probably wouldn't call him.

She loved Brett; she couldn't betray him with another man. Even if he'd betrayed her.

She spent over two hours in the lobby, alternately riding the bikes, climbing the StairMaster, and sitting at the juice bar. Brett did not show up.

Cilla and her girlfriend Eleanor Dishman met occasionally for Saturday brunch and a long gossip session. Today, Cilla realized as she was finally standing in the shower, washing off the fluids from her lovemaking with Shane Gancer, was her day to see Eleanor.

Well, she'd certainly have a lot to tell her, wouldn't she? Cilla could feel every tissue in her body glow.

As she exited the shower, her phone rang. Naked except for a towel, Cilla answered it.

"Don't you play back your answering tape at all?" demanded Lou Hechter. "I called you about six times last night. I was working on something and wanted your take on it."

Cilla felt her glow flicker like a candle going out.

"Sorry, Lou, I was out for the evening," she said evenly.

"Oh? Well, I'm going into the office today and I need your input. I want you to come in for a couple of hours."

"Lou, I've already made plans for the day."

"What plans?"

"Just personal plans, Lou."

In the background, Cilla could hear a woman's voice saying something sharp. Lou was married to Marty Seligman, of the automotive Seligmans, and Marty was also a senior partner in a prestigious Bloomfield Hills law firm. Cilla had always wondered how much Marty knew, or suspected, about her and Lou. There were wild moments when she thought about phoning Marty and telling her everything, but Cilla knew that would be the end of her job for sure.

"Cilla, I'm working up the new TV ad campaign, trying to get some ideas. I have a kickoff meeting next week with Ruhnau Bravo, our new ad agency, and I want to have something decent to bring them so they can run right out of the gate."

"But—"

"*Be* there, all right?"

Cilla agreed to go in for a few hours after her brunch with Eleanor.

She hung up, feeling a flood of irritation mixed with fear. She had no doubt that when she played back her answering tape there'd be the messages from Lou, each one more demanding than the next. Lou Hechter seemed to labor under the impression that he owned her—an impression Cilla certainly hadn't managed to dispel, had she?

Lou was a huge problem. He was the albatross around her neck.

She had to do something about him, especially now that she was seeing Shane Gancer.

Especially now.

"So you have a new maaaan," Eleanor teased when she and Cilla were seated at a table at Sanford's. Both had ordered toasted bagels, along with coffee. Cilla specified that her bagel was to be unbuttered, with no cream cheese. Tempting odors from the adjoining baked goods counter drifted through the room, but Cilla didn't dare even think about getting a raspberry Danish, which was what she really wanted.

"New man?" she parried the question.

Eleanor laughed. "Hey, I can tell by your bloodshot eyes. You look as if you haven't had a wink of sleep since yesterday. Tell Eleanor *all* about him."

Eleanor Dishman was fifty-two, dieted reed-thin, and had been divorced for nearly ten years, in that time going through at least five serial relationships. Lately, though, she hadn't been able to find a man who appealed to her—or so she said.

"There's not a lot to tell," demurred Cilla.

"Oh, right. You've got that postcoital look in your eyes, big-time. Come on, you can tell me. Who is this guy? What does he do? Or more to the point, what did *you and he do*?"

Cilla couldn't help laughing at Eleanor's irrepressible nosiness. "We went to a party last night."

"Oh, whose party?"

"A skydiving club."

"Skydiving? Just who is this guy anyway?"

"His name is Shane Gancer, and he's in the Legal Department at Cybelle," Cilla began, and then she rushed on. "He's twenty-six years old, Eleanor."

Eleanor put down her coffee cup. "Twenty-six? Did I hear that right?"

"Yes."

"Let's see, that's . . ." Eleanor began counting on her fingers.

"You don't have to count it up, Eleanor. It's a lot of years."

Eleanor gazed at her, her glance both curious and admiring. "Well, it looks as if you still have what it takes, Cilla. I'm assuming this guy is a real hunk."

"Why do you assume that?"

But the remark rolled right over Eleanor's head. "Is he good in bed?"

"I don't know; I haven't been to bed with him yet," said Cilla, telling the literal truth. "Not to *bed*. But he was very good."

Eleanor giggled. "Maybe this is just what you need, Cilla, a good fling with a handsome younger guy before you really settle down and get your life squared away."

"I suppose." Pensively, Cilla nibbled her plain bagel. A fling? Was that what this was? It didn't feel like a fling at all to her. It felt as if something a lot more was happening.

"I'm thinking of getting some lipo done," said Eleanor, changing the subject.

"Liposuction?"

"Yes . . . my stomach is getting loose and poochy, and my waistline has gotten two inches bigger in the past two years. My clothes aren't hanging right anymore."

Eleanor was always talking like this—she and Cilla had been debating the pros and cons of liposuction, collagen injections and plastic surgery for years. But before, they'd both agreed that it was silly to take surgical risks, and what if the doctor botched the job? Eleanor's college friend had actually died on the table while getting a neck job.

"I'm serious this time," said Eleanor.

"But you're thin. You're too thin, Eleanor. I've always told you, you'd look better with ten extra pounds."

Eleanor tossed her carefully streaked blond hair. "You can never be too rich or too thin. Well, I'm not rich so I'd better go for thin. Besides . . ." She hesitated. "When I go to a party now, it seems as if I'm not getting the attention I used to. Guys aren't interested in fifty-two-year-old women who look their age. They want the younger chicks."

Cilla frowned. "It's not all looks, Eleanor."

"Is that what this twenty-six-year-old tells you? Face it, Cilla, he probably thinks you're rich and wants to be your boy toy."

Cilla caught her breath. Eleanor could sometimes be cuttingly frank, but this was too much. "I really can't believe you said that."

"But—the age thing. Aren't you worried about the fact that he's so much younger? Twenty-four *years,* Cilla."

Cilla heard the sharpness in Eleanor's tone.

"Both of us are handling it," she said. "And to think that just a few minutes ago you were glad I was having a good fling."

"Cilla, do the math. You're fifty now and you're very attractive. No wonder he wants to take you out. But when he's forty, you're going to be sixty-six. And when he's sixty-six, you're going to be either dead or in a nursing home celebrating your ninetieth birthday."

"Oh, thanks for helping me figure that out," snapped Cilla angrily. She tossed her napkin onto her plate. "Anything else you want to tell me about why this will never work?"

"Well, there's the fact that you're always going to be worried about younger women coming along. You'll end up having a lot of plastic surgery, always being afraid you'll lose him if you don't get it. You'll become a plastic surgery junkie."

"You mean like you're going to be?" Cilla snapped.

Eleanor bit her lip, reddening unbecomingly. "Cilla . . ."

Cilla grabbed her purse, fishing in her wallet for a $20 bill. She dropped it on the table. "Enjoy breakfast on me, Eleanor. I've got to drop into the office this morning, and I really have to fly."

"Cilla, I'm sorry—"

"Look, so am I. But I'm not ready for the damn nursing home yet. Sorry to disappoint you. And oh, by the way, if you'd focus a little more on being fun to be around instead of a stupid two extra inches on your waistline, you'd probably get asked out a hell of a lot more."

Cilla rushed out of the restaurant, her eyes stinging. She and Eleanor had had their tiffs before, but never like this—

never about a topic that seemed to cut right into Cilla's vulnerability.

Cilla managed to put her tiff with Eleanor out of her mind, and helped Lou brainstorm ideas for the ad campaign, snapping at him when he suggested lunch.

"I came here to work, not to ingest calories," she heard herself say.

Lou had nodded. Female diet strictures were very familiar to him. Besides, he was enough of a workaholic not to want to stop to eat anyway.

Cilla left Cybelle by 4:00, driving back to her condo. She had a couple of Weight Watchers dinners in the freezer but they didn't sound appealing. Actually, what she wanted was a half order of baby back spareribs—totally forbidden fare now. She decided to have some water-pack tuna right out of the can, with a small salad. She exercised to her video, pushing the workout. Sweat . . . get past the pain. . . .

She had showered and was looking at the previews for pay-per-view when the phone rang.

"Cilla," said Shane, his voice low, sexy.

"Hi."

"I just called to say I've been thinking about you . . . a lot."

Again that slow, all-body flush crept over Cilla's skin, coupled with alarmingly sensual feelings that radiated up from her genitals. Those orgasms he had given her . . . it was as if parts of them had remained in her body cells and were now regenerating.

"Well, I had to go into the office for a few hours," she said.

"Work, on a day like today?"

"It's been known to happen."

"I know a place where we can go and see a boat race tomorrow on the St. Clair River," Shane said. "Since we never got over there the other week. High-powered boats that go about a hundred and fifty miles an hour. Are you game?"

Cilla laughed. Did he ever do anything "nice and easy," as the old Ike and Tina Turner song said? He was so brimming with energy that he wanted to go all the time.

"Whoa. Whoa, there. Sunday is my day to unwind, not rev up. How about if we do something peaceful?"

"Like what?"

"Like . . . oh . . . maybe renting a movie. Tonight I was going to see what was on pay-per-view but there's nothing on except slasher movies and some flick about U.S. soldiers fighting giant cockroaches the size of three-story houses. Who watches those things anyway, psychopaths?"

He laughed. "I think fifteen-year-olds. I've got a great rental place near my condo. What movie does milady wish to view tonight? Oh, and it comes with Chinese takeout, popcorn and me."

Cilla felt a stab of sexual desire so intense that she stopped breathing.

"The American President," she said. "I know it's an old one, but I've seen it twice and I just love the romance."

"Well, I've never seen it. I'll pick it up. What time do you want me over there?"

Her heart. Pounding, pitty-pat. She tried to imagine sitting on the couch holding hands with Shane while watching one of her favorite "girl flicks." He'd probably have his hand on her knee or thigh . . . she could feel herself melt.

"As soon as you can get here," she whispered.

On Monday morning Karyn was typing a travel itinerary when Cilla came striding in, nearly two hours late and looking wonderful.

Karyn looked at her boss. Cilla's face seemed more glowing, her color high. Her eyes sparkled. She was wearing a fitted Gemi suit with a wide collar and no blouse—a trendy, sexy look that Cilla carried off exceptionally well. And her hair. It feathered appealingly around her face, looking brighter, more glossy.

"You really look great today," Karyn couldn't help saying. Raquel had told her that Cilla was fifty, but Cilla didn't seem like any fifty-year-old that Karyn had ever met.

"Thanks. I had my hair cut *and* highlighted. Not too red? God forbid I should look like Lucille Ball."

"Trust me, you don't look a thing like Lucy."

"Good." Cilla walked into her office, her steps swingy and young.

Ten minutes later there was a call from the security desk—flowers had arrived for Cilla Westheim. Karyn trotted down to the door to pick them up.

"*Somebody's* got somebody special," remarked Cherise, handing her the heavy arrangement swathed in the usual green floral paper.

But when Karyn carried the flowers into her supervisor's office, Cilla made no move to open the wrapping. "I'll open them later," she said, flushing. "I really don't like getting flowers at work. I'll have to find some inconspicuous place to put them."

Karyn nodded and left the room, dying of curiosity. Cilla obviously hadn't wanted to open the flowers in front of her—so who had sent them?

Half an hour later, Karyn was leaving voice mail messages regarding a meeting Cilla had called, when Lou Hechter paused at her desk.

"Did anyone ever tell you what a sexy voice you have?"

Startled out of her concentration, Karyn stopped in midmessage.

"A *very* sexy voice," he repeated. His eyes raked up and down her, lingering on the swell of her breasts beneath the white blouse she wore. "In fact, you could get a job on one of those phone-in sex lines if you wanted to, Karyn. *I'd* certainly call your number. In fact, I'd call it again and again."

Karyn stared at him, startled and repelled. As usual, no one was around; Raquel had gone off somewhere, and Cilla's office door was closed. The hallway was temporarily deserted, not even a maintenance man in sight. Lou seemed to have the uncanny ability to pick times when no one would hear his off-color remarks but her.

"Please, Mr. Hechter, I don't appreciate being spoken to like that."

"Oh? What have I said? I was just flirting a little, Miss Karyn. Surely you've been flirted with before. It's all very harmless. Just a little fun."

Fun? Being compared to a sex line worker?

"I prefer to stick to business," she said firmly. "And I do need to send these phone messages, Mr. Hechter," she added, hoping he would go away.

Lou's eyes glinted. "Well, don't let me stop you, Karyn. By all means send your messages. Be a *good little employee*."

He walked into his office, shutting the door loudly.

Tears suddenly stung Karyn's eyes, and she got up from her desk, walking quickly to the women's room. She went into a stall and closed the latch, sitting on the commode with tears running down her cheeks. They were as much tears of anger as they were of frustration.

It wasn't that she couldn't handle this. She could. She'd run into jerks before on her previous jobs. One boss regularly had yelled obscenities. The office had reverberated with words like "shit," and "fuck," but management had condoned his behavior, promoting him. Fed up, Karyn had phoned her temporary agency and asked for another assignment.

She could do that again; Aunt Connie's agency could get her another temping job within days. But Karyn didn't want to temp any longer. She couldn't afford to. Now that she was divorced, she had the full responsibility of Amber. She desperately needed benefits and some kind of job security. Besides, she loved Cybelle. It was more than "just a job."

It was fun and interesting every day, and the people—except for Lou—were great.

All jobs had their downside, she reminded herself. Difficult people . . . unpleasant personalities . . . you found them in almost every company. You just had to avoid them as much as possible, stay out of their way.

She blew her nose and left the ladies' room, returning to her desk.

Her phone rang.

"Karyn?" said Roger Canton. "How about going across the street with me today for lunch at a different place? I know a really great Italian place and it's only a short hike."

"I'd love to," said Karyn, but without her usual enthusiasm.

"Everything okay? Your voice sounds a little funny."

"I'm fine."

She wanted to pour out her feelings to Roger. She could really use a little TLC and sympathy right now, but quickly she stopped herself. Lou was Roger's boss, too.

No, she would fight her own battles, she wouldn't involve Roger. And she didn't want to say too much to Raquel, either. She was afraid of what might happen if Lou heard she'd been complaining about him.

That night, Jinny Caribaldi didn't have to work her usual shift and could stay home with the girls, so Caitlin invited Amber to sleep over.

"Can I? Oh, can I?" Amber begged. "And Caitlin says bring my kitty. Missy can play with Fluff Ball."

"It's a school night, honey. And it's Mrs. Caribaldi's night off; she probably needs the rest."

"Mrs. Caribaldi says it's okay. She says we have to go to bed at nine. Caitlin has bunk beds and she said I could sleep on top. Please, Mom! Huh? Huh?"

"All right," agreed Karyn, after calling Jinny to confirm that Amber was welcome. The two women made arrangements that Caitlin would sleep over one weekend night so that Jinny could go out.

Karyn then called and invited Roger Canton over for dinner. "If you don't mind simple cooking," she specified.

"I love simple cooking."

Karyn had found a new chicken recipe that could be prepared in half an hour, adding a salad from one of those prepackaged envelopes that already contained baby mixed lettuce, garlic croutons and raspberry vinaigrette dressing. With it she warmed up a loaf of French bread she had sprinkled with herbs.

Roger raved about the food as if it was of gourmet quality.

"I can't tell you how pleasant it is to have some home-cooked food," he told her. "I have to confess I eat so often at the Big Boy near my house that all the waitresses know my name."

Dessert was freshly sliced Michigan-grown peaches served over ice cream. Then Karyn and Roger cleaned up the kitchen together like a couple married for fifteen years. She had to admit it felt very comfortable to be doing that. Mack had never helped in the kitchen. He'd acted as if anything in the kitchen was all her domain.

"Tell me more about Lou Hechter," Karyn said casually as they were loading the apartment-size dishwasher. "I mean—what is he really like?"

"Lou? He's quite a force at Cybelle. Well, you already know that by now."

"How long has he been around?"

"Oh, forever. Lou was manager of a Cybelle in Shaker Heights before he came to the International Headquarters. He's really done a lot to build up the business and give Cybelle the glamour image it has now. You have to give him credit for that."

Roger went on telling her Lou stories, some funny, some not. Once Lou had given fifteen buyers Christmas stockings with lumps of coal in them. Another time he had asked Maintenance to dump over fifteen hundred pounds of unsold merchandise in a man's office, piling the unwanted garments all over the buyer's desk, chair and floor. Shortly after that, the man had quit.

"Lou is . . . well, Lou. His talent is undeniable, Karyn. No one disputes that. But the way he chooses to express himself, well, you have to develop a tough shell when you're around him. And woe to you if you don't produce."

When the kitchen was cleared up, the counters wiped, Karyn suggested they go into the living room. She had rented a movie at Blockbuster Video.

She slid the tape into the VCR, but before she could push Play, Roger gently pulled her into his arms. They sank onto the couch, awkwardly locked together. Karyn's heartbeat pounded thickly as Roger opened his mouth on hers.

His kiss felt unfamiliar. She'd only kissed three other men before, two high school boyfriends and, of course, Mack. Mack had had very thin, hard lips. Roger's lips were fuller, softer, and there was the mustache.

Roger planted soft kisses on her cheeks, her neck, her ears, then groaned with desire as he returned to her mouth, deep-kissing her until Karyn thought she would collapse from nerves and desire. Did this mean . . . Were they going to sleep together? She could feel her heart fluttering, but abruptly the anticipation faded.

She barely knew Roger Canton. She liked him, yes, but . . .

"Is everything all right?" asked Roger, pulling away slightly as he sensed her change of mood.

"It's . . . I guess . . . I think maybe we'd better stop right here before we go too far."

"All right. I'm sorry if I got too pushy."

"It wasn't that." She sat up. "It's just that I'm new at divorce, and . . . I didn't really expect to be dating this soon."

"I understand," he said quietly. "Look, Karyn, I have plenty of time and plenty of patience. I like you, and you like me. We don't have to rush."

She smiled at him, feeling a sense of deep relief. "You're a nice man."

"I aim to be."

"So let's turn on the movie, huh? Let's see what Harrison Ford is up to."

"Sounds like a plan to me," agreed Roger comfortably.

Cilla was running on adrenaline.

All week she'd felt that way, as if her own, personal body time was on double speed. At work she flew through her daily meetings, phone calls and computer work. Yet still her mind kept breaking off for short, intense fantasies that were almost impossible to put aside. Shane holding her . . . kissing her . . . bringing her to fantastic orgasms . . .

By the time she went home from work she was still wired, and she dictated letters and worked on her laptop, waiting breathlessly to see whether or not he was going to call that night.

Those phone calls. Hours long.

They talked about *everything*, from their preferences in wine to crazy things they'd done in high school. Once, Shane told her, he and two friends had hitched a ride on a freight train and traveled all the way to Atlanta, where they'd been stranded in a railroad yard, unable to get off the train car because a security guard would see them. They'd been trapped there for more than twenty-four hours, parched with thirst, until the guard finally went away and they could sneak off.

"That's really adventuresome," said Cilla. "A lot more than me."

"What's the craziest thing you ever did, Cilla?" Shane wanted to know.

"I don't think I was that crazy, actually."

"You must have done something wild."

"Well, I did get a tattoo once."

"A tattoo!" Shane laughed. "What kind of a tattoo?"

"It was the name of the Beatles." Cilla flushed scarlet. "I was wild for them. I had it tattooed on my shoulder. My parents made me have it taken off. I still have a scar there."

"I wish I could have known you then, Cilla," he'd said softly, not making any remark about how old the group was or how it dated her. "I'll bet you were awesome."

On Wednesday, Cilla glanced up as Karyn brought her in the typed agenda for a meeting.

"Good job, Karyn," she said, looking it over. "No changes, just copy this and have it in the meeting room in fifteen minutes. I'm going to run down to the vending room and get myself some coffee."

"I'd be glad to get it for you," offered Karyn.

"Oh, no. I never ask my assistant to fetch coffee for me. But I do want to say, Karyn, that I am just so pleased at the way you're catching on here. Your attitude is definitely great."

Cilla found some change in her desk drawer, got up from her desk and headed down the hall to the vending room. She put three quarters in the coffee machine, pushing the button for cream. The machine was slow, taking its time about dribbling fluid into the flimsy-looking plastic cup.

She heard the door open and glanced up automatically to see who had entered.

Lou.

"Well, helloooo," he drawled, closing the door behind him.

"I was just getting some fast coffee before my meeting," Cilla said, not liking the gleaming look in Lou's eyes.

"How about a fast something else, right here and now?"

"Lou." Cilla was horrified.

"It'd be exciting, wouldn't it? I'd pull your panties down,

pull your skirt up around your waist. We could do it standing up, Cilla. You could straddle your legs around me and
I'd hold you right against my dick . . . push it in and out of
you. . . . You'd come until you screamed."

Have sex right there in the coffee room, where anyone
could walk through the door and catch them in the act? Cilla
realized that Lou was only bluffing—he had to be. Even he
wouldn't risk his job and reputation by being caught with
his pants down, screwing his coworker . . . would he? Anger
filled her. Lou loved having her in his power, pushing her
further every time.

The machine had finally finished dispensing her coffee,
and she opened the plastic door and grabbed the cup, lifting
it up high, putting the hot liquid between her and him.

"Got to get back, Lou. Better move, because I don't want
to spill this on you."

"We're going to get together soon, Cilla," he said, but he
did back away. "By the way, I saw the flowers in your
office. You hid them in a corner, didn't you?" His voice
mocked her. "Who're they from?"

"A friend," responded Cilla defiantly.

"Yeah, right." He laughed nastily, but she knew him well
enough to know he really did want to know who it was.
Thank God she'd torn up the card from Shane and thrown
it away in the women's room wastebasket. She should have
tossed out the whole bouquet or taken it home, but she'd
been afraid Lou would see her in the hall with it.

Holding up the coffee, Cilla managed to slip past her
employer and push open the door, just as a couple of accounting clerks were walking in. She nodded at them, making her escape down the hall, walking so fast that the coffee
sloshed onto the floor.

How could this have happened to her? Cilla wondered as
she proceeded to the meeting. Where had she gone wrong?
It had to be her fault. If she hadn't gone to bed with Lou
that first, foolish time . . . If she'd been stronger . . .

She'd started out in the business so starry-eyed. She'd loved retailing from almost her first day of work. It held such excitement for her.

And now . . .

That night Cilla didn't stay late, but left at 5:00 along with everyone else. She just wanted to escape . . . to put Cybelle behind her for an evening.

Walking through the kitchen of her condo, Cilla saw that the hand-painted wicker basket was still piled up with bills. She was going to have to juggle Peter to pay Paul, she realized with a sinking feeling, but she didn't have the heart to get into it tonight. She decided to procrastinate again.

She played back her answering machine messages, two cute, sexy ones from Shane that made her laugh, and a message from Mindy asking her to call her at the dorm.

She dialed Albion and managed to catch her daughter.

"Mom, your voice sounds funny," said Mindy, her own voice sounding as if she was chewing.

"Are you eating something?"

"Just some microwave popcorn. Look, Mom, I really need another check. I know you just sent me one, but I need to get another dress and some clothes and things. And my roomie and I need a new microwave; the one we have is practically broken."

"But you're eating microwave popcorn right now," Cilla protested.

"Yeah, and it blew a fuse and it's shooting out sparks."

Cilla thought about the humongous stack of bills, and reluctantly agreed to send a check to cover the microwave and a few clothes. "You have Kelly pay half of the cost of the microwave," she told her daughter, feeling frugal. "How are things with Dylan?" she added.

"Oh, he—he has another girlfriend," Mindy responded, starting to cry.

"Honey, I'm sorry."

"All guys are jerks. I hate guys, I really, really do." Mindy went on in this manner, telling Cilla all about how Dylan had asked two girls to attend the same dance, then bailed out on Mindy after he had the second girl locked in. He also had told everyone that Mindy's breasts were too small.

"He *is* a jerk," said Cilla, surprised.

"I wish I could get saline implants," Mindy went on. "I know three or four girls who have them. Mom, they have this new procedure now; they go in through this little cut above your navel, you hardly even have a scar."

"Mindy, you don't need implants. And the jury's still out on this breast implant safety thing."

"Mom . . . saline ones are the safe kind, and I'm practically flat."

"You are a very pretty, slender girl, and you don't need implants. Besides, it's elective surgery and I haven't got the funds right now."

"I'm ugly this way! He laughed at me, Mom."

Cilla felt a pang of sympathy for Mindy. She remembered how unsure she had felt about her own body when she'd been her daughter's age. And young men always sensed that vulnerability, didn't they? They'd tease a woman about being chubby, or having big hips or tiny breasts. . . . It was terribly ironic, Cilla thought. By the time you finally developed some self-love of your own figure, if you ever really did, it was already beginning to sag into middle age.

"Mindy, if you could see my bill basket you wouldn't even ask about elective surgery."

"But I want—"

"Mindy."

The college student expelled her breath in an irritated sigh, making sure Cilla knew her disappointment. "I'll go to Dad. *Dad* will listen to me. I'll make him listen. . . . Mom, are you still dating that guy you told me about, that Shane guy?"

"Yes, I am."

"He's not Shane *Gancer*, is he?"

"Why . . . yes."

"Because this girl at school knows Shane's younger sister, Jennie. She says he's a lawyer and just got a job at Cybelle so I knew it had to be the same guy . . . but it can't be, can it?" said Mindy. "I told her it wasn't the same one, because this Shane Gancer's only twenty-six years old."

A beat of silence throbbed along the phone wire. Cilla felt totally stopped, unsure of what to say.

Mindy jumped in. "You're dating a guy who's only twenty-*six*?"

"Well, yes."

"Mom . . ." Mindy's voice rose in a wail. "It's disgusting! He's only six years older than me!"

Cilla caught her breath, stung by her daughter's careless, hurtful statement. "Mindy, it's not so simple," she began.

"I think it's really, really gross and disgusting. It's just a horrid menopausal crisis! I hate you. You're so selfish. You never think of me, Mom, not even once! If my friends ever find out about this they'll laugh at me, they'll say he's your boy toy!"

"Mindy—"

But then Cilla heard the dial tone. Her daughter had hung up on her.

She rubbed her burning eyes, tamping down the anger she felt at Mindy's reaction. When adolescence had hit Mindy at age twelve, she had changed drastically from the loving little girl who used to cuddle up to Cilla. She'd always used Bob against Cilla, even though Bob wasn't the one who paid out the serious money, nor was he the one who was dependable and available. Now his second family took all of his attention and poor Mindy was only an obligation—if he remembered her at all.

Mindy was in denial about a lot of things, and she would be devastated to have reality rubbed into her face. Even though Cilla was angry at her daughter right now, she didn't wish that on a vulnerable young woman.

Cilla sank into a chair. She wished she could go back, somewhere along the line, and change things between her and Mindy. But where would she start? It all seemed so complicated.

Her whole life was complicated.

When am I going to be happy? Cilla wondered. She had waited all her life for some far-off dream called "happiness," and now she was fifty and it still hadn't arrived.

Karyn and Roger were in the living room watching television while Amber sat at the kitchen table, scrunched over a book report she was writing. The kitten crouched on the table top next to the young girl, waving its fluffy orange tail. Every two or three minutes, Amber would reach out and pet the cat, then return to her work.

To Karyn the sight was beautiful. Amber looked happy, content. Karyn just hoped she could keep things that way for her daughter. The strain of worrying about Lou Hechter and her own job was beginning to tell on Karyn, and she hadn't been sleeping well for several weeks.

"How's the book report coming, Amber?" called Roger.

"Okay. How do you spell *awesome*?"

Karyn smiled as Roger spelled out the word.

A local news program was playing on the TV set.

"And going back to two big cases that garnered a lot of attention, the accusations of misconduct against Sergeant Major Gene McKinney in the military, and the accusations against Bill Clinton, I would say that both of these cases certainly sent a negative message to women."

A caption underneath one of the women speakers said that she was Kathy Ellefson, president of a group called Concerned Women for America.

"What sort of negative message?" said the anchor.

"That if you speak out when you are sexually harassed,

people are not going to take you seriously." Ellefson explained, "Number one, your character is going to be verbally attacked, and number two, you may not get your day in court."

"Let's see if we can get a movie," suggested Roger.

But Karyn was still staring at the screen. The host was now introducing the second guest, an African-American woman about thirty-five years old, wearing a gray business suit coupled with a red silk blouse, its color reminding Karyn of a red flag.

"Malia Roberts, a Juris Doctor graduate of the University of Michigan Law School and a member of several feminist groups, has been specializing in sexual harassment cases. Malia, have we become too worried about sexual harassment? Has the definition of it become too broad? Remember that little boy who was suspended from school because he kissed a little girl?"

"Yes, I remember that very, very well. Diane, there's a huge difference between what an innocent little child does, or a few flirtatious words, and downright crude or suggestive things. Most people know where that line is; they know when they've offended someone. Except for a few, and those are the harassers."

"Harassment has become a weapon on both sides," put in the host. "I've talked to men who say they were unfairly accused of—"

"Now, wait a minute," said Malia. "Wait *just* a minute. I've been in the trenches here. I've prosecuted cases for women who were actually raped on a factory floor. Women who were forced to walk down a row of machines with the men reaching out and grabbing their butts. Who had to put up with pornographic pictures in their lunchroom and being taped to their computers. These women did not abuse the weapon of sexual harassment. They told the truth. And we proved it in court."

Karyn sat with the clicker in her hand, fully absorbed in the discussion.

When the half-hour program was over, she sat still for a minute, her mind whirling. This Malia Roberts seemed so tough and savvy—she had really impressed Karyn. And she was local; she had her offices somewhere in Detroit, the anchor had said.

But of course she wouldn't be seeing a lawyer about Lou Hechter. No one in Karyn's family had ever seen a lawyer, aside from Karyn's own divorce proceedings. And the harassment in her case wasn't really severe. It was bearable. And it sure beat the alternative, which was losing her job.

"Karyn?" Roger was saying.

"What?" Karyn was jerked away from her thoughts.

"Anything wrong? The way you stared at that program . . ."

She reddened. "I was just interested, that's all."

Roger hesitated. "Karyn, I hope I'm not prying too much here, but something's going on with you, isn't it? You're worried about something. Can you talk to me about it?"

"I . . . I don't know if I can or if I should."

"I promise whatever you tell me I'll keep in confidence."

She drew in a deep breath. Part of her wanted to tell him, but she was afraid of the repercussions it could have if for some reason Roger wasn't able to keep her secret or chose not to.

"It's . . . something I have to deal with," she finally told him.

"I see." He bit his lip. "Well, I brought some work home tonight, so maybe I'd better leave and try to catch up on it." He got to his feet, and Karyn could tell that she'd offended him.

"Roger . . ." She jumped up, too. "I didn't mean . . . This is just something that I have to work through by myself. I will tell you all about it, I promise, but I can't do it right now. Please understand that I would never hurt you. I would never want to do that."

"I know." They both looked at each other, and Karyn saw the love plainly in Roger's eyes, shining out of them.

"I . . ." she started to say.

He moved toward her, pulling her into his arms, and she stood pressed against his solidness, breathing in the clean, familiar smells of the fabric softener he'd used on his shirt, his skin and shampoo. Gratefully she stayed in the circle of his arms, loving the safe feeling, which she had never had with Mack.

"Karyn, is it sexual harassment that's happening to you?" he whispered into her neck.

"I . . ."

"Is it Lou Hechter?"

"Oh, God, Roger." Anxiously, she pulled away. "Yes, but . . . Please don't say anything. Please! Not yet. I'm not ready. I'm handling it right now."

"I'm so sorry, Karyn."

"It happens sometimes," she choked.

"I've heard rumors about Lou over the years. Some of the women who've worked for him before . . . they've said things."

"Like what things?" she couldn't help asking.

Roger hesitated. "I heard it fourthhand, so I can't really speak for the truth of what was said. Just that some things were said. Anyway, I'm there for you, Karyn. Anything you need—anytime. I don't care what."

She hugged him again. "Thank you," she responded. Her eyes blurred with moisture. "But I don't want you to get involved, Roger. Lou is your boss, too. No sense both of us getting into trouble over this. Really and honestly."

Roger lingered for a few more minutes, saying good-night to both Amber and Karyn before heading for home. He and Karyn walked out of the apartment and stood in the hallway, wrapped in each other's arms for another long minute. His kisses were sweet and deep. He was much gentler than Mack had been, much more loving. But she was still afraid.

"I love you," whispered Roger. "Karyn—"

"I'm beginning to love you, too," Karyn whispered back. "At least I think I am. But I just don't give my emotions as fast, so please give me time."

"All the time you want. Whatever you need. I'm so glad you're in my life, Karyn."

Finally he left, walking out of the building. Karyn moved to the narrow glass panel that had been installed by the building's outer door, watching him cross the parking lot to his van. An ordinary man, no one who would stand out in a crowd, just a regular Joe. Rather like her father, Karyn realized.

He loved her. She was starting to love him. Was that what she wanted?

"Mom," Amber said a half hour later, as Karyn tucked her in, the kitten curled up on the child's pillow, a purring ball of yellow with green eyes. "Do you like Roger?"

"Yes, babydoll. I like him."

"A real, real lot?"

"Yes, but I like you more," Karyn reassured her daughter. "You'll always be number one in my life, Amber, forever and ever and ever."

Amber sighed, hugging her mother, then sinking into the pillow. "What about Daddy?" she said.

"Daddy loves you, too, even though he can't see you right now."

"When will I see him?"

"We'll talk about that later," said Karyn reluctantly. She had no intention of keeping Amber away from her father forever. That would be much too cruel. "When your daddy's better and is back to living his regular life again, we might be able to drive down to Atlanta and you could see him for a while."

Amber nodded. "If he doesn't throw spaghetti."

"That's right. If he doesn't throw spaghetti."

Shane called and wanted to take Cilla out for pizza. "I know it's last-minute, but . . ."

"I'd love to," said Cilla, realizing that she badly wanted to escape from the condo and her gloomy thoughts about her own life. And she wanted to see him. Just being with him seemed so pleasurable. She realized she was beginning to think and fantasize about him more and more.

"You look a little pensive tonight, Cilla," remarked Shane when they were seated in a booth at a popular pizza establishment and had ordered a pizza with low-fat cheese, sweet red pepper, chicken and sun-dried tomatoes.

Cilla sipped at her wine. "It wasn't the greatest day in the world," she admitted.

He looked at her questioningly.

"Work . . . well, you know how that goes." She couldn't possibly tell him about Lou's sexual proposition in the coffee room. "And my daughter hung up on me."

She started to tell Shane about Mindy's conversation, then decided to leave out the demand for breast implants because she felt that would be violating her daughter's privacy. She also omitted Mindy's horrified accusations about Shane's age, and her calling him a "boy toy" and Cilla "menopausal." Which actually left not much else to describe.

"She's at the age where she thinks parents are money machines," Cilla explained awkwardly.

"She doesn't work part-time at school?"

"No. She's an officer in her sorority, and that takes up quite a bit of time. She does work summers temping for Kelly Services, though, as a receptionist. Not that she puts in a full summer, but it's something," Cilla admitted. "She has excellent grades, though I don't know how she manages it with her extensive social life. It must be a special talent you have when you're twenty."

"Does she look like you?"

"She doesn't think so, but yes, we do have quite a resemblance."

"Then she must be very pretty."

"Oh, she is."

"Will I meet her sometime?"

Cilla hesitated, picturing the possible fireworks. "Sometime, but . . . we'll have to see."

"The age thing," he said. It was a statement, not a question.

Cilla flushed. "She's young. Her father left us for a twenty-three-year-old bimbo and she's still very angry, even though she blocks most of it out. You'll have to be patient with her, Shane. God knows I'm trying to be."

Later, Shane drove Cilla back to her condominium and came inside for coffee, but when he slid his arms around her and began kissing her neck, Cilla moved out of his embrace. "It's not you, Shane," she said uncomfortably. "It's just—well, today took a lot out of me."

"I understand. I'm sorry if I was insensitive."

"You could never be insensitive."

"I'd certainly feel badly if I ever was. Cilla, I wonder if you realize just how special you really are. I've never met a woman quite like you."

Suddenly she wasn't in the mood for flattery—if that's what this was. Maybe he meant it, maybe he didn't—Lord, how was she to know? Maybe this was what a twenty-six-year-old thought a fifty-year-old woman would want to hear. Or maybe she was just wasted from her long, disturbing day.

"I'm really tired, Shane," she said. "Ordinarily it would be great if you stayed longer, but not tonight."

"I want to see you again."

"Yes. All right."

He kissed her gently and left. Cilla went into her bedroom, slipping into a comfortable nightie, a cotton one, not the type she'd ever wear with a man around. She had two or three novels she'd been meaning to read, one of them the latest Patricia Cornwall.

But she'd read only four or five pages when her thoughts segued back to Lou. Lou, her great tormentor. If Lou even suspected she felt this way about another man, a man young enough to be his son . . .

Waiters bustled back and forth, moving with swivel-hipped alacrity while holding huge trays on their shoulders. Lou Hechter stared across the table at his wife, Marty, who was pushing her bass-and-lobster Veronique around on her plate. She was still an attractive woman at forty-nine, the soft femininity of her appearance at odds with the steel power of her mind.

"I'm going to bill nearly eighty hours this week," Marty boasted, taking a bite of lobster. "That's more than our hungriest associate; he only billed seventy-eight hours last week."

"How can you bill eighty hours when you don't work eighty hours?" Lou couldn't help asking.

"Everything counts—even the dictation I do in my car," his wife told him with a smirk of satisfaction. "Too bad you don't get paid for *your* commuting time, Lou—maybe you could buy that condo at Myrtle Beach if you did."

Lou pressed his lips together. "Who said I wanted a condo at Myrtle Beach?"

"You did, dear—just the other week. Well, I'll have you know it's not coming out of my checkbook, it's all going to be your expenses, *if* you can afford it."

He couldn't, and Marty knew it full well. Lou had invested in a theme restaurant last year that had gone belly-up. He was still paying off sizable debts and would not be clear of them for some time.

"If I want one, I'll get it," he snapped.

"Oh? My, we're assertive today, aren't we, Louie-Louie? If we had talked to a few people, learned the restaurant business, done our homework, we wouldn't be in this situation, would we? I told you it was a poor location but you wouldn't listen to me. You don't like listening to women's advice, do you?"

He didn't; she'd gotten that right. But Lou clamped his lips shut on a sarcastic remark. Marty had inherited a sizable trust fund from her father and was also due to inherit more millions from her mother. He was still hoping eventually she'd help him clear off his debts. Still, it rankled to be subservient to her . . . to know she was the one in the household with the major money, not him, the one who truly called the shots.

"How was everything?" queried a young waiter, sidling up to their table with an expectant smile.

"Not great," Lou snapped. "The service was abysmally slow. It'll be reflected in your tip, believe me."

As the waiter looked shocked and tried to apologize, Lou felt his bad mood come to a peak. "We won't be coming back here, believe me," he said, tossing his napkin down on the table, along with a bill just large enough to cover the cost of their lavish meal. For a tip, he fished out a dime from his pocket and plunked it on the tablecloth.

He rose, perfunctorily helping Marty up from her chair, and the two of them walked out of the restaurant without another glance back at the crestfallen waiter.

"Pansy little shit," Lou remarked as he and his wife reached the parking lot, where they would take separate cars back to their offices, both of them to put in more hours at their desks. "It took him forever to bring the menus."

"You're a sweetheart, Lou," murmured Marty as she got into her Lexus, showing plenty of long, lean, nyloned leg. "No wonder you're so beloved."

Lou grunted something and got into his Mercedes, starting up the motor. Glancing to his left, he could see their waiter standing on the steps of the restaurant, gesturing angrily.

Ignoring him, Lou proceeded to drive out of the lot, turning in the direction of Cybelle. His stomach was still churning. He fumbled in his pocket for a Gaviscon and began chewing down the antacid tablet.

Then gradually his thoughts turned to Karyn Cristophe.

Sexy. The way she walked, showing off that sweet behind of hers . . . Lou believed that she did it all deliberately. She was being provocative just for him, and her protests over his flirtatious advances were only token no's.

Lou smiled, grinning to himself inside the privacy of his car. He knew all about women like Karyn. You approached them gradually, escalating the game just a bit more every week. Soon they were caught up in it, confused and aroused. *Excited.*

And then you let them know who had the power.

As was her daily habit, Karyn phoned home around 3:30 to make sure Amber had gotten home from school all right.

"How was school today, gumdrop?"

"Boys. You know," responded Amber, giggling. "They're so weird."

"I guess so. What are you doing right now?"

"I'm watching Animal Planet. I'm watching a program about vets. I want to be a vet when I grow up, and I'll take care of kitties like Missy and Fluff Ball. I watched a lady vet give a kitty a shot. And there was this dog that swallowed a cassette tape. The tape stuff was hanging out of his mouth. That was really grotty."

Karyn finished the conversation, then left her desk to go to the basement level of the building, where she had to pick up a stack of reports that had been copied and spiral-bound in the company's print shop.

By the time she returned to the department, lugging the big box, over an hour had passed.

Walking into her alcove, Karyn was startled to see that her usual screen saver—the Microsoft Star Field—had been replaced by Marquee, a scrolling banner with a pink background and white lettering. There wasn't much contrast so she had to strain to read the letters as they slowly crawled past on her screen.

I'd like you to lick my dick and balls. . . . I'd like you to lick my dick and balls. . . . It repeated itself endlessly.

Karyn slammed her hand on the mouse, the movement causing the screen saver immediately to vanish. Who had done this?

She glanced at Raquel's alcove, then remembered that Raquel had taken several hours off for a doctor's appointment. If Raquel had been here, she would have seen anyone walking into Karyn's alcove. But with her gone, and if no one had been in the hallway, it would only have taken someone a few minutes to reformat Karyn's screen saver.

Perspiring, Karyn gazed down the hallway, where Lou's office door stood halfway open. She heard amplified voices as he conversed on the speakerphone. Lou could have done it. He knew his way around a computer, and his own screen saver, she happened to know, was also a Marquee banner that said simply *Whatever works. . . .*, repeated again and again.

Quickly she went into the Windows program and erased the obscene screen saver, putting her usual Star Field back in place. Her head was pounding, stress pinching the center of her forehead between her eyes.

It *was* Lou who had done it.

She just knew it. Who else in the department would dare to enter such a profanity on her computer screen? She felt soiled, dirty. She wanted to go home and take a long, hot shower just to wash the ugliness off herself. Instead she settled for walking down to the women's room and dampening several paper towels.

Returning to her alcove, she obsessively cleaned her computer keyboard, monitor screen, keyboard and desk top, wip-

ing off all traces of the man's body oils. For good measure,
she also washed her phone.

By this time, Raquel had returned carrying a fragrant-
smelling bag from Burger King.

"Want some fries?" she offered.

"No, thanks. I'm not very hungry."

"You spill something on your computer?" Raquel asked,
observing the way that Karyn was trying to clean between
her keys with a straightened-out paper clip.

"No, I wish I had. Somebody came into my alcove and
wrote a dirty message on my computer screen."

Raquel's eyes widened. "Again?"

"You mean it's happened before?"

"Yeah, off and on. The woman before you, Angela, she
used to get nasty messages once in a while. Nobody ever
found out who did it. What did yours say?"

Karyn couldn't repeat it. "It was just sickening, that's all."

"Tell you what," said Raquel. "I'll show you how to do
a locking screen saver. Then nobody can get in your computer when you're gone unless they have the password."

Karyn's headache lasted all the rest of the day. Even a
couple of ibuprofen didn't lessen its intensity.

She did her usual work, resenting Lou Hechter for forcing
her to worry whether or not the culprit might be him. Why
couldn't he have been nice and courteous and laid-back, like
some other male bosses she'd had in the past? *They'd* been
a pleasure to work with. Cilla, too, was a great supervisor,
piling on the work but seeming to really care about Karyn,
and never scolding her or being bitchy.

Good bosses did exist, she had to remind herself.

The rest of the week passed in a nervous haze. Karyn had
put the lock on her computer, so she didn't have to worry
about further intrusions there, but now her working hours
became pervaded with tension. She found herself always
checking out the hallway to see if Lou was in his office. If

he was, her stomach began churning. Only if he was out of the office or in a meeting could Karyn completely relax.

Karyn was relieved when the weekend finally came and she didn't have to think about work for two whole days. Amber's birthday was on Saturday, and Karyn was giving a small party for her daughter. Roger had begged to come over and help.

Karyn's first instinct was to say no. She still didn't want to take the chance of disappointing Amber if the relationship should break up, but Roger was so smiling and appealing that she couldn't bring herself to refuse.

"Do you know a really good place to get a cake?" she asked him.

"Let's see ... There's a bakery in downtown Birmingham, but it's really expensive. But Farmer Jack's has pretty good cakes. I think I saw a Barbie doll cake there once ... that's what you should buy her." Roger smiled. "Twenty years of NOW and kids still want Barbie. Can you believe it?"

Roger arrived at noon, and together they hung the decorations and blew up party balloons. Karyn had bought small prizes for each girl, and those had to be wrapped as well. Six children were coming, including Caitlin, all of them from Amber's class in school. Jinny Caribaldi was keeping Amber upstairs until the party began so it wouldn't spoil the surprise.

Roger helped Karyn decide how much pizza to order, and then he helped her wrap her gift for Amber, an enormous Barbie dollhouse for which Amber had been begging for months. Roger's own gift was already wrapped in shiny pink paper.

Suddenly the apartment door burst open and Amber and Caitlin burst into the living room. Ten minutes after that the apartment was overrun by little girls.

They watched the Walt Disney video Karyn had rented. They screamed and giggled; they munched pizza, fastidiously picking off the pepperoni; they told stories and teased; they played Barbie dolls.

Roger and Karyn retreated to the kitchen, where they watched CNN on a small, portable TV and munched their own pizza, taking about comfortable things.

Suddenly. Amber burst into the kitchen, demanding that Karyn and Roger come into the living room so she could open her presents.

Watching her daughter tearing off paper, her eyes alight as she uncovered boxes of games, clothes, jewelry, and various Barbie accessories, Karyn felt a rush of pure love for her child.

Yes, it was tough trying to survive in her job at Cybelle, and the job hadn't turned out exactly as she'd fantasized. There were definitely some major drawbacks. But she was doing it for Amber. And Karyn had such big plans. As soon as she was permanent at Cybelle, she was going to start saving for a down payment on a small house. . . . Or maybe she could get a rental with an option to buy.

Now Amber was tearing open Roger's pink package.

"Barbie clothes!" she squealed, lifting up the shrink-wrapped package.

The package contained a long, blue lace evening gown trimmed with sequins. There was a tiny plastic pair of high heels, a little evening bag, and a matching shawl. Plus a comb and brush for Barbie, and a tiny package of "makeup."

It wasn't an expensive gift, but it had been unerringly chosen.

"Thank you," said Amber shyly, looking at Roger. "She needed another evening gown."

"And now you have one."

By 4:00 the mothers began arriving to collect their daughters. Roger spent a half hour helping Karyn clear up the mess, and then left, saying that he was sure both Karyn and Amber would probably like some well-earned rest.

"You want to enjoy your little girl, and I don't want to horn in too much."

Karyn was touched at his thoughtfulness. "Yeah, we've done a lot of giggling today, haven't we?"

"She's a beautiful girl, Karyn. You've raised her well."

"Thanks so much," Karyn said, saying good-bye to him at the door. "It was nice having you here."

Amber was still hyperexcited from the party, insisting on having all of her presents out and playing with all of the Barbie dolls and accessories. She wasn't hungry for dinner, but agreed to drink a glass of milk and eat a small bowl of cereal.

"Mom," she said as she was fitting one of the Barbies into the gown Roger had given her. "That guy, Roger. Do we like him?"

Karyn smiled at the "we." "Yes, I do, and I hope *we* do, too."

"He can come here lots of times," Amber decided.

That same day, Cilla and Shane drove up to Mt. Pleasant, where the Sky Jumpers had scheduled a one-day course for beginners that would culminate with a jump from 3,500 feet. The club had insisted that all first-time jumpers get a physical exam before they jumped, which Cilla had completed the previous day.

"You're healthy enough, and your bone density test shows you don't suffer from osteoporosis," said Cilla's doctor, Jenny Wagner. "Your heart's in great shape, and your lung capacity is excellent. In many ways you're physically more like a woman of forty than one of fifty. Still, I have to wonder. Most jumpers are in their twenties or early thirties. Why are you going to do this?"

Cilla blushed. "I'm still not sure I am. I'm going to take the course, though."

Jenny Wagner had eyed Cilla. "Well, you've got more guts than I have."

"I've met a man," Cilla finally had confessed. "He's . . . younger."

"Ah."

"I don't know if I'm doing this to please him or to please myself. I guess I want to feel that I can do it," Cilla tried to explain. "I don't want to feel old in front of him."

"Cilla, you know as well as I do that age is a relative number once we pass forty. I've got forty-two-year-old patients who suffer from high blood pressure, stomach problems and bad backs, and they act like they're sixty. And I have another patient, she's seventy-four. This past summer she biked all the way across lower Michigan. Who's younger? Who's more fit? Who has more fun?"

Cilla had grinned. "Thanks for the encouragement."

The class sounded do-able, Cilla thought now. It would last four hours and cover everything from equipment to aircraft exit, count and position, plus (the brochure had said) "unusual situations and emergency procedures," which she devoutly hoped she would never experience firsthand. The activation of her main chute would be done by the jumpmaster when she let go. Five seconds later the canopy was supposed to be completely open, and an instructor on the ground would assist her, via radio, in providing guidance during the descent.

The ground instructor would be Shane.

"You really don't have to do it," said Shane, touching her hand. "This isn't mandatory for us to have a relationship, you know."

"I said I would, and I will."

He grinned. "You're awesome, Cilla. You really are."

The other two people in Cilla's class were Tom and Derek, young men who attended nearby Central Michigan University. The two college students kept staring at Cilla, as if wondering what she was doing there. The class was interesting, Cilla had to admit, but by the time they broke for a box lunch she was so nervous she could barely pick at the ham-and-cheese croissant sandwich and crisp apple that had been provided.

Indian summer had touched the area's farms and fields with seventy-five-degree temperatures. The sky was a fresh-washed blue, brushed with only a few faint cirrus clouds. The wind was perfect, Shane told her.

They sat at picnic tables watching as two others jumped from the Cessna 182. Dark spots ejected from the small plane. Suddenly the chute packs opened and puffed out, balloons of red and yellow, tiny black dots hanging from them. Cilla watched in awe and fear as the jumpers floated to earth.

"Okay," said Jill Brewton, the fifty-eight-year-old woman she'd met at the party, who was the class instructor. "We'd better double-check your gear."

Cilla lunged to her feet. Shane was behind her, checking straps, clips, pins.

"Too tight?" said Jill, yanking each one of Cilla's shoulder straps.

"No, I think they're fine."

"They'd better be fine, because once you get up there, it's a little bit too late to make adjustments."

"Okay," said Cilla nervously.

"Make sure your privates are free of the leg straps."

Cilla gave a ladylike wiggle. "They are."

Nervously she waited while both Shane and Jill checked her again, rechecking her radio and her pack, hooking and unhooking the clips again. There were two square chutes in her pack—that she knew for certain. She had passed beyond fear now and was merely numb. What if she got killed today? What if her chute never opened and the emergency chute failed, and she just kept on falling and falling until she crashed to the ground?

The Cessna was circling down to the small airfield for a landing.

"You and Tom go up in the next group," said Shane, sliding his arm around her. "Are you excited?"

"Yes," she said in a monotone.

He laughed. "Just hang in there, because this is the tough part right now, the waiting. Oh, Cilla, I love you for doing this. You are such a trouper."

"Mmm," said Cilla, fighting a sudden urge to be sick.

"I'm going to be right with you, as close as the earpiece in your ear. I'll talk you through everything. Just relax and let it happen. The weather is perfect; we couldn't ask for a better day."

The Cessna's motor roared in Cilla's ears, wind battering the small plane.

Jill Brewton pointed her finger at her eyes to remind Cilla that she was supposed to maintain eye contact with her instructor.

"Ready?" she shouted above the roar of the wind.

"Yes." She had to yell it twice to be heard. Her heartbeat was pounding, and she felt sick, vertiginously afraid. Why, why had she agreed to do this?

"Get your feet out the way I told you!"

Slowly, Cilla moved her behind to the edge of the hold, placing one leg, then the other, outside the door. She put her feet on the step that had been positioned alongside the plane. God . . . oh, God . . .

"Don't look down!" Jill shouted into the wind.

Cilla swallowed dryly, fighting not to stare downward. She knew if she did she'd be dizzy and sick; she'd make a terrible screaming fool of herself.

Jill leaned closer and shouted into her ear. "Climb all the way out!"

Automatically, Cilla's hands reached out to the beam connected to the wing of the plane. She was supposed to pull herself to a standing position now—*outside the plane.*

Oh, no, she thought desperately. She couldn't do it.

Never, never. Still, somehow she was doing it, her hands clutching as the wind attacked her, lashing her jumpsuit, flapping the cloth, nearly blowing her off the step. Desperate for her life, she clung to the beam and cursed herself for her foolishness.

"Okay, okay!" Jill was calling. "Cilla, remember the training. Your chute is safe and you're going to be safe. I'm going to activate your chute so you don't have to. It's going to be beautiful."

"God in heaven," said Cilla, and then she looked down.

The plane vanished above her and Cilla realized that she was falling. She uttered a hoarse groan, or maybe it was a scream, and suddenly the roar of the aircraft motor was gone and she was falling into perfect blue silence.

The noise, the clamor, the fear were gone.

There was just . . . her and the sky, and the softness of air. It didn't feel as if she was falling; she was just floating.

Beautiful.

Abruptly she felt a jerk, and looked up to see her chute, fully deployed, snapping above her in the wind, a huge, rainbow-colored balloon of cloth, suspending her.

Then she heard the voice from the earpiece, coming from Shane on the ground. "Cilla, it's Shane. Your chute looks great. After clearing your brakes do a hard right turn so I know you can hear me."

Cilla pulled the right-hand toggle, the way she'd learned in class, and obediently the chute shifted around.

"Great . . . great . . . you're doing fabulous," called Shane. "Just relax. The hard part is over. Look around. Isn't it beautiful?"

As she continued to float down, Shane's voice in her ear like a heavenly guide, Cilla became so exhilarated that she shouted and laughed. Her life on earth fell away from her, all of her problems that seemed so weighty when she was down on the ground. Her credit card debts, her problems with Mindy, her job, the horrible situation with Lou Hechter. Up here they were less than motes of dust.

Blue sky surrounded her, searing her eyes. A patchwork of farmland and highways spread itself below her, fading to blue-gray at the horizon.

She descended in the blue, and she knew she had never been happier and never would be this happy again. *Oh*, she prayed, all of her emotions surging to the surface. *Please, God. Help me to be happy. Help me to be loving.*

Was that the right prayer? Should she have prayed for something better or different? Cilla felt such peace and calm that she knew the words of her prayer did not really matter. She was alive. She was part of life, part of the sky, part of the sun.

She reached the ground, bending her knees and running forward as the chute fell, and in the distance she could see Shane, running toward her.

Cilla laughed, sitting down on the grassy field, her knees suddenly so rubbery she couldn't stand. She watched her lover run toward her, and saw what a beautiful man he was, sun and wind tousling his light hair.

He reached her, kneeling down to take her anxiously into his arms. "Are you okay? You didn't sprain anything, did you?"

"Not a thing." She laughed joyfully. "It was . . . I was part of God! Oh, Shane. I'll never forget it. Never."

"I love you," he said hoarsely, pulling her close.

Cilla hugged him back, knowing he'd said it just in the flash of exhilaration—it didn't mean *love* love. But still, to hear him say it gave the final, wonderful cachet to her beautiful day.

"Jazzy Kulture is just what Cybelle is looking for in a new celebrity line," said Cilla, pacing Lou's office the following Monday. She had a few muscle aches from her skydiving adventure, but otherwise she felt energetic and rejuvenated.

She'd even tentatively told Shane she might jump again . . . provided that he went art gallery hopping with her in downtown Birmingham, one of her favorite occupations for a Saturday afternoon with nothing to do.

She continued, "You know what a star she is, and that sexy new video of hers . . . well, girls are dying to dress exactly as she does. I've already been in touch with her manager and he's very enthusiastic."

Lou shrugged. "Isn't she into that grunge look? Ugly to start with and good riddance now that it's finally going out."

"Not the old grunge look but a totally new one!" cried Cilla. "Lou, you said yourself that Cybelle isn't attracting enough women age fifteen to twenty. Well, Jazzy's the answer! They love her. They're imitating her style all over the country right now . . . sleeveless tanks with low-cut armholes. Girls are actually cutting their own tanks. The tabloids are calling her the tank girl. I'm telling you, Lou, if we don't grab onto this, someone else will."

"Let me think about it," said Lou.

Annoyed, Cilla pressed her lips together.

"Dammit, Lou, don't do this to me," she said. "This is a great idea. It'll boost our numbers, which we need," she emphasized.

"I said I'll think about it," Lou snapped, but in a way that told Cilla her idea had taken root.

Lou waited until Cilla had left his office before jotting down detailed notes on the Jazzy Kulture promotion. Of course, since Cilla worked for him, all of her ideas were basically his, and he felt no compunction about taking Cilla's idea and running with it.

Maybe they'd commission some mannequins to be made that would be modeled on Jazzy herself. Yeah, girls would walk into Cybelle, they'd see Jazzy everywhere.

Lou leaned back in his chair, beginning to embellish on

Cilla's idea, making it his own. When his private phone rang, he picked up.

"I've got a business trip to Chicago; I'm leaving from the office tonight," said his wife's crisp voice. "I'll be back Thursday." He heard voices in the background, someone laughing. "And now I've got to get back into a meeting. Oh, and when I get in on Thursday night I have a dinner meeting, which means I won't be home until elevenish."

Lou and Marty were often ships that passed in the night, each putting in workaholic hours that frequently did not mesh.

"No rest for the wicked," he said flatly.

"Let's not talk about who's wicked," she said. "They need me in the meeting. See you at the end of the week."

"Fine," he said, hanging up.

He sat for a minute, rubbing his temples.

What had his wife meant by saying, "Let's not talk about who's wicked"?

The idea of her knowing about Cilla Westheim, or even suspecting, made him shudder. Not to mention all the other little escapades he'd had over the years.

But swiftly he calmed himself. He'd been circumspect, and Marty didn't know anything. Besides, he was getting weary of Cilla. She'd begun to lose her freshness and enthusiasm. Fucking her was beginning to be a chore.

But now there was the new secretary, Karyn, rejuvenating him every day with fresh interest. He was in the game with her now; they were both playing it. Oh, hell, yes, she knew exactly what was going on. She wasn't fooling him with her pretense of being angry when he flirted with her. It was a blatant case of no really meaning yes.

Suddenly, Lou was in the middle of a sexual fantasy so intense that it rocked him.

Karyn Cristophe.

The prettiest woman he'd come across in years . . . and this was one game he was definitely going to win.

TWO

IN THE COURTYARD A CHILLY DECEMBER RAIN SPRINKLED down, puckering the reflecting pond and causing Cybelle's group of smokers to huddle under a protective awning while they puffed on their cigarettes, most of them jacketless despite the cold.

"Karyn, I'm on my way to the marketing committee meeting," said Cilla, stopping by her assistant's desk where Karyn was sorting color swatches for one of the merchandisers. The vibrant colors—cranberry, burgundy, raspberry, lavender, kiwi—would be appearing in the stores a year from now.

Karyn looked up, smiling.

Cilla went on, "I wanted you to know, I just got a call from HR. Your ninety days are up and they want to talk to you about benefits and all that. So why don't you call down there and make an appointment?"

Karyn's mouth fell open, her complexion blazing pink. "You mean—I'm going to be a full-time employee?"

"Congratulations." Cilla smiled to see her assistant's delight. "I'll schedule a formal review with you later in the week, but I want you to know that I'm very, very pleased with your job performance. Welcome aboard. Oh, and I've approved a raise for you."

Karyn jumped to her feet, impulsively coming out from behind her desk to hug Cilla. "Oh, I'm so happy! That's such awesome news."

"I hope you still find it awesome after you've been at Cybelle for a year or two," Cilla said dryly. "I can be a slave driver sometimes."

"I love working for you," said Karyn, meaning it.

"Good. I'll be in the meeting at least until four. Take messages for me, but if Jazzy Kulture's manager calls, phone down to the meeting room, okay? Oh, and I'm expecting a call from Dom Carrara, too."

Karyn nodded, her cheeks still stinging pink. As soon as Cilla had disappeared down the hallway, she rushed out of her alcove and hurried to Raquel's desk.

"I'm in! I'm an employee now! Cilla wants me permanently!"

"That's *great* news," said Raquel, dropping the work she'd been doing to high-five Karyn. "We've gotta have a cake for you, Karyn. And definitely a lunch. The whole department can go out and celebrate."

Karyn sank down into Raquel's guest chair. "I've been waiting and worrying, waiting and worrying," she confessed breathlessly. "I just wanted it so much."

"Well, what are you gonna do now that you're one of the peons at Cybelle?" Raquel inquired teasingly.

"Oh . . . learn this job really well and then . . . I don't know!" Karyn laughed with pleasure. "Maybe go to school and learn buying."

"Well, they have tuition reimbursement, you know. Cybelle'll pay for the whole thing."

Karyn squealed and grabbed Raquel and they danced around the hallway, laughing so loudly that several employees passing by in the corridor turned to stare.

News traveled fast—and Raquel helped spread the word around. People in the department, and other friends Karyn had made elsewhere in the company, started coming up to her desk, congratulating her. Karyn hadn't realized so many people liked her. Even Antwan, the mail clerk, stopped by to offer his good wishes.

And there was an E-mail from Sondra Zapernick: *Congrats! So glad you're on board. Sondra.*

Karyn felt adrenaline buzzing through her system, making

her feel as if she'd drunk one or two glasses of Asti Spumanti.

When the congratulations finally slowed to a trickle, Karyn made the appointment in HR to take care of her benefits. Then she called Aunt Connie, giving her the good news.

"This calls for a celebration," said Connie jubilantly. "How about if I take you and Amber out to dinner this weekend?"

"You're on," said Karyn. "Oh, Aunt Connie. This wouldn't have happened if it hadn't been for you. It's just—" She blinked back moisture. "It's just so super. I'm just so happy. I never thought I'd ever get a job like this."

"Well, I see you're going to be among us for the long haul," remarked Lou an hour or so later, returning from some meeting, his arms loaded down with a stack of three-ring binders.

"Yes, I'm very happy to be here," Karyn said, keeping her smile.

She was—except for Lou.

Fortunately he'd been out of the country in London and Paris for nearly a month and was slated to travel again soon—good news as far as she was concerned. The office rumor mill had also been saying that Cybelle was negotiating to buy a small chain of mall stores called Girlrags, now in Chapter 13. Some people said that Lou would be taking over as CEO of Girlrags if the deal went through. Karyn hoped he would. Having him transferred out of the department would make her job just about perfect.

"You know, this is a very, very good job for you," he told her now. "The benefits here are super good, especially for clerical-type personnel. If you stay here long enough you'll actually receive retirement benefits, and hardly any jobs offer that perk anymore for people at your level. I mean, 401k is about all most secretaries get."

How patronizing he was. And was there a warning in his

words, a warning of what she stood to lose if she protested his advances?

"I realize that," she said, her mouth going dry.

"So just keep it in mind . . . your good luck at being here. And if you do have any problems, you can always come to me. You know I'd be more than willing to do everything I can."

He'd said that on her first day, and she'd believed him—then.

Now the words "everything I can" sounded vaguely sinister to her.

Karyn's celebratory lunch at Don Pablo's was hectic and fun. Nineteen people from Fashion all crowded together at two long tables, laughing, gossiping, and consuming vast quantities of burritos, enchiladas and soft tacos. Roger Canton joined them, sitting next to Karyn. Cilla attended, and even Lou made a brief appearance.

"To a terrific secretary, and it's only going to get better," he told her in front of her coworkers, as if he were her supervisor, not Cilla. "You have a bright future here, Karyn."

"Thank you," she murmured, not knowing where to look.

"Thank God I've got a good secretary," Cilla put in quickly. "Karyn, we're all glad you're part of the team but I have to be selfish and say I'm the gladdest, because you've already made order out of the chaos around here."

"Hey, way to go," said Roger to her as the two of them drove back to Cybelle afterward in his car. "You deserved to be taken on full-time and I'm glad they saw it."

"I'll be able to save money," she burst out. "And I love the hospitalization plan—the company pays for nearly all of it, and there's dental and vision, too! Oh," she added in confusion, "you already know that."

He smiled. "It's great just hearing you be excited, Karyn."

"I'm going to save for a down payment on a house

maybe. With fruit trees in the backyard. I've always wanted a peach tree. And I'll build a little tree house for Amber, so she and Caitlin can play up there with their Barbie dolls."

"I'll help you with it," volunteered Roger. He glanced at her, his glance softening tenderly. "Karyn . . ."

"Maybe we can buy some plans for the playhouse," she said cheerfully, deflecting whatever it was he had been going to say.

"Sure," he agreed.

The past several months had advanced her relationship with Roger Canton, slowly turning it serious, at least on his part. Karyn was still scared; her marriage to Mack had left her with scars. It was going to be hard for her to relax and put her trust in another man.

But she wouldn't think about that right now, Karyn told herself. Nor would she think about Lou Hechter. Today was a day to celebrate. . . .

Karyn drove home that night with the Cybelle Employee Benefits folder on the seat beside her, subtly edged in pink and decorated with the famous Cybelle *C*. In it were the papers for her insurance policy that would provide Amber with six times her salary if something happened to Karyn, the short-term disability policy that provided for twenty-five weeks at three-quarters pay, the 401k plan, the retirement plan, the stock options and the Blue Cross/Blue Shield hospitalization policy she'd chosen from a cafeteria plan. Cybelle paid nearly all of the premiums.

As she drove she kept glancing at the folder, touching it just to make sure it was real. Before, Mack had always been the one to carry the decent benefits, while Karyn had taken jobs at small companies that didn't provide much beyond an hourly pay rate. He'd expressed his attitude about her various jobs by telling her that he was "working to support them" while she was working for "extras."

No more. She was the primary wage earner now. She'd

be able to take care of Amber without help from anyone.

Karyn stopped at Papa Romano's and bought a medium Sicilian pizza to share with Amber, Jinny Caribaldi, and Caitlin, half of it cheese-only for the girls, the other half covered with mushrooms, onion and green pepper for the two women.

"Pizza?" Amber squealed, running up to her.

"Pizza!" echoed Caitlin.

"To celebrate," Karyn announced. She lifted up the big cardboard box that smelled deliciously spicy. "I'm full-time at Cybelle now, and they gave me a raise. Plus benefits like you wouldn't believe."

"That's just great," enthused Jinny, seeming genuinely happy.

"Mom got a raise!" echoed Amber, her petite, intense face lit up with pride.

Karyn hugged her little girl, at last beginning to relax a little and feel the joy she should feel at this turn of events in her life. Everything was beginning to open up for her now. Her move up north from Atlanta, taking the job as a temp, all the hard work and hoping she'd put in. It was finally paying off.

"Okaaaay," said Jinny, taking the pizza box and putting it on her kitchen table. She got out paper plates and began handing out slices. "This *is* a momentous day, kids. Because, hey, I just got promoted to head floor nurse. I start next week. Same shift, but lots more money. Lots more paperwork, too, but I guess I can handle that."

"Wonderful," Karyn cried.

Jinny's grin was ear-to-ear. "We're finally kicking butt, Karyn. And doesn't it feel good?"

Later that night Karyn phoned her parents, bubbling over with her good news. It took her several hours to fall asleep, she was so excited.

*   *   *

The following morning Karyn came in to work to find a bouquet of three dozen long-stemmed roses on her desk with a congratulatory card from Lou Hechter.

Later, he stopped by her alcove, and she thanked him for the flowers.

"Have they taken care of you in Human Resources?"

"Yes, excellently."

"Good, good." Lou stood by her desk, dressed in one of his usual, expensively cut suits that made him look like he belonged on the cover of *Fortune* magazine. She could see that he was in an expansive mood: he practically oozed good cheer.

"I have great plans for you, Karyn," he added, lowering his voice slightly. He paused and winked. "Employment-wise, that is. I expect to move up the ladder, and when I do, I intend to take some first-rate secretarial help with me, too, if you get my drift."

"Why, I—t-that's . . ." Karyn stared at him, shocked into stammering. What on earth could he mean? Had the Girlrags purchase gone through? And what about Raquel Estrada? *She* was Lou's secretary, not Karyn. Raquel was the one who should move up the ladder with Lou, not Karyn.

"But—" she began awkwardly.

"Trust me, Karyn, you'll be taken care of," Lou said, smiling at her. He glanced at the roses. "By the way, a packet of rose food was supposed to come with those flowers. See to it that you put it in the water so they'll last longer."

He walked off.

Glancing to her left, Karyn saw that Raquel sat ramrod straight in her alcove, her cheeks reddened. How much of the conversation had she overheard? Shit . . .

Karyn got up and went over to Raquel's alcove.

"Did you overhear that? I'm really sorry. I don't know why he said such a thing. I don't want to take away your job. I'm just glad to have the one I have."

Raquel said stiffly, "It's all right. I'm Hispanic, that's why he doesn't want to take me to the top with him. He doesn't want a woman with brown skin sitting up there on the executive floor."

"Oh, God, Raquel, you're the best friend I have here. I'd quit before I'd take away your job. . . . I would."

Raquel's eyes teared up. "It's just that I'd like a nice promotion, too. And that asshole will never give me one. He likes having me around to make me miserable." She grabbed a tissue out of a box she kept on her desk. "Besides, Lou's never going to make president around here. He's got too many enemies. And I'm one of 'em."

"Anyway," Karyn said. "Let's go out for a drink tonight, okay?"

"All right!" agreed Raquel, her irrepressible smile appearing on her face again.

"I'm buying."

Forgetting about his expansive boasting to Karyn, which he felt sure had impressed her, Lou sat in his office leafing through *Women's Wear Daily*. A new designer named Li Su was making waves in the rag trade. He studied photographs of her hard-edged clothing being worn by a black model so skinny that her collarbones stood out in sharp relief. A little too cutting-edge for the Cybelle customer, he decided. He turned the page, looking at some dresses by Chloé that they might be able to have a manufacturer in Taiwan knock off for the Career shop. They had one firm under contract that did exquisite work. . . .

His phone rang and he picked up.

"Mr. Hechter, I have Mr. Carrara on the line for you. Will you hold?" said the well-modulated voice of Sondra Zapernick.

"All right, put him on," Lou snapped.

He was forced to wait nearly three minutes on hold, listening to canned music, before Carrara finally came on the line.

"I've just finished an hour-long meeting with Randy Caravaglio, reviewing the quarterly numbers. Women's figures have been going flat, Lou. I want to have a meeting with you and the other members of the Executive Committee tomorrow morning, seven forty-five A.M. sharp, and we're going to discuss this at length."

"We've had these flat periods before," Lou defended himself. "We've bought some hot new—"

"Flat can turn into a downward trend in a day, Lou. You know that as well as I do. Tomorrow morning. I'll have breakfast brought up here to the executive conference room."

Lou agreed to be there, then dropped the phone into the cradle.

A wave of fear rippled through him. Dom Carrara had been on board at Cybelle for only twenty months, but he hadn't hesitated to fire some deadwood and offer early-retirement deals to others age fifty-five and up. A few of Lou's friends had gotten the "golden handshake" and were now out of it.

He shuddered, picturing himself being shunted aside with a buyout. He'd last in retirement about a week. He'd have no clout with Marty if he got booted out; she'd despise him. Work was his life. It was everything for him, the most important game of all.

But then Lou reassured himself that it could not happen to him. In the first place, he was only fifty-one and looked years younger. He'd helped mold Cybelle into what it was today; everyone recognized it. Even old LaRivière, the company's founder, had been a special friend of Lou's before he died.

Right now Lou had a buyers' meeting in five minutes. He'd drop something on them, all right. There would be no more flat numbers, not so long as Lou Hechter was still around.

Lou darted his eyes rapidly around his office, settling on two brass Degas dancer statuettes he'd purchased while he was in Paris one time on a buying trip.

Cilla, too, was headed for the buyers' meeting.

It was being held in a large third-floor conference room made cramped by the presence of three rolling racks hung with women's suits, trouser suits and tops. The room had been set up with PicTel teleconferencing equipment that included a small video camera so that Cybelle executives could hold conferences with manufacturers or buyers around the world.

The room was full as Cilla walked in. She knew everyone and was immediately pulled into the usual greetings, asides, laughter and jokes.

"Hi, Cilla, how are you?" said Sally Gazzara, an assistant buyer for Women's Fashions, in her early forties and single. Sally leaned forward and whispered, "I hear you're dating up a storm with a new guy down in Legal."

"Isn't there any privacy around here?" complained Cilla, smiling.

"Actually, I think it's great that he's a few years younger than you. Why should guys be the only ones who get to date young stuff, while we women have to stick to guys with gray on top because that's who they think is appropriate for us?"

Cilla had known people at Cybelle would eventually find out. Although she and Shane had attempted to keep their relationship discreet, they'd been spotted several times in restaurants, and had also been seen at the Star Theater in Rochester, standing in line to buy movie tickets. Still, what was she supposed to do? Cilla didn't feel she should have to sneak around to see her lover. She had done nothing wrong and she was damned if she would feel guilty.

Aaron Vishnek began telling one of his usual off-color jokes. Cilla must have heard a hundred of them. "Did you hear when Nancy Reagan realized that Ronald had Alzheimer's?" Aaron asked loudly.

There was a chorus of no's.

"When she sent him to the video store to pick up a copy of *Scent of a Woman* and he came back with *A Fish Called Wanda*."

There were groans, laughter, and then Lou Hechter walked into the room, closing the door behind him with a sharp click.

The laughter immediately died.

As he took his place at the head of the table, Cilla noticed that Lou was carrying a briefcase with him—a little unusual for Lou. Usually his briefcase stayed in the corner of his office unless he took work home.

"Well, people, prepare for Armageddon," Lou began, putting his hands on the polished table top and leaning forward aggressively. "You think that sounds extreme? You think I'm just talking, pulling some rhetoric to get you to sit up and listen? Well, I've just gotten word that women's fashions are flat—and they've been flat for a whole fucking quarter. Now, is that a fluke? A blip on the charts? Or does it show some serious tendencies? And if it does, are we going to sit around on our asses *laughing about it* and *making jokes about it*?"

Lou's words created a painful silence in the room that only a few moments before had been erupting with laughter.

"You know what a flat line means in the medical profession. It means the patient is dead. Well, here at Cybelle it's just about the same thing. Why?"

Lou certainly had their attention now. His eyes moved around the dead-quiet conference room.

"Why? Because you people haven't got your finger on the pulse of what our shoppers really want. Oh, you've been *told*. Over and over. Haven't we gone to a hundred buyers' meetings? Haven't the fashion merchandisers hammered into your heads, over and over, just what styles are hot and which ones are not, who our Cybelle customer is and what she likes to wear? But you people can't listen, or maybe you don't *want* to listen, which is it?"

Lou swiveled his head, glaring into the eyes of first one buyer, then another.

Aaron Vishnek began staring at the table top, and several others were squirming uncomfortably.

"It's only the past three to four weeks that figures have really started to flatten," pointed out Roger Canton, obviously hoping to cool things a little. "Most of this year our numbers have been quite good."

"Figures are one thing, trends are another," Lou snapped. "I say a new trend has begun, and it's got to be nipped right now, in the bud. Sally!" he snapped.

Sally Gazzara stiffened, her cheeks turning red.

"I walked through a couple of Cybelle department stores yesterday and I saw a big bunch of those Eastlight pointelle knit tunics on the remainder tables. You bought those misfits, didn't you?"

Sally began examining the table top.

"Quit looking at the table," Lou snapped. "Miz Gazzara, do you want to go to work for Kmart? Or Wal-Mart? Or Montgomery Ward?" He sneered out the names of the low-end chains.

Her face grew even redder. "Of course I don't—"

"Well, you might be planning some blue-light specials on panty hose if something doesn't turn around and damn quick."

Lou went on, lambasting the buyers one at a time, while most of them squirmed lower and lower in their seats, or stared back, afraid to argue with Lou.

Abruptly, Sally Gazzara pushed back her chair and exited the room, sniffling. Cilla felt a wave of pity for her. She'd suffer later. Lou was merciless on people who he believed "couldn't take it."

Lou waited until Sally had gone, letting the silence build. "Cowards," he cried, opening up the briefcase and taking out two statuettes of Degas ballet dancers that until now had decorated the credenza in his office. "We have too many of those at Cybelle . . . too damn many. What Cybelle needs is a breath of fresh air. Don't you agree?"

There was a stricken silence.

"A breath of fresh AIR!" Lou suddenly shouted. He lunged to his feet and hurled one of the heavy statuettes through the floor-to-ceiling tinted window. Glass shattered.

There was a blank second of silence, then people jumped out of their chairs and began trying to exit the room.

"Lou! No!" Cilla yelled as Lou picked up the other statuette. "Lou—stop!"

She tried to grab the statue, but Lou wrenched it away from her and threw it at the broken window, smashing away an even larger portion of the huge glass pane. "Fresh air!" he said softly, his mood suddenly dissipating into smiles. "That's what we need, is to let some fresh air into our work."

But no one was listening; everyone was fleeing out into the hallway.

As soon as the last person was out, Cilla closed the door, leaving herself and Lou alone in the room.

Breathing hard, Cilla looked around. The conference room looked as if a fire alarm had just sounded. There wasn't much broken glass since the glass had fallen outward, but papers were scattered everywhere. Two or three of the buyers had exited in such haste that they'd left their Franklin planners behind. A woman's black pump lay on its side near the door.

Lou sank into a chair and stared fixedly at the broken window, his breath stertorous. He looked like a man on the verge of a heart attack. Or one who'd just completed a manic episode.

"Lou?" said Cilla tiredly. "Are you all right? That was quite a display."

He wiped sweat from his forehead.

"Are you all right?" she repeated, wondering if she was going to have to call 911.

"Of course I'm all right!" he snapped. "Don't look at me that way. I'm damn fine. I just opened up a breath of fresh air in this department; I just instituted some major changes, and you can damn straight bet I'm all right."

Cilla's heart sank. Lou was known for making a strong point—like putting coal in people's Christmas stockings—but he had never totally lost control like this.

"Lou," she whispered. "Look at that shoe on the floor—you frightened that woman so much she ran right out of her shoe."

"She's a pussy then." Lou's voice strengthened. "They're all pussies if they can't see that I was trying to send them a message they would never forget. Extreme measures," he told Cilla. "That's what I gave them. Extreme measures." He waved at her in annoyance. "Go on, Cilla, get out of here, go join all the other pussies. I've got work to do."

Cilla was glad to escape. Lou wouldn't listen to her anyway—not in this mood. Not in any mood, she recognized with a surge of anger. He was a force majeure, like a tornado or a typhoon.

She quickly left the room. Cilla hurried down the hallway, knowing where they'd all be . . . in the buying area's "back room," an untidy place jammed with rolling racks, tables, an ironing board, a small refrigerator and microwave, stored boxes of hangtags, scrapbooks of color samples from years past, a few tables and chairs.

As she walked in, she saw the buyers gathered in groups. Mary Malcolm, an assistant children's buyer, wore only one shoe. Roger Canton had a small bandage wrapped around his thumb. Sally Gazzara was talking fast, waving her hands. Something about "that bastard."

"Is everyone all right?" asked Cilla.

"Oh, we're fine," said Sally. "We found a bandage for Roger, and he'll live. Just another day of fun and games at Cybelle."

An angry murmur.

They were all looking to her for guidance.

"Look," she finally said, "the best thing is to go back to your desks, get back to work. We'll have another meeting tomorrow, without Lou, and we'll talk about this and get ourselves a game plan, all right? You're all talented people, and I know you can do it."

As they started to file back to work, Cilla left. Her stomach was already beginning to well acid into the back of her throat. Lou'd always been a maverick, arrogantly believing that because of his great track record with the company he could do no wrong. And truthfully, in the past this grandstanding type of behavior had sometimes worked.

Karyn sensed that something had happened when she saw Lou come striding back into the department, his jaw jutting out and his face patchy with red. However, she passed it off as one of his usual spates of ill temper.

Out of the corner of her eye she saw Lou open the door of Cilla's office and peer inside. Then he approached Karyn's desk.

"Karyn, I need that blue binder Cilla was working on. Will you look around her office and find it for me? Bring it into my office." He continued down the hall to his office.

Karyn quickly found the binder and carried it into Lou's office.

For a moment she thought he wasn't in the room. His desk chair was empty, his computer screen running a screen saver. She was about to put the report on his desk and leave when she noticed that the door of Lou's executive bathroom was standing half open.

Suddenly, Karyn heard the unmistakable spattering sound of male urine hitting a toilet bowl. She jumped back, appalled.

"Karyn," he called. "Don't leave. I'll be right out, hon."

She withdrew to the hallway door, feeling sickened as she couldn't help hearing the sounds of his urine stream, finally ending in a few short stops and starts.

Finally Lou emerged from the bathroom, his hands fondling himself as he took his time about pulling up the zipper.

"Now, I need five copies of that report by—"

"Right away, Mr. Hechter," she snapped.

Pulling the binder to her chest, she hurried out. Fighting revulsion, she strode to the copy room and took the three-hole-punched sheets out of the binder cover, feeding them into the copier and setting it for five copies, sorted and stapled.

Lou was a *vice president*. Flaunting bathroom behavior in front of his employees was unthinkable. Even factory workers with ninth grade educations were capable of having better manners than that.

Karyn finished the copies and piled them on her desk—she was darned if she would deliver them to Lou when he was in this mood.

Was this her fault? Had she provoked him somehow?

But Karyn could not see anything she had done that would cause Lou to behave as he had done.

She fled to the rest room, staying there for over twenty minutes, trying to compose herself, and finally went back to her desk, beginning to work on a presentation in Power Point that Cilla needed.

Just as she was formatting some bullet points, Raquel came sidling over to Karyn's desk, her dark eyes aglow.

"You'll *never* guess what."

"Probably I can't," said Karyn, trying to smile. "But

have a feeling you're going to share it with me."

"It's my boss—Lou the Terrible. He's gone berserko."

Karyn nodded, uneasily wondering if someone had witnessed what happened in his office.

Raquel's eyes danced. "He threw some statues out the window in the buyers' meeting."

"What?" Karyn stared, remembering Lou's red face when he had arrived back at the department. "He broke a window?"

"Big hole," said Raquel, stretching out her hands wide. "Said he was letting fresh air into the corporation."

"Was anyone hurt?"

Raquel giggled. "Not really. They ran out of the room so fast that Mary Malcolm left one of her shoes in there."

"But . . . what's going to happen?"

Raquel sobered. "Who knows? Maybe someone will report it to HR, and they'll send an E-mail to Lou about it, but they're not going to *really* do anything. What are they going to do, take away his stock options? And if he ever finds out who reported him, he'll find a way to make them pay, so probably nobody will say a damn word."

Lou's body hummed with unspent adrenaline. He'd enjoyed scaring silly little Karyn by zipping his pants in front of her, making her think he might actually pull out his dick. But it hadn't been enough. He was still revved up like a high-performance engine. He needed to release some of his energy or he was going to explode.

Impulsively, he reached out his hand and dialed Cilla's extension.

"Yes?" she said crisply, finally back in her office.

"Meet me in our usual place . . . one hour."

There was a pause. "Lou, it isn't convenient. And things are going to have to change."

"One hour," Lou snapped, and hung up.

He was pacing again when Raquel buzzed through. "It's Mr. Carrara's secretary on the line."

"Mr. Hechter, Mr. Carrara would like you to come up to his office right away." Sondra Zapernick's voice was steely-sweet.

Lou stifled surprise and annoyance. "Now?"

"Please be prompt, Mr. Hechter."

Sondra Zapernick hung up in Lou's ear with a soft, official click. Lou stared at the phone and then lowered it into the cradle, something squeezing deep in the center of his stomach. Dom Carrara had heard about the broken window in the meeting . . . that had to be what this was all about. Well, he didn't have to worry, because he could justify everything he had said and done.

By the time he left his office and was proceeding down the marble walk toward the lobby elevator, Lou had reassured himself that all was well. He was Lou Hechter, a legend at Cybelle; he'd brought this corporation millions in profits. And legends were by tradition cut some slack. At least, they had been in Vic Rondelli's regime, before Dom Carrara was hired as president and CEO.

"What in the hell were you thinking about by breaking that window?" demanded Dom Carrara, gazing at Lou with eyes of cold granite.

Lou gave him the same look back. "I was jolting them, prodding them out of their dangerous complacency. Letting a little fresh air in, both literally and figuratively."

Dom had shut the door of his magnificent office but hadn't offered Lou a seat, so Lou had simply sat down on the arm of one of the chairs, a position that left him head and shoulders higher than Dom, a little bit of a one-upmanship that Lou felt appropriate for the occasion.

"Run this past me again, your reasoning in this," said Carrara.

So, Lou explained at length, basically repeating his speech to the buyers about flat lines and downward trends.

Dom Carrara got up from his desk, and stood with his arms folded across his chest, staring down at Lou.

"And weren't you worried that you might injure one of our employees?"

"It was just an attention-getter," Lou insisted, minimizing the incident. "I was thinking only of Cybelle. I maybe did get a little carried away, I can see where people might think that, but that's my stock-in-trade. That's who I am. Trust me, they'll start pulling together now. I personally guarantee you that the flat line is going to be heading up, starting in the next three weeks."

"Fine, but from now on, I want you to stay within conventional bounds when it comes to meeting room histrionics," said Carrara.

"Fine," Lou agreed.

Carrara brought up a couple of other points, extending the meeting for another ten minutes, and finally Lou was released when Carrara said he had a conference call. Lou left the CEO's office and stalked past Sondra Zapernick's desk without looking at the attractive, silver-haired woman who had probably heard about this on the company grapevine and informed her boss.

She was just another bitch—like all of them.

He entered the executive elevator, pushing the Down button. He had just about enough time to make a few phone calls, then leave for his "meeting" with Cilla Westheim.

Cilla, meet me in our usual place . . . one hour.

Cilla's hands were shaking as she sat at her computer.

Maybe she just wouldn't show up, she thought, feeling a surge of nausea. She could phone the hotel room, explain to Lou why this had to stop . . . but even as she was thinking this, Cilla knew it was not going to work. Lou really, actually, believed that he had a right to have her, that she was his property in the same way that his desk was, or the photographs on his office wall.

Cilla phoned Karyn, telling her assistant she would be comparison-shopping for the afternoon and would not be in until tomorrow. Then she remembered that she'd agreed to meet Shane Gancer for dinner in downtown Rochester.

Oh, Christ. She was going to have to break the date.

Reluctantly, Cilla dialed Shane's extension in the Legal Department, and was relieved when his voice mail picked up, so she wouldn't have to give her excuses personally.

"Shane," she explained onto the tape, "something has come up. I have to drive to Albion tonight to see my daughter, so I won't be able to have dinner with you tonight. A raincheck, huh?"

She hesitated, not knowing what to add to the lie, hating herself for the fact that she had to lie at all. What would Shane think if he knew she was on her way to a sexual assignation with her boss? An *enforced* assignation?

"I'll call you when I can," she finally finished, hanging up.

Her afternoon was now cleared for Hell Day.

Five minutes later Cilla was on her way to her car. She was a coward, she lambasted herself as she made the long trek across the parking lot. But somehow she had to change that—she had to stop this horrible situation with Lou or she knew she'd never be able to live with herself.

Once Cilla left to go shopping, and Lou disappeared somewhere, Karyn thought she might be able to relax a little, but her stomach was knotted up with tension, actually hurting underneath her diaphragm, to the left.

"I don't suppose you have any antacids, do you?" she asked Raquel when the pain became persistent.

"I've got some Gaviscon," said Raquel, who used one drawer in her cabinet as a departmental first aid kit.

"I guess I'll take one," sighed Karyn.

"You have stomach problems?"

"Not usually. But . . ." Karyn hesitated, then burst out

with it. "I walked into Lou's office to take him a report and he was in his bathroom peeing with the door half open."

"He's a slug," said Raquel. "He does that sometimes with new women, or women he thinks he can intimidate. You've gotta develop a harder shell when it comes to Lou, honey. He only picks on the ones he thinks he can get to."

"Has he done it to you?"

"Yeah . . . once when I first came here. I turned around and left the room fast. And I kept his hall door open, too, so anyone out in the hall could hear him peeing."

Karyn began chewing on the big, chalky tablet.

"Hey," Raquel added. "While the cats are away, the mice can play. Let's go down to the Cybelle store and see if we can find any good bargains. I usually check them out at least once a week. Come on, let's go."

So Karyn went, and she found a blouse in Amber's size with pictures of cats on it, and a Patagonia jacket for herself that would be warm with winter coming on—all for about what she'd pay at Kmart. By the time she and Raquel were in the cafeteria, getting yogurt, her stomachache had mostly gone away.

Lou seemed in an odd mood, restlessly pacing the hotel room. He kept talking about the "attention-getter," as he called it, framing and reframing the broken window incident, painting himself as a company hero. The more he raved, the crazier he sounded to Cilla. Couldn't the man grasp that he had gone around the bend? That he'd terrorized everyone in the meeting?

"Lou," said Cilla after a while, "we have to talk."

"No, Cilla, we don't have to talk. What good is talking? It's just a bunch of emotional bullshit."

"This has to end. I can't do this anymore."

"Why not? It never bothered you before. In fact, you love everything I give you."

Cilla rubbed her forehead. "I don't. I don't love it. I want it to stop."

Lou's face started to turn brick-red again, the way it had in the meeting.

"Don't give me that *bullshit,*" he snarled. "You want this as much as I do, if not more so. How long has it been since we've been meeting like this? Almost three years. And it's been consensual sex, sweetheart. So don't give me that bull-crap now, because it just won't wash."

"Lou," she whispered. "Please. Please, let me stop doing this."

"Oh, ho, it's *way* too late to stop, Cilla. I like it and you like it, and you want to keep your job, don't you? I can't believe how forgetful you can be, darling, sweet Cilla." He slid his hand underneath her hair at the back of her neck, pinching the tendons tightly in his thumb and forefinger.

"Lou!" She uttered a cry of pain. "Please!"

"Get your clothes off, Cilla," Lou ordered.

She was weeping as she slowly began to comply. If only she'd never slept with Lou that first time. If only she'd accepted the job that time with Dayton-Hudson; they'd really wanted her. If only she didn't have so many credit card debts, if only she wasn't a shopaholic who'd gotten in way over her head, if only she didn't have those huge tuition payments. If only she wasn't such a fucking coward.

"That's it," said Lou in triumph as Cilla unfastened her bra and dropped it on the floor. "Take off your panties, Cilla. Yeah . . . yeah . . . You still have a good body for a lady of fifty. A great body. But you better take care of it or you'll lose it and then these little sessions *will* end."

Oh, great, Cilla thought in despair as Lou lay on top of her. She could stop all of this by getting fat . . . what an irony.

She was dry, and Lou had to shove painfully in order to enter her. He came almost immediately, within three strokes, his premature ejaculation a problem he'd had from the first

time they'd been together. Cilla often had wondered whether
he had the same problem with his wife. But right now she
couldn't have cared less. Lou was a monster. If she could
think of a way to make his dick drop off, she'd gladly en-
gineer it.

Cilla drove home, her body feeling sticky and unpleasant
underneath her clothes. She hadn't showered in the hotel
room, wanting only to flee as quickly as possible. Now she
could hardly wait to get home and wash all traces of Lou
Hechter from her body. And maybe, she thought angrily,
she should fix herself a chocolate milkshake when she got
home. Two of them. Obliterate herself under seventy pounds
of extra blubber and then Lou would cease to be a problem.

As she pulled into her condo complex, she caught sight
of a florist's van exiting toward the main road. She drove
into her driveway, seeing a green package sitting on her
front steps—something wrapped in florist's paper. Great!
Flowers. From Shane, probably, anticipating their now-
canceled date. Just what she did not need right now.

She sat for a minute in her car, feeling too tired and despairing to push the garage door opener or to deal with the
unwanted floral arrangement on her front steps. He must
have ordered them before she canceled, and not yet played
back his voice mail to listen to her message.

Shane. How young and naive he was. He was still young
enough to think that he could conquer anything, too young
to know the humiliations and compromises that adulthood
could throw at him. He had no idea what Cilla was going
through—what she was up against.

What she had let herself become.

Wearily, she used the remote, drove into the garage, then
went around to the front steps to retrieve the flowers from
Shane. She punched her security code and carried the arrangement into the kitchen.

Two dozen salmon-colored roses this time, their fragrance
spicy. Cilla went through the motions of finding a vase,

snipping stems, adding the little packet of rose food to the water.

She ought to call Shane to thank him.

But of course he had no idea she was home already. He thought she was in Albion visiting Mindy. Shane knew nothing. He didn't know her at all, and if he did he probably would not *want* to know her, she thought.

As usual, Cilla managed to do a little mental legerdemain, and by evening she had managed to push her rage at Lou deep down inside herself, blanking out the memory of her most recent, ugly session with him.

Mentally blotting it out was the only way she could survive.

By the time Friday came, Cilla had immersed herself in work again, her usual anesthetic for her problems. She'd thanked Shane for the flowers, not telling him she'd seen the florist's van driving off after leaving them on her doorstep. When had her life become so complicated?

She found herself browsing the travel section of the *Detroit News,* glancing over the list of exotic holidays and cruises. She hadn't taken a vacation, a real one, in years, not since her divorce from Bob. She studied the listing of cruises, wondering if she'd like to go to Hawaii or maybe the Mediterranean. But who would she go with, Shane? In a way that would just be carrying the complexity of her life with her.

Maybe she should just call and make reservations—for one. Go far away from the telephone and all her responsibilities. Lie on a chaise lounge somewhere and drink Mai Tais and get a sunburn, thinking about nothing more pressing than where she would eat dinner. A fabulous, healing escape.

But Cilla knew she could never do that, not with her credit cards maxed, her bills filling up her wicker basket, and more tuition bills looming on the horizon. She just had to trek on, doing the best she could. She'd failed once to get rid of Lou, but she'd have to gear herself up to try again, that was all.

On Friday night Cilla and Shane went to a movie at the Star Theater in Rochester, holding hands through a love story with Charlize Theron in it. Charlize had the glowing yet down-to-earth beauty you didn't often see on the screen anymore. It was definitely the kind of quiet, cozy evening that Cilla usually loved. She didn't have to jump out of a plane, nor did she have to watch boats racing at 140 miles an hour, and she didn't have to hike in the woods—another activity she'd recently enjoyed with her young, fit lover.

There were plenty of funny moments and sexy scenes, and Shane began running his fingertip up and down Cilla's wrist, creating ripples of desire along her nerve endings.

As they filed out of the theater, he whispered, "Cilla, how about coming back to my place and I'll make us some bananas flambé."

"Bananas flambé?"

"Actually, it's rather good, or we can skip it and have each other for dessert."

He lived in a duplex near downtown Birmingham, owning the entire building and renting out the other half to help pay the mortgage.

"A necessity, since I owe about forty thousand dollars in student loans," he'd admitted ruefully.

Shane had bought some vanilla-scented candles, Cilla's favorite scent, and they lit them together in his bedroom, which was slightly untidy, books and clothes strewn about, a bachelor's lair. Shane's bedspread was a quilt his mother had made for him, a red-and-blue log cabin pattern.

They each undressed the other, Shane pausing frequently to kiss Cilla's skin, paying particular attention to her breasts, which he cupped reverently in his hands. She was no longer self-conscious about her breasts, thrusting them out toward him in a way she never could have done with Bob during their marriage.

"Small, like peaches. Perfect in size, and so edible. Much better than bananas flambé," Shane murmured, licking her nipples until electricity shot straight through her, creating a warm loosening of wetness between her legs.

By now Cilla was brave enough to caress a few parts of his anatomy, too, and she was learning about the wonderful textures of the male body . . . the crispness of his pubic hair, the soft furriness of his testicles, his rock-hard penis sheathed in velvet, its tip silky beneath her caressing, exploring fingers.

Cilla put her leg over him and straddled him, slowly lowering herself onto him. Unlike the vaginal dryness she experienced when she had sex with Lou, she was creamy moist. She arched her back, as she had seen movie stars do in love scenes, and threw back her head, grinding in a feral rhythm.

Then two strong arms grasped her sides and rolled her over, and now he was on top of her, pulling her knees up until she was exposed to him like a peeled plum.

"My Cilla . . . come to me . . ." he demanded hoarsely. "Come to me."

He pushed in and out of her, thrusting in a semicircular motion until she was panting and uttering little screams.

Her orgasm was noisy and wild, her screams so loud that they reverberated in the room. In the middle of her climax, Shane came, too, shuddering in paroxysms of pleasure.

Later they sat in bed by candlelight, propped up on pillows, eating the dessert that Shane had prepared for them while wearing nothing but a towel around his waist. He had even garnished it with fresh springs of mint.

Her own naked chef, Cilla thought complacently, allowing herself to swim in relaxation. This was much better than any cruise ship, and it far surpassed any other fantasies she'd been having recently.

"So what do you think?" Shane asked her when they had finished the dessert.

"About what?"

"Me."

"I think you're . . . There are no words," she said simply.

"Am I going to meet your daughter?"

She'd told Shane that Mindy was coming home for the weekend on the following day, and obviously he'd been thinking about it.

"Why—I think so," she said, surprised, touched that he wanted to meet Mindy, yet also more than a little alarmed. "It's just that I'm not sure I'm ready. I'm not sure *she's* ready. It might not be great."

"Cilla, I won't push you. I'd never do that. If you don't feel ready, then we won't do it. But if we're going to be a couple, you can't hide me forever."

Cilla could feel redness flush her chest, and was glad of the concealment of the semidarkness and flickering candles.

"Is it that obvious? Me hiding you, I mean."

"It's that obvious." He smiled at her to take away the sting.

"I'm sorry, I didn't—I mean . . ." Her voice trailed off. How could she tell him that she hadn't wanted to go through the hassle of taking him around her friends and family because she thought it wouldn't last?

"Maybe just a quick introduction at first," he said. "That'll probably be more than enough for everyone. Later, we'll see."

Cilla's daughter arrived home for the weekend lugging a stack of textbooks, a duffel bag full of laundry, and a suitcase full of weekend clothes.

Cilla eyed her daughter. Mindy was wearing jeans and a sorority T-shirt, with a golden Delta Gamma pin affixed just over her left breast. Her blond hair flowed down her shoulders. Cilla had hoped that Mindy would not pledge a sorority, but her daughter had insisted, and now Mindy was a golden girl who could have appeared on a poster advertising the Greek life on campus. Nervously, Cilla wondered what Shane would think of Mindy.

"How about a kiss?" Cilla said, smiling.

"Kiss-kiss," said Mindy, hugging Cilla and casually giving her a couple of air kisses. "Are we going to eat out tonight, I hope?"

"As a matter of fact, we are," said Cilla, who had made plans for Shane to drop by for a few minutes before they left.

"Oh, where're we going? I hope not that Szechwan place we went to last time. Mom, the egg rolls were just full of fat. They were soooo greasy."

"Don't worry, this place will have low-fat items on the menu. I hope you brought something besides jeans," Cilla added.

"Yeah . . . I brought a dress." Mindy wandered into the living room, walking right over the area of the carpeting where Cilla and Shane had made love for the first time. The college student threw herself on the couch with the boneless movements of the young and flipped her head forward, then back, running her fingers through her hair.

Seeing this gesture, Cilla winced. All through high school Mindy had been obsessed with her hair, and her hair mannerisms had been a constant source of friction between them. To Cilla the flipping of a blond ponytail seemed such an airhead gesture, and every time Mindy did it, she cringed. She didn't want Mindy to be an airhead. Of course, no Albion student was an airhead, she reminded herself. Mindy had managed to keep her grades at a B-plus level.

"You know, Kelly almost had an accident," Mindy remarked. "She nearly sideswiped a stupid semi."

"Kelly?"

"Yeah, she drove me this time; my car's in the garage again. Something about the suspension. The man in the garage says it's going to need new tie-rods, too, whatever those are."

"No," said Cilla, paling at the idea of a near-accident with a semi.

"We had to drive off on the shoulder. You know Dad always says you should never pass a truck on the right because they have that blind spot, but I guess Kelly doesn't know that, and I could have been killed," said Mindy casually. "If I'd been driving it wouldn't have happened. Mom, I need a newer car, not that old tin can I've got. It's already got ninety-five thousand miles on it."

Cilla sighed with frustration. "Mindy, I told you when you picked Albion that we couldn't afford both a car and the tuition. Then I relented and we got the used car. Even with your scholarship it costs more than sixteen thousand dollars a year to send you, and your father has not sent any money in nearly two and a half years."

Mindy flushed. "He has—I'm sure he has."

"I'm sorry, honey, but he has not." Cilla tried to keep the bitterness out of her voice. Bob had stopped sending the money almost as soon as he married Trisha, apparently deciding that he didn't have enough resources to cover both a new family and an old daughter.

"I bet he's sent it and you've spent it on something else."

It had been a long, tiring week, exacerbated by Lou's nightmarish sexual demands and the fact that Cilla had stayed over at Shane's duplex until 3:30 A.M. Now he was due over here any minute. The last thing she wanted was for Shane to get here and find her and Mindy fighting.

"Honey, you're welcome to discuss this with your father. In fact, I suggest you call him right now and get it settled. Meanwhile, we've got reservations at seven-thirty, so you might want to hop in the shower and get out that pretty dress you brought. And someone's dropping over in a few minutes, someone I want you to meet."

Mindy unfolded herself from the couch. Her eyes glittered

with tears. "You always say that, Mom—go and call Dad. You know he won't be home. You know he'll be out with Trisha—you know he spends all his money on her now."

There. At least Mindy was facing facts.

"Then why do you keep asking for things I can't afford?" Cilla asked quietly.

Mindy's eyes glazed with tears. "Because I hate being poor when we're not poor. If you'd spend your money like a normal person—if you didn't keep going to the mall all the time and maxing up your plastic—"

"Mindy." The accusation was disconcertingly accurate. "I wouldn't be having so many financial worries if I didn't have your tuition to pay. I've been trying to carry the load, but you've got the rest of this year and next, and you're going to have to assume some of the burden yourself now, too."

"What do you mean?" asked Mindy suspiciously.

"I mean you're going to have to take out a student loan."

"What?"

"Lots of students take out loans, and they pay them back later, when they've found jobs."

"But I won't make enough money to pay back a big loan!" Mindy wailed. "Mom . . . I don't even know if I can get a job. If I have to pay back humongous debts I'll never be able to get a good car, and I won't be able to get an apartment . . ."

"You'll manage," Cilla said, amazed at the cool control in her voice when she felt like screaming. "You'll have a business degree, for God's sake. Business graduates make good starting salaries. I might be able to get you in at Cybelle if it comes to that."

"I hate Cybelle! Cybelle is just a stupid store."

"You're behaving like a brat, Mindy," said Cilla, shaking. "Get a job wherever you want. But you will take out a loan."

They glared at each other.

It was just at this moment that Shane pulled up in his Explorer.

"Who's that?" inquired Mindy suspiciously, peering out of the glass side panel of the front door as Shane parked in the driveway and started to get out of his vehicle.

"Honey, at least meet him."

"This is the guy, Mom? It is, isn't it?"

"Mindy, all you have to do is say hello."

"I don't want to meet him! Mom, I've told you what I think of you dating a guy like that. It's really sick. You're too old, to date some guy who's only twenty-five."

"He's twenty-six, Mindy. He'll be twenty-seven in a few months."

"Oh, great! That makes it all right?" Mindy snatched up her suitcase and started upstairs. "I'm not hungry anyway. I'm going to call around, call some of my friends. I think Jill is home, and Kelly. Maybe we'll go out. So you two don't have to worry about me. You can do . . . whatever."

Cilla heard the slamming of an upstairs door. Fury rose inside her, and she felt like rushing upstairs, flinging open her daughter's door and . . . then what?

More fruitless arguing. Face it, Mindy resented her, had done so ever since the divorce. Cilla felt as if her daughter was moving farther away from her with every passing week.

She felt a lump ride its way up the column of her throat as she waited for Shane to ring the doorbell.

"Are you all right?" asked Shane. He looked handsome and casual in a pair of jeans and a dark red denim shirt open at the throat, worn underneath a black windbreaker.

"I'm . . . fine," Cilla lied, rubbing moisture out of her eyes. "Okay, I'm not fine. Mindy and I had a . . . she's not ready to meet you, she made that plain. I was going to take her out to Max & Erma's but she decided to go out with her friends instead."

"I saw her look out the window. She's very lovely."

"And also very rude."

"It takes time, Cilla."

"Yeah . . ." Cilla fought tears.

"Look." Shane smiled. "You don't have to eat alone. How about if I take you out to eat?"

Cilla nodded. "I'll give Mindy another chance to join us."

She went upstairs and knocked on Mindy's door, but her daughter refused to open it.

"Mindy?" Cilla opened the door a crack and called through it. "Shane and I are going over to Max & Erma's. Would you like to come with us? I promise we'll keep the conversation light."

"Ugh! No thank you!" Mindy called. "But could you leave me some money on the dining room table? We're going to go over to St. Andrew's Hall and I need money for concert tickets."

Cilla felt something inside her freeze. To Mindy, Cilla existed only to shell out money. No matter how furious Mindy was with her mother, the money was supposed to keep on coming.

She quietly backed away from the door, going into her own master bedroom to freshen up. But instead of combing her hair, Cilla leaned against the wall and gave herself up to hot tears.

Against her better judgment, she left $20 on the table for Mindy. A token amount not the $50 or $100 her daughter expected. They were going to have to talk more about money. She was dreading it, but it had to be done.

Max & Erma's, located in a shopping center in Rochester Hills, was crowded, the noise level high. Tonight, dining with Shane felt constrained and awkward. Cilla glanced around the room several times but saw no one she knew. She made conversation, trying to sound vivacious, but her heart wasn't in it.

Finally, Shane looked at her pityingly. "Poor Cilla," he

said. "This really bothers you, doesn't it? My age. Your daughter's reaction."

"No," protested Cilla, but then she nodded.

"Don't worry about it, all right? Mindy will come around, and if she doesn't, we'll deal with it."

Cilla again nodded, looking down at her plate, where she'd barely touched her breast of chicken stuffed with ricotta and herbs. Suddenly a picture of Lou stabbed into her mind. Lou was the one most likely to come between her and Shane, not Mindy. Or, horror of horrors, a whisper might come out about her and Lou, and Shane would hear it. . . . She shuddered, her good mood of the evening rapidly draining away. Her life was chaos. When would she admit it?

"Cilla, what are you thinking?" inquired Shane. "You haven't said a word in five minutes. Is the food all right?"

"The food is lovely." She pasted a smile on her face.

"Then maybe it's the company?"

"The company is lovely, too."

Shane touched her hand. "It'll be fine," he repeated.

Jinny Caribaldi's mother had a cold this week, so Karyn had taken Caitlin for four nights, and the two young girls enjoyed their "sleep-overs" to the hilt, giggling and gossiping and talking about boys. Karyn loved watching her daughter have fun. Already, Amber was much changed from the timid little girl she'd brought up from Atlanta. Just being here in Michigan . . . free of Mack . . . had opened up both of their lives.

However, that Friday morning, Karyn received another of the anonymous phone calls in the morning, just as she was getting ready for work.

"I want you to lick my dick and eat my come," said the hoarse male voice.

Karyn slammed down the phone, her heart racing. God . . . this was the third time he had called, always the same husky, muffled voice, as if the caller might be holding a handkerchief or cloth up to his mouth. Sometimes she felt sure it was Lou, but then she would doubt her instinct. Surely an important man like him wouldn't stoop to anonymous calls . . . would he?

She sank down at the dinette table, rubbing her throbbing forehead.

"Mom? Are you sick today?" inquired Amber, coming up to her mother with a worried expression.

"I'm fine, Amber. Tell Caitlin to get her book bag. I'll drive you girls to school."

She was going to have to get Caller ID, she decided, watching the two young girls run into the grade school. She didn't need the extra expense, but what if Amber picked up the phone sometime and heard that scary, sleazy voice? She would call the phone company today and arrange it.

Arriving at the huge office building, Karyn greeted Cherise at the #2 door, then proceeded to her own department, her eyes feeling grainy with tiredness. Usually she approached her day with expectation, but this morning she felt dulled and out of sorts.

And it was going to be a busy day, too. Lou was making a presentation for the executive committee. Cilla had to give a speech to her merchandisers' group. And there were more travel arrangements to make.

Karyn stopped by her desk to turn on her computer, noticing that Raquel was late. Cilla had left a stack of dictation tapes on Karyn's chair, and there was a big pile of interoffice mail to deliver, too.

Karyn sighed, and decided that maybe some coffee would perk her up—like about two cups of it. Deciding against making the long walk to the large cafeteria, she decided to visit the nearby vending room.

Walking in, she stopped, startled. Lou Hechter was standing at the coffee machine.

"Good morning, Miz Karyn," he said, smiling.

"Good morning." Nervously she hung back, hoping someone else would come into the room.

"My, you look sexy today," he remarked, staring at her teal-colored rayon blouse, which she wore with a gray herringbone skirt that grazed her kneecaps. "That color is magic with your complexion. And it works a little magic with your nipples, too. Or did you rub them before you came to work or pinch them erect?"

"Mr. Hechter!" She backed away, but not before he'd quickly moved, putting himself between her and the door.

"Does talking about nipples excite you?"

"Please—I have to get back to my desk."

"You love to show off your figure, don't you, Miz Karyn? Oh, yes, lovie, and you've got a wonderful one. You like being looked at, you like showing off, don't you? Have you had implants or are they naturally yours?"

Angrily she moved away, hoping to slip around him and make her exit. What made Lou think he could do this?

"Let me guess," Lou went on, eyeing her chest. "About the implants, I mean. You bounce a little when you walk, but not all that much, which is consistent with a good set of silicone. In fact . . ."

He started toward her, his hands out.

She backed farther toward the window, but it was too late. Lou's outstretched hands connected with her chest, and his spatulate fingers splayed themselves around each breast, cupping her firmly.

Karyn uttered a small, shocked scream.

"Hard ones," he announced. "Nice little nubs is what you have. I like that in a woman."

She gave a twisting wrench and managed to slap out at his hands at the same time, extracting herself from his grip. Giving him a shove, she ran past him, hurrying out of the vending room. She fled down the hallway, joining a group of arriving employees who were heading toward their work spaces.

Karyn stopped in the women's room to straighten her clothes. Bitterly she stuffed some toilet paper into her bra so that if her nipples did turn into "nubs" this biological event would be concealed. Apparently just wearing a blouse without a jacket had been too revealing, too tempting for an asshole like Lou.

From now on, she vowed, she would wear loose, baggy jackets.

Karyn was breathing fast as she finally went back to her desk and opened up her bottom file drawer. She riffled through the folders until she'd found the Cybelle Employee Brochure they'd given her in Human Resources that first day. She flipped to the table of contents and finally found the section on sexual harassment.

Sitting with her arm partly over the booklet, shielding the pages from any passerby, she scanned down the page.

It is the policy of Cybelle that employees be free from sexual harassment by other employees of the company. For this purpose, "sexual harassment" is defined as including unwelcome sexual advances, requests for sexual favors, and other verbal or physical conduct of a sexual nature, whether or not it is directly linked to the grant or denial of an economic consideration, where such conduct has the purpose or effect of unreasonably interfering with an individual's work performance or creating an intimidating, hostile, or offensive working environment.

Cybelle's sexual harassment policy is posted. In order to permit Cybelle to take appropriate action to enforce this policy, employees are encouraged to bring any complaint of sexual harassment, whether directed toward themselves or any employee, to either their immediate supervisor, the Human Resource Manager, or any one of the persons identified in the posted policy statement on the bulletin board in the company cafeteria.

All such complaints will be investigated by Human Resources and will be handled, to the extent feasible, with confidentiality. Persons found violating this policy will be subject to disciplinary action, up to and including discharge.

Her stomach knotting, Karyn reread this edict, trying to picture just how it would work out in real life. It would be handled "to the extent feasible" with confidentiality, but what did that really mean? They'd have to talk to Lou. And suppose Lou denied everything? He could—of course he would. There'd been nobody else in the vending room when he had fondled her breasts. Nobody in the fax room when he'd pressed his body against hers, nobody in his office when he had peed with the bathroom door half open, then fondled himself while zipping his pants.

There were no witnesses, so it would be her word against that of a company vice president. And would they fire a vice president on the word of one woman?

Karyn's mind whirled as she remembered the Paula Jones case against President Clinton. Then Monica Lewinski. And in the end, all the polls showed that Clinton was the country's most popular president in spite of his sexual behavior. Clinton had kept his job. Powerful men usually did keep their jobs, she thought resentfully.

After a few minutes Lou arrived in the department carrying his coffee cup, walking past Karyn's alcove without a glance in her direction as if nothing at all had happened.

Karyn continued to work, her hands shaking.

And then she thought—maybe Human Resources wouldn't be able to help her but she knew someone else who could.

*   *   *

Dressed in an ecru suit with a darker silk blouse, Sondra Zapernick was on the telephone when Karyn approached her desk.

"Thank you so much for letting me come up. I know I don't have an appointment, but could I possibly see Mr. Carrara for five minutes?"

"I'm so sorry but he has gone to Atlanta and won't be back for two or three days, and after that he's going to be tied up in meetings for a week, then another trip to L.A." Sondra smiled to take away the sting. "Usually he's so very overbooked, I'm sure you understand."

How naive she'd been. The man was superbusy. He wasn't even here! Karyn remembered how kind Dom Carrara had seemed when she'd met him, and felt suddenly lost.

"This is—important. It's personal," she pressed on awkwardly.

"I am sorry. What about if you were to send a memo addressed to his attention? I'll make sure he sees it."

Karyn felt a crushing disappointment. Lou's behavior. No way could she write that down in a memo. What if Lou saw what she'd written? Dom Carrara might show it to him. Either that or Mr. Carrara would toss the memo away, dismissing Karyn as being vindictive or a troublemaker. Or the memo would go into her employee folder and follow her for years and years. Why hadn't she thought this all the way through before coming here?

"That's fine, I'll write a memo," Karyn replied in a low voice, knowing she never would.

"Oh, by the way," Sondra went on. "Has anyone told you about the secretaries' lunch I have every year for all the secretaries in the company? It's coming up next month. It's a very nice luncheon up here on the executive floor, and this year the speaker is going to talk about 'win-win' negotiating. She's just an excellent speaker, very inspiring."

"It sounds wonderful," said Karyn. "I'll be there."

She thanked Sondra and left, getting into the executive

elevator for the trip down to the lobby floor. As the elevator traveled downward, Karyn rubbed her aching temples. "Win-win" negotiation? In her case, it was more like "lose-lose."

She was going to have to do something about Lou Hechter, but what? Quitting her job was an option, but Karyn didn't want to do that.

Anyway, she'd think of something, Karyn assured herself. She came from a family that had weathered many hardships. Her grandfather had been one of eighteen survivors of a Navy ship that had been torpedoed in the Atlantic during World War II, fighting 45-degree water and circling sharks. His grandmother had fought off a full-grown mountain lion, saving the lives of her three daughters, ages six, eight, and nine.

Karyn believed she was a survivor, too.

Around 4:00 Cilla came walking down the hallway looking preoccupied, a frown marking two parallel lines between her eyebrows. She looked about as stressed as Karyn felt.

"Karyn, I need you to make arrangements for a trip to New York for me on the eighteenth. I'll fly out after work and return on the red-eye that same day. LaGuardia."

Hastily, Karyn slid the employee booklet under a stack of papers. She grabbed a notepad and jotted down the date and times Cilla wanted.

"Good—have Travel give me the E-ticket as soon as possible," Cilla said crisply. "Oh, and Karyn, I'm finishing up another stack of dictation tapes for you to transcribe, can you get them out by tomorrow close of business?"

"Certainly," Karyn said, trying to sound cheerful.

"Plus I want you to reserve the West B meeting room for Thursday from nine-thirty to noon, and Friday the same. Send E-mails to all the buyers that we're meeting both days, and do reminder voice mail messages if you would."

"Of course." Karyn jotted all this down.

"That's it for now." Cilla sighed, and Karyn noticed the dark circles under her employer's eyes. "It gets busier around here every day, Karyn—the fun never stops."

Karyn nodded, not knowing what to say.

Cilla turned and hurried away. Karyn watched as Cilla went into her office and closed the door behind her, the universal signal for privacy. The employee manual said she should talk to her "immediate superior." That was Cilla. But Cilla's door was closed right now, and even when it wasn't, she always seemed so busy, springing from one task to the next, seldom stopping even to breathe.

Besides, Karyn would feel funny talking to a woman so much older than her who was so important to Karyn's own job. Suppose Cilla didn't believe her? Or, worse, thought Karyn was a troublemaker? And even if Cilla did believe her, Lou was her boss, too.

Bad idea, she thought glumly.

Her head had begun to pound. Karyn fumbled in her purse for a bottle of Advil and got up to go to the drinking fountain to take two. Bitterly she thought back to her first day of work here, how impressed and excited she'd been.

Well, some of the excitement had certainly worn off, hadn't it? She still loved her job, the part of her job that didn't include Lou, but . . .

When Karyn returned to her desk, her phone rang. It was Jinny Caribaldi. "Sorry to bother you at work, Karyn, but Amber came home from school with a bruise on her face. I've put ice on it, but maybe you'd better come home. She seems kind of upset."

Karyn felt her heart give a horrible twist.

"Is she okay? Should we call 911?"

"I think it's just a bump. Some boys did it to her, she said. There's nothing seriously physically wrong, but she's upset and wants her mother."

"I'll come right home."

Karyn quickly dialed Cilla's extension.

"Yes?" Her boss sounded tired.

"My daughter had an injury at school and the sitter just called—I need to leave to go home and make sure she's okay. I'm sorry. I'll see if Raquel can finish the meeting arrangements."

"It's okay, Karyn. I remember when Mindy was that age. She was a little tomboy and used to fall off the playground equipment all the time. I was always being called to school to pick her up. You go right ahead and do what you have to do."

"Oh, thank you," said Karyn gratefully.

Karyn pulled into the parking lot of her apartment building, parked, and jumped out of her car, half running to the building. She fumbled with her key, managed to get the front door open, then raced upstairs to Jinny Caribaldi's apartment.

"Hi," Jinny greeted her at the door. The TV set was playing in the background, some after-school show on the Learning Channel. "Well, she's settled down a little. I've got her drinking Pepsi and eating Keebler's cookies, so I think the patient is going to live."

"Amber?" Karyn rushed inside, where she found Amber and Caitlin sitting on the couch together watching a silly-looking man talking about the speed of light. Amber was holding an ice bag in her lap. There was a purplish bruise on the side of her jaw.

"Mom!" Amber cried, looking up. "Mom, these sixth grade kids . . . they had these baseball bats and they were hitting all the girls' titties with them!"

"What?" cried Karyn. "They were hitting with baseball bats?"

"Foamy bats," explained Amber. "The foam rubber kind. I didn't get hit in the titty but Michelle did, and the teacher came out and the aide and they were yelling and all the girls ran away. Michelle kept crying and her face got so red and her mom came, an' . . ." Amber seemed to run out of steam.

Karyn knelt down and examined her daughter's petite, pointed chin. The bruise there was already starting to turn yellow. "If the bats were foam rubber, what happened to your face?"

"I fell on the playground," said the girl. Her eyes were saucer-wide, blue and scared. "Mom, they kept yelling 'Titty, titty.' "

"Oh, baby." Karyn hugged her daughter, feeling a surge of anger.

"Mom, I hate those boys!"

"I know, Amber. What they did was wrong."

"Why?" Amber wailed, while Caitlin snuggled against her, appearing to be upset as well. "Why'd they do that?"

"Because—" Karyn hesitated. What she said now was so important. She mustn't make Amber feel afraid, yet she had to teach her little girl to be cautious.

"Because boys like to feel powerful around girls and they think doing this will help," she finally said. "But they're wrong, Amber. When boys harass girls it shows they're weak, not strong."

"But they had those foamy things . . . baseball bat things!"

"They were wrong, Amber. Nobody has the right to touch your body unless you give them your permission. Nobody has the right to hit your breasts with any object or touch them with their hands unless you say it's okay."

Karyn decided to take the girls' minds off the day's trauma by going out and picking up a Little Caesar's pizza for the four of them. The girls munched pizza, watching a rerun of *Splash* on television. Later, while she and Jinny were clearing up the dishes, her neighbor, dressed now in her nurse's uniform for her night shift, said, "You're going to have to call the principal, you know. That school needs better supervision. There's no excuse for what those boys did."

"I'll call tomorrow morning," Karyn decided.

Jinny frowned. "I'm going to call her, too. Caitlin saw everything, and she was just as scared as Amber was. I hate it, that we had to go through this when we were growing up, and now our daughters do, too. Isn't it ever going to end?"

The door buzzer rang. It was Jinny's mother, arriving to stay for the night.

Karyn brought Amber back down to her own apartment and helped her with her bath, then tucked her into bed.

"I really, really, really hate boys," Amber whispered as Karyn turned out the light.

"Boys sometimes don't know how to act," Karyn agreed. "But most of them eventually learn. Meanwhile, if you see them start to act silly like that, you go off someplace else, Amber."

Troubled and upset, Karyn went out to the living room and switched on the TV set, hoping to lose herself in a couple of hours of sitcoms. But the actors on the screen were just a blur as she wrestled with the dilemmas of her own problems. Lou Hechter might not yell "Titty, titty," but he was a grown-up version of the same boys who had tormented Amber, Caitlin, and the other girls. And much more terrifying because he didn't carry a foam rubber baseball bat but brandished the threat of taking away Karyn's job.

The phone interrupted her. It was Roger, calling to see how she was.

"A little frazzled," admitted Karyn. She told him about the boys at school harassing Amber.

"Oh, brother," said Roger. "With baseball bats? That's serious stuff."

"I think they were foam rubber bats. That soft, cheap kind you see in the drugstore."

"Still, it must have been traumatic for her."

"It was. I'm just so mad," Karyn fumed. "I'm going to

call the school and give that principal hell. I'll go to the school board if I have to."

Roger hesitated. "Are you sure that's the right thing to do? They might retaliate against Amber."

Karyn felt a fresh surge of anger. She was close to tears, and she knew it wasn't only because of Amber's situation but also her own with Lou Hechter. "That's the way those bullies control their victims, isn't it? By threats and fear over what might happen if they tell. Well, it sucks!"

"Of course it does. It's a shame it happened to Amber. Calm down, Karyn—"

"I won't calm down. I'm just so frustrated. She asked me why the boys do it. I gave her some sort of answer, but I don't really know. Did you ever harass little girls when you were in the sixth grade?"

Another hesitation. "I tried to kiss a girl once and she slapped my face. Hard."

"Really?"

"I tried to grab the kiss—you know, steal it. I thought that's what you had to do. Boy, did she set me straight." Roger laughed, a little uncomfortably. "It was at least seven years before I tried kissing another girl, and I asked her permission first. That worked much better."

"But boys like the ones that harassed Amber and the other girls. What do they get out of it?"

"It's the gang mentality, I suppose. Boys egging each other on. Showing off. Trying to be Mr. Big. It got out of hand and they didn't know how to stop."

"Maybe." Karyn bit her lip. Right now she was too angry to try to see the boys' point of view. She wanted to tell Roger about Lou but something stopped her. Anyway, there was nothing he could do about it. She was the one stuck with Lou and his ugly sexual behavior.

"Mom, I don't want to go to school today," said Amber, coming into Karyn's room the next morning just as Karyn's clock radio was going off. "My stomach hurts."

Amber's bruise was fading to yellow. By tomorrow it would be nearly gone. Karyn tried to rouse herself. "I'll bet some waffles and strawberry syrup would help the pain."

"Maybe . . ."

Karyn pulled the child onto her bed and ruffled Amber's tangled golden hair. The cat jumped up with them, its body warm on Karyn's legs. "Look, sweetpea. School's going to be just like usual today, you have my word on it. I'm going to call there as soon as I can and talk to the principal, and she'll be sending out extra teachers to recess so you won't run into those problems with the boys again."

"She will?"

"Yes, trust me, she will."

"Well, okay . . . but I want my waffles cut up, okay? In the heart things like you do."

"Heart waffles coming right up, because you're my special heart, Amber Marie."

Jinny was driving the girls today, and the instant they left the apartment building, Karyn dashed for the phone and called the grade school.

"Mrs. Carthena, please," she said crisply, when a secretary answered.

"I'm sorry, Mrs. Carthena is on another line."

"I'll hold," said Karyn, using her best imitation of Sondra Zapernick's patrician, firm tones.

"It might be a few minutes."

"That's quite all right. I'll hold."

She waited, grabbing up a kitchen sponge and using the time to wipe off her counters and dust her flour and sugar canisters. Amber had spilled sugar all over the counter. Finally she heard a live voice.

"Yes, this is Mrs. Carthena speaking."

"Mrs. Carthena, this is Karyn Cristophe. I'm calling because my daughter, Amber, was one of the girls sexually harassed yesterday by the boys with the foam baseball bats.

She fell down and bruised her face and has been quite traumatized. I want to know what safety measures you're taking to see that this never, never happens again."

The school principal, a woman in her sixties sighed as if she'd already been dealing at length with this issue. "Mrs. Cristophe, I'm dreadfully sorry about the occurrence. I didn't know that Amber had hurt herself; she didn't tell anyone. Is she all right?"

"Her bruise is better today, but she didn't want to come to school. I did make her go because I trusted that the school would take care of this problem and make it right."

"Well, we have suspended all five boys involved for the rest of the week. We are going to add several more teachers' aides to our playground supervisory staff, and we're going to be talking in class about what is acceptable behavior and what is not. Sexual harassment is an issue on everyone's minds these days, and you can be sure it's on our minds as well. We will make sure your daughter is safe."

"All right," said Karyn.

"Would you consider joining the PTA, Mrs. Cristophe? It would give you an opportunity to be in much closer touch with the school, and you could be a part of solving some of these problems we face here."

"Yes," said Karyn. "I'd like that very much."

"Good. There's a meeting next Wednesday night at seven-thirty P.M in the school library, if you'd like to come."

A gray rain was falling this morning in keeping with Karyn's mood, and she felt relieved that the weather would probably be too rainy for her daughter to go out for recess anyway. Let the kids have time to calm down and get back to their normal routine.

On the car radio she flicked from station to station, catching a Cybelle ad for holiday dresses. The female announcer was supermodel Ila Britt—a coup that Lou had somehow pulled off. The man did have amazingly good ideas sometimes. Then a PBS talk show drew her attention.

Karyn's stomach began knotting up as she drew closer and closer to the big Cybelle International Headquarters Building. She wished her problem with Lou was as easy to solve as the one that had involved Amber.

"Did you hear what happened?" said Annie Fiacci as Karyn walked into the department.

"No, I just got here."

"Lou fired Vicki Tourneau."

"Really?" Vicki Tourneau was a "hangtag clerk," in charge of organizing the huge number of hangtags that Cybelle required to label its own Cybelle and celebrity lines. Vicki was constantly on the phone to several dozen manufacturers and also did a lot of routine data entry work. "But why?"

"He called her into his office last night and told her that she had been encouraging business from suppliers that had been cut off our list and he wanted her to pack her stuff and get out—like right then. I mean, he didn't even give her a warning."

"We didn't even have a chance to say good-bye," mourned Raquel, coming up to them. "And I just don't understand. Vicki worked so hard. She never even took breaks, sometimes."

The women continued to gossip while Karyn tried to compose herself. A rush of guilt ran over her. The incident in the vending room when Lou had touched Karyn's breasts and she had pushed him . . . Lou had pretended later it didn't happen, but she felt sure he was very angry. He hadn't fired her, though.

Vicki had gotten fired.

Was the firing meant to be a message to Karyn, to show her that he had control over her and her job as well?

What if it was?

This was getting serious—and scary. Karyn's mind went

back to the radio talk show she'd been listening to, the First Lady's knowledgeable attorney.

And then a name popped into Karyn's head.

Malia Roberts. The female attorney she'd seen on TV that time, the one who worked with sexual harassment cases.

A few minutes later, Karyn went into the department's fax room, where a shelf was packed with phone books.

It was still morning-quiet in the department. Elton John was singing the song from *The Lion King* over the company PA system. The two fax machines were silent, and the phones had not yet started to ring, the way they would later in the day.

She began leafing through the North Woodward Area book under Attorneys, looking for Malia Roberts's name. She didn't find it, and finally realized that if Ms. Roberts worked for a large law firm, her name might not be individually listed.

She tried the white pages.

And there it was.

"Malia Roberts, Attorney."

Karyn stared at the name, her heart beginning to pound. It was one thing to try to put up with Lou, to adjust her life and her thoughts to his behaviors, to fume at night and try to hold back her anger, suffering sleepless nights and—increasingly—an ache in her stomach.

She was a plain, ordinary woman making plain, ordinary wages. For her, it was quite a thing to actually see an attorney.

Even if she only talked to her—this was still taking a very major step.

She jotted down the phone number on a Post-it note and carried it back to an empty office where she could have privacy, quickly dialing before she lost her courage.

"Good morning. Hanson, Young and Guthrie," said a cheerful female voice. "How may I assist you?"

Karyn moistened her lips. "I'd like to speak to Malia Roberts, please."

"May I ask what this call is regarding?"

"I'm a—I need some information on sexual harassment. Just information, that's all," Karyn finished hastily, hoping no one would barge into the office while she was having this personal conversation.

"Ms. Roberts does offer free half hour consultations," said the receptionist. "Would you like to come in for an appointment?"

Karyn felt a wave of relief. She'd been afraid that she'd have to pay $150 or more, when she wasn't even sure if she wanted to do this yet. "If I could."

The woman set her up with an appointment for Thursday afternoon at 4:30 P.M. Karyn agreed to the time, writing it down. She'd have to leave work a little early, and Jinny would have to keep Amber for an hour or so longer, but she felt sure she could work out all the logistics.

Karyn returned to work, her stomach jittering nervously.

"Okaaaay," said Raquel at lunch. They were sitting at the far end of a long table in the cafeteria, both of them with big plates of salad from the salad bar. "Something's wrong, isn't it? I can tell from the look on your face, Karyn."

"I'm just—" Karyn had confided in Raquel about some things regarding Lou but she was afraid to tell her coworker too much. Raquel, she had come to learn, could be a gossip, and this was just too sensitive to spread on the company grapevine. If Lou could fire Vicki that easily, then he could have Karyn fired just for talking.

Instead, she began telling Raquel about the incident at school with Amber and the boys.

"The little shits," exclaimed the Hispanic woman. "Next thing you know they'll be demanding those girls play doctor."

"Play doctor? Oh, God."

"Hey, my mama taught me what to do when a boy gets fresh and once or twice I actually had to do it."

"What did you mother teach you?"

"You know." Raquel's dark eyes twinkled. "Kick him where he's soft, if you get my meaning. I did that to a boy in seventh grade when he kept snapping my bra and wouldn't stop."

"Great," said Karyn, in no mood for such tales. "I can just see Amber trying to do that in her school, especially with schools getting so tough now. They'd probably call in a psychologist—for her."

They began trading stories about things boys had done to them when they were in school, and the conversation turned to their first sexual experiences.

"Me, I got laid the first time by this boy who worked in the convenience store. We went out on a real date and wrestled around and then we did it in his dad's truck. I cried all the way home. I'd lost my most precious possession and all that religious stuff. I was only fifteen, and if my Ma ever found out we did it, she'd have killed him and probably shot my butt off, too. In my family, you had to be a virgin or tell pretty good lies."

Karyn looked at her friend. "My first guy was Mack, my ex. But we were married when we finally went all the way."

"Yeah?"

"We met when we were both working at this car dealership. He was a salesman, the top seller, so full of confidence, and he dressed great. I remember I loved his clothes, he had so many. We could hardly keep our eyes off each other. . . ." Karyn frowned as the memories came flooding back. There had been good ones. "That seems like a long time ago now. I was a different person then."

"Don't you ever worry that he'll, you know, come back or something or try to get Amber?"

"I have a restraining order against him. But . . . he's Amber's father, after all. I'm just hoping that his counseling will work." Karyn sighed. "When he was stalking me like that I really started to hate him. I just wanted him to go away and drop off the end of the earth."

She didn't notice the dark flush that started on Raquel's chest and rose all the way up to color her face.

Cilla had managed to get the buyers galvanized, staging a series of meetings designed to pump them up with enthusiasm. She arranged more trips for the buyers to attend runway shows in New York and Paris, and even sent two over to Israel, where trend-setting fashion was happening again. When Sally Gazzara quit, Cilla decided to replace her with a young woman fresh out of design school. Nathalie Cohen had earned her way through school by marketing her own beaded evening purses, and was incredibly fresh and creative.

The campaign to start a line of Jazzy Kulture clothes was moving along—the Cybelle Legal Department was now negotiating with Jazzy's lawyers.

Lou said nothing, which meant that he approved. If Cilla was successful, he'd take the credit; if she wasn't, she'd face his wrath.

Still, Cilla found herself dreading going into work each day.

Would Lou pull another crazy stunt as he'd done in the buyers' meeting, throwing the statues through the window? She hadn't heard of any investigation going on, so once more, as usual, he had gotten away with it.

Dom Carrara called Cilla later that week to ask her if she would fly out to L.A. and visit several branches of Girlrags, buy up samples, talk to the managers and customers, and report back to him.

"A gut reaction, Cilla, that's what I'd like from you. There's only twenty stores right now, but if Cybelle buys it we'll expand to at least a hundred and twenty, possibly more."

Cilla hung on to the phone, surprised that Dom would be asking her to do this instead of Lou. "Certainly," she agreed. "I'll fly out there this week."

"I trust your judgment, Cilla. You haven't got an ax to grind and that's what I want, an honest, gut-level opinion. I'll E-mail Lou to tell him you're on a temporary assignment for me. Write me up a report when you get back. Nothing fancy, just your thoughts."

"Happy to," Cilla responded crisply.

Lou acted very testy an hour later when he barged into her office to confront her about the E-mail he'd just gotten from the company president. "I'm in charge of Fashion and I've got a hell of a lot more years of experience under my belt than you do," he accused.

"I think it's that Dom wanted a fresh eye."

"I've trained myself to have a fresh eye. What are you doing, currying favor with Dom in hopes of getting out of my department?"

Cilla's face burned. "In the first place, I'm not currying favor. I had no idea he was going to call; he must have heard about some of my other accomplishments, that's all."

"Well, let me see your report before it goes out. I might want to tweak it a little."

Cilla made a sound that could have been yes or no. She wasn't going to revise her report to Dom based on Lou's input when he hadn't even made the trip or seen the Girlrags stores. No way. This was her project and she wanted to show Dom Carrara what she could do.

That night she and Shane met for a drink at a small bar/restaurant near where Cilla lived, and she told him about the trip to L.A. and how excited she was. "Getting the attention of the CEO . . . it's things like this that can make or break a career."

"I think your career is going swimmingly. I've heard from

various people that you're quite a dynamo in the Fashion Department. One person said that you're like a younger version of Lou without all the temperament and bullshit and ego. Just the talent part of Lou, is what I think they meant."

"Well, thanks . . . I guess." Cilla laughed. "At least Lou went far up the ladder, which I'm hoping to do sometime."

"You will, Cilla. And there won't be anyone prouder than me."

Cilla gazed at him, at his honest eyes, and wondered if Shane could be for real . . . a man who wasn't competitive with a woman, who could handle her success. But obviously he must be, or he wouldn't have asked her for a date at all.

Later that night Cilla called Mindy to give her the hotel number where she'd be. She always did that whenever she traveled. She never wanted Mindy to have the feeling that Cilla wasn't there, or couldn't be there, for her.

The following day, Cilla was on a Northwest flight to L.A., feeling an odd sense of freedom as the jet reached cruising altitude.

She desperately needed a getaway, and she was looking forward to seeing some old friends in L.A. once she'd done her thing with Girlrags. She opened a copy of *Cosmo* she had bought at the airport newsstand and began turning pages, looking at the clothing ads. A Cybelle ad appeared on page 133, the model a beautiful Eurasian with airbrushed skin. The midriff blouse she wore was mostly lace. On the facing page was another ad, this one for a Gemi pantsuit, sexy and low-cut, that would set office environments ablaze.

At least Lou knew his advertising, she had to admit. It wasn't as if he was a stupid clod. Cilla knew that he loved merchandising and attacked every problem with zest, even if that zest was sometimes misplaced. Like those lumps of coal he had given out a few years back . . .

Her mind returned to Girlrags. She did love the name. It sounded young, fresh, just the thing to appeal to girls aged twelve to seventeen. But why hadn't the small chain done well? What mistakes were they making? She hoped to discover some clues on her visit.

"Are you heading toward L.A. on business?" said the man in the seat next to her, a businessman with a laptop opened on his knees.

"Yes," responded Cilla shortly, turning another page of the magazine.

"Yeah, I'm going there on a sales trip," he persisted. "I sell network server software. We have some really cutting-edge stuff."

Cilla didn't answer. Another airplane Romeo. How many had she encountered during her years of travel for Cybelle? More than she could remember. Long ago she'd learned not to share a cab while traveling if she could help it, and never to eat dinner in a public restaurant by herself. Room service was boring, but at least she didn't have to deal with the guys who wanted to be her dessert.

Finally she was alone with her thoughts as the plane flew over the beautiful patchwork fields of the Midwest, then the foothills of the Rockies sugared with a light dusting of snow.

Shane Gancer. What was she going to do about him? Were her feelings merely those of infatuation, pleasure that she'd been chosen by a young, attractive man? Or were her emotions running much deeper than that?

She frowned, staring down at the landscape. Oh, God . . . if what she was feeling for him was love, then she was in for a very rough ride. Because she didn't see how it could last very long. Maybe in a romance movie or a Danielle Steel novel, but in real life?

A couple with ages so disparate? There was just no way.

Cilla visited three Girlrags stores, in strip malls in Beverly Hills, Lompoc and Carmel, and found them to be bright and flashy, designed to appeal to rebellion-oriented girls who wore rows of earrings in their ears and plenty of funky leather. The clothes were displayed on skinny black plastic mannequins wearing wigs dyed black, purple or both. Some of the salesclerks, obviously dressed in Girlrags clothing themselves, looked positively predatory. Industrial-type rock music pulsed out of each store, but although curious crowds of young girls entered the stores, not many were buying.

Maybe this was because the clothes were too hard-core, Cilla decided. A certain percentage of girls went for the rock club look, but millions more wanted fresher, cleaner-looking styles that still were sexy.

She purchased a suitcase full of samples and talked to managers and customers, making detailed notes to take back to Dom. When this was done, Cilla visited a former co-worker who now lived in Laguna Beach.

"You're dating a young one, huh?" said Ramona Fisk, whose skin was suntanned a warm California gold. Ramona had started out as a buyer for Cybelle but now was a physical trainer at a posh health club, her forty-eight-year-old body honed to solid muscle and sinew.

"Yeah. The good news is that a twenty-six-year-old actually wants me; the bad news is that a twenty-six-year-old actually wants me." Cilla tried to laugh.

"Look, we're hitting the fifty-years mark," said Ramona. "Out here in Hollywood the female stars are over the hill at forty. Here, old guys still think they deserve to get a younger woman. Look at Jack Nicholson in *As Good as It Gets*. He was sixty-one; she was thirty-four, and everyone thought it was perfectly okay. And Woody Allen, he looks like an old street person half the time; he was sixty-two in that film, *Deconstructing Harry*, and Elizabeth Shue was, yeah, thirty-four."

"Not fair," agreed Cilla.

"We still punish women for aging," insisted Ramona. "A white-haired old fart deserves to get a twenty-five-year-old, but let a white-haired woman try that . . . no way, baby. She doesn't deserve it."

Cilla's hand automatically flew to her auburn hair, which she'd recently had colored and highlighted by her stylist.

"But you . . . you look beautiful," added her friend. "I hope you turn the whole system upside down."

A chilly wind whipped across the Cybelle parking lot, blowing dead leaves before it in mini-vortexes. Raquel Estrada hurried down the steps and got on the yellow-painted pedestrian walkway that led across the parking lot. She walked as fast as her three-inch high heels could carry her, afraid of not reaching Brett's car in time.

What a crappy day, she thought. Lou yelling at her— again. And then she'd called Brett's work extension at 4:30 only to discover that he had changed it. She'd reached someone else instead, a man in the International Department. The new extension wouldn't appear in the company directory for three more months, and she knew none of Brett's friends would give it to her.

If he wouldn't even talk to her . . .

By the time she reached the back parking lot, Raquel's anxiety had intensified. She half ran the last few feet. What if Brett had decided to leave early for a change? What if she'd already missed him?

But no, there was his familiar black Jeep Cherokee with the ding in the right bumper, parked at the far end of the lot. Raquel hurried toward it, positioning herself behind a van so that she wouldn't be clearly visible from the walkway.

She waited impatiently while two or three more people got into their cars and joined the slow-moving line of exiting cars.

Then she saw a flash of white—Brett's white shirt.

"Brett," she said softly.

He turned, his shoulders tensing.

"Bretty," she pleaded.

"Oh, Jesus, Raquel. Please. Please, no," he said, looking at his Cherokee, parked a few feet away.

"Brett, you changed your phone extension."

"Yeah. I don't want any more calls from you, it interferes with my work. My supervisor doesn't like it."

"But I know we could work things out if we could only talk for a few minutes. Ten minutes, Brett. It's all I ask."

"Ten minutes won't do a thing," he retorted, digging his car keys out of his pocket and thrusting one into the door lock of the Cherokee. "Ten thousand minutes isn't going to change my mind."

Tears made Raquel's voice ragged as she thrust herself toward Brett, grabbing blindly for his hand. "Don't drive away on me again! Don't!"

He shook her away. "Stop it, Raquel. You've got to stop this."

"No—Brett."

"Raquel, we broke up in August. We're not getting back together again. Why can't you understand it?"

"Please . . ."

"It's finished," he told her, opening the car door and sliding quickly inside, clicking down the automatic door locks so she could not climb in after him. He started the engine, putting the sport utility vehicle into reverse.

"Brett!" she screamed as he backed the Cherokee into the aisle. She ran after it, banging on the fender for him to stop. "Brett! Stop! Please!"

He slowed down the car, and for one glad, heart-racing moment, Raquel saw him roll the driver's window down. But instead of inviting her to get inside the car, Brett said, "Raquel, if you ever try to follow me again, I'm going to call Security. Do you hear me? I'll get the regular police. I'll have you charged with stalking."

"Brett!" she screamed, but the window went up again and Brett drove out of the lot. She tried to run after the vehicle but her high heels teetered, slowing her down, and then he was gone.

Raquel was so blinded by tears that she nearly couldn't find her own car. Two or three employees, walking to their cars, stared at her, but they were just from Accounting, nobody she knew.

Raquel felt dizzied with grief.

If love was true, a woman kept on loving through hardships. Raquel had learned this at home and in church, from the time she was small. Even her mother, Modesta, still made efforts to find Raquel's father after all these years, and had never remarried, waiting for him.

Feverishly she got in her car and started the engine. If she hurried she could still catch her fiancé on his way home. She knew the route he followed, she knew his favorite restaurants, she knew his health club and what days he usually worked out. He couldn't keep himself from her, not if she wanted to find him.

Raquel drove around for more than two hours, making a tour of all the places where she and Brett used to hang out. She cruised the parking lot of his health club but did not see his car. He wasn't at Bennigan's, a restaurant located a short drive from the club, either.

By 7:30 P.M. she was back in Troy, driving past the three-bedroom brick ranch house where Brett lived. The house was still dark, the wind still blowing, mixed now with a fine, spraying rain. Raquel bit her lip, wondering for the thousandth time where he was. Out again with that woman he'd been seeing? She gripped the steering wheel tensely, deciding to drive around the block again.

Eight trips around the block, ten, twelve, and the house was still dark. Frustrated, Raquel decided to stop at a nearby Denny's for some eggs and a cup of coffee. Then she'd be back.

The restaurant wasn't crowded, and Raquel just picked at her omelet. A couple in the booth just opposite hers had two dusky-skinned toddlers that kept peeking over the back of the booth, making eyes at Raquel.

Raquel finger-waved and smiled, thinking they were just the kind of children she pictured herself having with Brett. Her heart ached. When, if ever, would she herself get pregnant? Without Brett she could not fully be a woman.

Brett *did* love her. At least some part of him still did, and that's why he'd let her continue to wear his engagement ring. He just didn't know he loved her, she reassured herself.

Parked several houses down the street from Brett's house, Raquel drifted into an uneasy sleep, slumped back against the headrest, but she woke up immediately when she heard car tires on pavement.

Raquel jumped out of the car and began running toward Brett's vehicle, hoping to catch her fiancé before he went inside the house. It was wet, and her heels slipped on soggy fallen leaves. She nearly fell, but managed to catch herself.

"Bretty!" she cried, breathlessly hurrying up. "Brett, please . . . please can we talk?"

"Oh, fuck," Brett said, staring at her coldly. The driver's window was rolled down a crack, the car rolling to a stop. "Can't I ever get rid of you?"

"If we could just talk for five minutes."

"I thought it was ten."

"Ten. Please."

"Raquel, I've asked you over and over to leave me alone. I told you today after work that it was finished. I've told you a hundred times." He got out of the car and stalked toward the back door he usually used, his expression twisted with annoyance.

Raquel felt her heart break as she followed him.

"Brett, don't be like this."

Brett thrust his house key into the lock, quickly letting himself in. The door closed behind him and Raquel could see him through the square pane of glass, shooting the dead bolt in place. As if she were a criminal.

She waved at him through the glass. "Please! Please! You haven't talked to me. If we could only talk—"

"We talked until we were blue in the face," he shouted at her through the glass. "It's over. Why can't you get it? *I don't love you. I want you out of my life. You're stupid, Raquel. Why can't you get a life?*"

Losing all control, Raquel began weeping, pounding on the glass pane. If he saw how devastated she was, he'd open the door . . . he had to. Her whole life could not be going down the drain like this.

But Brett was no longer there. He'd gone elsewhere in the house, leaving Raquel to stand on the back steps, her hair getting wet with rain, peering desperately inside at the back hallway at a blue recycling bin stuffed with bottles and cans.

"Bretty!" she kept calling. She pounded on the back door some more, and then went around the side of the house to peer into the living room window, which was partially blocked by a set of drapes. "Brett! Please! Come out! Please talk to me!"

But there was no response, nothing to indicate he had heard.

"Oh, Jesus." Raquel wept, feeling abandoned, the way she'd felt as a tiny girl when her father had arrived for a brief visit, then left without even kissing her, never to reappear again. "Oh, Mother Mary."

She made several circuits of the house, still crying.

In the distance, Raquel heard the whine of a siren, the sound growing closer. Brett lived only a mile from a hospital, so Raquel thought little of it, continuing to cry and to pace around the perimeter of the house. Then a police squad car pulled up, and one male and one female police officer got out of the car.

"Ma'am," said the woman officer. "Are you Raquel Estrada?"

"Yes . . ."

"We've had a complaint that you're disturbing the peace."

"I . . . I . . ." Raquel said, appalled.

"Can we please see some identification? Hold your purse out in front of yourself, then drop it on the ground. I'm going to look inside and take out your ID."

Too shocked to argue, Raquel did as she was told.

The woman picked up Raquel's shoulder bag and expertly shuffled through it, finding her wallet. "No weapon," she told her partner. "Your name is Raquel Maria Estrada?"

"Yes."

"You own a 1995 Pontiac Grand Am, license number YLN 453?"

"Yes, yes." Raquel pointed to where her car was parked. "Please," she began. "I just wanted to talk to him."

"Ma'am, what are you doing here at this hour? It's after two-thirty in the morning," said the male officer.

"I was just trying to talk to my fiancé."

"He doesn't want to talk to you. Now, I'm going to have to ask you to get in your car and leave, right now, Ms. Estrada. If you don't, or if you come back here again, we're going to have to take you to jail."

"Jail?" Raquel gasped.

"Yes, ma'am. We'll book you for disturbing the peace, and if your friend files a stalking charge, and you violate it, we'll put you in jail for that, too."

Jail. Raquel felt faint. Her knees sagged, and she found herself kneeling down on the driveway.

"Are you all right? Have you been drinking?"

"N-nothing but coffee," Raquel stammered. "Three cups." She shook her head wildly. "I . . . I'm sorry. I didn't mean to . . . disturb anything. Can I leave now?"

"Are you sure you're all right?"

"I'm sure," croaked Raquel.

"Then you can leave, miss, but please don't come back here again. Stalking is against the law in Michigan, Miss Estrada. Our stalker laws have teeth in them now, and you can get in serious trouble. If Mr. DiMaio decides to get a court order from a judge, you could seriously end up in jail."

Trembling, Raquel got into her car. To add to her shame and ignominy, the squad car followed her out of the subdivision all the way to her apartment building.

She cried the entire way.

She made it inside her apartment. Again her roommate, Heather, was out. Raquel threw herself on the couch and thought about some horrible stories she'd heard about jail. Women being beaten or raped by other inmates or guards. Especially if you were black or Hispanic, things happened. And she might be feisty but she was less than five feet tall. What if some big guard, 240 pounds or more, came after her?

Raquel stared into the distance, her heartbeat filling her throat so that it felt as if she were being choked. Brett's eyes . . . that coldness she'd seen in them. He *would* carry though with his threats, she realized with a sinking feeling of dread. He was totally fed up with her and saw no other choice.

Hail Mary, full of grace.

Raquel began to repeat the prayer she'd learned at Modesta's knee and said in church thousands of times since she'd been a small girl. She said fifty Hail Marys, then fifty Our Fathers, then repeated the cycle six more times. Finally she added, *Mother Mary, please help me. Please . . . I know I sinned when I had sex with him . . . but . . . I'll make it up to you. Just . . . please . . . give him back to me.*

Karyn was sound asleep, having an ugly dream about Lou Hechter. He was chasing her along the mazelike hallways of Cybelle, brandishing a big baseball bat and screaming at her that she was "luscious enough to fuck." She ran into the vending machine room and tried to close the door behind her but Lou swung at it, smashing holes in the wood.

She began to scream, but because she was asleep the sounds came out as raw, animallike chokes.

"I'm going to fuck you blind," Lou yelled. "I'm going to fuck the top of your head off and come into your brain."

The shrilling sound penetrated her dream, jolting her awake. Karyn sat bolt upright, her heart slamming.

The phone.

An emergency? Her parents? Or maybe Mack, finally locating her and calling to make trouble? Fear filled Karyn as she fumbled for the portable phone, hoping its ring would not wake Amber, who was asleep in the next room.

She nearly knocked it off her nightstand trying to pick it up. "H-lo?"

"Karyn! Oh, God! I nearly got arrested!"

"Who is this?" asked Karyn thickly, not recognizing the agitated voice.

"It's me—Raquel!"

"Raquel?"

"I don't know what to do," the other woman said, beginning to cry. "Brett . . . he called the police . . . they thought I might have a weapon . . . they followed me in the police car . . ."

"Raquel?" Karyn was beginning to wake up a little. "Slow down, you're talking way too fast."

"I have to talk to someone or I'm going to go crazy!"

"Are you all right?"

"He called the police on me."

"Who did?"

"My honey. Brett. Why? Why would he do that? Oh, Karyn, I know I've been, well, following him around some, and he didn't like it, but it was only so we could talk."

"You followed him tonight?"

"Yeah, a little. I drove over to his house. He wasn't there, he didn't get home until real late, so I parked down the street. He wouldn't let me in. He wouldn't even open the door."

"Oh, Raquel." Karyn sighed, feeling a pang of deep sympathy for her friend. Raquel was acting toward Brett much as Mack had done toward her. She'd wanted to talk to her about this before, but Raquel had built a wall that didn't allow anyone to climb it.

Fighting off groggy sleep, she listened as Raquel told her the details of the evening and what the police officer had said about jail and stalking.

"I . . . I didn't stalk him! I'm not that way, Karyn," pleaded Raquel desperately.

"But you followed him a lot, right?"

"Yeah, but I—"

"And you left a ton of messages on his phone at work and his answering machine at home. I'm talking a couple dozen messages a day sometimes. Plus you've called all his friends, haven't you? And now they won't talk to you, either; they hang up on you, too."

Silence from the other end. Finally, Raquel said in a small voice, "How do you know all that?"

"That's what Mack did to me when we were breaking up," Karyn explained. "He really believed that if we could just talk, everything would somehow be all right again. Only it doesn't always work that way, Raquel. Sometimes talking isn't any good. Sometimes it's just over."

"It's not over," insisted Karyn's coworker.

"But it is, Raquel. It's over when one person doesn't want to talk to the other one. That makes it over, don't you see?"

"It's *not over*."

Whoa, Karyn thought. Raquel was a lot worse off than she'd suspected.

"Didn't you say that Brett called the police?"

"Well, yes, but—"

"Raquel, he doesn't want it to go on any longer. He doesn't know what to do anymore. Trust me, I've been there," said Karyn gently. "It's horrible when you loved someone and now they won't leave you alone. It's a nightmare. And you want to put that on Brett; you want to punish him because he loved you once?"

"Punish him?" cried Raquel in a choked voice. "I'm not punishing him."

"Yes, you are. This has nothing to do with love when you follow him around like that. It has to do with your controlling him, your trying to feel power over him."

Raquel began sobbing again. "Karyn . . . what shall I do?"

Karyn caught her breath. "You can't become a stalker, Raquel. If Brett ever files charges . . . jail would be a horrible experience."

"I don't want to go to jail," her friend whispered.

"I don't want you to, either. Oh, Raquel. You have an obsession. It's just like alcoholism; that's what the psychiatrist said about Mack. An addiction. But you can be helped. It doesn't have to be this way."

"I just want him." Raquel wept. "I love him. There was this guy at the health club . . . he came on to me. But it wasn't the same; I couldn't call him for a date. I'm stuck on Brett, Karyn. Can't you understand? It's like he's the only man. No other man matters. If I don't have him, what will I do?"

Karyn breathed deeply. She had her own problems and was trying to find solutions. But she knew she had to be strong for Raquel. Raquel's family was no help. They tried to push her into marriage, and look where that kind of pressure had gotten her.

"Raquel, I'll help you through this. I promise. We're friends, aren't we? I won't let you go to jail."

They talked for a few minutes longer.

"It's really late," Karyn finally said, looking at the display on her clock radio. "Look. You'd better get some sleep. And call in sick tomorrow, why don't you? You need to be away from the office for a day or two, away from Brett."

"Okay."

"See if you can get through one day without calling him."

"I will." Raquel sounded totally wiped out.

"I'll call my Aunt Connie, get the name of a therapist you can start seeing. The company's Blue Cross will cover half the cost, so it shouldn't be that expensive."

Raquel managed a choked laugh. "Nobody in my family ever saw a therapist before. They all think you're crazy if you have to get help for something in the head."

"They don't have to know you're going. Raquel, I'll call tomorrow with the name. Promise me you'll call right away and make an appointment. Your life will get better," Karyn assured her friend. "Listen to me. It will get better."

After they'd hung up, Karyn lay awake in bed, too much adrenaline revving through her to allow her to fall back asleep again.

Raquel did not show up for work the next day, and Karyn arrived tired and red-eyed, in no mood to have a ton of work piled on her. Cilla was still out of town. Fortunately, Lou had meetings most of the morning and would be out of harm's way.

She decided to make her call to Aunt Connie first thing, before her aunt's employment office became too busy.

"A therapist?" said Connie. "For you? Is everything all right, Karyn?"

Karyn hesitated. She was going to have to tell Connie about Lou, but she could not do it here at work; her alcove, positioned in the hallway, didn't allow for many private phone conversations.

"A friend needs a recommendation," she told her aunt. "Truly, it's a friend, not me."

"Is your friend female?"

"Yes. It's a . . . relationship problem," said Karyn, not wanting to betray Raquel's secrets.

"Well, I do happen to know several very good people.

There's an excellent psychologist in Birmingham. I have several friends who've gone to her, and they rave about her—and I see her myself."

Karyn took down the name and number, thanked her aunt, and then waited several hours, until she felt sure Raquel would be up, before phoning her friend with the information.

"I'll call her right now," said Raquel, yawning and seeming subdued.

"Good. She's supposed to be wonderful."

"Karyn . . ." Raquel's voice was hoarse. "Do you think if I call Brett one time—"

"No," said Karyn firmly, lowering her voice so no one passing by would hear. "You can't, Raquel. Don't you see? If you do, you'll be a stalker. Another guy will come along, ten times better than Brett. I promise."

"I don't want another guy."

"You will, when the time comes."

Karyn began obsessing nervously about the upcoming meeting with Malia Roberts. She wondered if she had done the right thing in making the appointment with the attorney. But the first meeting was free, she reminded herself. She wouldn't allow herself to be pushed into anything she didn't want to do.

She didn't tell anyone what she had done. She felt partially ashamed that she should be reduced to this, that she couldn't have handled the work situation on her own. Besides—she didn't want people talking. This was still a very private decision.

Karyn often ate lunch in the cafeteria with Roger, but he was on a buying trip in New York, so on Wednesday she ate with six or seven other women from the department.

As usual it was talk about clothes, men, work, and company gossip.

"Guess what," said Annie Fiaccci. "I've heard this from

two people. Cilla's dating Shane Gancer, in Legal. He's only *twenty-six*."

Raquel had whispered something about this, too. "More power to her," said Karyn, feeling that she should stick up for her boss.

"Cilla's fifty, you know. *I'd* never have a guy that much younger than me," declared Annie. "Hey, what if he wants children? What are you supposed to say? Sorry, guy, I can't do it because I'm having hot flashes?"

All the women laughed, but Karyn felt uncomfortable doing so.

"I've heard of women over fifty having babies, but some of them have to take all these hormone pills and they have to use someone else's egg," said Jenny, a graphic artist. "I know a girl who sold her eggs to infertile women. She got three thousand dollars. And remember those models selling their eggs on the Internet?" Everyone giggled.

Annie went back to the original topic. "And, hey, there's other rumors about our Cilla, like the fact that she sometimes goes out with Lou Hechter."

"Lou?" Stunned, Karyn stared at the fashion designer. "You can't mean that."

"Well, no one's been able to prove it, but every once in a while they're both gone from the office at exactly the same time, and neither of them have meetings scheduled . . . if you catch my drift."

An affair? Karyn found herself wondering.

Or was it something else? She couldn't help remembering that afternoon when Cilla had left work in one outfit and returned later that day wearing a totally different blouse and skirt that didn't even go with her jacket. Cilla had seemed upset that day. And there were other days when Cilla seemed not herself, Karyn now recalled.

The psychologist's office was decorated like a charming sitting room, with a rose-colored carpet, hand-embroidered cushions on the couch, and a fantastically comfortable La-Z-Boy chair, which Raquel was sitting in now.

Sharon Stein was a small-boned woman of about forty-eight, with blond hair styled attractively short, and a cast on her right leg. A pair of crutches rested beside her elegant rolltop desk.

"I fell off my bike several weeks ago and broke my ankle." Sharon's smile was warm. "Trust me, it's tough getting around on these awful crutches even with padding on the arms. I should have gone to the gym and worked out for about six months before I decided to fracture myself."

Raquel felt herself begin to relax a little.

"I broke my leg when I was ten," she confided. "I fell off the monkey bars. I hated the crutches, too. I used to cry when my ma said I had to use them."

"Well, then, I guess we have something in common." Sharon's eyes twinkled. "Now, you told me a few things over the phone, and I want to know more, but first I need to get some basic information about you, Raquel. Just for my records."

Raquel was relieved that she just had to answer questions about her childhood; her mother; her four sisters; the different jobs she'd held; what sort of job she held at Cybelle. This wasn't so hard.

"Nobody in my family's ever done this," she told Sharon, twisting the engagement ring on her finger. "I mean . . . you know."

"You mean, you're the first one to ever see a therapist?"

"Yeah. They'd think I was crazy."

Sharon smiled, reassuring Raquel that thousands of people got help with short-term problems in their lives. "Trust me, none of these people are 'crazy,' or even close to it. They're just trying to live happier lives."

"That's me." Raquel stared down at her hands. As she moved her left hand, the engagement ring glinted, catching the lamplight.

"A very pretty ring," commented Sharon.

"Yes."

"Would you like to tell me why you're here?"

"I guess I'm here because I'm ... my fiancé ... I've been, like, following him around a lot. I tried to stop but I can't. He called the p-police ..."

She poured it all out, mopping tears with a tissue from a box the therapist handed her.

"I'm not like that. Not really. I'm a nice person." Raquel wept. "It's just ... I love him so much. It hurts me all the time, here in my stomach. I keep feeling if we could just talk ... but he doesn't want to talk. To him I'm like a ... a ..."

She broke down again, ashamed, and yet relieved to get it off her chest to someone who was listening, and nodding her head sympathetically, and not casting blame.

At length, Sharon Stein said, "Well, Raquel, you've definitely been going through some stress. What is it you'd like to accomplish in therapy? What would you like to see happen?"

Raquel held up her hand with the ring on it. "I just want—" She stopped. "I don't know. I just want not to hurt."

"Look, our fifty minutes are up, but I want you to try something this coming week. Are you willing?"

"Yes. Please. I'll do anything."

"See if you can go until next week without calling Brett or driving past his house or approaching him at the office. If you do get any of these urges, instead of acting on them, I want you to get a piece of paper and write down all your feelings about it—what you were doing when you got the urge, why you feel you have to talk to him, what you hope to accomplish, what you think will really happen if you do call."

"I ... I can try that."

"Wonderful. Can you come in at this same time next week?"

They made arrangements for her next appointment, and Sharon showed Raquel a second door in her office she could leave from. Gratefully, Raquel slipped out of the office and into the hallway of the building, hurrying out to her car.

Darkness had fallen, and the air was moist and chilly, yellow circles glowing around the parking lot floodlights. Raquel pushed the automatic door locks, enclosing herself safely in the car, but she didn't start the engine yet.

Instead, she stared at the mist, thinking that she'd like to call Brett right now . . . this very minute. She wanted to do it more than anything else on the whole earth.

But she'd made a promise.

There was a Dunkin' Donuts shop across the L-shaped shopping mall, with a phone outside it. Raquel riveted her eyes on that phone. Brett might be home right now . . . at least his answering tape would be running.

With a sharp intake of breath, Raquel grabbed for her shoulder bag and began digging around in its voluminous side pocket. She found an old grocery list and a ballpoint pen.

Turning the list over, she began to write.

I want to call him so bad. It's all I can think about. It will feel so good just to know he might hear me, that I will have his attention even for a few minutes. . . . But I can't do it. He is like an alcoholic drink to me. He makes me drunk with things I can't have, and dreams that will never happen. . . .

The law firm where Malia Roberts worked was located in a high-rise office complex in Rochester Hills near I-75. The firm had the entire fifth floor of the building.

Karyn found a place to park, gathered up her purse and adjusted her lightweight jacket, feeling like a sneak as she walked into the building. If Lou Hechter knew she was here

. . . if he even suspected . . . he would be livid with anger.

The elevator opened right into the main lobby of the law firm, where a well-dressed receptionist sat at a desk working a busy, multiple-line phone. The furnishings were sleek and modern, an enormous soft sculpture dominating one wall. The floor was polished oak.

Karyn introduced herself, and in a few minutes a secretary appeared, escorting Karyn down several corridors lined with offices and conference rooms. The center of the building held the usual array of cubicles occupied by—Karyn supposed—secretaries and paralegals. Phones rang, people hurried back and forth, some people inside an office were arguing.

Malia Roberts's office had her name on the door in polished brass.

"Hello, Karyn. I'm Malia Roberts. I hope you didn't have any trouble finding us. They've had some nasty construction out on Crooks Road. This whole area is getting way too built up."

An African American woman with short, straight hair rose to greet Karyn, extending a hand to shake Karyn's. Malia wore a silk suit in a deep rust shade that complemented her crème de cacao skin. Her brown eyes gleamed with energy and intelligence.

"No, I managed to get around it just fine."

"Sit down, won't you? Would you like coffee?"

"No, thank you."

Karyn glanced around the office, noticing the diplomas from the University of Michigan and photos of a slim, laughing, teenage girl, some of her alone, others taken with Malia, their arms around each other. Was the girl Malia's daughter, or a niece? Malia looked too young to have a child that old.

"My daughter, Kira," explained Malia. "She's going to Penn State, studying engineering, can you believe it?"

Karyn smiled, beginning to feel more at ease.

"Let me tell you a little bit about myself before you get started on telling me *your* story," the female lawyer began. "Just so you'll know me and where I'm coming from." She gestured toward the busy corridor outside the room. "This office is very profitable, but I'm not your typical law firm lawyer.

"I started out as a fourteen-year-old unwed mother on welfare . . . but I worked my butt off and won a scholarship to the University of Michigan, then two more scholarships to law school in Ann Arbor. They only had three or four other black women students there at the time—they have about forty-five percent women now, but back then it was twenty times tougher for me than the men." Her laugh was rich, chuckling and slightly bitter. "They didn't want me there—those arrogant white guys. But I stayed, and I participated in Moot Court, and I made Law Review. I graduated J. D., that's Juris Doctor, when some of the guys who gave me a hard time barely graduated L. L. D. A lot of them flunked their bar exams two, three times. I passed mine first time out of the gate."

Karyn listened eagerly, beginning to feel as if maybe this intense, dark-skinned woman might actually be able to help her.

"So that's my story, Karyn. I'm a fighter. Around here they call me Malia the pit bull." Malia laughed again. "But I win cases for my clients. I just won one; it was a real doozey. The client was a salesperson, and every week there were sales meetings the workers referred to as 'Pie Night.' Can you guess why?"

Karyn shook her head.

"Well, they had a charming little ceremony. And the ceremony was that the winning salesman got to throw a pie at the salesperson with the lowest sales record for the week. And they took it seriously, yes, they did." Another rich chuckle. "The winner could tell the loser to 'expose his chest or behind for pie throwing.' So this one Wednesday night, my client was the loser. Her boss told her to take off her blouse and bra, and she was surrounded by several yelling, laughing, swearing, intoxicated male salesmen who rubbed a pie over her exposed breasts."

Karyn gasped in horror. "Really? That's—that's awful."

"Yes, we thought it was, too, and so did the court. Especially when the regional manager of the company's explanation was, 'That's what we do.' We sued the asses off them, Karyn. We sued them until they screamed. We sued them for nine million—and won."

Karyn sank back in her chair, her mouth falling open.

Malia's smile was wide, warm and slightly predatory. "Now, I can't promise you I can do that for you, Karyn. Only a small percentage of sexual harassment cases ever go to trial. And you have to have a very, very strong case to reap those kinds of awards. Most cases of sexual harassment are never reported, because the women are too scared, or unaware of their rights, or too fearful of retaliation to dare to file. Which brings us back to you, Karyn. What brings you to my office today? Tell me what's been going on."

Karyn told Malia about Lou, trying to summarize rather than go into a lot of details because she knew she only got one free half hour. Malia nodded and made encouraging comments, her dark eyes glistening with sharp interest. She took detailed notes as Karyn spoke.

"So let me get this straight. He gave you a full-body touch. He showed you sexy pictures of prostitutes. He put a nasty message on your computer screen—which, by the way, might not hold up in court. Not unless you've actually got a witness who saw him type the stuff in; anyone might have done it. *But,* he did tell you to dress in a sexy manner, and he asked sexually oriented personal questions. He urinated in your presence and zipped his pants, fondling himself. He got you in a corner in the vending room and touched your breasts. He unreasonably fired another woman, possibly to scare you into meeting his demands. And he implied that your job depended on his approval."

"Well, yes. He doesn't have to imply it. It does depend on him—he's a vice president. And there might be more. I've been getting really awful obscene phone calls that could be from him."

"Who have you told about this, Karyn?" Malia asked when Karyn had finished telling about the calls.

"Well . . . I told some of it to another secretary at work, Raquel. But I didn't tell her everything. I was too ashamed," Karyn admitted. "The time he touched my breasts . . . I didn't say anything about that."

"Well, you should," said Malia. "Has he harassed any other women that you know about?"

"I think so. I . . . I'm not one hundred percent sure, though. He's fired a lot of secretaries or had them quit. And I was warned not to dress sexy around him."

Malia nodded as if this didn't surprise her.

"Karyn, I'm going to be blunt with you. We may have a lawsuit . . . I say *may* . . . but only if you assist in every way possible to build your own case. If you file just as it stands now, it'll be your word against his, a big important executive at your company. Poof. He can say you were disgruntled because you got a bad work assignment or got reprimanded, something like that. He can say you're lying. The company wants to believe *him* because he's the big cheese, not you."

"I know," Karyn said, clenching her hands together in her lap. "That's the problem—"

"We'll go more into this later, but there are several legal principles involved in sexual harassment cases. One of them we can use is called 'contaminated workplace.' It means that the whole workplace has been contaminated by sexual harassment, that it hasn't been directed just at you alone but at other women, too, and maybe even men. *And* the company knew about it and tolerated it. Do you understand where I'm leading with this, Karyn?"

Karyn twisted her fingers together. "Yes . . . it means I've got to report Lou."

"Absolutely. Start with your immediate supervisor. Is it Cilla?"

"Yes." Karyn shivered. "That's such a big step. I really love my job, Malia."

"I know, but is your job worth the sleepless nights, the sick stomach, the headaches, the strain, the stress, the doctor visits? The fear? Many women who are sexually harassed, Karyn, are fearful that the harassment might progress as far as rape. Is that a concern with you?"

"I . . . yes," whispered Karyn, recalling the way Lou had trapped her in the vending room.

"Then all right. And now we have to talk money, Karyn."

"I make about twenty-six thousand dollars a year right now," Karyn said. "I might be able to pay something every month—"

"I appreciate that you're a secretary and don't have deep pockets, so I'm going to put you in touch with a couple of feminist groups I know—if we get lucky, they'll help you with the legal fees until we know whether or not there's going to be a case. I charge one hundred and fifty dollars an hour, and that includes phone calls, writing letters—anything I do for you. Everything is billed in ten-minute increments. However, if someone else in the firm does something for you—for instance, an associate or a paralegal or secretary— his or her time will be billed at a lower rate."

Karyn swallowed, shocked at the high fees in spite of her knowledge, going in, that it would be costly. "I'm not sure I can—"

"I'm charging you what's called a split fee. The one-hundred-fifty-dollar rate will be only until we decide if we have a case. Once we actually file suit, I'll take the case on a contingency fee. That means I get one-third of anything you win. And if we settle out of court, it'll be the same thing. You get two-thirds; I get one-third. Can you handle that?"

"Yes. Do you want any payment today?"

Malia smiled. "Nothing today. I'll talk to my friend in the feminist group. She just might be willing to cover you until we go to trial. You can pay her back if you win, all right?"

Karyn nodded.

Now Malia began instructing Karyn on what she had to do.

"You have to be my main assistant, Karyn, because that will save you a lot of money. First, get Caller ID so we'll know if those obscene calls belong to Lou Hechter or some other conehead."

"I've already gotten it."

"Good. Also, we're going to need the names of other women this man has harassed—and get them to give a deposition. Ask around. Their names will turn up, believe me. Talk to them and see if you can get them on your side."

"All right."

"You'll need to keep a journal. Make daily entries. Write down the date, what happened, where it happened, exactly what this man did and said, what you did and said, and whether there were any witnesses, and if so, who those witnesses were."

"I can do that," said Karyn.

"If he sends you any nasty E-mail messages, print them out and save copies—keep them at home where they can't be confiscated. Any dirty notes, or dirty pictures, write the date on them and take them home to use as evidence later. Anything salacious that is posted on a wall or in your cubicle is public property, and you have a perfect right to take it down.

"Get copies of your employee records if you can. Also, every time something happens, I want you to tell someone about it—so later we can document that this did happen and it did bother you. Tell people in the workplace, but also tell someone outside of work, just in case the company gets to those witnesses at work and makes them afraid of losing *their* jobs if they help you."

Karyn's eyes widened as Malia said this. The seriousness of what she was undertaking was beginning to hit home.

She hesitated only a minute before saying, "All right. If the feminist groups will help with the fees, I'll collect all the evidence you need, Malia. I can do it."

Malia jumped up and leaned over the desk, high-fiving Karyn with her palm. "Way to go, woman! We're gonna be a team. We're going to fix that man's sorry ass, Karyn. We're going to make him whine and squeal for mercy. And the same with the company that allows him to get away with this. At his age, I bet he's been doing it for *years* and never got caught until now."

Karyn was late arriving home, and stopped at the drive-up window of Wendy's to pick up chicken sandwiches and fries for dinner.

She felt so nervous.

She and Malia hadn't actually discussed the amount of the lawsuit yet, but Karyn remembered that the other woman had won $9 million, which seemed like a huge sum to her, even split down to two-thirds of the original amount.

Should she call her parents and tell them what she'd done? But she decided not to, at least not right away. Her father, semiretired because of back problems from his job as a finish carpenter, would only worry, and her mother would be upset. And if they heard the things that Lou had done, her parents would urge her to quit the job and move to Norwalk.

She'd promised Amber they'd stay here. . . .

Roger Canton dropped by her apartment while Karyn was helping Amber with her homework.

"I'm writing a story about Missy and a bunch of other cats," announced Amber proudly. "They all go to a magic land looking for gold."

"Sound like very enterprising cats to me."

"Yeah . . . they bring back gold necklaces and crowns 'n' stuff. And they all get famous like on TV and they go on *Oprah*."

"Mmm," said Roger, amused.

"Time for bed, cupcake," said Karyn.

"I want to stay up longer!"

"You have another day to finish the story, and it's already eight-thirty, Amber. Maybe you can write a little more after breakfast if you get up early enough."

"Okaaaay," Amber grumped.

Karyn put her daughter to bed, returning to the living room to brew a cup of coffee for Roger. He said he could only stay a few minutes because he had brought some work home on his laptop and needed to get back to it.

Karyn told him about her visit to the lawyer, enthusing about Malia. "She just seems so fierce. I know she'll fight for me. But I have to gather the evidence."

"But will you be filing a lawsuit?" asked Roger, troubled. "Karyn, I'm afraid you're going to get in way over your head on this. She said you had to notify the company about the harassment—that means telling on Lou. Right there you're asking for major trouble. Lou Hechter isn't going to take this lying down, and he has a lot of friends at Cybelle, cronies who would stand up for him. Vic Rondelli is one of his buddies, and there's Chuck Krantz, he's one of the old guard, too. It could get ugly, Karyn."

"I know that. But I have to notify the company in order to have a lawsuit at all."

"They'd call you a liar, Karyn. Word would spread all over the company, and you'd get treated like Anita Hill, or even worse, all those women who tried to challenge President Clinton. Monica Lewinski is going to carry a certain

label around with her for the rest of her life. I just don't
want to see you hurt," he finished emotionally.

"I just can't live my life being afraid that I'm going to
be felt up or harassed or assaulted at work." Karyn swallowed over a dry knot in her throat. "I love this job but . . .
I can't put myself through torture every day. A workplace
is supposed to be safe!"

"Oh, honey." Roger pulled her to him. "I wish I could go
through this with you. I've seen some bad stuff go on
around Cybelle," he admitted. "Not just women, either."

"Oh? What kind of stuff?"

"Well, a gay buyer. They put obscene messages on his
screen saver, they dumped used condoms on his desk, they
overturned his desk chair and taped his cubicle with so much
duct tape that he couldn't get in it. They put porno pictures
in his cube . . . a two-headed dildo . . . It was not a good
scene, Karyn. Lou knew about this and didn't stop it, either.
Even when the guy complained, Lou did nothing."

"When did this happen?" Karyn asked. *Contaminated
workplace,* Malia had said.

"A few years back. The man quit, said he couldn't take
it anymore. I helped him get a job in New York and he's
doing very, very well, I hear. Making more money than he
did at Cybelle and being treated well."

"Can you put me in touch with him?"

Roger nodded. "I don't have his home phone, but as far
as I know he's still working at Jeri Jeri; they're in the Manhattan white pages." He gave her the man's name. "Karyn,
just be careful, is all I ask."

"I will."

"You know you'll never have to worry financially,"
Roger went on. "Not as long as I'm in the picture."

She stared at him, seeing the seriousness on his face.

"I've been trying to take it slow, not to push you too
much—I was afraid I'd scare you off. But I care about you,

Karyn. More than just care. I'm in love with you, and I'd like us to follow that as far as we can."

Was he talking marriage? He was. There was no doubt in her mind whatsoever. Karyn's mouth came open, and hot blood rushed to her cheeks.

"Roger, I . . . I want to be with you. I . . ." She couldn't say the word *love* yet. "I'll follow as far as I can."

"I hope that's pretty far."

She gave him something that approximated a nod.

They looked at each other, then Roger pulled her to him for a long, breathless kiss. Karyn's breathing grew way out of control as she realized she had just changed the whole course of her own life and Amber's . . . or had she already done that this afternoon by talking to Malia Roberts?

"I love you, I love you," Roger murmured into her neck.

"Me, too," she whispered.

The day after Cilla returned from L.A., she arrived at work at eight forty-five as usual, feeling hyped up, eager to get to her office and start work on the report for Dom Carrara. She whizzed into the cafeteria, bought herself a double coffee and carried it into her office, where she booted up her computer, going immediately into Microsoft Word.

She felt . . . exhilarated. The investigation of Girlrags had been fun and challenging, and she wanted to fill her report with plenty of good merchandising ideas that would spur Dom to want to purchase the chain.

She began typing an executive summary, each point only a sentence long, that would summarize the rest of the report, to aid Dom in completing it quickly.

1. *Girlrags, with its funky displays and salesclerks dressed in leather, its "techno music," does attract a lot of customers in the targeted age range who venture into the stores to browse.*

2. *However, not many of the customers actually make*

> purchases, and those that do purchase usually buy
> small items under $15, such as a sale-priced tank
> top or funky socks.
> 3. Interviews with managers, employees, and custom-
> ers reveal the following points:

She paused to think and collect her thoughts, and then began furiously typing again. Actually she was having fun, Cilla realized after a while. Maybe the most fun she'd had in several years. This chain did have appeal . . . but that appeal needed to be widened to bring in the much-larger customer base it needed. Cilla believed she could do that. In fact, she knew she could. It was just a matter of proving it to Dom.

The next morning was rushed and hectic. Amber had overslept and was crabby, and Karyn didn't feel very cheerful, either. She knew she had to talk to Cilla today about Lou and she was dreading it.

"Come on, honeybear, eat some of those good raisins I put in your cereal dish."

"I don't like raisins. They have *stems*," Amber whined.

"What stems?" Karyn asked.

"I just found one." Amber held up her spoon. "Stems are made out of wood. I don't like to eat wood. I hate eating wood."

"Well, at least eat the wheat squares then. And hurry, Amber . . . you have to be at school in less than ten minutes. Jinny's driving you today."

Amber stared into the soggy pool of cereal. "Could I have pizza for breakfast tomorrow instead of cereal?"

"Pizza?"

"Caitlin eats cold pizza in the morning lots of times, and so does Megan, and so does Jasmine, *allllll* the time."

"Maybe once in a while," Karyn finally agreed, thinking that she could hardly protest pizza when she'd allowed the child to eat Wendy's only the previous night.

As soon as Caitlin knocked on their door, Amber rushed out, and Karyn drove to work, arriving in time to get her usual parking space.

When she reached the department, everything seemed sane and calm. The usual elevator music was playing on the PA system. A group of designers was gathered in one of the art rooms, gossiping over coffee and a bag of bagels some-one had brought in. Raquel was in the fax room, and through the half-opened door Karyn could see Cilla hunched in front of her computer, absorbed in her work.

To Karyn's vast relief, Lou's office was dark.

Karyn had another cup of coffee to give herself courage. Finally she knocked on her supervisor's door. "Cilla? Can I have about five minutes with you?"

"Sure, Karyn." Cilla stopped typing and smiled at her assistant. A mug of coffee sat beside her, barely touched. "I'm working on this report about Girlrags for Dom Carrara. Later in the day I'll have corrections for you to do. Just a few tweaks, I hope. I want him to have it on his desk by close of business."

"Great." Karyn entered the office, closing the door behind her, a signal to everyone that there was a private conference going on.

"What's up, Karyn?"

Karyn sank into a chair, folding her hands nervously in her lap. "It's . . . I'm having a problem . . ."

"Oh?"

"It's about Lou," Karyn admitted with difficulty.

"What sort of a problem?" Cilla touched her coffee mug, but her hand must have jerked a little, because a few drop-lets of coffee spattered onto her desk pad.

"It's . . . he's . . . said some off-color things to me, some things that were on the offensive side. And he's done some other things."

"Has he? What kind of things?"

Karyn described some of the things that had happened to her since she arrived at Cybelle. But finally her voice trailed off. Maybe it was the set expression on Cilla's face, but she began to feel more and more uncomfortable.

"You know Lou is a very outspoken person," Cilla began after Karyn had wound down and was nervously rubbing her sweaty fingers together. "A difficult person. Sometimes he goes a little too far—well, you certainly know that by now, you've worked here long enough."

"Yes." Karyn wet her lips. "It's very upsetting."

She sat there waiting for Cilla to respond with sympathy, indignation . . . something. But the seconds ticked on, and with a little twist in the center of her stomach, Karyn realized it wasn't going to turn out that way.

Cilla sighed. Her face looked strained. "Oh, Karyn. I wish I could tell you there is an easy solution to this, but there isn't. Lou has been at Cybelle a very long time. He's a vice president here and has brought millions of dollars' worth of business to the company. Do you want to go down to Human Resources and fill out an incident report? They'll probably launch some kind of a sexual harassment investigation, but I warn you, it probably won't come to anything unless you have some witnesses to what happened. Do you, Karyn? Do you have witnesses?"

"No. I don't." Karyn rose to her feet. "Everything happened when no one else was around. I'm sorry; I shouldn't have bothered you with this. I know how busy you are."

"Karyn, I sympathize with you, I really do. These men in the workplace can be a pain sometimes. But Lou is one of the most important men at Cybelle, and, well, it wouldn't be easy at all going up against him. You'd probably only be hurt. I don't want to see that happen. My advice is to stay out of Lou's way as much as possible. If you do that, he'll probably get the hint and leave you alone."

"I'll do that," said Karyn politely.

She left her supervisor's office, her throat tightening with disappointment. Cilla hadn't been supportive at all, not in any meaningful way.

But what had Karyn really expected her to do? Talk to Lou? He was *her* boss, too. What a mess all of this was.

As soon as Karyn got to her desk, she took out a steno pad and began jotting down as much of the conversation with Cilla as she could remember, documenting exactly what both of them had said.

At least she'd told someone at Cybelle. She'd done that much.

She had begun her fight.

Cilla closed her office door when Karyn left, and put her phone on "do not disturb." The Girlrags report, still sitting on her monitor screen, faded from her view as she sank into her swivel chair, feeling as if all the energy in her body had just seeped out through her pores.

Dammit! So Karyn was getting the harassment from Lou, too. Just like Cilla herself, and all those other secretaries in the past. What a nightmare. She'd been so afraid of this. How long would it be before Lou had Karyn in bed, threatening to take away her job if she didn't comply with his sexual demands?

Cilla felt a wave of deep shame that she hadn't been more supportive of her secretary. She should have said more, done more. But she herself had learned the reality the hard way. So she'd told Karyn the unvarnished truth—little would be done, if anything; and without witnesses, Lou held the winning hand.

Sighing again, Cilla turned toward her computer. But the report she'd been so excited about now seemed just another screenful of words. Damn him! He contaminated everything around here.

She could see where the road was leading with Karyn, and it filled her with despair. She didn't think Karyn was going to persevere against Lou. Karyn was too young, too sweet, and a bit naive, not strong enough to fight a tough old reprobate like Lou. The minute she voiced a formal complaint, he'd retaliate. And his retaliation would be hardball all the way. Cilla knew. She'd seen it happen before. The other women had quit, unable to take the pressure.

Why? Why? Why was the man such an asshole? What made him so sick? What made him think he could do this to woman after woman, year after year?

Cilla picked up a 1½-inch ring binder and threw it against the wall, venting her frustration. Right now she didn't like herself at all.

By 4:30 P.M. Cilla had finished the report for Dom, and with Karyn's help had "tweaked" it. She reread it one final time, decided that it was brilliant and had hit on all the store's basic problems, with solutions that could turn them around. Fortunately, Lou was in a meeting. She sent Karyn upstairs to hand-deliver it.

At 5:45, she was surprised to receive a phone call from Dom.

"I read it right away, Cilla. Beautiful report, very complete and well done, and enough creative ideas to spark a real changeover, too, I might add. I'm very, very pleased with this, Cilla. It's going to be very good ammunition for me when I go to the executive committee with this."

Cilla flushed a happy red. "I'm so pleased you like it."

"I like talent, Cilla. I like that a whole bunch, and I believe you have it."

"Why . . . thank you," she said, thrilled and surprised.

"I'll keep in close touch with you on this," the CEO said, ending the conversation. Cilla hung up, bemused, adrenaline again racing through her, along with a wild hope that the report might actually lead to something. To have Dom Carrara on her side . . . taking her along with him . . . helping to pull her through the glass ceiling . . . Oh, if it would only happen.

She was gathering up her purse and laptop, preparing to leave for home, when Lou popped his head around her door. He was in a truculent mood. "What about this Girlrags report?" he demanded. "Have you got it for me to read? I want to go over it before you send it up to Dom in case I have any changes I want to make."

Cilla smiled pleasantly. "Dom wanted it by close of business and you were in a meeting, so I had Karyn hand-deliver it to him. I didn't think you'd have any objection."

Lou scowled. "Well, I do. You're working as my manager, and everything that goes out of this department goes out under my name basically."

"You're welcome to view a copy if that's what you wish, and you can E-mail Dom with any of your further comments," she told him, struggling to remain gracious. "I'm sure Dom would be glad of any additional input."

"And I'm sure you sent that report up there *knowing* I was in a meeting and wouldn't get to see it, isn't that right, Cilla baby? Taking matters into your own hands, that's the way you like to work around here, right? Going behind your boss . . . it suits you, eh?"

"Lou—it isn't like that—"

He approached her desk, standing within a few confrontational inches of her, close enough so that she could smell his deodorant and the aftershave lotion he'd used, now mixed with a faint tinge of stress sweat.

"Look here, madam," he snapped. "We have a procedure in this department and we will follow that procedure at all times, even when it comes to special projects that come down from on high. You'll keep me in the loop on everything you do, is that clear, Cilla? No more just forging ahead on your own. *I'm* the department head."

She nodded. God, she hated him. He would get his hands all over her report and muddy it up and claim her ideas as his.

"Well, don't expect any more time this week to help out

our savior, Dom Carrara, because I'm going to keep you too busy to think," was Lou's parting shot.

Cillia pushed the speed limit driving home to her condo, getting honked at by some man in a van when she nearly ran a red light. Cilla banged her horn back, taking out her anger on him. Great. She was exhibiting signs of road rage. Lou made her crazy sometimes. Now he was exhibiting signs of jealousy about Girlrags. She should have expected this. She wished he'd be forced to go in for a quadruple bypass and then retire to a condo in Myrtle Beach and she'd never have to look at him again.

A long hot shower improved her mood only slightly. She blow-dried her hair, put on makeup, and dressed in a pair of slim navy pants and a light aqua buttonless cardigan worn over a matching sweater tank. With this she slipped on a pair of glacée macramé slides with three-inch, stacked heels—another little self-indulgence that had nudged up her credit card balance just a tad closer to bankruptcy.

"Hey, lovely lady," said Shane, arriving to take Cilla out for dinner. "Don't you look awesome." He carried a large foil-wrapped box and a bouquet of roses. He thrust both into her arms, looking pleased with himself.

"My goodness," was all Cilla could say. The bouquet was huge, and so was the box.

"Well, aren't you going to open the box? I have to confess, I spent a very happy hour and a half picking everything out."

"What's the occasion?" she dared to say.

"Our four-month anniversary."

"What?" For some reason Cilla felt rattled. Had it really been that long? She'd just let the time slide by, both thrilled and fearful about this new relationship, hardly daring to think where it could possibly go.

"You mean you don't celebrate anniversaries, Cilla?" His blue eyes teased her.

UNDER PRESSURE   255

"Yes, but . . ." She felt a flush travel across her face. "Which shall I do first, arrange the flowers or open the box?"

"Try the box."

Cilla put the roses down and carried the box to the kitchen, where she began the task of removing the thin, gold elastic ribbon and four pieces of tape that held the box shut.

Lifting the lid, Cilla stared inside at a froth of lace in saltwater taffy colors. "My God," she whispered, pulling out a little strapless lace bodysuit with padded push-up underwire cups and a plunge vee-center. "What have you done?"

"I thought they were rather sexy," said Shane, grinning. "I was in Ann Arbor this week. There was this lingerie store downtown, Pepper's, and I couldn't help myself—I had to buy these."

Cilla's mouth fell open as she sorted through the expensive, sexy lingerie. A lavender silk jacquard gown with a stretch lace bodice. An exquisite lace demi-bra with adjustable, scalloped lace straps and a matching bikini panty, both in pale coral. And more.

"Shane . . ." she said helplessly. "My God . . ."

"Do you like them?"

"I love them— but —this is way too expensive—and I'm not sure I—I mean—what if they don't fit?" For some reason, this gift terrified her.

"Of course they'll fit. I took the liberty of looking at your bra size one morning after we'd made love. I hope you don't mind, Cilla."

She folded the beautiful things back into the box, her hands shaking. "My ex-husband bought me lingerie about twice in ten years," she said shakily. "I can't believe you did this, Shane. They're so lovely, but . . ."

Shane looked at her sadly. "I wasn't trying to pressure you. I just wanted you to feel as beautiful as you really are. If you want me to, I'll take all of it back and buy you a flannel nightgown, would that make you feel happier?" His gentle laugh took away the sting.

He moved closer to her and took her gently in his arms. "Do you think you're not sexy enough to wear these things? Well, let me assure you, you are. I guess this gift was just a way for me to tell you that I think you're incredibly desirable—in every possible way."

Cilla buried her face against his shirtfront, drinking in the attractive, clean-skin scent of him. How had she happened upon this kind, sexy, always surprising man? If only she'd met Shane when she was twenty-one instead of fifty. But she had him now, she reminded herself. For this month, this year, anyway, if she was lucky, and beyond that she didn't dare to think.

"Do you want to test out some of these things now, or shall we go out to dinner first?" he whispered.

"Let's test."

"Great. I was hoping you'd say that."

She lit vanilla-scented candles in the bedroom and modeled several of the garments for him, grateful for the dim, flickering light that made her look as sexy as she wanted to be. But then Shane peeled away the straps of the silk Jacquard gown, whispering to her that she was beautiful and he wanted her.

Sighs and cries, whispers and moans. Naked, her head flung back, her hair tousled, she rode astride Shane, rocking her hips back and forth on him, crying out as she came.

And came again. And again.

And finally a fourth time, her body shuddering so deeply that she gritted her teeth and moaned hoarsely. To hell with dinner. She wanted this night never to end.

On the following Monday, Lou Hechter was just finishing a meeting with Chuck Stark about a lawsuit one of their coat suppliers was filing against Cybelle. They'd gone through a lot of papers, and Lou had given his opinion, and now they were wrapping up their meeting. "We'll win it, no sweat," said Chuck. "I'll put Gancer on it to do the grunt work. He's damn sharp. Gonna be nipping after my heels one of these days, I'd say."

Lou nodded, his attention on the next meeting he had to get to.

"So," said Chuck, smiling. "Speaking of Gancer, what do you think of the latest little office romance? Sort of an interesting connection between our two departments, don't you think?"

"Office romance?" Lou was jotting down some notes in his Franklin planner, which he carried everywhere with him.

"Apparently Cilla likes to rob the cradle."

Lou glanced up.

"Gancer. You know—tall, blond. Twenty-six or -seven maybe. Barely shaves. Waistline of about thirty-two inches."

Lou felt a stab of anger. "Hey, Cilla's fifty. This guy is what, just a baby lawyer."

"Baby lawyers get around these days."

Lou stalked down the marble walk to his next meeting, anger pushing through him. Gossip . . . ordinarily Lou hated it, but today he was furious that he had not heard this particular item of hearsay sooner. What the *hell* did Cilla Westheim think she was doing, whoring around with a much younger man while the whole corporation observed her behavior? Was he the jerk who had sent her the flowers that time? The ones she'd tried to hide from Lou?

And was the man better in bed than Lou was?

It was 6:30 P.M., and everyone in the department had left for the day—not that Cilla really noticed. She was hunched in front of her computer, again engrossed in writing a report, this one for Lou, who'd kept her In box stacked with work since she'd returned from L.A., burdening her as if to ensure she'd have no time for any of Dom Carrara's special projects. He was so transparent it made her sick. Well, Lou was going to have to get used to the fact that Dom had noticed her.

Dom had already called her four or five times about the Girlrags project, asking her to cost out some of the ideas she'd presented. Maybe her career at Cybelle was actually taking a new and encouraging turn.

"Cilla," said Lou, suddenly appearing at the door to her office. He walked in without knocking and planted his rear end on the edge of her desk, crushing several file folders.

Cilla jumped, her heart climbing up into her throat. "Lou! You startled me."

"Did I?"

"Please don't sit on those folders. I'm reaching the end of the tunnel on this," added Cilla, recovering herself and starting to tap the keyboard again. "I should have a rough draft for you by tomorrow morning."

"Good. I hope you're reaching the end of the tunnel on a couple of other things, too."

Cilla glanced up. "What do you mean?"

"Really," he sneered. "I mean *really*. Do you have to make yourself a laughingstock?"

Cilla felt the blood drain from her face. "You'd better be a little more specific, Lou."

"Shane Gancer. Aged twenty-six. In Legal. Is that specific enough for you? The grapevine has really been active around here. Everyone's talking about you."

"Lou—"

"Do you suck him off? Is that how you do it with him, is that what he likes? They say the young studs like it all ways, Cilla. Upside, downside and from the rear."

Cilla jumped up from her computer and went to stand by the window, breathing so fast that she felt sick to her stomach. "Lou, I've had some dates with the man, that's all. It's a social relationship, nothing more."

"Well, not in my department it isn't. I want you to stop seeing this guy, Cilla."

"You don't have the right to dictate my social life."

"I do when it concerns the company." Lou got up off the desk and followed her to the window. His fingers dug into Cilla's upper arm. "You little bitch, don't you remember all of the things I've done for you? They were going to get rid of you back in 1992 and I saved you from the ax. I was the one who promoted you to the position you have now, you stupid little cunt. If it wasn't for me you'd still be a merchandiser, sorting color samples and going out shopping two afternoons a week." Lou's voice was a garlicky-smelling hiss. "I saved your sweet white ass. And now you dare to tell me you aren't grateful? That you don't give a fuck for everything I've done for you?"

Cilla looked at the man who controlled her job. His face was a congested shade of red, and spittle sprayed from his mouth as he spoke. She prayed to God that no one from another department, or even a maintenance person, was passing by her office door to hear this.

"Our sexual relationship is over, Lou. I can't go on with it anymore."

Suddenly, Lou was shoving at her, pushing Cilla backward so hard that her hip banged against the corner of her credenza. His wide, spatulate fingers squeezed around her neck, partially cutting off her air. "It's *not* over, Cilla, not until I say it is. I made you. I own you, do you get it? I own you and your stupid-ass job and your stupid-ass condominium and your pitiful, lame bank accounts and your blondy-ass daughter . . . they're all mine, do you see? DO YOU SEE THAT, CILLA?"

Struggling to breathe, Cilla felt a swooping sensation of sheer horror.

Mindy. Why had he mentioned her daughter? Instantly her mind began to trip on horrible images of Lou forcing Mindy into his car, Lou taking Mindy to a hotel room . . .

"You know," said Lou, letting go of her and stretching his mouth in a thin-lipped grin. "I've always wanted to drive

over to Albion, see the college there. They say they'v
poured millions into a lot of new academic buildings. It'
quite the little showplace, hmmmm? And of course I woul
need someone to show me around, someone like you
daughter, eh? I think she would do just nicely."

"You stay away from my daughter," Cilla gasped.

"I could. But what *motivation* do I have to do that? It'
a free country, Cilla. I can take a nice little Sunday driv
and I can go anywhere I want."

"You stay away from her or I'll kill you."

"No, you won't. You're a coward, Cilla. You're afraid c
losing your job," Lou sneered. "And you know what? Yo
are exactly right; you will lose your job if you don'
straighten around."

He turned and left her office.

As soon as he was gone, Cilla rushed to her door an
shut it, then she copied the report to disk so she could wor
on it at home, grabbed up her purse and tote bag, and hurrie
down the hallway toward the #2 door.

Her high heels clacked noisily on the gray marble veine
with swirls of pink.

Lou had never mentioned her daughter before. Not unt
today, when he'd learned she'd been seeing Shane.

With a squeeze of fright, Cilla remembered just how stut
born and rebellious Mindy could be. And Mindy's shoppin
neurosis, so like Cilla's. Mindy loved clothes, shoes, cos
metics, jewelry. Her wardrobe of jeans alone was mind
boggling. Mindy was asking for clothes, a new car . . .

Lou could exploit that, Cilla realized fearfully. Mind
longed for acceptance from her own father; she might accer
gifts from a rich, older man.

Lou was an expert at manipulating women. . . .

She had reached the #2 door. Cherise had ended her shif
A young black man in a security guard's uniform was stanc
ing at the desk, looking bored. He gazed curiously at Cil
as she hurried past. Cilla was sweating all over, one of th

hot flashes pouring over her skin, soaking her bangs with wetness.

As soon as she reached her car, Cilla switched on her car phone and dialed the number of Mindy's dorm room at Albion.

Trembling, Cilla listened to the repeated ringing of the phone.

Answer, answer, she begged as the phone continued to ring.

"Hello?" came her daughter's voice at last, sounding muffled.

"Mindy! Where have you been?" Cilla snapped.

"In the shower."

"Don't you turn up the ringer on your phone?"

"Mom, I was in the *shower*."

"I know. I just—" Cilla struggled to calm her wild breathing.

"Is everything okay?" her daughter inquired.

"Yes—I'm fine—" A lie. She wasn't fine at all. She was distraught and terrified and shamed and desperate.

"Is Daddy okay?" Mindy wanted to know.

"I haven't talked to him, but I'm sure he's just fine. Mindy . . ."

"Yeah?"

"Mindy, if you should receive any phone calls from, well, an older man perhaps, I don't want you to talk to him."

"What?"

"Mindy. Don't accept any phone calls or any dates with people you don't know. Especially older men."

Mindy uttered an uncomfortable laugh. "Hey, what older guys are we talking about? You're not talking about that Shane guy, are you? You don't think he's going to try to call here at Albion? That's stupid. He's suuuuch a geek, I wouldn't talk to him if he begged."

Cilla moistened her dry lips with her tongue. "No, I'm not talking about Shane Gancer. Mindy, look, you're a very

vulnerable young woman in a lot of ways. I just don't want
anything to go wrong for you, that's all."

"Hey, what is this? Mom, why are you talking like this?
What's going on?"

Static was beginning to interfere with the phone call, fading Mindy's voice in and out.

"Just be careful, Mindy. I mean that."

"So okay," responded the girl sullenly. "I will."

Cilla drew a deep breath. "Mindy, I know we've had our
differences and it's been, well, the divorce wasn't the
greatest thing, but I want you to know I love you. I love
you so much." Her voice cracked.

"Mom? You're on the car phone, aren't you? The connection is terrible."

"I love you, I said. Mindy . . ."

"I . . . I love you, too, Mom," said her daughter.

During the next two weeks, Lou Hechter was in Europe for
some fashion showings, and then his trip would take him to
Taiwan and South Africa to visit several dress manufacturers.

The absence of Lou seemed to send the department into
a flare of well-being and hilarity. Designers lingered in the
halls to talk. Every morning someone brought in bagels,
doughnuts, or often both. Even Cilla brought in bagels one
morning, and seemed much more relaxed than she had in
weeks.

People went out in groups to lunch at Hernando's or TGI
Friday's. Birthday parties, forbidden when Lou was in town,
now took up to an hour, with participants spilling out from
the conference room into the hallway, laughing and social-
izing. The leftover cake was placed on a file cabinet near
Raquel's desk, where people passing back and forth in the
hall could help themselves if they wanted.

How nice it would be if Lou never came back, Karyn
found herself thinking.

She had installed the Caller ID on her phone, but the obscene caller, whoever he was, still didn't call again. Was it because Lou was out of the country? She had a horrid feeling that as soon as he arrived back in the States the calls might start up again.

She began asking discreet questions, collecting the names of women whom Lou had harassed. Angela Ferrara, Linda Rickert . . . Raquel had given her those names. Roger gave her a few more. She hoped the women themselves could provide more names.

Calling Human Resources and saying that Cilla wanted the information, Karyn managed to get the home phone numbers of several of these women.

"I can't," said Angela Ferrara, who had been Cilla's secretary immediately before Karyn hired in. She was the one who had left one noon hour and never returned, the one Raquel had accused of being in a "clique" that didn't include Hispanics. Karyn had been forced to leave over eight answering machine messages before finding Angela at home.

"There will be other witnesses, other people speaking up about this," said Karyn quickly. "You won't be the only one."

"Oh, I couldn't. I'd be too—I just couldn't look at him again."

"I'm told it might never come to a court trial. We might only have to give depositions and that's all."

"I don't care. The very idea makes me feel sick," said the woman. "After I quit Cybelle I was so depressed that I couldn't work for over two months. I just can't tell you how that man made me feel. He's terrible and I hope he rots in Hades, but I—I can't put myself through that again."

"All right," said Karyn. "But maybe you know of some other women he harassed. Could you give me their names? I won't tell them where I got their names from."

Angela sighed, and there was a long silence on the other end of the phone wire.

"Are you still there?" Karyn finally said.

"Yeah. Okay. Well, he isn't a woman, but they were really terrible to Toby Holzer, and Lou knew all about it." Karyn nodded; this was the same man Roger had told her about.

"Anyone else?"

"One time I walked into the vending room and I saw Lou in there with this woman named Nancy Shertzen. He was grabbing all over her and she was fighting him off."

"Do you know where this Nancy Shertzen works now?"

"She transferred to the Cybelle in Grosse Pointe. That's all the names I have. There's probably a lot more women, though. I heard rumors, about him. He was at Cybelle a long time, if you know what I mean. There was always some high executive to protect him. I have to go now," added Angela hastily.

Karyn thanked the woman and hung up, breathing in deeply.

He was at Cybelle a long time, if you know what I mean. There was always some high executive to protect him.

She expelled her breath, then drew in another one. Yes, yes! Lou had been at the company for years, and if he made a habit of harassing women, then there had to have been dozens. . . . How many were still around? How many would be willing to give depositions?

"I can do a deposition, yes," said Toby Holzer, the male buyer both Roger and Angela had mentioned. "I'd be more than happy to. In fact, I'd be damn delighted to."

Karyn was on the phone long-distance to New York, having driven out at noon to find a phone booth behind a Shell station, where her call was not likely to be overheard. She had reached Holzer at the designer's studio where he was now employed.

"That's great," she exclaimed. "Can I give you my attorney's phone number? She'll set it up so you can give the deposition in New York."

"I certainly will. I've thought long and hard about this, Karyn. Back when I worked at Cybelle I was too afraid to rock the boat, but I wish now I'd done something like what you're doing. Same-sex harassment has been in the news enough now; I could have filed a suit and had a chance. Anyway, I'd have slept a lot better at night."

"I . . . I'm a little nervous about this, I'll admit," she confided.

"It's rough . . . I know. But listen, Karyn. Cybelle isn't the only good job in fashion—I found that out. I'm really happy here in New York, and if you ever feel like moving to the Big Apple, give me a call. I'll give you a list of contacts, see if we can't get you set up with a job here."

Karyn was overwhelmed with the generosity of this man she had never even met. "I promised my daughter we'd stay in Detroit," she told Toby. "But I can't thank you enough for your help. I'll keep in touch, let you know how things are going."

"You do that. This shit people pull at work has got to stop," said Toby. "Oh, by the way, I have a couple of other names you might call. Lisbet Frankl, she was a hangtag clerk when I was there. A sweet thing, very pretty. She told me that Lou showed her pictures of prostitutes in Amsterdam."

"I called that therapist you told me about," confided Raquel one afternoon. "I've been going in to see her."

"And? Do you like her?"

"She's nice, but I can see she's tough, too. I really have to work on this."

Karyn nodded, happy that her suggestion to Raquel was working out.

"I . . . I haven't called Brett since I was in her office the first time," Raquel went on. "I have to keep a diary and write down every time I want to call him. I have to write down exactly what I was doing at the time, and what triggered it, to make me want to call."

"Interesting," said Karyn, remembering her own instructions from Malia Roberts. "Raquel . . ." She hesitated. "I'm keeping a diary, too. About Lou."

Raquel's eyes flashed. "You are?"

"Yeah." Karyn began telling Raquel about all the things Lou had done.

"The pig! The sexist pig!" Raquel kept repeating. "He's still at it. The ugly jerk, I hope his dick falls off."

Karyn moistened her lips. "Has his—behavior—been going on a long time, Raquel?"

"Oh, yes. When I first started here I heard stuff. . . . He's had dick problems for years. He wanted to do it to me but I got my priest to come in. I think he's afraid to fire me because he knows I'll bring Father O'Meara back again." Raquel giggled. "Next time I'll ask Father to bring in holy water and sprinkle it all over Lou." She made hissing sounds as if water were landing on a vampire. "That'll fix the old bloodsucker."

Was there really a priest, or was this just a story Raquel chose to tell?

"Would you be one of my witnesses?" Karyn said at last. "Be on my side, give a deposition, maybe appear in court if I file a lawsuit?"

Raquel hesitated. "Hey. I like you, Karyn, and we're good friends, but . . . I've been on this job for five years. I've already got money vested in my 401k and I get three weeks' vacation now. I hate Lou, but I'm hanging on here because I get paid more here than I could anyplace else. Sooner or later, he'll quit or have a heart attack, I just know it."

She looked at Karyn pleadingly. "I'm *Hispanic,* Karyn. It isn't so easy, getting a good job when you've got brown skin. My ma struggled for years waiting tables at banquets, getting paid minimum wages, fighting off the guys who tried to pinch her butt. I've worked hard for what I've got. Lou isn't bothering me, not anymore, and I just don't want to rock the boat."

Karyn hid her disappointment. "It's okay, Raquel. Honest."

Raquel's eyes watered. "You still gonna like me?"

"Yes, Raquel, I'm gonna like you."

Lou was due back the following week.

On Thursday night, Karyn had one of her "Lou" nightmares, the one where he was chasing her through Cybelle with the baseball bat. This time he was attacking her desk, smashing the bat on her pictures of Amber, then destroying her computer monitor, causing smoke to billow out of it.

Her desk phone started to ring and Lou banged at it with the bat, crushing the plastic into shards.

Karyn woke up at 2:00 A.M., breathing fast, with perspiration soaking her body.

Suddenly the phone rang . . . or maybe it had been ringing all along, and that was what had created her nightmare.

Karyn fumbled out her hand, managing to grab up the receiver.

"*You think you're such a lady, don't you?*" came the familiar, muffled, heavy-breathing voice. "*You think you can do whatever you want. Well, you're a bitch just like all of them. I bet you're thinking about me right now, aren't you? You want me to slip it to you, don't you? Well, that's exactly what I'm going to do. I'm going to fuck you until the top of your head flies off. And then I'm gonna fuck you again.*"

Karyn didn't hang up this time. Disgusted, she listened to the full message, and when the man finally slammed the phone down, she jumped up and switched on the light so she could see the number displayed on the LED screen of the Caller ID machine.

Her throat closed.

It was Lou's home telephone number. She knew this because there was a book in the department that listed everyone's home numbers, for emergency purposes. It was probably how he'd gotten her number in the first place.

She grabbed for her journal and began writing down as much of the obscene message as she could remember.

On her therapist's advice, Raquel had finally told the truth to her sister Ana.

"You mean . . . you guys broke up?" said Ana, who was becoming plumper, in the first stages of another pregnancy.

Raquel nodded. "He said he couldn't spend the rest of his life with me. He says I made him feel smothered."

"I thought so. That son of a bee. Honey, you should have told us."

Raquel started to cry. "I was too ashamed. I didn't want Ma to know. I've been following him around, calling him. I've done it a lot, Ana. I . . . stalked him, Ana. He called the police on me once."

"The police? Oh, Mother Mary."

Raquel began telling her sister the entire story, including the fact that she'd gone to a therapist. "She's nice, real nice, Ana. She listens to me and everything."

"But you're not crazy, you're just mad," said Ana.

Raquel stared at her sister. Mad? Maybe she was. Maybe it wasn't love at all that she felt for Brett but anger.

"It's so hard not to call him. I keep wanting to. It's like I have to call him."

"You gotta leave the man alone, honey. And you've gotta take off that engagement ring, Raquel. You aren't engaged anymore."

"I can't," said Raquel, covering the ring defensively with her right hand.

"Did he say you could have it?"

"Yeah." Raquel hung her head, knowing Brett had let her

keep it because he didn't know how to get it away from her.

"Then sell it. Get the money for it, but you've gotta take it off, Raquel."

"I will. I'll do it," Raquel promised.

"Look, honey." Ana came over and enveloped Raquel in a big hug that smelled of cologne, fabric softener and baby powder. "How about if Fred and me invite a guy over to dinner this weekend? Fred knows this really nice guy from work, he's a salesman and he makes good money. He's not married and he's a Catholic. He's a little younger than you but not too young."

"I don't know ... maybe not. I still have Brett in my heart."

"You start getting out some, meet some guys, and you'll forget that jerk," advised Ana. "I'll tell Fred maybe next month then, he can bring this guy over. If you need to talk, I'm here, Raquel. I know Ma gets down on us sometimes; she tries to run all of us. Marriage! Babies! That's what Ma wants. But she's gotta know what's going on, huh? She can't go on thinking she's got a bride-to-be on her hands. She wants to sew your wedding dress, Raquel."

"Oh, no," moaned Raquel.

"Yeah ... she's already looking at patterns to surprise you. Hey, I'll tell her if you don't want to. Break it to her, you know, easy."

Raquel grimaced. "I'll do it—but I have to do it in my own time."

"But soon, huh?"

"Yeah."

"Look, we all love you, honey."

Raquel smiled a watery smile. "But you'd love me more if I was married. You'll kill me if I'm not married by age thirty."

Ana mock-smacked her. "Yeah, sure. Look at Mercedes in New York. Big sister, already thirty-three years old. She's not married and we let her live, didn't we? Anyway, you're gonna wear a beautiful wedding dress when you do walk down the aisle, this year or next or whenever. And I'm going to be your matron of honor. I know it's gonna happen."

I care about you, Karyn. More than just care. I'm in love with you, and I'd like us to follow that as far as we can.

Roger Canton's declaration of love had softened up a part of Karyn that had been tight and tense since years before her divorce from Mack. Mack had been a demanding man, very controlling. When he lost his temper, he shouted. Or threw things. He'd never made her feel safe the way Roger did.

Roger made her feel comfortable. He went shopping at the mall with her. He repaired the rust spots on her Tempo and helped her buy a new battery for it. He bought Karyn an ice cream machine, and to Amber's delight, the three of them made homemade chocolate ice cream.

"Next time we'll try peach," Roger promised. "That's really good, too."

The one thing they had not yet done was sleep together. Karyn knew that most men would have expected sex long before now, but she still held back. To her, giving her body to a man was a serious commitment.

Karyn's car needed a tune-up, and one Saturday afternoon Roger brought some tools and a new air filter over to her apartment complex. After he finished the tune-up he was going to outline the windows of her apartment with holiday lights.

It was a sunny afternoon in the low forties, and Karyn brought Roger a cup of coffee, then hung out near the car and chatted as he bent over and did things inside the engine of her old Tempo.

"Do you think Mack will reappear in our lives sometime?" he suddenly said, standing up to look at her.

Karyn flushed. She had told Roger most of the sordid

story of Mack's compulsiveness, his stalking of her at work, the several times when he'd thrown food and VCRs in front of Amber. Thank God for the restraining order. The first week she'd arrived in Michigan, Karyn had taken the precaution of getting another one, valid in Michigan, just in case Mack ever found out where they were.

"I sure hope not."

Roger touched her hand. "If he does, we'll handle it. You've been through a lot, Karyn. And now Lou Hechter."

"He makes Mack look like an amateur," said Karyn. "Thank God I had a good divorce lawyer then—and Malia Roberts is going to help me get free of Lou."

Jinny had offered to take Amber for the night, so Karyn and Roger could go out to dinner by themselves, if Karyn sat for her the following day so Jinny and her "friend" could drive up to Frankenmuth and do some shopping at Bronner's, famous for its huge collection of Christmas artifacts of every known type.

Roger took Karyn to the Olive Garden on Rochester Road, the place sparkling with small white lights and redolent with the smells of oregano, fresh ricotta and fontina cheese.

"You look beautiful tonight," Roger told her as they ate big helpings from the huge salad bowl that had been brought to their table.

"You're not so bad yourself."

"Hey, I know I'm not handsome."

"You're a teddy bear," she told him, smiling. "Trust me, that's far better than being handsome."

"Well, I hope this is one teddy bear you really want to hug," he commented.

Flushing, knowing he was referring to possible sex between them, Karyn looked down at her salad, then she glanced up again. Her pulse started to hammer.

"This is *definitely* a teddy bear I want to hug."

They finished dinner, then Roger tipped the waiter generously and they left the restaurant, getting into his car. Without discussing it further, Roger turned in the direction of Karyn's apartment.

Karyn felt calm as they drove into the apartment development. It was here. It was going to happen. But Roger was a good man, kind and loving and sweet, and she was sure that sex with him would be the same way. And it was time, more than time.

When they walked toward the building, Karyn could see the flicker of the TV set in Jinny's apartment. Obviously her daughter was happily watching television one floor above.

They went inside her own apartment and Karyn switched on a lamp. Its light seemed too glaring but she did not have a dimmer bulb. Suddenly she felt awkward, unsure of herself.

"Would you like coffee?" she asked Roger nervously.

"No, thanks, I'm coffee'd out."

It felt too quiet with Amber not home. Karyn wondered if she should turn on the radio. She found her small radio and twisted the dial until she'd located some soft music. Then it seemed too soft, so she fiddled with the dial again, getting something by Celine Dion.

Then she excused herself and went into the bathroom, where she rummaged under the bathroom vanity until she found her diaphragm in a box that hadn't been touched in over a year. Hopefully, nothing had happened to it. She carefully inserted it, finding a tube of spermicidal jelly as well. Now she *was* getting nervous. A pregnancy wasn't in her plans at all, and she didn't have any condoms. She hoped he would have those. Only in romance novels was sex really romantic. In real life, there were these embarrassing other matters, spoiling the spontaneity.

When she came out, Roger was sitting at the kitchen table in the semidark.

"Karyn, I have to tell you I haven't had sex with a woman in over a year and a half. And then it was with my ex-wife. I'm not good at this sexual seduction thing. In fact, you could say I'm pretty lousy at it."

"Do you have condoms?" she blurted.

"Yes—I did remember those."

"Then you're good at it."

They both laughed nervously.

"I love you," he said. "We'll get through this." He rose from the table and took her by the hand. "Let's go into the bedroom."

"If you want."

Karyn's heart hammered as they walked down the hall to her bedroom, nearly tripping over one of Amber's Barbie dolls, which her daughter had left lying on the carpeting.

Roger bent and picked it up. "We don't want to step on Barbie's leg."

Karyn was relieved that she'd made her bed this morning—some days if she was in a rush she didn't bother—and she'd arranged a group of lace throw pillows on the bed and put everything away neatly.

"A pretty room," Roger murmured. "It smells like your perfume."

They both stopped at the same time, colliding with each other, and Karyn uttered a soft, almost anguished cry as Roger pulled her into his arms.

"Karyn, oh, Karyn," he whispered. "This is awkward but I'm still so happy that we're together. I don't want it to be just sex between us. That isn't what I want at all. I want us to make love, honey. Oh, Karyn . . . you are the most beautiful woman I've ever seen."

They lay on the bed for a long time with their clothes on, pressing their bodies together full length and exploring each other. Kisses, at first light, became heavy, and finally they were entwined together, both of their hearts beating so loudly that Karyn could hear Roger's as well as her own.

Roger chuckled in the darkness. "Does this take me back to high school or what?"

"I guess I'm a little nervous after all."

"Let's just get to know each other. We can take it as slow as we want."

Another forty minutes of kissing, full-body embracing and foreplay. She discovered that Roger's body was much more muscular than she'd imagined it would be. He had solid upper arms and muscular legs. He began unbuttoning Karyn's blouse, one button at a time, kissing her skin as he went.

Karyn sighed with nervous pleasure, and then she began unbuttoning Roger's shirt. His chest was wide and covered with fine, curly hair.

The sex wasn't great—in fact, it was hardly the stuff of fantasy at all. When Roger finally penetrated her, Karyn was wet and ready for him, but then his movements felt so unfamiliar that she stiffened up. The only other man she'd ever had sex with was Mack, and it seemed difficult to get used to a new person. However, as Roger began thrusting, she began answering his thrusts with pelvic movements of her own, and it got better.

He climaxed but she didn't. Karyn didn't say anything, afraid to break what little mood they'd managed to create.

"Is there anything I can do for you?" Roger whispered.

"I . . . maybe another time," she said. "I'm just not a hundred percent relaxed with this yet." She just didn't feel ready to discuss her own needs and how they might be met.

"I don't want our sexual relationship to be one-sided. I want to know that you're enjoying it as much as I did."

"I'll enjoy it a lot more next time," she promised.

"Good. I'm glad I got to feel close to you, Karyn."

They lay wrapped in each other's arms, kissing and stroking each other, Karyn finally beginning to feel the warmth of closeness with this man.

"I'm sorry," she whispered. "I guess I could have been more . . . passionate."

In the darkness she could tell he was smiling. "You're a very passionate woman, Karyn, and all of that is going to come for both of us as time passes. As I told you before, I'm a very patient man. You're worth waiting for, lovie. You're worth everything to me."

She hugged him, tears moistening her eyes. Roger finally drifted off to sleep, but Karyn was too keyed up to sleep. She felt as if something in her life had changed forever.

At 6:00 A.M. Roger slid out of bed, kissed Karyn on the cheek, and went into the bathroom for a quick shower before leaving.

"I'm going back home," he whispered into her ear as he emerged from the bathroom, smelling of Karyn's shampoo. "I'll call you later in the day, Karyn."

As soon as Roger had left, Karyn dropped into a deep, dreamless sleep that was interrupted only by her clock radio.

"Oh, Karyn, oh, dear me," said Aunt Connie on Sunday afternoon when Karyn called to tell her what was going on. "You've actually seen a lawyer?"

"Yes."

"You know it's going to shoot your job there at Cybelle. It's not supposed to, it's illegal to retaliate against people who make complaints about harassment, but this is the real world and it happens," said Connie, sounding troubled. "Are you sure you're ready for the fallout?"

"No, I'm not sure," admitted Karyn.

"Then why risk everything?"

"You mean quit. I don't want to quit. I like working in Fashion. I like working with Cilla. Why should I have to be the one who has to accommodate, who has to make a move out of fear?"

"Have you talked to her yet about this? Cilla?"

Karyn bit her lip. "Yes."

"And what was her reaction?"

"She said men can be a pain in the workplace, basically. She said I should try to stay out of Lou's way. It wasn't exactly the kind of supportiveness I'd expected," Karyn admitted.

"Well, she's right. Lots of women have to accommodate when it comes to this kind of unwanted workplace attention. If you put eight working women in a room, you'll find at least five of them have been sexually harassed at one time or another. They make do, get past it. That's survival. Women have to be tough."

Karyn felt her cheeks redden. "I hate to think that."

"It's true, Karyn. I went through hell with some of the men when I tried to start my own employment agency, but that was a long time ago."

Connie went on, detailing her own story, while Karyn responded politely.

". . . so be very, very careful," Connie was finishing.

"I will," promised Karyn. She was glad when they finally said good-bye and her aunt hung up. She owed a lot to her Aunt Connie, loved her dearly. But this wasn't 1965, it was now. Today women had recourse in court. They could fight back.

A few days later, Malia Roberts called Karyn with the good news that a member of a local chapter of NOW was going to pay $1,000 toward her initial legal fees. "She's a personal friend of mine, and she's giving you the money because she believes in your case and wants to see a real, solid sexual harassment case hit the Detroit area. She's going to canvass her friends and see how much more she can raise."

"That's . . . But I'll pay her back," Karyn gasped, stunned at the generosity of women she didn't even know.

"I told you, you'll do that out of your award, if we win anything. Now, when can you come in and go over the progress we've made?"

Karyn arranged to visit Malia's office early the next morning, before working hours. Once again it was Jinny, her neighbor, she relied on. Jinny arrived home from the hospital just in time to take a sleepy Amber and her school clothes, and tuck Amber onto her living room couch until it was time for her to get dressed.

"I owe you so big-time," Karyn told Jinny. "Without you, I'd—"

Jinny hugged her. "In two weeks or so, I want to take a weekend off, drive down to Branson, Missouri, with my boyfriend. I thought just maybe—"

Karyn smiled. "I'll take Caitlin, no problem. She and Amber are inseparable anyhow."

At 6:45 A.M., Malia greeted Karyn with a friendly smile. She was wearing another power suit in a gray herringbone, accented by a deep aqua silk blouse. A silver pin with an African motif decorated one of the suit's lapels.

"These are my courtroom duds," Malia told her, smiling. "I'm going to be in court nearly all day. There's coffee— hot and strong—and I've picked up some bagels, Karyn. With cream cheese mixed with pimentos, my personal favorite. Would you like something?"

Karyn had been too nervous to eat much breakfast, and gladly accepted a bagel, spreading the cream cheese mixture over it. She didn't much care for the flavor but was too polite to say so.

While they were eating, Malia began talking about various issues that might come up in the case, assuming Karyn did file a lawsuit.

"Attractiveness of the woman becomes a sticky issue," the attorney said.

"Oh?"

"Yes. If a woman is considered attractive she'll be more likely to be believed if she claims sexual harassment, but the court is also more likely to believe that she 'asked for it' by her dress, her mannerisms, or because she is alleged to project sexual availability."

Karyn sat forward. "I didn't project availability!"

"I'm not saying you did, I'm just telling you how these birds think." Malia changed her voice, making it deeper in a mocking imitation of a man. " 'She practically asked to be harassed, the way she dressed for work. She used to wear low-cut blouses and short skirts. That must mean she really wanted it.' And so forth."

Karyn felt her face go red. "I did wear a Gemi suit on my first day of work. I was trying to fit in, be fashionable, look the way I thought they'd want me to look on the job. But Raquel, this other woman at work, told me to cool it, so I stopped wearing the suit. I never wore it again." She hesitated, then went on. "The problem is, Lou Hechter wants all the women in his department to dress sexy. We all have to wear skirts, with hemlines at knee level or higher. And if a woman wears really short skirts, he compliments her in front of everyone."

Malia's dark brown eyes flashed with interest. "Exactly how does he express that? Does he say it verbally, in meetings? Does he say it to various individuals? Does he have a written directive? If so, we need to get a copy of it."

"Everyone knew. I guess he said it to individuals. He spoke to me about it several times. All the women in Fashion have to wear skirts, but the general policy at Cybelle is office casual. You know, pantsuits, slacks, blouses, all shirts or blouses have to have a collar, women have to wear hosiery, and so forth."

"Very, very interesting." Malia looked pleased. "Please get me a copy of the employee booklet with the dress code in it."

"Is this good news?"

"Very. It will help us prove that the whole employment atmosphere was contaminated by harassment, since Mr. Hechter forces the women employees under his jurisdiction to dress in a sexually provocative manner not required of other women at the company."

They conversed for a few minutes longer, Karyn telling the attorney that she'd used the Caller ID to confirm that the breather's call had come from Lou's home phone number.

"So he's an obscene caller, huh? Continue to monitor that, and write down everything he says on the phone as nearly as you can remember. If you have an answering machine hooked up, try to tape him."

Malia shared horror stories about other sexual harassment cases. "You're not going to believe this, but in one lawsuit a woman working at a paper-processing plant was harassed by several male coworkers who heckled her and put an air hose between her legs, simulating a penis."

"No!" cried Karyn. "My God."

"A real case. I couldn't possibly make that up. And that's only the tip of the iceberg, Karyn. A female police officer was harassed when the other male officers she worked with photographed a nude, life-size inflatable doll and posted the pictures in the squad room with a message that the doll was wanted for impersonating her."

Karyn had both hands over her mouth, appalled. It was hard for her to believe that such blatant events could happen in the United States, in workplaces that were supposed to be safe.

Malia continued telling stories for a few minutes longer, then sighed, expelling her breath. "Okay. Enough of that. Let's get to your own horror story. This Lou Hechter. Tell me how many women you've found who he's harassed, and what they said."

Karyn went down the list, summarizing the phone calls and interviews she'd had. "One of them was a man," she added, telling Malia about Toby.

"We may be able to use him to prove contamination of the workplace," said Malia. "Especially since Hechter apparently looked the other way while his harassment was going on. I want you to follow up on any names these people gave you. The more witnesses we can get, the better."

As Karyn nodded, jotting this down on a notepad, Malia cleared her throat. "Karyn, there is one thing. I didn't want to tell you before, not until I was sure."

"What's that?" Karyn glanced up and saw that Malia's eyes were glittering.

"This woman who's helping to finance your legal fees. She is a former employee at Cybelle. She worked in Lou Hechter's department fifteen years ago, before he became a vice president. That's why she's helping you with your legal fees, girlfriend. This lady wants a little sweet revenge."

"Oh, my God," said Karyn.

"Yes, she's anxious to be deposed."

"All those years." Karyn shook her head. "I can't believe . . . it's just so incredible that the man was never stopped."

"Society didn't want him stopped. That's the bottom line." Malia began fussing with the bagel box, reclosing it and putting away the container of cream cheese, their plates and knives. "I guess you think I'm a fanatic, huh? A real man-hater."

"I don't know and I don't care," said Karyn honestly. "I'm just glad you're here, Malia. I can't thank you enough. You're . . . you're changing my life."

"No," said Malia. "*You're* changing it."

The trip back from Durban, South Africa, had been a real bitch, two legs of the journey plagued by turbulence, so the seat belt signs had been on for most of the trip. The flight attendants had virtually ignored Lou, focusing on some male TV soap star who was also traveling in first class. A young shit, just like the one who was banging Cilla. The sight of the man irritated Lou, putting him in a savage mood.

It was still the workday. Lou took a cab home; I-94 was jammed with big semi-trucks making their daily Chicago-

Detroit run. At home he found a note from his wife, Marty, taped to the bottle of Scotch he always poured from.

Enjoy your drinkie or two or four. I've got a dinner meeting. Major client-to-be. I had a week with the toilet lid down for a nice change, so keep it that way, or drinkie bottle goes right down in the bowl and I don't mean punch bowl. As ever, your "devoted" Marty.

Lou scrambled up the sarcastic note and threw it away. His wife was definitely a ball-breaker. Defiantly, Lou peed in the bowl off the master bedroom and left the lid up. If Marty didn't like it, then she could use the guest bathroom, keep the seat down and flush all the tampons she wished. She knew full well how much that irritated *him*.

He showered, took some aspirin and a double Scotch on the rocks to fight his jet lag, and got into his Mercedes. Still in a vile mood, exacerbated by the note from his wife, he drove straight to Cybelle.

"Hello, Mr. Hechter," said Cherise as he entered. The security guard was standing with several others at the guard desk near the door, chatting and joking with them.

"What is this, a night at the Comedy Castle?" snapped Lou. "If you want fun and games, you take it on your breaks, not on company time."

The laughter died, and Lou strode on past, already forgetting about the incident as he progressed down the main corridor of the building toward the Fashion Department.

Emerging into the Fashion area, he drew in his breath sharply. A white-flocked Christmas tree now occupied a place of honor in the hallway, complete with mock holiday gifts arranged beneath it. He heard the peals of more laughter, apparently coming from a hallway conference room. What was this, another damn birthday party? The whole place had apparently fallen apart during his absence.

He stalked toward the conference room, jerking open the

door to see fourteen or fifteen people gathered around a sheet cake, two-liter bottles of Diet Pepsi and Sprite arranged on the table. Helium balloons emblazoned with the numeral 30 were everywhere, colored streamers hanging from the corners of the room. Marcos Allen, a graphic artist, was standing in front of the cake, grinning foolishly as he started to cut the first piece.

Lou stepped inside, strode up to Marcos and snatched the cake knife out of his hand.

"What is this? Another party on company time? You people seem to live in this conference room. Well, from henceforth this room is closed to employee use. Its only function will be meetings."

He gazed furiously around the room.

A trick of sunlight streaming through the floor-to-ceiling window had caught Karyn Cristophe in its ray. It silhouetted her from behind, showing the outlines of her legs through the cotton skirt she wore. The pretty shapes of her legs, which she believed hidden from view, titillated Lou and made his penis begin to harden.

Covetously, Lou stared at her. She'd selected a skirt with thin fabric, wanting to be seen . . . what other explanation could there be? This bore out his theory about her. She was a little flirt . . . she wanted everything she was going to get. No, she *craved* it.

The chastened group dispersed and Lou went into his office.

In his absence, Lou's office had been organized by Raquel. His desk was piled with mail neatly divided into stacks by category. Trade papers and issues of the *Wall Street Journal* were in one pile. There were piles of personal letters, stacks of interoffice mail, and another big stack containing letters from would-be vendors all over the world, many with misspellings or grammatical errors caused by the language barrier. He'd glance at these only if he felt like it.

Lou started to play back his accumulated voice mail, but stopped after the first eight or ten messages, irritated in a way he couldn't explain. Petty. That's what it was. Everything was petty and demeaning, and no one listened to him; they all paid lip service but they didn't listen.

He got up from his desk, went over to the door and locked it, then returned and sat down again. The exhaustion of jet lag swept over him, and Lou rubbed his eyes heavily. Shit— all this traveling. He was getting too old for it. He used to bounce back easily; he'd always boasted that jet lag never threw him. But now he felt like a jackrabbit that had been dragged behind a train for ten miles.

Lou took a twenty-minute catnap in his chair, managing to awaken refreshed, an ability that had proved handy on his world travels for Cybelle over the years.

He went into the bathroom, washed his face, combed his hair, then emerged from his office, feeling feisty—and ready for something to happen.

Immediately, Lou spotted Karyn walking toward the copy room. The cotton skirt had looked fabulous with the sun shining through it, but now he saw that it was quite long, mid-calf, and loosely cut, barely touching her hips.

"Karyn," he said shortly.

She stopped, turning, her expression changing as she saw that it was Lou who had stopped her.

"Your first day of work you wore a Gemi suit. It looked sharp, attractive, sexy. Now you look like something the cat dragged in. Baggy clothes that do nothing for you. That skirt is an atrocity and ought to be burned."

He noticed the high flush of color that flooded her cheeks.

"Get with the program," he told her shortly. "Here at Cybelle, in this department, women dress to look good. See to it that you do—starting tomorrow."

The red receded from Karyn's face, leaving her face pale. She nodded and turned away, her hips moving tantalizingly. Lou felt a burst of satisfaction. He made a sudden decision.

Enough of this screwing around with her . . . it was time to start playing hardball.

Making up his mind, he walked over to Raquel's desk.

"Welcome back," she said dutifully. "I sorted all your mail and put it in different piles on your desk. You received five or six binders from various people, and I've set those on your credenza with sticky notes on each one saying who sent them and when."

Lou shrugged. "Call the Four Towers Hotel in Southfield and set up a meeting with Ruhnau Bravo," he ordered. "Set it up for Monday, ten A.M. sharp. We're going to go over the spring ad campaign."

Raquel, very businesslike, reached for her steno pad to jot down notes. "How many people? What type of a room do you want? Do you want any audiovisual equipment? Food? Just coffee and pastries or a complete breakfast?"

Lou thought fast. "Just six people. Yes, a TV and VCR. Pastries. Oh, and I'll give you the list of staff at Ruhnau Bravo to call. Also, I'll want someone to come down with a laptop and take notes and transcribe them for me. Get Karyn to do it. Good practice for her. And see to it that a hotel room is set up with a computer and printer for the use of Ruhnau Bravo. They'll want to crash on some stuff right on the scene."

"Yes, Mr. Hechter."

Smiling wolfishly, Lou went back into his office. With a flare of satisfaction, he began reading the stack of personal mail that had piled up in his absence.

He had Karyn now. The flirtatious little bitch.

His idea was foolproof, and it would deliver her right into his hands.

Lou was back, throwing his weight around as if he had never left.

The arrival back in the department of her "albatross" caused a wave of depression to descend on Cilla. All around the world, especially in foreign countries, there were plane crashes, typhoons, riots, earthquakes. Why the hell couldn't one have hit Lou Hechter? She didn't wish him dead . . . but she wouldn't complain if he was trapped in a collapsed office building for about nineteen days, forced to drink rainwater and eat rats before some doctor arrived to amputate his leg on-site.

She laughed bitterly at her fantasy. Lou had traveled everywhere, had been mugged three times in foreign cities, once at knifepoint, but nothing ever fazed him. He'd probably live to be ninety-five years old, pinching nurses' butts in some wealthy eldercare facility for the sensitivity-impaired. With a flare of hope, she thought again about her report on Girlrags for Dom. Nothing had been done about the chain yet—at least nothing she'd heard on the office grapevine. Maybe she'd call Shane later, ask if he'd heard anything. Legal was always involved with these acquisitions. . . . She didn't dare call or E-mail Dom about it, of course. He'd think her pushy . . . or would he? He was such a nice man, but if she broke protocol . . . ?

Cilla was in her car, driving home from work, her mind racing over her options, when her car phone rang.

"Mom . . . Mom, it's Mindy. I tried you at work, I tried you at home . . . Oh, Mom." Mindy was crying. "Mom, I'm in jail here in Jackson."

"Jail?" Cilla wondered if she had heard it correctly. *"Jail?"* she repeated.

"This is my one phone call." Mindy's sobs were choked. "You have to come and bail me out, I can't stay here, they've got . . . prostitutes in here. Sleazy women . . . oh, God, this is all so horrible, I can't b-believe it. . . ."

"But honey." Cilla fought to make sense of this. "You're in jail in Jackson? For what?"

The town of Jackson was only a half hour's drive away from Albion along I-94, and many of the college students drove there to eat in restaurants or to shop. Jackson's chief claim to fame was Jackson Prison, an enormous state facility barricaded behind high guarded walls and barbed wire. But of course Mindy had to be in a municipal or county jail.

She pictured her beautiful blond daughter sitting in a cell with an open toilet and bars on the doors, and nearly swerved out of her lane, narrowly missing hitting an Aerostar van.

"I drove here to the mall to shop, and I . . . Mom, I put this necklace and some other stuff in my purse. When I tried to walk out the door, this security guard came over and she t-told me they have a policy about shoplifting . . . Mom . . . *please*. Come and get me out."

"Oh, Mindy. I just left work; I'll drive over there right now. Just hold tight. How much do you think the bail will be?"

"I don't *know* . . .". Mindy sounded panicked. "Please . . . hurry. I can't call one of my friends. . . . I'd die if anyone knew. This is like some horrible program on TV. Please, just get me out."

Cilla used her car phone, making several calls until she finally learned her daughter was in the county jail on West Wesley Street. She was informed by a bored clerk that Mindy's bail would be $350, payable either in cash or through a bail bondsman. Cilla didn't have that much cash on her, but she could stop at an ATM in Jackson and get the necessary funds to bail her daughter out. She gripped the steering wheel, fighting the urge to floorboard the accelerator just to get to the jail faster.

Entering Jackson, she was greeted by signs that warned her not to pick up hitchhikers, a message that under the circumstances felt chilling.

Uneasily she remembered various bits of costume jewelry she'd seen Mindy wear, a pretty, tiny purse, expensive lipsticks. She'd assumed Mindy bought these out of her allowance, which was plenty to cover such items. But what if she'd shoplifted them? Cilla's stomach was knotted with worry.

Cilla was kept waiting nearly forty minutes before finally Mindy was brought out to her by a female deputy. Mindy's blond hair was disheveled, her eyes reddened and puffy with crying.

"Mom!" Mindy ran forward and Cilla hugged her tightly, feeling a wave of love for her obviously hurting child.

"Honey . . . oh, baby."

"Can we get out of here? I had to be in a cell with *hookers,* Mom. I need a shower and my hair looks terrible. I hope I don't have fleas or anything!" Mindy wailed. "Or . . . lice!"

Cilla felt a pang of hurt at the psychological stress her daughter was going through.

"Hookers?" she queried.

"Yeah . . . there was a really fat one. She kept talking about . . . oh, I can't even say it. She works at *bachelor* parties, Mom. And people send Big Mama Grams. It's so gross!"

They walked out to Cilla's Mercury Cougar in the parking lot. It was already after 9:00 P.M. Cilla's first instinct was to drive Mindy immediately back to Detroit, but of course, her daughter couldn't miss class. Besides, Cilla was exhausted from the long, stressful drive, and Mindy looked pale.

"Mindy, how about if I get a motel room for the night and you can shower there, and we'll have dinner afterward? I'll drive you back to Albion in the morning so you don't miss class."

"I have my car," said Mindy shakily. "It's still in the parking lot of that awful shopping mall. I'm never going back there, Mom! They had this security woman, she acted like I was a criminal, it was so awful, people were staring at us . . ."

Cilla started her engine, recalling that there was a Holiday

Inn in town. The choice of hotels in a town like Jackson was small, and that would do as well as any. How should she handle this? If she scolded Mindy, she'd only widen the already huge breach between them, something Cilla desperately did not want to do.

"Mindy," she said gently, "you know, I was arrested for shoplifting when I was nineteen. It was the worst experience of my life. The security guard who caught me accused me of being a criminal. I was horribly humiliated, and my whole family found out, and they never let me forget it. My mother made me get a part-time job to pay back the cost of what I had stolen."

Mindy stared at her, openmouthed. "What was it that you took?"

"A designer scarf. It was very expensive, very beautiful. I didn't have any money and I . . . I didn't think anyone would see me."

Her daughter was slumped in the passenger seat, staring out at the nondescript city scenery. Jackson was an older midwestern factory town and looked it. "I took a little pewter picture frame, too."

"Was it something you really wanted?"

"It had a picture in it, one of those preprinted ones." Mindy's eyes filled again. "Of a little girl and her dad."

"Oh, Mindy."

"I was going to pay for it, really. I took it outside the store and I was going back in to pay when they stopped me. Mom . . . I've taken other stuff," Mindy admitted in a low voice. "Jewelry. Makeup. Little stuff that I can just drop in my purse. I . . . I just do it."

"Honey." Cilla felt so moved by this admission that her voice cracked.

"I'm a klepto, Mom."

"We'll solve this, Mindy, we'll help you. We'll get you a counselor."

"All the girls at Albion seem so rich, Mom. They come

from these rich families in Bloomfield Hills, a lot of them. They have anything they want. Their fathers give them Visa cards and they just charge, charge, charge. And what does my dad give me? Nothing." Mindy paused. "I—I guess that's no excuse. Do you still love me, Mom? I mean . . . after I did this?"

"Mindy. Oh, sweetie. Of course I love you." Tears rolled down Cilla's face so thickly she could barely see to drive. She wiped them away with the back of her left hand, fearful they would have an accident.

"Are you going to tell Daddy? And Grandpa and Grandma?"

"Do you want me to?"

"No."

"Then I won't."

They got a room with two queen-size beds, and while Mindy was showering Cilla drove to a nearby strip mall to pick up some fresh clothes for her daughter to wear. However, the stores had all closed at 9:00. Belatedly, Cilla remembered she had a workout bag in the trunk of her own car with a few things in it. They might not suit Mindy's taste, but they would fit and they were clean.

By the time she returned Mindy had just emerged from the bathroom, wrapped in towels.

"For once I'm glad we wear the same size," remarked Cilla, handing Mindy a pair of jeans and a Nike T-shirt, along with a T-back sports bra and a fresh pair of panties. "You might want this, too," she added, handing Mindy a canister of deodorant.

"Thanks." Mindy began to dress, her young body firm and perfect.

"Would you like to go out to eat? We could eat in the dining room here, or just find a coffee shop."

"I guess. Maybe a grilled cheese sandwich."

Cilla again felt her heart squeeze. This had been Mindy's

favorite meal when she was four years old—comfort food.

When she had finished dressing, Mindy threw herself on one of the beds, bunching up two pillows to put under her head. "I can't believe you really shoplifted, Mom," she said. "That's just so weird, that we both did it."

"We're very much alike," Cilla admitted. "We both love beautiful things. That's one reason I'm in retailing . . . because I love clothes so much."

Taking a cue from Mindy, she lay down on the other bed, propping herself against its pillows, and tried to think of what to say next. This was the first time she and Mindy had communicated in several years. She wanted it to last past today, to be more than an ephemeral event created by the stress of Mindy's arrest.

Somehow they'd made a breakthrough.

She wasn't sure how or why, but today Mindy wanted her, needed her.

She couldn't let that go.

Cilla thought of her relationships with her women friends, all the secrets they told each other, secrets that drew them together, binding them. Mindy was an adult now, nearly twenty-one. Maybe to be close to her child, Cilla herself would have to open up a little.

The idea scared her, but she was desperate.

"Mindy, we all have our problems, even your own mother," she began slowly. "I have a few . . . well, I've never told you about them."

"You have problems? You mean about that Shane Gancer?"

"No, Shane isn't the problem at all." Cilla inhaled, then blew her breath out. "Mindy, Lou Hechter has been . . . sexually harassing me in a very bad way for about three years."

"Oh, my God." Mindy turned anxiously, her eyes riveted on her mother's face. "What do you mean, a very bad way?"

"As bad as you can imagine."

Horror filled the younger woman's eyes. "Does that mean . . . he made you have sex with him?"

"Yes."

"But, Mom—why did you do it?"

Cilla's eyes moistened. "He threatened to take away my employment, darling. I was terrified I'd lose my job. It pays very well, but I had so many expenses. I just overextended myself. Unfortunately I had a big credit card debt, and I'd just bought this condo, and new furniture, and a new car, and I'd bought your car—"

"And my tuition!"

"Yes, but I wanted you to have a good education and you loved Albion so much. I thought I could hang in there for four years, until you graduated. But it kept getting worse. He's . . . really a terrible man, Mindy."

"Is he the older guy you warned me about?" cried her daughter. "The one you said to be careful with?"

"Yes," admitted Cilla in a low voice. "I told him I didn't want to be with him anymore and he started talking about you. He hinted that he might drive over to Albion and talk to you. I was just sick. I had to try to warn you. . . ."

By now Mindy had moved to the other bed and was sitting beside Cilla, putting her arms around her mother. "I can take care of myself. He couldn't have hurt me."

"I was afraid. . . . You don't know him, Mindy. You don't know what powerful men like him can do."

"I'd kick him in the balls," declared her daughter fiercely. "I had to do that once to this kid in high school. Mom, this guy is harassing you. Just like those women in Tailhook or . . . those women plebes at the Citadel!"

Cilla felt a wave of weary shame. "I know, babydoll. I should have fought back. I was just trying to preserve my life—our life. I kept thinking that each time would be the last . . . that I'd tell him no and he'd stop. Only he didn't. The nightmare kept going on. And now I think he's molesting my secretary, too."

Mindy tossed her head, her blue eyes flashing. Her cheeks were flushed with anger. "Well, you can stop now. Quit your job if you have to, Mom. I'll be all right."

"But your tuition . . ."

"You already told me that I should get a student loan. I'll get one; I'll go to the administration building and apply for one tomorrow. If I get one, that'll cover the rest of this year and next. As soon as I graduate I'll get a job and I'll start paying it back."

Cilla looked at Mindy, at the fire in her daughter's eyes. "It's going to be a big financial burden," she said gently.

"I can do it. I'll live at home for a couple of years if I have to. Mom, you have to listen to me. This Lou guy, he's evil. He's on a big power trip, just like all those senators and Army guys that harass women. Please, don't let him win. Please, fight back, Mom."

Cilla wiped a thin sheen of perspiration from her face, one of her "meltdown" hot flashes suddenly flushing her skin. "I'm going to be fifty-one on my next birthday," she told Mindy. "Maybe I'm not that much of a fighter anymore; maybe Lou knows that. Maybe that's why he treats me the way he does."

"Well, now you have me," said Mindy vehemently. "Kick butt, Mom! Kick his sorry white butt!"

That morning, Raquel told Karyn that Lou wanted her to go to Southfield and take notes for a meeting with Ruhnau Bravo, the company's new ad agency. The meeting was scheduled for Friday of the following week.

Karyn's heart sank. "But I don't know shorthand."

"You don't have to. You'll take a laptop and take notes on that. It's fun. The meetings are always pretty lively, and lots of times they show ads or visuals that are pretty interesting."

Raquel scribbled down a map to show Karyn how to reach the hotel, which was near 9 Mile and Lahser, and got out the laptop and showed Karyn how to use the trackball.

"Easy," she said. "And usually the meetings don't last all that long, so you can probably just go straight home afterwards. Lou'll be busy with the people from Ruhnau Bravo; he always shows off, and he'll hardly notice you."

Karyn started to protest, then closed her mouth.

If he touches me—

But how could she refuse? This was her job, after all.

Malia Roberts had asked Karyn to call her today with an update on what was going on, and Karyn managed to find a private phone in Annie Fiacci's office. Annie was out for three days, taking some vacation time, and Karyn felt sure Annie wouldn't mind if she borrowed her phone for ten minutes.

"How are you holding up, Karyn?" Malia wanted to know.

"Well, there's been a development."

"What's wrong?"

"I'm supposed to go to a meeting at the Four Towers Hotel in Southfield with the company's ad agency. Lou's going to be there, running the meeting. I have to be there all day and take notes on a laptop. I'm—nervous about it. I mean, it seems all right, but . . ."

"Hmmm," said Malia. "Well, I have several thoughts here. One, you're going to be outside the office environment in a hotel setting, and you know how these lecherous men feel about hotels. To them, a hotel is nothing more than a sexual playground. Two, I suggest you go out today and buy yourself a mini-cassette tape recorder—the small kind. Go to a store and pick up several hundred-and-twenty-minute tapes. Test it, make sure everything's operating okay. Practice using the on-off switch so you can activate the recorder by putting your hand in your pocket."

"All right . . ." Karyn agreed.

"Now, here's what I want you to wear. Do you have a nice, loose jacket with big pockets?"

"Yes."

"Wear that, and be careful not to let him feel you up."

Karyn uttered a tense laugh. "I hope it doesn't come to that."

"I hope it does. I'd love to have this asshole on audiotape. We might not be able to use it in court, but we could sure fry him if we're trying to get a nice, fat settlement out of the company. Trust me, Karyn. This man has been aggressive with you. Now it's your turn. Have you got the courage?"

"Yes," Karyn said, moistening her lips.

"When these jerks play, they're gonna *pay,*" said Malia jubilantly.

Karyn skipped lunch and drove out to a nearby Kmart, where she purchased two 120-minute tapes and a microcassette recorder, plus batteries for it. The clerk in the checkout line rang them up matter-of-factly, but Karyn's heart was pounding thickly as she paid for her purchases.

Mindy and Cilla had breakfast in the coffee shop, talking freely as they hadn't talked in years, since Mindy had gone into her stormy adolescence.

"I'm going to have to appear in court, aren't I?" said her daughter.

"Yes, I'm afraid so. We'll need to get you a lawyer."

Mindy's face clouded. "Oh, it's just going to cost you more money, isn't it, Mom? I'm sorry . . . I didn't mean . . ."

Cilla hesitated. "Well, Shane *is* a lawyer. Maybe he can do us a favor or knows someone who can give us a family rate."

"Not him! Not your boyfriend. Please—I don't want him to know!"

"Okay, then, we'll get someone else, someone anonymous out of the phone book, or I can call a few people I know."

Mindy uttered a choked laugh. "Mom . . . I'm s-sorry, Mom."

"Mindy, what's done is done. Fortunately the stuff you took wasn't expensive. Hopefully you'll be charged with just a misdemeanor. The judge will probably make you pay a fine or do community service. We'll get through this, Mindy."

Mindy sipped her orange juice. "Mom, I guess I thought it was your fault that Daddy left."

Cilla sipped her juice, too. "Life is very complicated. Your father wanted to be young; he didn't like facing his responsibilities. He loved you, he probably loved me, but we meant growing up to him, so he split. But I . . . I *picked* a man like that, Mindy. Do you see? Part of me loved that part of him—his boyishness, his—"

She stopped, putting down her glass. Mindy was looking at her.

"Mom, do you think that's why you love this Shane guy? Because he reminds you of Daddy, the way he used to be? Boyish and all that?"

Cilla was startled at the astute observation coming from the twenty-year-old.

"In some ways Shane is like Bob used to be, yes. But he's the best part of Bob. He's the part of Bob that should have been, could have been."

"Do you think you'll—marry Shane?"

Cilla smiled sadly. "I don't think it's an issue at this point. I'm not sure I'll ever remarry, but if I did, would that bother you too much?"

"I don't know." Mindy attempted to smile, but failed. "I guess I won't like it, but if he makes you happy . . . I won't stop loving you."

Cilla bowed her head, her heart suffused with emotion.

Later, she drove Mindy back to pick up her car, and they said good-bye, Mindy heading back to Albion, Cilla toward Detroit. Cilla turned on the radio to a Top 40 station, her mood beginning to pick up as she drove. She'd make some phone calls today and get Mindy an attorney who practiced in Jackson. But most important, she had her daughter back. Finally they were relating as women . . . not as mother and daughter. And, incredibly, Mindy was becoming a woman Cilla thought she would like.

"Thank you, God," she whispered. *"Oh, thank you."*

The cafeteria was doing a sporadic business in coffee, juices, bagels and doughnuts, people mostly carrying trays or bags back up to their offices. Holiday decorations had already gone up, swags of greenery decorating the cashiers' desks, giant-size wreaths hung in all of the windows.

Cilla ran into Shane as she was standing at the coffee machine filling a Styrofoam container. Looking handsome and young in a gray-heather blazer, he was balancing a bagel, a package of cream cheese and a double container of coffee.

"Well, hello," he said, giving Cilla a surprised look that was filled with pleasure. "Everything okay? You're frowning, Cilla. Just a tiny bit," he added, grinning.

"Just cranky in the morning before I get my first jolt of caffeine," she told him, remembering her promise to Mindy not to tell Shane what had happened in Jackson.

"Why don't we sit down and drink our coffee right here?" suggested Shane, pointing to an empty table near the window.

Cilla hesitated. *In front of anyone who came in?* was her first, ignoble thought, followed by, *Setting ourselves up for more gossip?* And another angry attack on her from Lou? The very idea turned her stomach.

"I'm not sure . . ." she began.

Shane nodded. "It's okay for two employees to enjoy a cup of coffee together, you know."

Cilla felt her face turn magenta pink. "Not here, and not right now, at this point in my life," she managed to say. "There has been gossip," she admitted.

"Are you okay, Cilla?" asked Shane softly, looking her in the eyes.

"I'm fine."

"Good. I'll call later on tonight, all right?"

He gave her one of his young, rakish, melting smiles and walked away across the room toward the door that led to the hallway, leaving Cilla to sink down at a table by herself, feeling suddenly . . . drained.

This year as soon as Raquel had caught sight of the first holiday decorations in a Rite-Aid drugstore two weeks before Thanksgiving, her mood shot downward in her usual seasonal funk. This year she'd thought it was going to be so different. She and Brett would be exchanging gifts, she'd get him a pair of Rossignol skis. She had been saving up for them for months. They'd love each other, and eat Christmas Eve supper in bed, and make love until all hours. Christmas Day they'd trade off between the two families, eating two holiday dinners until their stomachs burst.

Now none of it was happening.

She sat in her therapist's office, feeling so distracted she was barely able to concentrate.

"So nothing's been going on, basically. I still haven't told my mother, and she still thinks she's got to make me a wedding dress." Raquel rubbed her aching temples. "I've got to stop her before she's gone too far. She'll murder me. And . . . I still haven't called the guy I met at the health club. And . . . Christmas looks awful this year. I don't even want to be there for it."

"So, in a word, you feel stuck."

"Stuck, stuck and *stuck*!" exclaimed Raquel. "I just want someone over the holidays like everyone else. Someone to be with on New Year's. I'll end up over at Ana's watching the ball drop, something stupid like that."

The therapist smiled. "But didn't you tell me that Ana has a young man she wants you to meet? Maybe she can invite him for New Year's Eve. And you can all watch the ball drop together."

Raquel clenched her hands in her lap. "I . . . I don't think I'm ready for that. But . . ." She moistened her lips. "I might meet him sometime. Maybe . . . in a couple of months or so. But only if he's cute."

"Well, that's definitely making progress," said Dr. Stein. "Now, what about your mother, Raquel? And that wedding dress she's starting to make? Are you going to let her finish the whole dress before you tell her?"

"No," said Raquel, biting her lip.

This year Cilla bought a new artificial silver tree and hung it with her nutcracker collection she'd picked up during years of traveling abroad. Mindy loved the nutcrackers, and some of the decorations were hand-painted items Mindy had done when she was a child. Looking at each one as she hung it brought back memories of previous Christmases, making Cilla feel sad at the passage of time.

That weekend Shane took Cilla to meet his family. He'd been talking about it for several weeks and each time Cilla had put it off, but she had run out of excuses.

The Gancers lived in a subdivision in Rochester Hills, the yard filled with rock gardens and flower beds that would be stunning in the summer season. Shane's father owned Gancer's Gardens and Nursery, and his mother was a landscape designer.

As they parked at the curb, Cilla was trembling with anxiety. What if his parents were her own age? She'd die. There wasn't a family in the world that would approve of its only son getting serious with a woman twenty-four years his senior, virtually past the age of childbearing. That was one reason society frowned on these types of matches, Cilla realized with another spurt of nerves. Older women couldn't bear children, while some older men could father babies well into their seventies, even eighties. Look at Pablo Picasso. . . .

"You okay?" asked Shane lightly. He seemed amused at her nervousness.

"I feel like I've just arranged to go in for a high colonic."

He laughed. "Oh, come on, everyone will love you. And even if they don't, I don't care. You're special, Cilla, and they're going to see it, too."

But they didn't. Shane's father turned out to be a man, only three years older than Cilla herself, who kept making remarks about "women executives." Shane's mother, only four years older than Cilla, seemed terribly uncomfortable, and his college-age sister, Jenny, barely would look at Cilla. Despite Shane's efforts, the conversation dragged. Cilla tried to fill some of the silences by asking questions about gardening. But even then it was slow going.

Cilla was desperately relieved when the cake and cookies were finished, the coffee drunk, and they could safely leave.

"So it wasn't exactly the Brady Bunch," remarked Shane as they were pulling away in his car.

Cilla winced. "Your family is extremely nice, Shane, but the problem is, they just have never visualized you getting serious with a woman almost your mother's age."

"Yes, they have. They know I'll end up with an older woman and they have accepted that. They're not age bigots, Cilla."

"But I mean—"

"I know this was disappointing for you, but trust me, my family are all introverts. That's why they had such a hard time talking freely. After they get to know you better, they'll start opening up to you. Anyway, it doesn't matter what they think. I still want to marry you."

"What?"

"I said I'd like to marry you." Shane pulled over to the curb and leaned over the gearshift, sliding his arms around Cilla. "Beautiful Cilla, woman of my dreams. Did you think I'd let you get away from me? No way. I want to be with you forever. I love you so much."

"Shane . . ." She could barely get the word out. Oh, this was catastrophic. His family . . . and Lou hanging over her . . . and Mindy's dislike of her dating a younger man . . . despite their reconciliation she knew Mindy still had deep reservations about Shane and probably always would. Not to mention her friends' jealousy . . . she remembered Eleanor Dishman's comments. How could a marriage with that big an age disparity last?

"Baby?" Shane murmured. "Sugar?"

Baby? She was fifty years old. In another twelve years she'd be thinking about whether to sign up at age sixty-two for Social Security or wait until she was sixty-five—no, it would be age sixty-seven by then. Suddenly, Cilla started to giggle. She couldn't help it; the laughter erupted out of her as if propelled by gas.

"Cill?" Shane demanded anxiously, taken aback.

"It's—oh, Shane—I'm sorry—I just—"

She couldn't stop.

She laughed and laughed, rubbing her eyes. Then suddenly she was crying, bent over the seat, rubbing her damp forehead with her hands, beating her fingers against her skull.

"I don't know! Oh, God, Shane, if it could just be you and me. But it isn't! It's Mindy, and your sister, and your mother, and it's—that bitch Aileen Hanran, and it's Eleanor Dishman, and it's my boss, Lou, and it's—everyone—it is—just—*everyone*. It's the damn world! Older men marry young women all the time, but if an older woman tries it . . . it shocks everyone . . . they feel revulsion!"

She couldn't talk anymore, the sobs racked her so. She cried for a long time, while Shane held her and handed her tissues and gave her murmuring orders to "blow." He was tender and loving about it, and somehow that hurt Cilla even more, that he should have to be punished because of people's attitudes because *she* was the one over fifty.

"Cilla," said Shane gently, "it isn't exactly as if you're robbing the cradle by yourself. I'm fifty percent of this deal. I'm not ashamed of my love for you."

"But . . ." Cilla ran her hands through her carefully colored hair, which she'd had styled for him, then rubbed them down her front, cupping her still-curvy breasts. "My hair! My boobs! My hips!"

"What about them?"

"They're all going to fall."

"Your hair?" he inquired. "That looks nicely in place to me, along with everything else."

"I'm aging, I'm going to age, my wrinkles are going to get wrinkles, and I can have a face-lift but I can't keep on doing it. . . . I'm afraid of going under the knife," Cilla stammered.

"Do you think that loving me means you're forced to go under the knife?"

"I . . . I'd have to."

"Why?"

She stared at him, incredulous. "Shane, just to keep you. Get real! When I'm sixty-five, you're going to be a very young-looking and virile forty-one. For Christ's sake, *listen* to me. You might not want children now, but you may want them later. You're going to want a wife who—who—"

"Who is loving, sexy and kind? Who is bright and vibrant? Yes, I want a wife like that. Cilla," he went on, "let me tell you something about my family. My father has had five heart attacks. He lost four brothers, all around age forty to forty-five when they keeled over from heart disease. There are no guarantees, dear. I'm hoping I'll have a different health history, and I'm doing everything possible to stay healthy, but I just don't know what lies ahead for me."

"Oh, Shane."

"So can't we just let life unfold? What's more important,

what other people think or a love that could sustain both of us for many years?"

Cilla looked into his clear, honest eyes, and knew she had to be honest with him, too.

"Shane," she whispered, "there's another part of my life . . . I think you have to know."

They drove back to her condo, and Cilla brewed a pot of coffee. When she poured the coffee into two mugs, her hands shook so much that she spilled on the countertop.

"So I did it out of fear," she finished an hour later, after telling Shane the whole, humiliating Lou story, from that first, reckless drink right on up to the most recent encounter with him in her office, when Lou had shoved her into her credenza, squeezed his hands around her neck and threatened her daughter.

"My God. Jesus," Shane kept saying, gripping Cilla's hands so tightly that it nearly hurt.

"I wasn't brave. I wasn't ready to have my life wrecked, and I . . . I kept hoping each time would be the last, but it never was." She hung her head. "I have no excuse."

"Oh, Cilla, the pain you must have gone through."

She nodded, feeling devastated with shame and humiliation. "So that's it," she finally said. "That's the worst thing about me. My deep, dark secret."

"Cilla, you have legal options."

"I don't want to sue that man. I'd be connected to him for years . . . he'd never be out of my life. He's like a . . . a horrible disease. I just want to be cured. And I don't want this horrible nightmare to come between us," she said, choking.

Shane took her in his arms, stroking her hair back from her face. "Cilla, I love you, I love who you are and where you've been. No matter what that includes. Do you hear me, sweetness? We'll get Lou Hechter out of your life. I'll help you."

She pulled away a little. "This is one thing I have to do for myself, Shane. And I . . . I'll think of a way."

On Christmas morning, Karyn and Amber opened presents underneath the artificial tree Karyn had purchased, the only kind allowed in the apartment complex. Despite her many worries, Karyn had splurged on a pink computer for her daughter, complete with software and games, and Amber had bought Karyn some crystal earrings at Kmart. "They look just like diamonds, Mom!" her daughter said proudly.

Karyn oohed and aahed over them as if they'd come from Jules Schubot, one of the most exclusive jewelry dealers in the area.

Roger arrived in the afternoon, bringing four shopping bags of gifts, including a poster of Jazzy Kulture, autographed especially for Amber by the teenage singer.

Amber squealed when she saw it, and immediately had to hang it in her room.

"And I've got great news," Roger announced after he'd finished helping Amber to decide where to put it and they'd located picture hangers and a hammer for the job. "I've gotten a court order for reasonable visitation," he told Karyn joyfully. "Thank God. I can fly Anna out to Michigan next summer for five weeks. She is such a nice, kind, vivacious girl, she really is. I know you'll love her, and so will Amber. Oh, Karyn. My love. I want us to be a family so much. I promise this is the last Christmas you and I will ever be apart—if that's the way you want it."

Karyn nodded, unsure of what to say. She did want it, yes. She did love Roger. And yet—Roger offered choices to her, options that she wanted to explore yet still was afraid to.

"We have all the time in the world," he assured her, kissing her gently. "And no matter what happens with your lawsuit, we still have each other."

*   *   *

The following Saturday, Karyn drove to Ann Arbor to interview another witness whose name she had been given.

Linda Rickert had transferred to a job at the Cybelle store that co-anchored the big Briarwood Mall, and they'd arranged to meet at a coffee shop in the mall.

Linda was a tall blond, her body type very similar to Karyn's own. And the story was one that was now beginning to sound very familiar to Karyn.

"He used to do these obscene phone calls; I was sure it was him. One time he wrote a nasty message on my computer screen saver. Another time I was in one of the vending rooms, getting coffee, and he suddenly came in and closed the door behind us and he . . . he started asking me if I was wearing panties. When I tried to get out of the room he blocked the door and tried to put his hand up my skirt."

Linda agreed to give a deposition if it could be scheduled so she would not miss work, and Karyn gave her one of Malia's business cards. She also gave Linda one of her own new business cards that had been printed up for her when she was given permanent employee status at Cybelle. "I'll call you when we need you to come in to give the statement. And Linda . . . call me anytime you want to talk."

That afternoon, when Karyn arrived back at her apartment and had just picked up Amber from upstairs, the phone began ringing.

"I'll get it!" cried Amber. "It's probably Caitlin or Megan."

Karyn had a strange feeling. "I'll answer it, honey."

"But, Mom . . ."

"I need to use the Caller ID, cupcake. If it's Megan, I'll give you the phone right away."

She walked into her bedroom and looked at the Caller ID unit. The number on the indicator was Lou Hechter's home telephone.

Swiftly, Karyn picked up the phone, switching her answering machine to record.

"Bitch, you're going to suck my . . ."

Shuddering, Karyn held the phone far from her ear so that she wouldn't have to listen to the obscenity. This man was truly sick, she found herself thinking. For all the sexual harassment, but also for taking such major risks with his own career.

Or didn't he think he was taking a risk?

Did he really suppose that Karyn would be afraid like Angela, Linda, and all of the other women he'd done this to?

When Roger called later, Karyn was still tense from Lou's phone call.

"Your voice sounds strained. Is everything all right?"

"Everything is fine," Karyn lied.

"Good," said Roger cheerfully, "because I have three tickets to that ice-skating show at the Palace next Sunday with Tara Lipinski."

"Sounds wonderful," said Karyn, forcing enthusiasm. "Amber will love it, and she's also got a birthday party to go to. Caitlin's going to be nine."

They talked about the weekend for a while, Karyn trying to hide her apprehension over the upcoming meeting and the plans she'd made to deal with it. She felt sure Roger wouldn't approve of her carrying a clandestine tape recorder in her pocket.

In fact, he'd probably try to talk her out of it.

The week at Cybelle seemed to crawl by.

On Thursday, the day before the meeting in Southfield, Karyn was jumpy all day. She spilled a cup of coffee on her desk, soaking a stack of papers that Cilla had wanted copied. Then the copier jammed, and Karyn had to squat down to open the doors and pull levers, trying to find the crumpled piece of paper causing the jam.

While she was doing this, she burned her finger on the heat transfer mechanism and got a run in her panty hose.

Then a package Cilla had sent to London didn't arrive, and Karyn had to try to track it. The only thing that saved her sanity was that Lou was in meetings most of the day and they barely saw him in the department.

Surely nothing bad could happen at a major hotel ... could it?

Unless Lou caught her with the tape recorder in her pocket. Then, Karyn knew, things could get ugly. In fact, if he caught her ... well, she would have to make sure she did not get caught.

Roger had flown to Chicago on Wednesday morning on business, and Karyn didn't want to be alone, so she and Amber went up to Jinny's apartment, where they spent Thursday evening chatting and watching television until it was time for Jinny's mother to arrive to stay the night.

"You okay?" whispered Jinny in the kitchen while they were getting out cookies for the girls. In a minute she'd have to change into her uniform.

"I'm fine, I guess." She had already told Jinny about the possible lawsuit. "It's just that I have to go to this meeting down in Southfield tomorrow and I'm wearing a tape recorder."

"Whoa."

"Yeah ... I thought it was stressful being harassed. It's just as stressful fighting back."

"Maybe you're carrying this too far," suggested her friend.

"I can't stop now. I have to go through with this."

"Well, I'd be very careful."

"Don't worry, I will be."

Karyn tossed and turned most of the night. At 5:00 A.M., she crawled wearily out of bed, showered, and went to the kitchen, where she made herself a cup of instant coffee in the microwave. Outside the darkened windows rain was falling, water rattling in the eaves trough that ran at the corner of the building. It was the kind of rain that looked as if it might freeze later in the day.

Finally, Karyn went into her bedroom, throwing open her closet door, and began pulling out her blazers and jackets. She selected a boxy-looking navy blue jacket with big patch pockets. With it she chose a plain white blouse and a herringbone skirt she'd worn often. For shoes she picked a pair of flats that were very comfortable to walk in. Or maybe she'd have to run in them. God . . .

She called Amber and started breakfast.

Amber trailed out of her bedroom wearing a long nightgown printed with pictures of dancing cats which Karyn had bought for her at the Cybelle sample store. Her daughter spooned up cereal, Missy curled in her lap as she ate.

"Don't forget we have to buy Caitlin's birthday present tonight," Amber urged as Karyn was making sure her daughter put on a warm, rainproof jacket and remembered to put her homework in her book bag. "You *said* tonight we'd shop."

"I did?"

"Mom . . ."

"I won't forget."

"I want to get her some Barbie stuff."

"Barbie stuff it'll be."

They heard Caitlin pounding on the apartment door, and Amber blew Karyn a kiss and rushed off for her ride to school.

When Karyn left the apartment building, the rain had lessened but wind pushed at her raincoat. Her Tempo was parked underneath the carport, and after she got in, she checked to make sure she had everything with her.

The laptop computer in its black carrying case with the heavy strap. The mini-recorder, which she had already dropped into the pocket of the jacket she wore. She took it out and triple-checked to make sure it ran properly.

Finally, Karyn inspected herself in the visor mirror. Her eyes had violet circles under them, which she'd tried to cover up with a concealer stick. Other than that, she'd worn no makeup. She had pulled her hair back with a clip and assured herself that she looked totally businesslike.

She took I-75 south to I-696, finding herself caught in a crush of bumper-to-bumper morning traffic, made worse by several accidents. She ended up taking the wrong service drive and, because of the heavy traffic, found it difficult to exit.

Finally hurrying into the Goldenrod Room at the Four Towers, Karyn found Lou Hechter sitting alone at a conference table, papers, a briefcase, and his Franklin planner spread out in front of him. He was dressed in an expensive Armani suit and looked extremely well-groomed, the picture of the successful corporate executive.

"What took you so long?" he demanded.

"Traffic and construction, plus I took the wrong exit."

"Didn't Raquel give you a map?" He spoke to her as if she were stupid.

Karyn decided to ignore this remark. She took out the laptop and began setting it up. Lou began briefing her on the meeting. Six people from Ruhnau Bravo were due to arrive. They were "creative honchos," as Lou described them, and were going to do the initial presentation of a whole new advertising line of Cybelle-brand evening wear. No matter what they showed or how much she liked it, Karyn was not to comment and was to keep a poker face.

"No sense letting them see we like it," Lou informed her. "Keeps them worried."

The hotel catering department came in with carafes of coffee, fresh juice, and a selection of mini-pastries, muffins and bagels, while Karyn tried to quell her growing nervousness. Twenty minutes later the "creatives" from Ruhnau Bravo arrived. The four men were dressed in jeans and trendy sports jackets, one woman wore a trouser suit, and the other woman, Patricia Ruhnau, sported skintight purple leather pants, a matching satin blouse and stiletto heels. Her black hair was clipped short, no longer than a half inch in length, and was dyed flat black. Karyn tried not to stare.

"All right, folks, this is Karyn," Lou introduced her, speaking quickly, as if anxious to get on to more important things. "She's my laptop lady."

Karyn flushed at the demeaning way in which she had been introduced.

"Karyn Cristophe," she corrected firmly. "I'm a secretary."

"Hello, Karyn," said Patricia Ruhnau. "Nice to meet you. Hope you're keeping Lou in line. He needs it once in a while." Despite her flashy appearance, Patricia seemed nice.

"Oh, yes," said Karyn, smiling politely.

They broke at 12:30 for lunch, and it was just assumed that Karyn would make her own arrangements. She packed up the laptop and put it back in its carry-bag, afraid someone might pilfer it, and lugged it out to her car. Then she got out the directions Raquel had given her and proceeded to a Chinese restaurant where (Raquel swore) they had sweet-and-sour shrimp to die for.

Pouring plum sauce over an egg roll, Karyn felt herself begin to relax a little. Maybe nothing was going to happen. They would be reconvening at 2:00, and then she'd only have to work until around 4:00, when the meeting would break up.

Which meant she could take Amber out for pizza tonight before they went shopping for Caitlin's birthday present.

"All right, that's done," said Lou when the last agency person had filed out of the meeting room with hearty handshakes and even larger smiles. Lou had actually voiced semiapproval about one of the ads. "Thank God. What a raft of lizards. And did you dig Ms. Purple Leather? She looked like something you'd pick up on the Galápagos Islands. Probably carries her eggs in a pouch."

Karyn stifled a giggle. She had rather liked Patricia, but the leather pants did have a lizardlike texture. "I'll start on these meeting notes first thing on Monday morning," she said.

"Actually, I'd like them now."

"Now? But Raquel told me—"

"I have a dinner meeting later this evening with Dom Carrara, and I want to make the presentation to him tonight. Now, this is what I want. A topline summary of the notes— one page—and then a full transcription of what was said about each of the five ads."

"But I don't have a printer here."

"I've arranged for a laser printer to be put at our disposal. Let's go into the bar and have a drink. I'll fill you in on how I want the report to look, and then you can go up and transcribe the notes."

Karyn had promised to take Amber shopping, and the weather had worsened, which meant the drive home would take longer than she'd planned. She wanted to get started so she could leave. "Mr. Hechter, I really should get started right away if I'm going to finish in time for your dinner with Mr. Carrara."

Lou's dark brown eyes bored into hers. "I don't know about you but I need a drink, and you can't deny me that."

No, she couldn't. She, after all, was his employee

Karyn tried not to show her dismay as she walked behind Lou through the hallways to the lushly carpeted hotel bar, which featured a splashing fountain and enormous skylights hung with plants. Groups of businesspeople were scattered around the room, sipping drinks. Someone laughed, the sound sucked upward by the high ceiling.

"What'll it be?" asked a young, pretty waitress, coming up to their table.

"Scotch and water on the rocks," said Lou.

"Just a Diet Pepsi for me," said Karyn.

Lou acted shocked. "What? No mixed drink? Loosen up a little, Karyn. The lady will have a strawberry margarita—large."

Karyn spoke firmly to the waitress. "The Diet Pepsi will be fine."

Lou looked annoyed but then began gossiping about the ad people who'd been at the meeting. Karyn found herself laughing several times despite her dislike of the man. Lou had a sharp, sarcastic wit. However, he didn't discuss the meeting minutes at all.

Carefully moving her left wrist so that her watch face was visible, she sneaked a look at the time. It was 5:00 already. She was going to be here for hours. Where had they set up this computer anyway? Maybe she should again remind Lou of her purpose in being here.

"All right, time to get busy," Lou finally said before she could speak. He snapped his fingers as if she were a dog. "Time to go upstairs and whip me out a beautiful set of meeting notes."

"Upstairs?"

"Yes, of course. I had the hotel set up a computer and printer in one of the suites. Makes it a little nicer that way. We can order room service if we want, and there's a TV set for me to watch while I wait for you to get done."

"I don't want to go to a hotel room," Karyn blurted. She felt a ripple of fear as she quickly slipped her right hand into her jacket pocket, where she flipped the lever that would turn the mini-cassette recorder on. She hoped she'd done it right and that it wasn't malfunctioning.

"I don't want to go to a hotel room with you," she repeated, for the benefit of the now-running tape.

"Do you think I'm going to have sex with you? Not that I wouldn't like to. And I bet you'd enjoy it, too."

"Please, Mr. Hechter, I just want to finish the work I'm supposed to do."

Lou glared at her. "We're wasting time here, Karyn. Let's go."

Her mouth was dry as she followed Lou out of the bar to the lobby elevator.

The ride up to the twelfth floor seemed to take forever. Karyn nervously studied the floor indicator lights as they flashed upward.

"Did you know that you have beautiful breasts?" Lou said, leaning toward her.

Karyn stepped to the opposite side of the elevator. "I'm just here to transcribe the meeting notes," she said clearly.

"Well, well, and so you are," Lou sneered. "You know, Karyn, I can make your job easy or I can make it hard. Which one will it be?"

"My daughter will be waiting for me at home, and I'd like to get the work done as soon as possible," was all she could think of to say.

The suite was beautiful, the sitting room papered in a lush grasscloth print, with nice upholstered furniture, an oak entertainment center, a small refrigerator, and a floor-to-ceiling view of Southfield and downtown Detroit, the silver ribbon of the Detroit River glittering in the distance. Karyn usually loved high-up views. Ordinarily she would have oohed and aahed at the view, running to the window and trying to pick out familiar landmarks.

Instead, all she could do was stare at the round table on which a Gateway 2000 computer had been set up, with an HP Laserjet 4si printer.

"I told you," said Lou, smirking. "I told you there was a printer here. You should learn to trust your superiors a little more, Karyn."

Karyn nodded curtly and went to sit down in front of the computer, quickly calling up Microsoft Word, then inserting the disk she'd made of the day's meeting notes. In a few seconds she had her notes on the screen. Fortunately, she had typed them in coherent English, so now all she had to do was scroll down what she had typed, change some of the wording, reformat, and run spell check. She would print out the detailed notes first, she decided, then use them to write the topline summary Lou wanted.

She set to work, slipping her hand in her pocket when Lou wasn't looking to turn the tape recorder off again. The tape was only 120 minutes long, and she was afraid she'd use it all up on the sounds of keyboarding.

Meanwhile, Lou roamed around the sitting room, opening the refrigerator, then pacing into the bathroom, after which she heard the loud spray of urine hitting water, then the flush of the toilet. Karyn shuddered in revulsion, remembering his other bathroom display when he had been in his office. She sped up her typing, taking shortcuts, anything to complete this and get out of here.

When Lou emerged from the bathroom, he had taken off his tie and unbuttoned the top three buttons of his shirt. Good heavens, he was wearing a gold chain like guys in the 1970s. Karyn couldn't imagine anything cheesier. She began to feel increasing vibrations of anxiety.

She stopped typing and reached for the phone, dialing Jinny Caribaldi.

"I'm going to be home in about an hour, Jinny. I'm finishing up here. But if you need to reach me I'm in Room 1244 of the Four Towers."

"Everything okay?" inquired her upstairs neighbor, her voice sounding concerned.

"I'm not sure."

"Look, Karyn, don't be stupid. Hurry and finish up and get out of there. Amber's fine and I'm feeding her and Caitlin leftover spaghetti."

Karyn finished her conversation with Jinny and hung up. Lou was now restlessly clicking through channels with the remote. He had made himself a drink from the room bar—his fourth of the night. Karyn finished the basic notes, printed them, then opened a fresh document for the summary.

She could type over a hundred words per minute, and planned to whiz through the summary in ten minutes or less. Then she was out of here.

Karyn stood by the printer waiting for it to spit out the last few pages. It was then that she heard the noise at her side, a faint, metallic sound. Turning, she saw that Lou held a pair of small, gold sewing scissors. The sound had been him snicking the blades on air.

"Scissors?" Karyn blurted.

"Come on, Karyn. It's just a fantasy."

Karyn suppressed a cry, backing away from Lou and thrusting her hand into her jacket pocket, fumbling wildly for the on-off lever of the mini-recorder.

Lou moved toward her, brandishing the scissors.

"I'm going to cut your clothes off," he told her.

Gasping, Karyn dodged backward, instinctively hitting out at the scissors, which fell to the floor. Papers scattered too as she dropped the report pages.

"Leave me alone!" Karyn yelled, praying the recorder was on.

Suddenly, Lou grabbed her by her hair, dragging her into the adjoining bedroom. Karyn screamed and fought him, but he was too strong, his grip on her hair agonizingly painful.

"Bitch!" he roared. "Cock teaser! You've been flirting with me for months. So give it up to me or don't come to work on Monday."

"No . . . please!"

He threw her on the bed, pulling his zipper open. Instinctively, Karyn bent her knees to her chest, then kicked out, her shoes catching Lou in the chest.

"Christ!" he shouted hoarsely, staggering back.

"Don't you touch me!" she yelled.

He was on top of her again. "Give it, give it, do you think

it's that precious? I've had a lot better. Do it if you want a job on Monday, little bitch."

Karyn pushed and struggled, choking back sobs. He was going to rape her—all because she'd been a fool, arrogantly thinking she could tape-record him.

She fought underneath him, managing to get her right hand down between their bodies. She found something hairy and disgustingly soft, and squeezed it as hard as she could, her fingernails digging deep into Lou's testicles.

As Lou screamed a high-pitched yelp of agony, Karyn gave him a shove and rolled off the bed. She raced across the room, grabbing up her shoulder bag from the table.

"You hurt me, you hurt me," whimpered Lou as she slammed the door.

Lou Hechter recovered himself, wincing with pain as he hastily pulled up his pants and adjusted his zipper. He wiped his watering eyes. Jesus, his balls hurt. The pain had been excruciating. Had she damaged him?

He staggered out of the room, hurrying toward the elevator, his heart pounding sickly. Had he misjudged? Had he been a total fool? His only hope was to chase after the bitch and put fear into her. Otherwise—

But then Lou blocked the consequences out of his mind. Nothing bad was going to happen. He was a vice president, for Christ's sake. Stock options, two lease cars, five weeks' vacation yearly, the premium benefits plan, a retirement pay equal to 85 percent of his current income, plus a sizable bonus . . .

There were two elevators, and he noticed that the number indicator on the right one was already at ground level. It had to be Karyn, he thought furiously. The little bitch, she'd outrun him.

He smacked the Down button, pushing it repeatedly, then pacing back and forth like a man demented, until the elevator finally arrived. Two women were standing in it, one middle-aged, the other one elderly. They shrank against the back wall as Lou strode into the enclosure, hitting the Door Close button, then the Main Floor button.

Lou stood facing the door, smelling the sour perspiration rising from his body, mixing unpleasantly with the vanilla-scented aftershave he'd worn. Too late, he realized that his tie was loose and one of his shirttails was hanging out.

"What are you staring at?" he barked at the hapless women passengers.

As soon as the doors started to slide open, Lou rushed out, running toward the exit.

He hurried into the parking lot, but it was large and extended around three sides of the high-rise tower complex. He had no idea which direction Karyn had gone, nor did he know what her car looked like.

The bitch! How could he have let it get out of control like this?

Driving home, Karyn felt sick with fear. She alternately cried and gritted her teeth, clenching the steering wheel so tightly that her fingers hurt. Every time she thought of the feel of Lou's baggy testicles in her fingers, she wanted to throw up. She kept wiping her hands on her skirt as if they were contaminated.

He'd tried to rape her! And nearly succeeded.

She hadn't had time to see if the incident had been recorded on the tape. She'd been too frightened, wanting only to get out of there.

Her job . . . her wonderful job . . . it was gone. Totally wrecked.

How could they possibly keep her on after what had happened? There was no way she could continue to work anywhere near Lou Hechter after this horrible incident. She'd have to quit like those other women, assuming he didn't fire her first, which seemed very likely.

Back to being an ordinary secretary making less than

$18,000 a year. She'd never be able to support Amber alone on that kind of money. She'd have to borrow from her father, who really couldn't afford to help her. Get a second job on weekends in addition to a regular one, or else go back to Mack for child support and risk having him stalking them again, ruining their peace of mind.

No, she told herself, suppressing a sob. She wasn't going to give up that easily. She couldn't. And there was still the possibility of a lawsuit settlement or even an award of several million, as Malia had hinted could be hers.

The late rush hour traffic was even worse than she'd imagined. The icy rain had caused several fender-benders. Karyn found herself sitting at a standstill, caught in gridlock.

Cilla. Could Cilla possibly help her? She was her supervisor . . . she'd have to.

But then Karyn expelled her breath, remembering her previous unsatisfactory conversation with Cilla Westheim.

As usual, there'd been no witnesses. She had no proof, unless the tape recorder had been turned on. And right now, she didn't know if it had been. She'd been so scared, and her hands had been shaking so violently . . .

Karyn arrived home late, and Jinny's mother was already there in her role as baby-sitter while Jinny worked at the hospital.

"Are you all right, dear?" said the woman when she greeted Karyn at the door.

"I . . . I'm fine," Karyn lied, realizing her hair was a mess and her eyes were swollen from crying. "Just coming down with a flu bug, I think."

"Push fruit juices and chicken soup," advised Jinny's mother, waving good-bye to Amber.

"Mom, are we goin' shopping?" asked Amber eagerly as they were descending the stairs to their own apartment.

"What?"

"Caitlin's *birthday present*. We're gonna get her some Barbie stuff, remember?"

With dulled surprise, Karyn remembered her promise to take her daughter shopping. And wasn't there something about tickets to an ice-skating show at the Palace on Sunday? All of that seemed to have happened in another lifetime, to another Karyn.

"Mommy?" cried Amber. "Aren't you listening?"

"I'm listening, cupcake. We'll go shopping, yes. We'll go over to Kmart, all right?"

A "Big K" store was near their apartment, would be fast and easy, and doing a little Kmart shopping would be a red flag in Lou's face, Karyn thought disjointedly, trying not to break down in front of her daughter. Maybe she ought to buy herself a couple of outfits there, too—something really loud, she thought, fury overwhelming her. Let Lou give her a hundred rusty safety pins.

How could a company keep a man like him on the payroll? Didn't they know what he was like . . . or care?

Before they left for Kmart, Karyn went into the bathroom, locked the door, and took the mini-cassette player out of her jacket pocket. The On button was still on, she noticed, her heart slamming. Had the recorder worked?

She was breathing shallowly as she rewound the tape, turned the volume down to low and pressed Play.

"I don't want to go to a hotel room with you." That was her voice, the first section of the tape. Karyn expelled her breath and played a few minutes of it, then fast-forwarded to the next section.

"I'm going to cut your clothes off." That was Lou's voice, deeper, sexually charged, yet still recognizable as his.

Karyn shuddered, reliving her terror. She rubbed her aching eyes and cried silently, so that Amber couldn't hear her through the walls.

Grimly, tears still rolling down her cheeks, she played enough of the rest of the microcasette tape to make sure she had everything. Tonight, after Amber was in bed, she'd make extra copies. She wasn't sure how . . . maybe she'd play the tape to a regular tape recorder. She did have one in the hall closet. The copy might not be perfect, but Lou's voice would still be recognizable, she felt positive.

Stripping off her clothes, Karyn stepped into the shower and turned on the water full-blast. More tears streamed out of her eyes, joining the hot, sluicing water as she washed every last trace of Lou Hechter from her skin.

He was going to pay for what he had done . . . big-time.

The shopping trip turned out to be less than perfect. Karyn's upset nerves had infected Amber, who acted up when Karyn said she couldn't afford to buy two Barbie outfits and a plastic horse, in addition to some Pokémon cards Amber spotted.

Amber pouted as they stood in the checkout line. Karyn hadn't had the heart to buy a "revenge" outfit after all.

They drove home, and Karyn told Amber she could wrap the package if she wanted to.

"Are you crabby, Mom?" her daughter asked as she was putting six times as much tape on the package as was necessary.

"I . . . I guess so, honey," Karyn admitted. "I had a bad day."

"I wish we could've bought Caitlin that other outfit, too."

Karyn felt a stab of guilt. She might be jobless very soon, and all extras, including birthday presents, would have to go. "We couldn't afford it, Amber."

"But I wanted—"

"Caitlin's going to be very happy with what we did get her," said Karyn firmly, feeling as if she wanted to scream.

She managed to get Amber into bed by 9:30, kissing her good-night and telling her she loved her.

"Are we poor?" Amber wanted to know, snuggling into her Pocahontas sheets.

Karyn's heart felt as if it had been stabbed. "Cupcake, we're not going to be poor. I'm going to take good care of us. Don't you worry about it."

She hugged her daughter and they nuzzled faces, just as they'd always done since Amber was a toddler. Karyn again vowed to herself that she'd do what she had to, no matter what it took.

At 10:00, Karyn tiptoed back down the hall, making sure that Amber was sleeping, before she dialed Malia Roberts at the home number the attorney had written on the back of her business card.

Malia picked up on the first ring. "This is Malia Roberts."

Karyn felt a vast wave of relief just to hear the attorney's cheerful drawl. "Malia . . . it's Karyn Cristophe. I . . . I got the tape."

"Good, that's wonderful, but what happened? Your voice sounds awful. Are you all right?"

Karyn uttered a bleak, nervous giggle. "He . . . tried to rape me."

"Oh, my dear."

"He was all over me, yelling about how I had to cooperate and screw him or I wouldn't have a job on Monday. I squeezed his balls and he let go of me, though. I ran out of there. Do you want a copy of the tape?"

"I certainly do," said Malia. "In fact, can you drop it off at my office tomorrow morning first thing?"

"I think I can. I'll have to get someone to watch Amber, though. Maybe my neighbor can do it. I've used her so much but . . . I won't be able to stay long, either. My daughter's going to a birthday party in the afternoon and I promised I'd help."

"We don't have a receptionist on Saturdays, and a card-lock system is in use, but there's a house phone by the door. Use that. My extension's on my card." Malia added, "And, Karyn—make some copies of that tape right now. Give one to your neighbor for safekeeping, keep one for yourself, and bring one for me. Oh, and one more thing. Do you need to see a rape counselor? I have the names of several if you need to talk to someone about this."

"A rape . . ." Karyn shuddered. "I don't think so. I don't want to spend the money right now."

"Okay, but I could get you one who works on ability to pay."

"I know, but . . . it'll just make me feel like a victim," Karyn blurted.

By the time Karyn had finished making the copies it was well after midnight. She felt drained, wrung out from the dreadful day. She took an over-the-counter pill that promised "restful sleep," but it didn't do anything for her.

She lay awake most of the night, staring into the darkness. These horrible things might have happened but she was not going to think or feel like a victim. She was going to fight back—whatever she had to do.

On Saturday morning when she explained to Jinny what had happened, her friend offered to have Amber come upstairs immediately and she would give her breakfast.

Karyn's voice broke. "Jinny . . . I can't thank you enough."

"I've seen rape victims in the emergency room, Karyn. Thank God he didn't injure you physically. If there's *anything* I can do, if you just want to talk . . . Oh, Karyn, I hope this lawyer is half as good as you say she is."

"Me, too."

Half an hour later Karyn was pulling into the parking lot of the high rise where Malia had her office. As instructed, she phoned Malia in the lobby of the law firm, and in a few minutes the attorney came out to greet her, her full figure clothed in a pair of jeans and a long, flowing gold tunic. Malia wore a bronzy makeup that accented her dark features.

"Are you holding up?" said Malia, gazing at Karyn sharply.

"I'm here, aren't I?"

They walked through the firm, passing several offices where attorneys were working, and entered Malia's office.

"All right," said Malia. "First, tell me again if you're all right. Did you see a doctor?"

"No."

"It would have been better if you had. Did you make a complaint to the security staff at the hotel where you were?"

"No, I . . . I just had to get out of there."

"And I'm sure you showered about ten times. Never mind," said Malia. "Most rape victims don't report it, they feel too violated and ashamed. I was raped when I was fourteen, and I never told a damn soul. That rapist is the father of my daughter. Maybe he's why I'm the way I am right now. I don't trust men much, as you might have noticed. Anyway, girlfriend, how about if we play this tape of yours and I can hear what's on it?"

Karyn played the tape for Malia, pushing Stop when they reached the door slamming, when she'd run out of the room. Hearing it all over again seared her emotions, and by the time the tape was finished Karyn was again shaking.

"Are you all right? Do you want coffee, or a glass of water?"

"No. I'm fine. I didn't turn it off," Karyn explained. "I was too scared. I just ran for the parking lot."

"Mmmm, this is powerful stuff." Malia paused. "Okay. Here's what can happen. We have to play the tape for some of the executives at Cybelle—they have to know what their supervisory person is doing. If Lou retaliates, or the company retaliates in any way for what you've just reported— or even if they don't—" Malia grinned widely. "Bingo, woman! We have a serious lawsuit."

Karyn stared at the attorney. "You mean . . . we're going to *hope* he retaliates?"

"Yes. If he's gonna play the game, we are, too. Are you still willing to go through with this?"

Karyn thought of Amber's question last night. *Are we poor?* And she thought of the assurances she'd made to her daughter that she would take care of them. Karyn had broken free of Mack . . . she'd gambled by coming north to Michigan . . . now she could not let Amber down.

"I'm going to do whatever I have to," she repeated.

"Just so you can have this thought in your head," Malia interjected. "Suppose we do file suit. We could ask for as much as fifteen or twenty million dollars in punitive damages."

Karyn stared at her, too stunned to speak. That kind of money was almost beyond her comprehension. Her father had earned a living as a finish carpenter, and her mother worked in a doctor's office as an insurance specialist. They basically lived from paycheck to paycheck.

"But," Malia went on, "the odds of us actually collecting twenty million are not that high. The big tort lawsuit is a gamble—a form of lottery, really. It depends on a lot of factors, like how good a case we can build, how well the jury believes you, and how angry they get at Lou Hechter."

"I see."

"In fact, our real payoff may come if the company decides to settle for a sizable amount just so they won't garner any national publicity about this. Women aren't going to like learning that a glamour store like Cybelle harasses and nearly rapes its female employees. Those types of stores depend heavily on women customers, and they won't want to look bad."

Twenty million dollars . . . the money still didn't sound even remotely real to Karyn. And according to Malia, it probably wasn't.

"Getting some money would be good, yes," she finally said. "But Lou has to pay. I want him stopped; I want him fired from Cybelle."

"Don't worry, dear. He will be. He doesn't have a prayer there after people hear this tape. Now, here's what I want you to do. . . ."

THREE

KARYN GOT THROUGH THE WEEKEND ON AUTOPILOT. THE birthday party, the sweet giggling girls, the happy ritual of pizza, birthday cake, and the tearing open of presents. When Jinny hugged her as the party was ending, Karyn had to force back a sob.

"You'll be okay, Karyn. You're one of the strongest women I've ever met."

"I don't feel strong."

"You are, though."

Karyn wanted to call Raquel, but another part of her didn't. She knew Raquel was going to feel terrible when she learned what had happened, yet a small part of Karyn couldn't help blaming Raquel for getting her into this. Why hadn't Raquel been more explicit in warning her? But then she remembered that Raquel had thought Karyn would be leaving at 4:00 . . . she hadn't known, either, the events that would unfold.

Karyn also didn't call Roger. She'd be seeing him on Sunday afternoon, and she'd decide then whether or not to tell him about the attempted rape.

By Sunday Karyn was feeling ragged from lack of sleep, but she was determined to fulfill her obligations.

Amber loved the colorful ice-skating exhibition, which included not only Tara Lipinski but a roster of other skating stars. By the time they were back in the car, driving south on Opdyke Road from the Palace, the nine-year-old had already fallen asleep in the backseat, tired out from the long day.

When they reached the apartment building, Roger carried Amber into the building. While he waited in the living room,

Karyn undressed her daughter and put her to bed.

"All right," said Roger, when Karyn had brought him a cup of coffee. "Now, please tell me why you've been so upset since Friday. Something is wrong. I know you; I can feel it."

"It's—" Then Karyn stopped, unsure whether or not to continue. It was one thing to tell Malia—another woman— about the rape, but to tell a man . . . And what if Roger asked to listen to the tape? She couldn't bear it.

"It's about that SOB Lou Hechter, isn't it?" Roger demanded.

"How did you know?"

"Because you always get upset when his name is mentioned. Most people wouldn't see it, but I do. That meeting down in Southfield you went to on Friday . . . something happened there."

Reluctantly, Karyn nodded. "He . . . he harassed me again," she admitted. "It was . . . pretty bad, Roger."

"Bad? How bad?"

"He—it was an attempted rape," she said through dry lips.

"Oh, Karyn. Oh, darling. My God. That bastard. Were you hurt?"

"No. I fought him off."

"Thank God." Color rose to Roger's face, then receded, leaving his face pale. His lips had tightened and his eyes flashed with anger.

"I was able to tape-record it all, and I have the tape. I'm going to play it for Cilla on Monday morning," she explained.

Roger looked even more troubled. "Karyn . . . oh, Karyn. You do know that Lou and Cilla have a thing going? At least that's what gossip says."

"I know that."

"What if she plays that tape for him? Honey, if he tried

to rape you, then he's a violent man ... rape is all about power."

"So is harassment," Karyn said dryly.

"Suppose there's more violence? You could be triggering a very ugly thing."

Karyn drew in her breath. "Roger, it already is ugly. I can't let this go. I have too much at stake."

His voice shook. "Karyn, I just don't want anything to happen to you. It would kill me if anything happened to you."

Overcome, he leaned forward, pulling her to him. Karyn clung to him, and then the sobs came. He held her and murmured, and stroked her hair, which was dampened with tears, and still she kept on crying and couldn't stop.

Just as Roger was getting ready to leave, the phone rang. Karyn took the call in her bedroom. She could see on the Caller ID that the caller was Lou Hechter.

"Hello?"

"So, have you calmed down a bit?"

She slammed the phone down.

"Everything okay?" Roger asked when Karyn returned to the living room.

"It was ... him. I hung up on him. I just want to get this over with," Karyn added miserably.

"Darling. If there is anything I can do to help, anything, I want you to let me know. And I'm going to loan you my cell phone. I want you to carry it in your purse, just in case you run into any problems."

Karyn agreed to carry the cell phone. She kissed Roger good-night and promised to have lunch with him tomorrow in the cafeteria—if she still had a job. She still felt so numb ... so battered emotionally. Like a victim.

She wondered when she would ever feel normal again.

Cilla and Shane lay in bed, their bodies still lightly sheened with perspiration after some athletic lovemaking that had made Cilla feel almost thirty again. Her pelvis still throbbed from her two orgasms, and all of her thoughts were pleasant—a big change from the supercharged way her mind usually felt these days.

"Happy?" murmured Shane.

"Oh, yes. With you, here and now. I feel like I'm floating in a beautiful and safe bubble with only the two of us in it."

"That's how lovemaking is supposed to be."

"But so often it isn't."

"Hey." Gently he touched her jawline, turning her face toward his. "All that 'so often it isn't' stuff doesn't apply to us, Cilla. The average way that average people express themselves, the statistics of making love one-point-eight times a week, all of that . . . why should we listen to and believe that nonsense? What we have is unique. It's special. It's what only you and I have, and nobody can take that away from us."

"Life can take it away from us, Shane. All the pressures." Cilla rolled aside, propping a pillow underneath her head. "Sometimes I feel as if I've lived the last three years of my life under the highest kind of pressure. Fighting it, fighting it. And now I'm wound up so tightly . . ."

"Not that tightly." He began kissing her neck, butterfly kisses that drifted warmly over her skin. "As long as you have me there'll always be a pressure valve, Cilla. I'll be your pressure valve. And your lover and your best friend and your—"

"Oh, God!" She felt a swift rush of tears to her eyes and quickly swiped a hand across her face. Everything Shane said . . . she wanted it so badly. Maybe too badly. Things had changed for her so much recently, and she had this horrid, instinctive feeling . . . it was going to get much worse.

* * *

Light snow had been predicted for Monday—the season's first snow. The morning drive to Cybelle seemed to take forever. Karyn had put a copy of the tape into one of the pockets of her shoulder bag.

Caught in the long line of vehicles waiting to turn into the Cybelle parking lot, she chafed impatiently, wanting only to reach work, get this nightmare over with. It was somewhat of a shock to walk into the department and see it functionally normally. Everyone was in their morning mode, drinking coffee, eating bagels or doughnuts, killing time before actually starting work. Was it only her life that had been turned upside down?

"You sick?" Raquel greeted her. "You look positively green."

"Just didn't sleep much last night," Karyn admitted, rubbing her burning eyes.

"Hey, lunch today? Unless you're eating with Roger."

"Yeah, I promised I'd eat with Roger."

"You *sure* you're okay?" questioned her friend. "You didn't break up with him or anything, did you?"

"No, everything's fine with Roger." Karyn longed to tell Raquel everything, but she couldn't—not until she'd played the tape for Cilla.

Walking to her own alcove, she encountered Lou in the hallway.

"Good morning, Miss Karyn," he practically chirruped. "Snow's predicted for tonight—maybe six to eight inches."

The way he said it, *six to eight inches.*

She felt taken aback, unsure how to respond. Finally she nodded, feeling as if she'd stepped through the looking glass into some strangely askew Alice world. This was the way it worked, wasn't it? The man was all over you one day and then the next you were supposed to make small talk about the "weather," if that was really the topic at all.

She changed her mind about going to her desk, visiting the women's room instead.

Snap out of it, she ordered herself, wiping her forehead and upper lip with a damp paper towel.

Cilla was leafing through a copy of *Women's Wear Daily,* studying photos of garments that would be appearing in stores the following summer ... white knee pants, Capri-length pants, negligee-inspired dresses in shimmery, pastel satins. There was a little lavender bias-cut dress from Bisou Bisou by Michele Bohbot that Cybelle customers might love—

Cilla glanced up to see her secretary knocking at her door. "Cilla?"

"Yes, come in, Karyn."

Karyn Cristophe entered Cilla's office. Her face looked pale, her eyes huge. She was dressed in a dark green twill jacket and a long beige skirt, a dark green silk blouse completing the outfit. She carried her shoulder bag protectively across her chest. Cilla felt a sudden twist of apprehension in her gut.

"Is anything wrong?" she couldn't help asking.

"Is it all right if I close the door?"

"Certainly," Cilla said, an awful feeling coming over her.

Karyn closed the office door, giving them privacy. She then sat down in a chair and reached into the purse, pulling out a mini-cassette player.

She moistened her lips. "Cilla, you know I came to you about Lou before. I tried to take your advice and stay out of his way, because I love this job and I want to keep it, but I was advised to start keeping a journal of his ... approaches to me. And on Friday afternoon I made this tape. I'd like to play it for you."

Oh, God ... Lou had done something terrible, Cilla just knew. But she was through running from this, cowering in fear. Maybe it was her talk with Mindy, maybe it was just that she'd simply had enough.

"Please," she whispered through bloodless lips. "If you would play it. I'd like to hear it."

When the tape had finished, Cilla felt weak with revulsion. It was Cilla's own, personal nightmare, right there on tape, only it was happening to another woman, not her.

"That's the extent of it?" she managed to say, getting to her feet. She walked over to the window and stood staring out at the reflecting pond. Because of the season, the spraying fountain had been shut down and the water was grayish, partially frozen. Cilla's body felt damp with perspiration underneath the elegant suit she wore.

"It's what happened. It's all there," Karyn said, her voice low.

Cilla stared downward at the pond.

This tape. It was vile. Worse than vile. If Lou ever learned about the recording that Karyn had made, he would be enraged.

Karyn would be fired, of course—or, if Lou couldn't make that stick, he would be sure to have her transferred and demoted.

Lou was going to get away with his tricks yet another time, Cilla thought. And it would go on and on with other women who were yet to be hired, until Lou retired or quit. Even in retirement he'd probably find some woman to torment, she thought tiredly.

"Did you make copies of this?" she asked her assistant, walking back to her desk and sinking into her chair. Karyn's face looked so white.

"Yes, I've made several."

"Good. May I keep this one?"

"Yes." Karyn expelled her breath. "Cilla, I have to be very, very honest with you. I'm seeing an attorney about filing a sexual harassment suit. This tape might not be admissible in court, but my lawyer told me to get it anyway. I'm not sure how it can be used but . . ."

Cilla breathed fast, trying to absorb everything at once.

A sexual harassment suit! Oh, the upper management at Cybelle would not be pleased about that one. Companies like Cybelle that had deep pockets lived in fear of litigation, and this one could end up costing them heavily, especially if Karyn could prove her allegations and get other witnesses to testify.

"I think I can figure out a way to use the tape," she heard herself say. "And can I have the recorder for a while?"

"Of course." The younger woman was gazing at Cilla with wide, anxious eyes. "I love my job," Karyn blurted. "I love working with you . . . you're the best boss I ever had. I just want you to know that."

Cilla felt absurdly touched. She reached out and clasped Karyn's hand. "I love having you work for me. Karyn, I—" But then she cut off what she had been about to say. "I'll see to it that very good use is made of this tape. And you don't have to worry. As long as I have a job here, I'll do everything I can to protect your job, too. That's a solemn promise."

Later, after Karyn left the office, Cilla reclosed the door and sat alone at her desk. She let all of her calls go on voice mail. Picking up the cassette recorder, she turned it over in her hands, feeling sick.

She sat that way for a long time. Finally she picked up her phone again.

Karyn left Cilla's office, her forehead beaded with perspiration. Cilla's face had been so shocked, then repelled, as she'd listened to the tape. But at least her supervisor now had the tape, and the ball was in Cilla's court.

What was going to happen now? Karyn was almost afraid to find out.

Feeling too upset to work, she walked down to the company's smaller, snack cafeteria, and ordered a chocolate-and-vanilla-swirl yogurt, smothering it with chunks of Heath

Bar. But sitting down at a table, she was unable to take more than two or three bites.

Nothing was going to be the same after today, she thought. How could it be? Pushing away the dish of yogurt, she felt her eyes glaze with tears.

Sondra Zapernick listened to her voice mail message, at first startled, then stunned.

It began simply enough, with Cilla Westheim's crisp, businesslike voice. "Ladies and gentlemen, I'm forwarding a tape of an incident that happened on Friday at one of our company-sponsored meetings held at the Four Towers Hotel in Southfield. You'll recognize the voice of one of our own top executives, I'm sure. Please listen and draw your own conclusions. I'm sure you'll have some."

The next voice Sondra heard was that of Lou Hechter.

When the tape was done playing, Sondra sat shivering, remembering a day long ago, when she'd first come to work at another company as a nineteen-year-old secretary. A salesman named Wayne had tried to pin her against a wall, reaching his hand into her blouse. Sondra had fought him off, but she had not reported his behavior. Back then, no one had ever heard of sexual harassment. Sondra had been afraid that if she complained her boss and others would think she had somehow invited the behavior.

She sat for a minute thinking, and then she reached into her Rolodex, pulling out the card where she kept Dom Carrara's many phone numbers—his home, car, pager, boat, cottage, his condo, modem, the numbers of his children.

Dom had just left the previous morning for his condo on Siesta Key, where he planned to play golf, do some beachcombing with his wife, Lee, and take the grandchildren to Disney World.

Sondra found the correct number and punched it into her phone.

"Hello?" came the voice of the company CEO, sounding cheerful and relaxed.

"Dom, this is Sondra," she began. "I've received a very disturbing voice mail message and I'd like you to hear it in its entirety."

"What is it?"

"I'll forward the message into your voice mail here at Cybelle. Call here and play it back," she told him. "And, Dom—I think Cilla Westheim did the right thing in letting you know what was going on. I would have done the same thing if I had been her."

There. Sondra knew all the political games that were rampant in any corporate setting, and she also knew that because of her longevity and position here, Dom often considered her opinions before making an important decision. She hung up with a feeling of satisfaction.

She liked Cilla Westheim. She had liked Karyn Cristophe, too.

And if Sondra liked someone, that had weight.

Vic Rondelli, former CEO of Cybelle and now a titular chairman of the board, was semiretired because of a heart condition and only came into the office once or twice a week for a few hours. Today he was in his large office on the executive floor, wading through his E-mail and voice mail, which was about all he had time to do anymore. Right now he was listening to his voice mail on speakerphone with a sense of shock.

"You waved that tail at me. This is what you want, swee-tie."

It was Lou Hechter, all right. Vic knew that voice as well as he knew his own brother-in-law's. Vic had played about a thousand rounds of golf with Lou. He'd also covered up a few of Lou's "misadventures." Vic took care of his friends and expected them to take care of him as well.

Vic finished playing the message, then dialed Lou Hechter's private line.

"Hey, buddy. I'm forwarding you a voice mail message, a hot one. Better listen good, and hey, tell them it was all consensual. Tell them she's into kinky games. Then fire her little ass, and fire Cilla Westheim, too."

Lou had been feeling uneasy all weekend.

He'd had two meetings this morning, but his mind wasn't on them, and he excused himself from the last one, saying he had scheduled a conference call. Walking back to his office, he could feel his head beginning to throb. Was it his blood pressure again? Stress made Lou's BP rocket upward, but he assured himself that he would have the Karyn situation under control soon.

As he entered his office, Lou saw that his phone message light was blinking. He automatically put the call on speaker as he always did.

When he heard Cilla's voice, he felt a chill. When he realized that the message was about him, the chill became a shudder. He switched the phone off speaker, gripping the receiver with damp hands.

There were sounds of struggling, and muffled sobs.

"No . . ." Karyn's voice cried out. *"Don't you touch me!"*

And more. The sounds ugly, graphic. Even his own high-pitched scream when she'd pinched his testicles.

Lou drew a deep breath, fighting panic.

The bitch must have been wired. She'd audiotaped him!

Sweat began to pour freely down Lou's body, soaking his clothes. It ran down the creases of his neck, wetting his shirt collar. He started to play the next message, discovering it was the same thing, forwarded from Cilla. Jesus, who else had Cilla sent it to?

Lou mopped the sweat with an oversized tissue he kept in a box in his drawer.

Damage control, he thought.

He shoved back his chair and lunged to his feet, heading in the direction of Cilla's office. But when he got there, her computer had been turned off, and so were the lights.

She was gone.

Furious, Lou dialed her home phone and left a message on her answering machine. "Get me every last fucking copy of that tape, Cilla, and FedEx it to me at home today, or you'll be in more trouble than you ever dreamed possible."

Cilla drove out of the Cybelle parking lot with a squeal of tires, her breath coming fast.

Nervously she wondered if Lou had played back his voice mail yet. Maybe she shouldn't have sent it to him, too, but the temptation had been irresistible. She'd wanted him to be humiliated—to suffer, as she'd suffered. Let him worry who she'd sent it to. Let him obsess.

Let him panic.

She felt too adrenalized to go home yet, and she didn't want to face Lou's message on her home answering tape, his vituperations. She knew there'd be plenty.

She stopped at a Thai restaurant in Rochester and ate lunch, then forced herself to call her home number, where she accessed the machine with her remote code and listened to three messages Lou had left on the tape. He'd been yelling so loud some of the words were unintelligible, but she got the gist of it. He wanted the tape immediately or she'd pay dearly. Interspersed with this threat were words like *bitch, cunt* and *slut*. And he was screaming something about consensual sex.

Cilla shivered, hearing the rage in her boss's voice. Was it really possible he believed himself to be a wronged victim? Didn't he realize the heinous things he had done? If he did not, then it was sad and sick and terrible.

She was unable to finish her meal, and refused coffee, paying her check with a credit card, then leaving the restaurant. She began driving around aimlessly. Rochester Hills was an upscale community with huge new homes going up, boasting three- and four-car garages, often shoehorned on too-small lots. In one of these new subdivisions, two little girls were playing with their dog in a driveway. Both were blond curly-heads as Mindy had been.

Cilla reached for her cell phone and dialed her daughter at the dorm in Albion.

"I did it, Mindy. I . . . I took action."

"Against that creepy Lou guy? Way to go, Mom. What did you do?"

"My secretary brought me a cassette tape she'd made when Lou . . . tried to rape her after a meeting. I sent it out as a voice mail to several people in the corporation, including Dom Carrara and Vic Rondelli. I also sent a copy to Lou," admitted Cilla.

"No *way*. . . . Really? Oh, Mom . . ." Mindy sounded both proud and scared. "Mom, if he's that awful, are you going to be okay? I mean, what if he gets mad at you?"

"He's probably very mad, sweetie. He wants me to FedEx him copies of the tape and I'm not going to."

"Well, lock all your doors and put the security system on," said her daughter, sounding much like Cilla. "And, Mom, call me if you need me. I can always drive home; it wouldn't take that long."

Cilla was touched by Mindy's concern. "He's not going to hurt me, baby. I promise you that. Lou Hechter's days are numbered at Cybelle, and that, I'm telling you, will hurt him more than anything else I could possibly devise."

Cilla's nerves felt too jangled to go home right now. She passed a sign for the Star Theater in Rochester Hills and decided to see a movie. A flick with Sandra Bullock in it. Just what she needed to unwind for two hours.

When she finally pulled into her condo complex and started playing back her phone messages she found another one from Lou, equally vituperative, and one from Shane.

"It's all over the company, Cilla—that tape you sent of Lou. Bravo for you. I love you more than ever."

She called him back at work, and they spent a few minutes rehashing the event and its ramifications. "I have a bad feeling about this," Cilla said. "Lou can be very, very vengeful. I know him. He's out of control."

"Well, Lou is also going to have to watch his ass legally now," Shane pointed out.

Cilla frowned. "Lou's never been one for following rules, Shane. It's part of his whole charisma thing. And he's got a lot of friends at Cybelle still."

"Well, be very careful, Cil . . . and don't show up at work until tomorrow morning. Maybe by then Lou will have cooled down a little."

Cilla drew in her breath. "I don't think that's too likely to happen. And maybe I should go in again myself, just to give a show of strength here. I don't want people to think I've run off and am afraid."

After they'd finished the call, she went into the bathroom and combed her hair back from her face, applying "power makeup" to her eyes and mouth, and changing her jacket to a more assertive-looking black one.

It was 1:00 P.M.

Karyn was in the copy room making multiple, stapled copies of a report Annie Fiacci had asked her to duplicate, when Lou appeared in the doorway. His face was flushed a deep, unhealthy red.

"In my office," he snapped. "Now." He made a beckoning motion, then shook his forefinger at her in a threatening manner.

Karyn's heart rate suddenly speeded. Oh, God . . . Somehow he'd heard the tape.

She followed him down the corridor to his office. A couple of administrative assistants from another department were passing by, and they said "Hi" to Karyn, greeting her in a friendly manner. They knew nothing of the torment she was in. Karyn managed to say "Hi" back. She felt like a death row prisoner being walked down the hall to be given a lethal injection.

"Close the door," Lou snapped as they entered his big corner office.

Karyn defiantly left it open, continuing to stand as Lou sat down on the corner of his desk, as he often did, keeping his head high in order to dominate whoever was in the office.

"Sit," he ordered her.

Numbly she continued to stand.

"All right, if you won't obey orders," he snapped. "Miss Karyn, there have been some major problems with your employment here."

"There certainly have been," she began. "On Friday, down at the hotel in Southfield, you—"

"Kinky sex," he snapped.

"What?"

"You love to play your little scenarios, don't you? Asking a man to pretend to rape you."

She stared at him, stunned at the accusation, which came to her out of left field, so totally unlike the real circumstances that she could only gasp. "It wasn't like that—"

"You are a sex tease, Karyn. You were from the first day you got here. Dressed in sexy skirts with a long slit. Teasing and leading a man on, acting like you were eager and willing. Then luring me into that hotel room . . ."

"Luring you?" Karyn felt a hard jolt of anger. She wished she still had the recorder but Cilla had kept it. "I didn't lure you! You told me to go into that room to type up notes. I did that. When I was finished, you tried to rape me. I had to fight you off. In case you're not aware, Mr. Hechter, rape is a felony."

"You ungrateful little bitch. I approved a beautiful salary for you, far above what other women with only a high school diploma can hope to earn. And this is how you repay me. Get out of here. I'm calling Security. Go to your desk and have your personal things packed in five minutes. You're being escorted out."

"If you fire me, there's going to be a lawsuit."

"A laaaaawsuit?" He elongated the word, mocking her viciously. "Oh, sure: Yeah. Right. Maybe you don't know it, Miss Karyn, but secret tape recordings don't hold up in court and you have no way to prove that was really my voice. You resented me, didn't you? Because I reprimanded you and made you toe the line instead of goofing off. You could have hired an actor to sound like me, given him a script. . . . I wouldn't put it past your conniving, female mind. And by the way, anything we did together was fully consensual. Two adults getting together. That's all it was."

Karyn was stunned and amazed at the spin Lou had put on their interactions, realizing this was the story he'd tell to the corporation. She couldn't believe how twisted he was, how unprincipled.

"It was *not* consensual," she began, but Lou was already reaching for the phone. He punched in an extension with sharp jabs. "Security? Send someone over to Fashion immediately. I want Karyn Cristophe escorted out to her car and I want it done STAT."

"What's wrong?" Raquel cried, running over to Karyn's alcove as, fighting tears, Karyn began hastily sliding her desk photographs of Amber into a plastic shopping bag. "Are you packing up your *stuff*?"

"Lou fired me. He's sending someone from Security to escort me out."

Raquel seemed shocked. "What happened?"

"That meeting in Southfield on Friday? He tried to rape me. I made a cassette tape and I played it for Cilla. She must have played it for Lou, I don't know. Anyway, I'm out of here."

"That bastard. That fucking, dyslexic bastard." Raquel put her arm around Karyn. "Look, I'll stay with you, I'll walk out of the building with you. Anything you miss here I'll FedEx to you. Karyn . . . this is just a glitch. You're not gonna be gone permanently. Cilla'll take care of it, she'll get you hired back in again."

"I wish she could," Karyn said bleakly. "But the way he was talking . . . he acted like I faked the tape. . . . He said . . . . What if they listen to him? What if they believe him?"

"They won't; they can't." Raquel was almost as agitated as Karyn was. "Oh, shit," she cried. "There's Security now."

It was Cherise, the friendly African American woman who had greeted Karyn every morning of her employment here at Cybelle, and said good-night to her most evenings, too.

"Hi, ladies. Looks like I'm your escort out of here, Karyn," Cherise said pleasantly. "You got everything, honey? If you don't, I can wait a couple minutes. I don't think Mr. Lou Hechter is going to bust a gasket if you take a few more minutes to get your stuff."

By now Karyn just wanted to leave, before she burst into sobs. "Thanks, I'm fine," she responded tightly.

They left the department, Karyn struggling not to cry. Merchandisers in their offices barely looked up as the group passed, unaware of the little drama that was being played out. These were people Karyn had eaten lunch with, enjoyed birthday cake with, teased and worked with. She'd loved knowing all of them. Now she was being spirited out of here like a criminal.

They started down the marble walk, Karyn and Raquel walking side by side, Cherise a few steps behind them. Cherise was muttering indignantly under her breath about arrogant executives who don't know shit."

Karyn pressed her lips together. Everything seemed unbearably poignant. The gleaming gray marble floor with the delicate veins of pink . . . it was the most beautiful floor she'd ever seen. And the windows that looked out on reflecting ponds . . . the fashion photographs on the walls . . . the mail clerk, Antwan, with his rolling cart stuffed with mail, another person who had greeted Karyn twice a day with smiles. Karyn said, "Hi, Antwan," for the last time. She would probably never see Antwan again.

"I don't know what happened, Karyn, but I wish you the best of luck," Cherise said when they had reached the #2 door. "Remember, God always has a plan. You'll be in my prayers, girl."

"Thank you, Cherise." Karyn impulsively hugged the heavyset woman in her blue uniform.

Karyn and Raquel walked outside onto the broad steps that overlooked the huge parking lot.

"Remember when you lost your car on your first day of work?" said Raquel, her eyes wet.

"Yeah . . . and you helped me find it."

"Oh, Karyn!" Raquel hugged her. She was crying. "Call me in a couple of days. . . . I'll tell you what's going on around here. That asshole Lou. I hope he gags to death on a fax. I hope he pukes in the cafeteria in front of fifteen hundred people. I hope they fire *his* ass."

"They won't," said Karyn bitterly.

"I'll walk you out to your car."

"No . . . don't, Raquel. It'll just make me cry." They hugged again.

"Thanks for being my friend," Raquel whispered. "I should have stopped you from going on Friday. But I didn't think—I thought you'd be safe in a big hotel."

"You didn't know," said Karyn, wiping tears.

Then Karyn walked alone down the yellow-striped pedestrian walkway to her car. Memories of her first day of work assailed her. The sun shining on the glass building making it appear like a magical place . . . now it was cold a wintry wind whipping at her coat. Also, unlike her first day of work, she knew exactly where her car was and found

with no trouble at all. She had to drive home and call
Ialia Roberts, tell her what had happened.

Then she had the rest of the day to spend adjusting to the
ict that she'd been fired.

.aquel was crying as she got into her own car to drive home
or lunch—she just couldn't go to the cafeteria today. Then
omething made her get on the entrance to I-75, and instead
he drove to her mother's house in Ferndale. Poor Karyn . . .
h, it had been awful . . . and partly her own fault for not
eeing what that asshole Lou intended to do.

Suddenly, Raquel wanted to be near her own family,
round people who cared about her.

The house was a small, shabby bungalow located just off
Voodward Avenue behind a bunch of car dealerships, on a
reet lined with similar homes. The five sisters had made
e down payment and now were thinking about getting
eir mother some new aluminum siding to replace areas
at had faded to gray in the harsh Michigan winters.

But inside the house was cheerful, the TV set running,
e house full of delicious, spicy odors, Ana's baby running
ll over crowing cheerfully.

"Hey, hi," said Ana who often dropped by their mother's
uring the day.

Raquel went out to the kitchen, where she found her short,
lump mother stirring an enormous pot of spaghetti sauce.

"How's my girl?" Modesta wanted to know. "My pretty
irl. I've got a surprise for you tonight, something I've been
orking on. It's a real nice surprise, baby."

Raquel felt a chill, realizing what the "surprise" had to
e—a pattern for the wedding dress, or maybe, even worse,
er mother had already begun to cut out the expensive fab-
c. Oh, God, the cost of fabric and trim for such a dress
ould be outrageous, and she knew her mother couldn't
fford it.

"Mom . . ." she began.

"And where's that Brett? Why haven't you brought him? A big man like him, you'd think he'd be hungry for some spaghetti and garlic toast."

"Mom . . ." Raquel's eyes teared again. She glanced around the kitchen, then went over to the door and closed it, shutting out the noise of the TV and chatter from the other room. "Mom . . . I didn't bring Brett because . . . because he's not . . . I mean, we're not . . ."

"You broke up?" Her mother stopped stirring, gazing at Raquel with sharp brown eyes.

"Yeah."

"I was afraid. I kept thinking, no, she wouldn't do it, but I knew something was wrong. And then when we heard he was with another girl . . ."

"Ma, I couldn't help it!" Raquel choked. "I tried so hard to keep him. I did everything! I . . . I followed him all around, I kept asking him and asking him why, and he . . he said I was smothering him. He doesn't want me. He . . he wouldn't listen to my phone messages and I called him all the time, I kept trying to tell him but he . . . I know it's my fault that he . . . I . . ."

Modesta drew up her plump, 5' frame and tightened her lips, gazing at her daughter. "No, Raquel, it is not your fault. If a man doesn't want my daughter it is not her fault, it is his, for not seeing her beauty. *You* are not at fault. I cried about this but I know my daughter, and you're worth more than such a man."

"Mom." Raquel felt as if a huge burden had dropped off her shoulders. "But the dress, the wedding dress. Ana said you found a pattern. . . ."

"Yes, a very beautiful Vogue pattern, my honey. Yes, it is wonderful."

"You didn't get the fabric, did you?" Raquel inquired, alarmed.

"Not yet. But it will keep," said Modesta. She added, "O

course, you work at Cybelle, you know all about it, these fashions, they do not stay in style forever."

"I know that." Raquel laughed with relief. "But wedding dresses, Mom. They do stay in fashion a real long time."

Modesta made a facial expression very similar to ones that Raquel, Ana and the other sisters often made, although neither of them realized it. "But my sewing machine doesn't stay in repair forever, and I'm getting the arthritis in my fingers so it's getting harder to sew on beads. So if you want beautiful beading, remember my old fingers and get married before they get too crooked to sew."

"I'll remember your fingers," said Raquel, laughing as she hugged her mother. "But they're not old fingers, Ma."

"Oh, yes, they are." Modesta wiggled them. "Ancient."

Raquel laughed and hugged Modesta again. Suddenly she was enormously hungry, ready to eat a huge plate of spaghetti and two or three pieces of her mother's delicious garlic toast. Then she had to hurry back to work.

Cilla arrived back in the office around 4:45 P.M. striding quickly through the maze of offices toward the Fashion Department, feeling as if people were staring at her. The department seemed oddly quiet, nobody talking, everyone glued to their monitors. She had left her computer on, and began dictating some tapes before Raquel drifted into her office to tell her that Lou had fired Karyn and she'd been escorted out of the building under guard.

"No," breathed Cilla, feeling rocked.

"It was awful," choked Raquel, her eyes reddened.

"Shit, shit," Cilla couldn't help exclaiming.

"It wasn't fair."

"I'll take care of it," Cilla told Lou's shaken assistant. "Just go on about your work, Raquel, as if nothing has happened. And stay out of his path if you can."

"Mmm-hmmm," said the petite woman, nodding as she walked away.

Cilla continued to dictate, grimly concentrating on not letting her voice shake. Rage flooded her. Lou was monstrous. How dare Lou fire Karyn like that—her secretary? He was the one who should be fired.

"And now you," said Lou Hechter, walking into Cilla's office and closing the door behind him with an emphatic slam.

Cilla looked up, her heart squeezing. Lou looked like a heart attack about to happen, his black hair disheveled, his face brick-red and congested.

"You . . ." he growled. "Playing that tape was a big, big mistake. You ruined my reputation in this company!"

"Don't you dare speak to me that way." Cilla rose, anger and fear rushing through her. Instinctively she pushed a stack of papers over the mini-cassette player that Karyn had given her, hiding it from Lou's view.

"I should fire you, too, like I just did Karyn. Send your sorry ass out the door escorted by two security guards."

"You don't dare fire me, Lou, because I have a few stories I can tell Dom Carrara in addition to what's already been going on with Karyn," Cilla snapped. "Your old crony, Vic Rondelli, isn't in charge anymore, and I think Dom will listen to me."

"You and I had consensual sex," he told her.

"What? With you threatening my job every step of the way, telling me I had to put out or get out, words to that effect."

"I did not threaten you. That is an outright lie. You're as bad as that other little bitch, trying to make me look bad," he accused. She could smell the sharp, acrid odor of his perspiration.

"Lou, you forced me to have sex for over three years, telling me that I'd lose my job if I didn't."

"Lies, lies, lies!" He swung his head from side to side, like some large animal at bay. "All right then, Cilla. Little Cilla. You are out of here, too. Pack your things; I'll give you twenty minutes. Karyn got fifteen, how's that for seniority?"

Cilla was enraged. "You won't get away with this, Lou. I've got rights. As soon as I'm of here I'll phone Dom Carrara and we'll see just who he listens to! I've got a very good professional relationship going with him right now and—"

"He'll listen to *me*," Lou grated. "Last time I heard, I was a vice president and you're nothing but a director. So move your ass, get it in gear, because you are no longer an employee of Cybelle."

Cilla sat in her office, not knowing whether to laugh or cry. He'd really done it—tried to fire her. And how insulting, to be given twenty minutes to get out. She thought of calling Dom—right now—but then reluctantly put it out of her mind. Lou's long years at Cybelle, his proven track record as a profit maker, would surely outweigh her one contribution on the Girlrags project. She wouldn't humiliate herself by going begging to the president of the company. At least, she told herself, not right now, when she felt so burningly angry. Going in calm and secure was the way to handle the problem.

But she wasn't going to allow herself the humiliation of being escorted out by Security. No, she'd leave herself, now. Quietly she gathered up her purse and put a few photographs in one of the pockets. Tomorrow she'd call Raquel and have her pack up the rest of her personal things—if the firing even stood. Cilla didn't think it was going to. She felt sure that Dom Carrara would reverse Lou's decision as soon as he learned about it.

She left her computer running and simply got up and walked out, smiling at Raquel as if she expected to be back in an hour or so. Later, gossip would run rampant through the department. She was damned if she'd have anyone saying that Cilla had cried.

Anyway, this was only a temporary setback, Cilla felt sure.

There were a lot of politics in big corporations, and if she played her cards correctly, she might be right back in this office in only a few days.

Raquel watched as Cilla moved past her desk, walking gracefully, her head held high. She'd heard Lou yelling behind the closed door—the offices weren't completely soundproof—and she'd gotten the gist of what went on.

It pissed her off. First poor Karyn, trying so hard not to cry as she was escorted out the door as if she'd done something wrong. Now Cilla. Cilla was a nice woman, and she'd always been kind to Raquel, even occasionally giving her theater tickets or concert tickets if she couldn't use them.

As soon as Cilla had left, Raquel went into her office.

She discovered the cassette player immediately, pushed under a stack of papers near Cilla's telephone. Apparently, Cilla had forgotten to take it with her . . . or had left it on purpose. Raquel preferred to believe it was the latter.

She darted over and picked up the tape player, noticing that it was loaded with a tape.

She couldn't play it here. But she could play it in her car.

"I was fired," Karyn said, phoning Roger at his office as soon as she got home. Amber would not be home from school for several hours, and the apartment seemed cavernously empty. She told Roger how Lou had forced her to leave with a Security escort.

"Oh, Karyn. Oh, Jesus."

"It's okay," she lied. "My aunt has an employment agency and she'll—" Her voice cracked and she broke down.

"Do you want me to come over? I can leave work right now—I'll drive right over."

"Would you?"

While she was waiting for Roger, Karyn dialed Malia Roberts at her office but was put into her attorney's voice mail. She left a short message, asking Malia to call.

Within fifteen minutes Roger was at her place, and he pulled her into his arms, hugging her and wiping away her tears with his hands. "Honey, they've treated you like shit. Surely something can be worked out. I can make a few calls—"

"No," she cried. "I don't want you making any phone calls on my behalf. Please don't. It'll only hurt you in the long run. Anyone who tries to help me is going to be in trouble from Lou, I know it. He can fire you just like he fired me."

Roger tried to insist, but Karyn put her hand over his mouth. "Please. I know what I'm talking about. I have an attorney, and she's going to help me. Just . . . hug me, Roger."

Roger took her in his arms again, giving her a long, sweet hug that had Karyn crying again. Finally he pulled away and said, "Karyn, I want you to know one thing. Men like Lou . . . well, the majority of men are not like him. Most of us are pretty good guys. We don't hit on the women who work for us; we don't harass them."

"I know," she said quietly. "But all it takes is one, Roger."

Roger stayed the evening and took her and Amber out for dinner at the Olive Garden, and then brought them back to the apartment. Karyn felt so tired, so exhausted from the stress of the day, all of the lost sleep, that she kept on yawning and couldn't stop.

"Sounds like you'd better get some sleep, sweetie," said Roger, announcing that he was going to leave.

Outside the apartment in the common hallway they kissed good-night.

"You're going to beat this," he assured her. "Karyn, it's

going to come out all right, I promise. And if you need any money—"

"I can't take money from you."

"You can pay me back every cent with interest, if you want to. I just want you to know that help is there, no matter what you need," insisted Roger, his brown eyes full of concern. "I'd mortgage my house for you, Karyn. I hope you know that."

As Karyn was walking back into the apartment, the phone rang. It was Malia Roberts.

"I got your message. I'm sorry you lost your job but it's started our lawsuit rolling, girlfriend, and I need to talk to you as soon as possible. How about if you come in tomorrow at nine-thirty? I have to be in court all afternoon and that would be a good time for me."

Karyn agreed to be there.

Cilla spent the evening watching a movie on pay-per-view and finishing off a bottle of California Riesling that she and Shane had opened the previous weekend. She was restless, barely able to concentrate on the courtroom thriller. She'd hoped to achieve some sense of calm, but it wasn't happening.

She finally called Shane at home to tell him she'd been fired.

"No, Cilla . . . no."

"It wasn't the greatest day in the world," she admitted.

"But you have to fight it. You have legal options. You could file a wrongful firing suit, Cilla. I'm sure you could win it."

"Wrongful firing?" Cilla heard her voice rise. "Shane, I don't even want to go there. Even if I win the suit, I'll be a pariah. I'll probably never get any higher at the company than I am right now, and they'll probably offer me a buyout as soon as they feel it's safe. After all, I am fifty. It would be a very convenient way to get rid of me."

"But then you're going to let it stand?"

"No. I'll fight it; I'll go to Dom Carrara. I'll work it out somehow."

Shane hesitated. "I'm worried about you, Cilla."

"Don't be." She tried to smile.

"If there's anything I can do . . . I'll even punch Lou Hechter in the nose for you, honey. Us legal eagles do know how to fight, you know."

Cilla couldn't help uttering a choked laugh. She did love Shane so much, perhaps never more than at this moment. "A good punch in Lou's big nose? Pleasant as that sounds, it's the last thing I need right now, and we don't want your career to start circling the drain just like mine is doing."

The wine had made her sleepy, and she finally went upstairs and lay down on her bedcovers, pulling a throw over herself and drifting off to a seminap that wasn't really sleep at all but more like a trance. A worried trance, filled with all the ramifications of everything that had happened.

She was awakened at 1:30 A.M. by the sound of car tires screeching to a halt. Then a car door slammed. Stirring groggily, she heard yelling coming from her driveway.

"You did it, baby, you finally did it! You ruined me! You bitch! You ugly old piece of ass!"

It was Lou, of course, standing outside her condo glaring up at the window of the master bedroom, shaking his fist and shouting.

Cilla threw aside the covers and jumped up without turning on a light. Christ. His screaming was going to wake up the whole condo community.

She picked up the cell phone she'd brought upstairs with her and quietly dialed 911.

If she didn't make the call, one of her other neighbors was sure to. The residents here were all professionals, and the association had all sorts of picky rules about motorcycles, loud parties, tinkering with cars, and so forth. Yelling

obscenities had to be on the list somewhere—or it would
be by the next association meeting.

Standing behind her bedroom curtain, Cilla gazed down at
Lou as he attempted to explain to two Rochester Hills police
officers exactly what he was doing. Her employer gestured
toward Cilla's condo, moving his forefinger in a circle
around his forehead as if trying to explain that Cilla was
crazy.

Cilla began to seethe. He was the crazy one, not her.

Finally she heard her doorbell ring, and walked downstairs in her jeans and barefoot to disarm the security system
and answer the door.

"Ma'am, do you know this man?" asked a young black
male officer, his manner very polite.

"He's my employer," she said calmly.

She could hear Lou saying something loudly to the other
officer, who had remained with him in the driveway. The
word "bitch" was audible. Great. Cilla'd bet her elderly
neighbor on the left was sitting in her living room, listening
to all of this and being horrified.

"Ma'am, was there an argument going on?" queried the
police officer.

"He fired me today," she said, shrugging. "I want him out
of here and I want him out now."

The officer stared at her. "Ma'am, he's drunk and disorderly, but a man of his age wouldn't be comfortable in a
holding pen in jail, and we don't have room for him anyway.
So we're going to drive him home. If he bothers you again
tonight, please call and let us know and we will arrest him."

"Fine," she agreed. "I'll be more than happy to press
charges. Just get his car out of my driveway."

Cilla might even have felt sorry for Lou if she hadn't
been so angry. The two officers inserted the fifty-one-year-
old executive in the backseat of their squad car, courteously
pushing down his head to make sure he didn't bump it. Then

he second officer started Lou's Mercedes and backed it out of Cilla's driveway.

Even when you were drunk and disorderly, screeching out obscenities and threats, if you drove a Mercedes you got treated special, she thought bitterly. Lou's position as a vice president at Cybelle was a big, big advantage in his favor. Everyone from the police to the courts was going to treat him with kid gloves, she realized.

She went back inside her condo and rearmed her security system.

Finally she went upstairs and took off her clothes, pulling on an old cotton sleep T-shirt that had been washed about 250 times and was velvet soft. Comfort clothes. She combed out her hair and crawled into bed.

If she'd just refused Lou that first time, none of this would be happening now.

If she hadn't drunk too much wine, if she hadn't been angry at her husband . . . a thousand ifs.

The police officers dropped Lou at his home in Bloomfield Hills. Marty had left the outdoor floodlights on, and the 6,500-square-foot house gleamed like a palace. Two magnificent pines glittered with white holiday lights installed by the handyman the Hechters used. Hanging in the foyer was a Waterford crystal chandelier that had cost half of what one of these common police officers earned in a year.

As they pulled in, the black cop remarked, "A man from a nice house like this shouldn't be in a police car, buddy. Maybe you'd better think about AA. They have meetings every day around here, all over the place."

"I don't need AA," Lou snapped.

As soon as they let him out, he found his keys and let himself into the house, punching the security code so the alarm would not go off. The squad car waited until Lou had the door all the way open and was inside before it backed out of the driveway and left.

Lou sighed. His Mercedes was parked in a strip mal parking lot about a quarter mile away from Cilla's. Some how he was going to have to pick it up tomorrow.

The very idea made him feel weary.

He'd had enough today—more than enough. He fel thirsty, tired and drained, and all he wanted was to stand underneath the shower for about thirty minutes, then take sleeping pill and fall into bed.

But when he walked into the kitchen for a glass of water he met an unpleasant surprise.

"So where have you been, Lou? Christ, it's two-thirty i the morning and you look like shit warmed over. And heard a car drive off. Did a designated driver drop you of home?"

His wife, Marty, was sitting in the kitchen at the smal desk, her laptop opened in front of her. She still wore th business suit she had put on for work, but had taken off he panty hose and was barefooted, giving her an oddly youthfu look she probably had not intended. Her lipstick had wor off, and the expression on her attractive face was grim.

"Well?"

"None of your business," he snapped.

"Babe, I think it is very much my business. I received phone call from a certain anonymous person tonight, an you'll never guess what it was about."

Lou blanched. "What anonymous person?"

"Someone who works at Cybelle . . . someone who's a *li tle* bit pissed off at you. And for good reason, as far as can tell."

"Who?"

"What does it matter? You've got zipper problems, Lo dear, and you're in trouble up to your overplucked eye brows!"

Lou was unable to believe this was his wife talking. "M eyebrows aren't overpl—"

"Weren't you listening? According to this person, you'v

been screwing Cilla Westheim for three years, plus I don't know how many clerks and secretaries, and now you just tried to rape your latest secretary, and it's all on a god-damned audiotape! How could you be so stupid, Lou? I've never had a client even half as stupid as you."

Lou staggered to a nearby bar stool and sat down. He felt as if he'd been punched in the stomach.

"Who . . . who called you with this pack of lies?" he repeated, trying to take the offensive.

"Never mind."

Lou felt a surge of panic. The "anonymous" caller could be anyone, from Sondra Zapernick to Raquel, Cilla, or even Karyn. Or even someone Cilla had played the tape for. It could be anyone.

Marty's face hardened. "Hey, I don't think you're going to keep your job after this one, no matter what favors that creep Vic Rondelli tries to do for you or how many lies you tell."

Lou rubbed his forehead, sobering up fast. "They're not going to—"

"Oh, fuck, get real," exclaimed Marty. "You don't think they're keeping you on after this fiasco? Sweetheart, it's the new millennium. Maybe once companies kept reprobates like you on their payrolls, but those days are finished. Now they're going to want to dump you as fast as possible before the woman starts asking for big money. Which she probably will, Lou. It's what I would advise her to do if I were her lawyer."

"She . . . fabricated the whole tape."

"That's not what I was told." Marty's face was as hard as the Corian kitchen counters that had been installed in the huge kitchen. "Lou, I don't want you under this roof one more minute. Go in the bedroom and pack some suitcases, as much as you can stuff in them in ten minutes."

"I'm not going anywhere, for Christ's sakes."

Marty's eyes glittered dangerously. "When I heard you

let yourself in, I took the liberty of calling two of the security guards at the law firm, and they're on their way here now. They'll escort you out and follow you to a hotel."

"Shit!" He didn't even have his car. They would have to drive him to pick it up, then take him to the hotel.

"It's over, Lou. I don't want you in my life anymore. Get on upstairs and get your stuff packed. Anything you don't take I'll have put in storage until you get a place."

"Marty!" he cried out in anguish, but there was the sound of a car pulling into the driveway, headlights flashing along the side of the house, and Lou knew it was too late. He was finished, cooked, screwed.

Who had called his wife, anyway? Lou's thoughts began to go wild. He couldn't believe anyone would hate him that much. All he'd done was have a little sex, after all. The women had liked it. They'd wanted him, thought he was a stud.

Basically he had done nothing seriously wrong.

Karyn dropped into blankness, without any dreams—just flat, plain sleep. She woke up the next morning at 6:45 A.M., her usual time, only to remember that she didn't have a job to go to. She lay still, listening to the morning drive-time show, three or four immature "personality boy" disk jockeys making tasteless "Yo Mama" jokes.

Yo Mama is so fat that when her beeper goes off, people think she's backing up. . . .

Karyn flicked off the clock radio and forced herself to get out of bed. She had to get Amber ready for school—that hadn't changed—and then she'd decided to call Aunt Connie and see about getting a temping job. She might have been escorted out the door of Cybelle, and there might be a lawsuit in the offing, but that didn't change the fact that she had bills to pay.

"Mom, why do you look so sad today?" Amber inquired as they sat at the breakfast table.

"Honey bear . . . I had a problem at work and now I'm going to be working at another job for a while," she explained to her daughter.

"Did Daddy make the problem?" Amber wanted to know.

"No, baby. He didn't make the problem. And it's not really a problem," Karyn said bravely. "So don't worry, babydoll. Everything's going to be fine."

After · Amber left, Jinny Caribaldi driving the girls to school today, Karyn put away the breakfast dishes. At 8:00 A.M., she telephoned Human Resources at Cybelle and was told that she legally still had her job at Cybelle, only she was going to be transferred to a different department, Accounting. She would perform administrative assistant functions and start to learn Solomon software. She would retain her same pay and benefits.

"Thank you," said Karyn, stunned.

"You'll be reporting to Madelyn Vigo on Dom Carrara's orders. You can come in tomorrow."

After the call was finished, Karyn sagged into a dinette chair, relief pouring over her. Accounting. Not what she would have chosen. But at least there would be a paycheck, and she still had hospitalization insurance.

She placed a call to Raquel's work extension to tell her what had happened.

"Oh, man, that's great news!" Raquel enthused, but then there was a pause. "Accounting, though. That place is the pits. Have you ever seen all their papers and binders and storage boxes up there? They'll have you filing and shuffling papers until you go blind."

"Blind but employed," Karyn said as cheerfully as she could.

Snow dotted the air, flurrying lazily. Pale light streamed in the windows of Malia Roberts's law office, illuminating the photographs of Malia's daughter, the diplomas, and the African-American art Malia'd hung on her walls.

"Okay," the attorney said, leaning forward to gaze at Karyn. "Let's talk about this lawsuit. We can't go for actual monetary damages lost because you're being transferred to another department and you're being given equal pay and benefits. So you've lost nothing financially."

Karyn felt a stab of disappointment. "Does this mean I don't have a lawsuit?"

"It doesn't mean that at all. What we have to go for are punitive damages. A plaintiff can win those when the defendant has done something truly heinous or when the plaintiff wants to make a big point to everyone that changes should and need to be made."

Karyn listened carefully.

"The standard for punitive damages is this, Karyn. Willful, malicious, wanton, or vicious conduct. Does that remind you of anyone you know?"

Karyn felt a patina of perspiration dampen her forehead underneath her bangs. "Lou Hechter, of course."

"Sexual harassment is an arena that has hit it big in the media, and we do have a chance of collecting not only for your emotional pain and suffering but also punitive damages. But if we want to win big, big damages, then we have to get that jury angry. We have to get them hating Lou, hating everything he is, everything he's ever done, and everything he stands for. *And* we have to have them believing every word you say."

"I see," Karyn said, clenching her hands together.

There was more. Malia explained to Karyn the legal process of "discovery," which included interrogatories, written questions to the opponent that solicited information on any aspect of the case—and had to be answered under oath.

"We'll have requests for production of documents, most certainly your employment records at Cybelle, Karyn, and any written recommendations that were made to hire you on full-time. And they'll do the same to us. So you'll be providing them with a copy of the journal you've been keeping among other things. Then there are depositions, where a lawyer asks questions of a witness and the witness answers, and her statement is taken down by a court reporter who prepares a transcript."

"Will that take place in court?"

"No, we'll do that in a lawyer's conference room, Karyn. We'll depose all of the women you've managed to find as witnesses, and we can subpoena other witnesses who are a party in the case, for instance, people at Cybelle who may have witnessed the harassment. It won't be exactly like a courtroom situation; a judge won't even be present. It's essentially a disclosure of information as to what the other side has."

Karyn listened, her mind swirling with all of the legalities.

"How . . . how much will we be suing for?" she finally asked Malia.

Malia grinned. "I'm thinking in the region of twenty million dollars."

Karyn stared at the attorney. Malia had mentioned that figure before. "But that's—way too much," she admitted honestly.

"Yes, it is, and we probably never could win that much— not here in Oakland County. But the high figure will convince Cybelle to take us seriously. That's another reason I'm eager to do the discovery. Once their attorneys read the transcripts of the depositions, they'll realize we do have a very, very strong case. We'll also, as I mentioned before, provide them a copy of the tape you made of Lou attempting to rape you."

Karyn thought about that and felt her skin turn red.

"What comes next?" she said.

"Well . . . do you really want to go through with this? Lawsuits are stressful, Karyn, I have to warn you. Heavy-duty stress. And it could be with you not just for months but for years. And you're going to be working at the company you're suing. Not everyone can handle that kind of pressure. Some people realize they've made a mistake and drop out just to have it be over with."

"I can do it. I want to do it."

"You'll have to give a deposition yourself, you know. I'm sure the other side will subpoena you, along with our entire list of witnesses. It could get rough. And that's only the deposition, it doesn't even count being in court, where things really could get dirty. They'll try to make you appear like a whore, Karyn. Like you wanted and consented to everything this man did."

Karyn's eyes widened. "I didn't consent to anything!"

"Plus," Malia went on, "there'll be publicity if we file a big suit. Maybe lots of media publicity. Are you ready for that?"

Karyn thought about her life, the bad marriage, finally breaking free to come to Detroit, the excellent job she'd managed to fall into. What if her ex-husband, Mack, found out where she was because of all the publicity? Still, if she backed out of the case, wouldn't she be right back where she was before, scared of a man, uncertain, powerless? She had tasted a better life. And she wanted it. She'd take the risk.

She caught her breath. "I'll handle it."

"I think you will." Malia raised her hands, shaking them in a victory gesture. "I told you I'm a bulldog, Karyn. People like Lou Hechter are pond scum, and there's nothing I like better than vacuuming them up but good. Stick with me and you may find yourself a millionaire."

"So what's next?" repeated Karyn.

Malia grinned. "How about if I draft up a complaint? How's that for starters? Oh, and one more thing. Round up any more witnesses you can find. I'll need to compile a list of their names and addresses for the discovery."

Walking out of the building to her car, Karyn opened the door of the old Tempo and slid into the driver's seat, feeling alternate rushes of exhilaration and fear.

A $20 million lawsuit.

It just didn't seem totally real to her. More like those huge amounts the lottery winners got . . . totally out of the comprehension of most ordinary people. Karyn didn't even know what she would do with $20 million. Of course, it would only be two-thirds of that after she paid Malia, and she'd still have to pay back the woman from NOW. Still, she could buy a house for herself and Amber. A new car, God, she needed one. Maybe a trip to Walt Disney World, take Jinny and Caitlin with them. Put money in a savings account for Amber's college education. Purchase a new house for her parents, maybe a car for them, too. Beyond that her mind would not stretch.

She drove home, went for a walk, tried hard to absorb what was happening, this tremendous change her life had taken. Finally she dialed Cilla's phone line at work. She knew that Cilla frequently called, even on weekends, to check her voice mail.

She waited for Cilla's brief, businesslike message to finish playing, then began speaking.

"As you probably know, I was fired yesterday afternoon by Lou Hechter. He had me escorted out by a security guard. It was because of that audiotape I made. They're transferred me to Accounting though. I . . . I just wanted you to know that I'm going through with my plans to file a lawsuit against Cybelle. I saw the attorney this morning and she's ready to go ahead. It was a rough decision. I didn't make it easily. I enjoyed working for you, Cilla, and . . ."

She paused, wondering how to phrase it. "If there is any way you could assist me with my lawsuit, *any* way you can think of, please call me at home. I have an answering machine so you can call anytime."

She gave her home number and replaced the phone, perspiration shiny slick all over her skin.

Lou had sexually harassed Cilla as well as herself.

Karyn felt sure of it. *She just knew.*

But would Cilla help her? She hadn't acted as if she would. Still, Karyn had to try.

Although she'd been "fired," Cilla could still access her voice mail messages, at least until someone fixed it so she couldn't. The message Karyn had left reverberated in her head all evening, creating such unease in Cilla that she couldn't eat any dinner and had to take several antacids for her stomach, plus a headache pill.

If there is any way you could assist me with my lawsuit, any way you can think of . . .

Did Karyn even know what she was asking?

If Cilla did appear in court as a witness, she'd be forced to tell the world that she'd submitted to Lou's harassment for *three horrible years*. What would the jury think? Lou would certainly argue that the sex had been consensual; he'd accuse her of sleeping with him so she could get a promotion which she *had* gotten during the three years, from assistant director to director.

It would be a nightmare. Attorneys would pry, demanding all the sordid details. Shameful things Cilla had blotted from her mind now would become public. It would probably be in the newspapers, raked over by the media. She might even attract more attention than Karyn because her position was much higher than Karyn's, making her all that much more vulnerable.

In court, her daughter would hear all of it. Shane would know, too, details that Cilla was ashamed to repeat to anyone now becoming public knowledge. Maybe his love wouldn't be strong enough to take it. After all, they still hadn't been together even six months.

She paced the condominium, a hundred video flashes of Lou racing through her head. The time he had cut off her clothes with a pair of scissors . . . his ugly threats, repeated in a dozen different ways . . . the wolfish smile on his face as he dominated her in bed, listing for her the acts he wanted her to perform.

And she'd performed them.

Hoping it would end, hoping somehow the nightmare would cease, that each time would be the last, only it had never been. Always there had been another time, another demand, another threat. And Cilla had clung to her job as if it was a lifeline, as if she might drown without it. That was how Lou had been able to use her. Because of her desperate connection to her job.

Cilla found herself in the downstairs powder room, leaning over the commode, where she dry-heaved until there was nothing but stinging stomach acid to bring up.

Later, the red letters on Cilla's clock radio said that it was 4:48 A.M. Cilla pushed away her bedcovers and slid out of bed, shrugging on a bathrobe. She relinquished any idea of being able to sleep tonight.

She walked barefoot to the bedroom window and pulled open the curtains. Snow glinted on the blue spruces that decorated the communal lawn, sugar white. Everything looked so fresh and pure. Much purer than Cilla felt right now.

Huddled in her bathrobe, she stared out at the snow, wondering what would have happened if she'd spoken up sooner.

Would other women have been spared the humiliation of Lou's threats and malicious sexual advances? Certainly, Karyn Cristophe would have been. And now here was Karyn, a young, single mother without many resources, much more dependent on her job than Cilla, brave enough to face not only Lou but the whole establishment.

The idea filled Cilla with shame.

What if it had been Mindy, instead of Karyn? It could have been if Lou had carried out his threat to contact Cilla's daughter. How would she live with herself in later years if that had actually happened . . . if he'd hurt her child?

Cilla shuddered.

Finally she turned back into the bedroom and lifted the bedside phone, punching in the number Karyn had given her.

"Hello?" Her secretary's voice was hoarse but it did not sound as if she'd been sleeping much, either.

"Karyn, I know it's late. This is Cilla. I . . . I want to be a witness in your lawsuit."

"Oh!"

"He's been harassing me for three years, Karyn, forcing me to have sex with him under threat of losing my job. I'm so very ashamed of myself that I didn't come forward earlier." Cilla drew in a deep breath, then expelled it slowly. "But I'm here now, and I'll do whatever it takes. I'll talk to lawyers, I'll give a deposition, I'll appear in court."

"Oh!" Karyn said again, and then her voice started to shake. Cilla realized that Karyn was crying but trying to hide it. "Thank you," the young woman blurted.

"Look. It's nearly morning, and I haven't slept. I'll call you tomorrow—I mean today—and get the details about your suit."

After she had hung up, Cilla blew out a long gust of air, feeling as if she was releasing something dirty and festering. She took in another gulp of air, then pushed it out, releasing more of the bad feeling.

Her job? There were always jobs.

Mindy could get a college loan—she'd survive. Cilla herself could go to a debt-consolidation place and figure out a payment plan for her credit card debts. Maybe she'd buy a small house that did not cost her $350 a month in condo fees on top of a whopping mortgage. Learn how to mow her own lawn. It might take her a long time and some sacrifice but she'd feel a lot cleaner inside, in the way that counted.

Now it was time for Cilla to start getting her self-respect back.

* * *

Cilla had called again as Karyn was eating breakfast, and Karyn had talked to her for a few minutes and given her Malia's office number. It felt good to have Cilla on her side. Karyn dressed in a trouser suit for the first time since September, and drove to work.

Accounting was located on the third floor, not far from the area where the data entry clerks toiled. It wasn't one of the glamour departments. Rows of gray-fabric cubicles housed various accountants, payroll and accounting clerks, and a few offices accommodated their supervisors, along with the vice president of Accounting, Randy Caravaglio.

Karyn knew that Dom Carrara had meant well when he had placed her here to assist Madelyn Vigo, one of the accounting supervisors. She'd be buried up here in the rows of cubes, just one more worker, much less likely to experience any kind of harassment.

Madelyn Vigo was about sixty, a thin woman whose face was slightly reddened, as if she'd had some kind of a chemical peel that had gone bad. Deep wrinkles grooved her face, and the corners of her mouth turned downward. She wore a light blue polyester pantsuit outfit that Lou Hechter would have sneered at.

"Well, we can certainly put you to work," said Madelyn, eyeing Karyn curiously, as if wanting to see just what sort of woman filed a $20 million lawsuit against the company. "Have you ever used Solomon software?"

"No."

"Well, it's our accounting software program, and you're going to be using it a lot here, entering data. Also, our filing has piled up and we need to transfer all of our 1996 and 1997 batch files to boxes for temporary storage." Madelyn went on, "Come on, we'll start you off with the filing. There's really a ton of stuff to do. We had a woman quit last month and haven't been able to replace her."

Karyn noticed that everyone looked up as Madelyn led

her down to the end of a row and introduced her to a chubby
young woman named Alex.

"Alex will show you what to do."

Madelyn left, and Alex stared hard at Karyn. Her expression looked hostile. "Did you really sue this place for twenty
million dollars?"

"Yes."

"What are you going to do with twenty million dollars if
you get it?"

"I doubt if the award will be that much," Karyn finally
said. "Where's the work that needs doing?"

"You probably won't even have to work if you win. You
can just lie around and sun yourself all day, or buy a home
in Florida. While we have to slave here. I wish *I'd* been
harassed so I could get rich."

"Please. I came here to work."

Alex sighed and led her into a cube at the back that had
been stacked everywhere with big three-ring binders stuffed
full of printed reports.

"This will be your cube. These are batch files," explained
Alex. "Every time we make out a batch of checks, the batch
is given a number. First you need to check to see that all of
these batches are placed in numerical order. We had a girl
working here and she got it all screwed up, some of it. Then
you'll file them in storage boxes by number, using a labeled
divider for every thousand. I'll show you where the boxes
are when you're ready for that."

Karyn looked at Alex's sly smile and realized that she
was being given the "scut" work, the work no one else
wanted.

"I'll get started," she told Alex firmly. "I'll come to you
if I have any more questions."

The woman nodded and left. Karyn sank into the chair
and looked at the binders. The stacks of them seemed overwhelming. She'd put the binders in order first, she decided.
Then the individual batches.

All day long, people kept coming up to her cube.

"Are you the woman who filed that humongous lawsuit against the company?" was a typical question.

Or, "Why are you working here if you're going to get twenty million dollars?"

"What are you going to do, use your twenty million to buy up a Cybelle store?"

"Don't you think you asked for a little too much? Twenty million dollars is enough to feed a whole country full of starving children in Ethiopia."

Karyn at first tried to reasonably answer the questions, but there seemed to be no satisfactory answers. The questions weren't really questions—they were hostile remarks. The employees around here resented the fact that she had asked for so much. She ended up just glancing up, smiling, and saying, "I did file the lawsuit but right now I'm here to do my job."

"But twenty million is a lot—"

"I'm just here to work," Karyn insisted firmly.

The day seemed to stretch on forever.

Karyn got the binders in order, then began checking the batches. Her back ached from sitting in one position for so long, and her eyes burned from constantly trying to read the small print of the numbers. Only occasionally did she find one out of order. It was boring, grueling work, but she didn't want to get up and take a coffee break. She was afraid her fellow employees would only converge on her with more questions.

At 3:00 in the afternoon, her phone rang and Karyn picked it up, relieved for something to break the tedium.

"How's it going, bitch? You'll find out what happens when you lie about a vice president, dearie," said a strange male voice.

"Who is this?"

The man hung up on her.

Karyn sat shaking, then recovered herself enough to jot

down the gist of the conversation in the steno book she
carried everywhere with her. She resumed her work with the
batch numbers. About half an hour later, the phone rang
again. A different man, with a scratchy, old-sounding voice.

"It was consensual sex, baby. So don't make the company
pay just because you wanted a big, thick dick."

This time Karyn slammed down the phone. Lou's friends.
Someone had given them her extension number and they
were tormenting her—or trying to. She phoned down to the
Security office and told the head of Security that she'd been
receiving obscene phone calls on her work extension, demanding another number. Fortunately, the security chief, a
woman named Toddy Gearring, seemed sympathetic.

Finally, about 3:45, a man came up to replace her phone
with another one. Karyn knew that eventually Lou's friends
would get the new number, but she hoped she might have
some peace for a few days before this happened.

She phoned down to Raquel to let her know her new
extension, begging her not to give it out, especially to Lou
or any of his friends. It would take several months for the
number to appear in the company's printed phone directory.

"Uh, oh. Are they treating you okay?" her friend wanted
to know.

"Do vultures circle around a piece of roadkill?"

"That bad?"

"Almost. I've been getting these really bad phone calls,
the kind where they call you dearie and baby and refer to
big, thick dicks." Karyn said this in a low voice so as not
to be overheard.

"Whoa," said Raquel. "Those dickfaces."

They whispered about the calls for a while, poking fun
at the perpetrators until Karyn began to feel a little better.
Then Raquel began telling her some of the departmental
gossip she'd missed.

Raquel giggled. "In fact, did you hear about Renee Bugossi?"

"No."

"She's pregnant with twins and the father is a pro baseball player. And he's married!"

The gossip session cheered Karyn a little, although she felt sorry for Renee.

"I'll bring you up some yogurt," Raquel finally decided. "I know those old bean counters up in Accounting. They don't like you to go to the cafeteria; they're afraid you might lose ten minutes of work."

Karyn could hardly wait for Raquel to arrive. She missed the Fashion Department so much, the brightness, the life and laughter, the birthday parties and the gossip. She felt as if she'd been banished to northern Estonia.

"How is it going?" asked Madelyn Vigo as Karyn was still going through binders at 5:00.

"The work is going fine."

"Good. We have plenty for you."

Karyn looked at the woman, hard. "Mrs. Vigo, I've accomplished quite a bit today, and I believe I'll be a valuable employee to you. But I must say this. It's illegal for the company to fire me because I filed a lawsuit against them, but it's also illegal for me to be harassed because of that suit. All day long I've been receiving harassing remarks from people in this department, as well as obscene phone calls from other people in the company. I'm counting on you to protect me so that no one in this department has to be subpoenaed to appear in court."

The accountant's mouth fell open, and she stared at Karyn in shock. Probably no one had ever spoken to her that way in her life. "I'm . . . I didn't realize . . . I'll speak to them."

Karyn smiled. "Thank you very much. I knew I could depend on you."

Karyn was late leaving the building, and she walked slowly to her car, feeling the stiffness and kinks in her back. She felt both elated that she'd stood up to Mrs. Vigo and depressed because she'd been forced to do it. She was no longer the same Karyn Cristophe who'd arrived at Cybelle the first week in September, innocently happy about her new job.

She was taking control—standing up for herself now.

Cilla Westheim walked fast into the lobby of Cybelle, the glamorous front area with the colored fountain where Dom Carrara often held his showy press conferences. He was going to have to hold one soon about Karyn's $20 million lawsuit, Cilla realized. He'd have a lot of explaining to do if he allowed Lou's firing of her and the attempted firing of her assistant to stand.

She gave her name to the security guard at the main desk and waited while she called upstairs to the executive floor.

In a few seconds she had boarded the express elevator. Riding upward, she tried to quell the anxious beating of her heart. Dom Carrara wasn't like Vic Rondelli, the previous president of Cybelle. She'd finally overcome her inhibitions about talking to Dom, and felt she could handle the situation. He was warm and vital, a reasonable man. Well, she was going to find out if he was reasonable.

"Hello, Cilla," Sondra greeted her, looking up from her computer screen. Sondra wore winter white today, with jade jewelry, and looked fantastic. "He'll be five or ten minutes. He's just flown up from Florida. Would you like coffee?"

"No, thank you. I'll just wait."

Cilla strode to the beautifully appointed waiting area and lowered herself into an upholstered couch, reaching out for a copy of *Cybelle,* a glossy quarterly publication that the corporation used as part of its press kit.

"I'm so sorry for everything that has happened," Sondra said after a few minutes.

Cilla looked up sharply. "Yes, it is very much a shame I expected better of this company."

"I know, and I've spoken to Dom about this at length,"

said the executive secretary. "I've spoken out on your behalf, and Karyn's."

"Thank you," Cilla said, realizing that Sondra was a powerful ally.

In a moment, Sondra's private line rang, and she said a
few words into the phone, then nodded to Cilla. "He'd like
you to go in now."

Cilla rose, drawing a deep breath.

She walked down the hall to the CEO's office, knocking
on the door and then entering.

"Well, Cilla, hello." Dom Carrara, looking suntanned and
fit, was standing in the middle of his office with a putter
and a small putting device to hit balls into. He was in shirtsleeves, with no tie, and his full head of prematurely white
hair was rumpled, apparently from repeatedly running his
hands through it. Not the way he usually appeared to his
employees.

"Good afternoon. Thank you for seeing me," Cilla said.

Carrara put the putter away in a closet and invited Cilla
to sit down on a leather couch with him, near the window.

"See that view down there?" he said, pointing to the six-
lane street below, already beginning to clog up with the first
of the rush hour traffic. "I look out at it every day, and I
think that thousands of those people, a bigger and bigger
percentage every day, are shopping at Cybelle, or wishing
they could afford to."

"It's an exciting thought," Cilla said, uncertain where this
was leading.

"Yes, very exciting. Cilla, I want you to know that that
Jazzy line you sponsored is one of the innovations that is
going to take Cybelle into the year 2001 and beyond. Lou
tried to take the credit but I was informed where the idea
came from. It was brilliant."

Cilla clasped her hands tightly in her lap, then released
them, trying to keep her body language relaxed. "Dom, Lou
did a lot more than just take credit for my ideas. He sexually

harassed not only me but my secretary, Karyn Cristophe, and dozens of other Cybelle employees over the years. He made our jobs a living hell and he openly and blatantly threatened to have us fired if we didn't comply. As you know, there is proof of these allegations."

"The audiotape," said Dom, his face stone serious.

"Yes."

"You know it probably won't stand up in court."

"No, it probably won't. But you heard it, and you recognized Lou's voice and you know in your heart that tape is genuine."

Dom gazed at Cilla. "Yes, I do. I've met with Lou Hechter's attorney and we are arranging his severance package. Unfortunately, that may not be enough to stop the lawsuit that was filed this week against Cybelle by Karyn Cristophe in the amount of twenty million dollars."

"Yes, Karyn told me."

"People think that a Fortune 50 corporation like Cybelle has deep pockets, and they like to shoot for the moon."

Cilla flushed. "Lou fired me unreasonably," she began.

"Why didn't you come to me about this harassment?"

Cilla's eyes moistened. "Because it started when Vic Rondelli was CEO, and Lou was his crony. And when you first came, I didn't know you. And by then—I didn't see any way out. I'm going to be a witness in the lawsuit. I am sure they will subpoena me."

"I see." Carrara walked back to his desk and sank heavily into his swivel chair. "Cilla, this presents problems. We are required by law not to retaliate against you, but that's all on paper; it doesn't mean shit in the real world. There will be plenty of resentment against both you and Karyn if you remain here. I've tried to protect her, but people are people. Lou's friends will be your enemies, and they'll be out to get you in a big way. He'll probably orchestrate it himself from home, and you know what a wily political infighter Lou can be when he wishes."

"Yes. I . . . I see."

Carrara steepled his hands, frowning. "The thing is, you're a real asset to the corporation, or you were. I'd go so far as to say you were a rising star."

Cilla nodded, rising quickly. Disappointment seared her like acid. Girlrags. All her hopes about that now were sliding away, impossible to recapture. Her being a witness in the sexual harassment suit made her situation here impossible. "Well, thank you for your time."

"Whoa. Wait a minute. Sit down."

Cilla lowered herself back into the couch.

"I'm not trying to fire you. I want to keep you. I just want to figure out how."

"Just let me keep my job. I'm sure I can work out any problems."

Carrara thought a moment. "I need to do some housekeeping around here, Cilla. There is an element that I inherited from Rondelli, along with Rondelli himself. Jay Gaines, Chuck Krantz, a few others. These people contributed to an atmosphere around here that I can no longer tolerate. I'm going to set some early-retirement packages in motion. This is all very confidential, do you understand me?"

"Yes." She was perspiring lightly. Did he really mean to help her?

"Meanwhile, I'm putting you back on the payroll. You'll receive the same benefits and salary package as you were getting before, but you'll be working at home heading up a three-hundred-thousand-dollar market research study we've just commissioned. Phone interviews and focus groups in six cities. You'll be our liaison with the research firm. That will keep you busy and politically safe until I can clean house and decide where to put you next."

Cilla nodded. "And my secretary, Karyn?"

"I've had her put in Accounting. She'll be off the beaten

track and maybe the wolves will leave her alone. Let's hope."

Cilla got to her feet again. "Well, I thank you for what you've been able to do for me, Dom, and I'm sure Karyn is grateful, too."

"But not so grateful she'll withdraw her suit," he said wryly.

"Probably not."

"I'll messenger you a copy of the specs for the research and the proposal submitted by the research firm. You'll deal with the project director, and you'll make sure everything is running along the time line that was set up. You'll communicate with me by phone and E-mail, and the company will provide you with a fax machine, laser printer, scanner, copier—any type of office equipment you need."

Roger hadn't seen his little girl, Anna, at Christmas because the child and her mother had been with his ex-wife's parents. Now he flew out to Carlsbad, California, near San Diego, to spend a week with his daughter and take her to all of the tourist attractions.

Karyn's parents phoned. Karyn reassured her mother that she was fine, but her mother was worried about the lawsuit and concerned that the company wasn't treating Karyn right. "You're an administrative secretary, not an accounting clerk."

"It's boring work," Karyn admitted. She wasn't going to tell her parents about the obscene, anonymous calls from Lou's cronies. "But I'm surviving it, and it's tolerable."

"You should quit," said Holly Cristophe. "There must be other jobs out there, just as good."

"I'm not going to give them the satisfaction."

Karyn sat at her computer, entering check amounts into the Solomon software program, using the right-hand keypad as

he other women did, working it like a cash register keyboard. Her speed was going up every day.

Her first few weeks here had been mostly filing and sorting. Nothing in Accounting was a small job. If you filed,
there were stacks and stacks. If you sorted, there were usually big binders full of printouts or thick reports that took
hours to carefully check. When checking numbers you had
to slide a ruler down the list so you wouldn't look at the
wrong figure. It was grueling work that hurt both the eyes
and the back.

Still, she was finally doing some higher level work now,
even if it was only entering numbers. And Madelyn Vigo,
true to her word, had spoken to the other clerks, who had
stopped asking her about the lawsuit. Most of them ignored
Karyn, but a few had begun to say "Hi," and Karyn would
say "Hi" back. If she stayed here long enough it would not
be so bad.

Her phone rang, and Karyn reluctantly picked it up, remembering the phone calls she'd received from Lou's
friends for more than three weeks. Lou Hechter's cronies
hadn't let her alone, quickly getting her new extension number.

Karyn had stood the calls as long as she could, then she'd
been forced to go to Madelyn Vigo again.

"Those SOBs," said Madelyn with feeling. "I'm going to
go to Randy Caravaglio about this. Nobody treats one of
my people like this."

"Thank you so much," Karyn said. She realized she'd
totally misjudged Madelyn, reading her as a dull, dry, bean
counter.

"No problem. I'll talk to Randy now."

And Madelyn had. Within a few hours the calls stopped.
Karyn would never know how he did it, but Caravaglio had
accomplished a miracle. Later, Karyn encountered Caravaglio in the hallway and he'd greeted her cordially, telling her

he'd already heard good things about her work in the department. He'd seemed sincere—and nice.

Thank God there were men like Randy Caravaglio, Roger Canton, and many others she'd worked with here at Cybelle, decent people who treated women well. Those men made the office a fun place to be in. They helped women, not hindered them. She had to hang on to that idea, especially now. She didn't want to become bitter because of Lou and a few jerks like him.

Karyn's fingers flew as she added more check amounts, careful to be accurate.

The depositions were coming up in two more weeks.

The beginning of her case . . . She was scared, as she'd never been before.

She had to win. She had to!

One day Malia called Karyn with some bad news.

"Honey, I don't want to alarm you but the other side has got something they're going to use against you. Apparently they've been researching your employment history, all the way back. And something's come up."

"What is it?"

"It's—well, I'm afraid it has to do with your ex husband."

"Mack?" Karyn felt a stab of fear.

"You met him on the job, right?"

"Well, yes. We were both working for this auto dealership in Atlanta. A Ford dealership."

"And what was his position there?"

"He was a salesman; I was a cashier."

"And you started having sex with him while you were still working there?"

"No. We didn't make love until our wedding night."

"Karyn, they've got a deposition from a woman who' the head cashier there, some woman named Betty Slocum and she says she walked into an empty office and caught ou and Mack, well, getting pretty hot and heavy."

Karyn sucked in her breath in shock. She'd forgotten all
bout that day. "But . . . but that was years ago! And we
ever—I mean, we were just kissing—"

"They've already deposed this Slocum woman, and she
ays it sounded more like you were having sex, Karyn."

"I told you, I was a virgin when I married Mack," Karyn
nsisted sharply.

"I know that, Karyn, but I'm just telling you that the other
ide has a deposition from Betty Slocum and they've also
eposed your ex-husband. His deposition claims that you
nd he frequently met in that unused office to kiss and neck
nd at one time he exposed your breasts."

"Oh!" Karyn uttered a despairing cry. "He did it before I
ould stop him. Malia, that was so long ago; I was just a
id then. He was all over me, and I was flattered, I guess.
: wasn't . . . dirty. I married him; he became my *husband*."

"Well, that's the only bad thing they've been able to dig
p about your previous employment, but that lawyer Wallin
; going to make it appear as if you were easy to get, at
:ast once, so maybe you were easy to get a second time,
o. And if we get the wrong kind of jury, they might be-
eve it. Lawsuits are all a big crapshoot, honey. Even when
ou believe you have a sure thing, there's still about a thirty
ercent chance the jury will screw you."

"But—that's so unfair!" Karyn's eyes filled with angry
:ars. Mack was angry at her for divorcing him, getting an
ijunction against him, taking Amber north. He was unpre-
ictable. What if he lied under oath? She breathed deeply,
ying to control herself.

"Calm down, Karyn. This is just part of discovery, finding
it what the other team has. We have plenty of heavy-duty
mmunition, too, don't forget."

But after the call was finished, Karyn went into her small
tchen and microwaved herself a cup of coffee, her heart

filled with sudden dread. Malia had warned her that a lawsuit could be very stressful, and now she could see why.

The early-February morning Karyn was to give her deposition was cold and snowy, traffic snarled up because of drifting snow and several fender-benders. The depositions were to be given in the office of the outside law firm that Cybelle had hired, a firm called Buskin, Devers, Goodenough and Wallin. Their offices were on Telegraph Road, in Bingham Farms.

According to Malia, Cybelle's own legal department would serve as advisers, sitting "second chair," but the company was going with Barry Wallin, a tough, aggressive, accomplished litigator, as their counsel. Cilla Westheim's own "friend," Shane Gancer, had withdrawn from the case pleading personal involvement. That, Cilla hoped, would shield her from having him know *every* shameful detail about what she and Lou had done.

"Now remember everything I told you," Malia said as they waited in a small, empty conference room for a few minutes before the depositions were to begin. Tall windows gave views of a freshly plowed parking lot.

Malia went on, "When you answer the questions, always pause a little in case I want to object—that'll give me time to do it. Listen to the whole question before you start answering. You'd be surprised how many people just jump right in before the question is even done and somehow they say the wrong thing. Only answer the question that was asked, don't keep rambling on and explaining. The more you say, the more openings you give the other side."

Karyn nodded; they'd been over this two or three times already. "I'm kind of nervous," she confessed.

"You don't have anything to be nervous about—I'm here and my job is to protect your rights at all times, Karyn. You're going to do fine. Just go in there and tell the truth, that's all you need to do."

The conference room where the depositions were to be taken doubled as a law library, its floor-to-ceiling bookshelves crammed with legal tomes. A middle-aged female court reporter had set up her machine at a small side table. A video technician had also set up his equipment and would be videotaping all of the depositions. This was the current trend in depositions now. Malia called it "extra insurance" if a witness died or could not appear in court.

They were the first to enter the room.

"Have a chair," Malia invited, breezily seating herself.

Karyn sat down next to Malia at the long, polished conference table, making an effort to appear calm. She was wearing a navy blue blazer, a white blouse, and a lighter blue skirt, her hair combed neatly back from her face. On Malia's advice she wore light makeup for the camera.

They heard footsteps and four men entered the room. One of the men was David Nichols, an attorney for Cybelle. He introduced another Cybelle lawyer, and then Barry Wallin, counsel for Buskin, Devers, Goodenough and Wallin. Wallin was the litigator who would defend Cybelle.

"Good morning, Ms. Cristophe, Ms. Roberts," Wallin said genially. He was about forty, with sleek black hair, a slender man who reminded Karyn of Pee Wee Herman without the humor. She felt sure his put-on geniality would last only a few minutes, and after that he'd be as aggressive as a ferret.

The last man to enter the room was Lou Hechter. Karyn sucked in her breath. Her former employer was dressed today in a dark gray suit that seemed loose on him. He had lost weight, his cheeks much more hollow than they'd been previously, but the aura of arrogance and entitlement still surrounded him. He glared at Karyn as if she were some ugly form of underwater animal life.

"Miss Karyn," he greeted her sneeringly.

Karyn reddened. Malia had warned her that Lou might try to intimidate her.

"Now, let's keep this meeting peaceful or I'll object and have Mr. Hechter removed," Malia said.

The three attorneys surrounded Lou and placed him in a seat at the far end of the table, as far away from Karyn as possible.

"Are we ready? Mr. Wallin will be asking questions for the defendant," said the Cybelle attorney, "Ms. Roberts for the plaintiff."

The preliminaries began with a formal introduction of all those present, which the court reporter dutifully typed into her machine for the record. Karyn was given an oath to tell the whole truth.

"Would you please state your full name for the record?" Wallin asked Karyn, smiling in a friendly manner.

"Karyn Anna Chadwick Cristophe," Karyn responded, her voice clear.

"Chadwick is your maiden name?"

"Yes."

"Do you have any children?"

"Yes, I have a daughter."

"What is her name?"

"Amber."

"How old is she?"

"Nine. She just had her birthday."

"And what is your profession, Ms. Cristophe?"

"I've worked as a secretary."

"How many years' experience do you have in secretarial work?"

Karyn paused to think. "Nine years," she responded.

The basics, the boring details needed to establish who Karyn was. The court reporter's fingers moved lightning fast, taking every word down. She was also audiotaping the proceedings as her own backup. From the other end of the table, Lou's eyes bored into Karyn, making her adrenalin flow.

She tried her best to follow Malia's instructions, her pulse

ate speeding up as she realized that soon she would be
elling these people about Lou Hechter's sexual behaviors.

"Okay," said Wallin. "Now let's go to that incident in the
ax room that you've mentioned in this little 'diary' you've
so assiduously kept. How big is that room?"

"About ten by twelve feet, I guess."

"And what sort of office equipment is in the room?"

"Two fax machines, one incoming and one outgoing. A.
ong table and a metal shelf with mail slots in it."

"Would you say that the room is a little cramped?"

"It was adequate for our work space," Karyn responded
cautiously.

"Isn't it true that occasionally if two or more people were
n the room they occasionally bumped into each other?"

"Yes."

"So when Lou Hechter bumped into you, as you state,
his was an event that did occasionally happen in that
oom?"

"Yes," Karyn admitted, her cheeks flushing. "But it
vas—"

"Isn't it true that when Mr. Hechter did accidentally bump
nto you, he moved away from you immediately as soon as
e discovered his error."

"Yes, but—"

"Let Ms. Cristophe respond to the question," interrupted
Malia.

"Yes, but it was the way he looked at me," Karyn ex-
lained. "Like . . . he knew he did it on purpose."

"Did Mr. Hechter apologize for colliding with you?"

"Yes," said Karyn, feeling defeated. At the end of the
able, Lou grinned as he leaned over to say something to
he Cybelle lawyer.

How are you holding up?" Malia asked Karyn during a
wenty-minute break. They took it in the smaller conference
oom, drinking Diet Pepsis and eating some pastries the law

firm had ordered sent up from a nearby bakery.

"I'll make it," said Karyn. Actually her stomach was ach
ing, and her appetite was completely gone. She took on
bite out of a cream-filled doughnut and put it back on th
paper plate, unable to finish it. "They're trying to make m
look like a jerk."

"They're just trying to use the same facts to paint a
entirely different picture. It's what lawyers do, Karyn. Jus
remember to keep on being honest and follow all the in
structions I gave you. You've doing great so far."

They were back in the conference room again. Lou chatte
with the Cybelle attorney, saying something in a low voic
and laughing. He presented the picture of confidence.

Now Malia was asking the questions.

"Ms. Cristophe, when you were told to go to Southfiel
to take notes for that meeting with the advertising firm, wer
you told that you would have to work late?" Snow outsid
the windows had started to fall down thicker—the road
would be slippery later.

"No. I wasn't."

"Were you informed that you would be expected to typ
up your notes and print them in a private hotel room rente
by Mr. Hechter?"

"No."

"Were there public areas in the hotel where you migh
have had access to a computer and printer?"

"Yes, they advertised they had a special section just fo
businesspeople. It had faxes, modems, printers and so forth.

"Were you surprised when Mr. Hechter told you to go t
a hotel room with him?"

"Yes."

"Why did you do it, Karyn?"

Karyn moistened her lips, feeling her eyes begin to wate
"Because he'd made it clear that I had to . . . if I wanted t
keep my job."

"Mrs. Cristophe, I know this is a very personal question, but what sort of financial resources do you have—beyond your job, I mean. Do you have a savings account?"

"Yes."

"How much money do you have in the account?"

"Around twenty-five hundred dollars."

"Where did you get it?" Malia wanted to know.

"My dad loaned it to me. I'm planning on paying him back in monthly payments."

"And do you have an IRA account?"

"I . . . no. I had to cash in my IRA account in order to move to Michigan."

"Do you own your car outright?"

"No. I'm making payments on it. A hundred-forty a month."

"And your rent is?"

"Seven-fifty a month."

"Do you receive any sort of child support?"

The questions about her financial situation went on.

"So you need your job very much, don't you, Ms. Cristophe?" Malia concluded.

Karyn wrung her hands in her lap, feeling them moist and sweaty. "Yes. My job is all I—was all I had."

"So when Mr. Hechter told you that you had to stay late and work on the notes in a private hotel room with him, you felt you had no other choice but to comply? Isn't that right?"

"Yes," Karyn whispered. "I was afraid to lose my job."

"How many times, over the course of the months you worked at Cybelle, did Mr. Hechter tell you directly that your job was dependent on your pleasing him and allowing his sexual advances?"

"I'm not sure." Karyn said, her voice shaking.

"One time? Two times?"

"He'd hint that my job depended on his—sufferance. And he was the boss. My boss's boss," she corrected herself.

"That alone made me feel he had the power. And then in the hotel he told me I'd better have sex with him if I wanted my job. Do it if I wanted a job on Monday, he said."

"And how did this make you feel?"

"I felt . . . very afraid." Karyn paused.

It went on, everything recorded by the court reporter and the video camera.

Malia took Karyn through the attempted rape in the hotel room step by agonizing step. Forced to relive it, Karyn felt perspiration begin to sheen her face. Her heart was thudding, and she felt as if she could scarcely breathe enough air.

"Exactly what did he do next, Karyn?"

"He got out some scissors and said he was going to cut my clothes off."

At the other end of the table, Lou was stony faced.

"How do you have such a clear memory of what he said?"

"I . . . I was afraid when I was told to go to a hotel with Mr. Hechter, so I took a tape-recorder with me. I tape-recorded what he did and said."

Malia turned to the pair of defendant's lawyers. "I would like to introduce this tape recording as a part of the discovery process."

Lou whispered to his attorneys, his face congested.

"Objection!" snapped Wallin, jumping up. "Plaintiff has no way to prove that it was really Mr. Hechter on that tape or that the tape hasn't been altered or tampered with."

An argument began over whether or not the tape should be introduced as evidence, Malia insisting that the tape was used by Karyn as an audio "diary," much like the written one that had already been placed into evidence, to refresh her memory of what had occurred.

"That tape is inflammatory!" cried Wallin. "It could have been prepared at any time or place, even by an actor, and if it's entered into evidence it will be very prejudicial to my client."

"But what's the difference between written notes and au-

io notes? You allowed Ms. Cristophe's diary to be admitted
ut now you're going to balk at a tape, even though it cor-
borates what the plaintiff says, testifying under oath?"

More arguments. Karyn felt her head begin to throb. It
as decided that a judge would make a decision on admis-
bility later, if the case actually went to trial. The attorneys
ecided to resume the deposition the following morning.

Karyn felt drained and wrung out as she got to her feet
d left the room, again walking down the hallway with
alia.

"But do you think the tape will be admitted?" she asked
er attorney when they reached the room that had been al-
tted to them. Karyn's voice was hoarse from talking so
ng, and she felt totally drained. She'd had no idea that
ving a deposition could be so physically tiring, although
alia had tried to warn her.

"I hope so, but if it doesn't, that won't stop me from
aying it for the defendant's attorneys in private, now, will
? Its big purpose, Karyn, is to notify them that we have
em down cold. We have the slimebag down on tape, and
yone who knows him is going to recognize his voice and
ey damn well know it. In fact, that's the main thing about
scovery, to let the opposite side know that we do have a
lluva good case. If and when the time comes to settle,
ey aren't going to discount us."

Karyn felt too tired to think. She just wanted this to be
er with. She thanked Malia and rose to leave, saying that
e had to get home to prepare dinner for Amber.

Malia had stayed behind to speak to the opposing attor-
ys, so Karyn was alone in the hallway as Lou Hechter
proached her.

She attempted to brush past him without speaking, but he
ood in front of her, blocking her way.

"Please let me pass," she said.

"You're not going to get away with this travesty," he told
r hoarsely.

"You're the one who started this, not me."

"No, *you're* the one who started it by waggling those sex
hips of yours."

Karyn had been intending to remain calm and try to ig
nore Lou as much as possible, but it had been a long, stres
ful day, and as soon as Lou mentioned "waggling her hips
she lost it.

"What's the matter, Lou? Are you upset because I'm n
your employee anymore and you can't control me? Or didn
you get your allotment of Viagra this week?"

Some women employees of the law firm were walkir
down the hallway, chatting about an office party, and Kary
seized the opportunity to back away from Lou and head f
the elevator.

Snow had been falling all day. Cilla sat in her home offi
studying a moderator's outline that had been submitted t
the market research firm.

The depositions on Karyn's case had started today, Cil
knew, and Malia Roberts had told her that she was sche
uled to be deposed the day after tomorrow. She'd been su
poenaed; there was no backing out now, not without bei
in contempt of court. Lou Hechter was going to get wh
was coming to him, she reflected. She felt a wild jolt
elation. She was going to tell the truth, every smidgen of
No matter what it cost her.

Her phone rang and she picked it up.

"Cilla, this is Dom Carrara."

"Hello, Dom."

They discussed the research project for a few minute
The focus groups would be held during the following tw
weeks in Detroit, Dallas, Los Angeles, Boston, New Yo
and Atlanta, each conducted in a local focus group facili
with viewing rooms where clients could observe from b
hind one-way glass. Cilla had booked herself to travel to a
five out-of-town locations.

"Have you read today's *Wall Street Journal* yet?" Dom finally asked. "Or looked at the news channel on Excite?"

"Why, no."

"Cybelle has finally completed the deal with Girlrags. It's ours now. And I need someone who can take charge and hit the ground running. I want to double the company's size in two years, triple it in four. I'd like to put you in as CEO, Cilla. You're the one I want. I've been saving this for you."

"As . . . my God . . ." For a moment she was totally speechless.

"Girlrags will be a subsidiary of Cybelle, and I'm the only one you have to report to. I'll support you in every way possible. There's an office building down on Big Beaver Road, and I happen to know the fifth floor is for lease. When the company gets bigger, you can expand, but if this is agreeable to you I'd like you to lease it as your temporary headquarters. I want you to bring in the top management people from Girlrags, the ones you want to keep. What do you say? I'd like a decision in the next day or two."

Cilla's mind raced. Her own company! And she'd be the CEO! Girlrags was small now, only twenty mall outlets, but she could grow it big. It would be a struggle at first to revive a failing chain, but Cilla knew she could do it. But best of all, she'd be autonomous. She could, in effect, start fresh.

"I don't need a day or two," she told Dom Carrara. "I think I can make that decision right now. The answer is yes."

After they completed their conversation, Cilla dropped the phone into its cradle, her heart jumping with excitement. She couldn't help doing a little dance around her office, raising her hands over her head in a cheerleader victory wave.

Her brain spun with plans. She'd keep the best of the Girlrags management, promise them a future if they produced, hunt down a few more young stars like Jazzy Kulture . . . oh, and she'd have to call Karyn, see if she'd be willing . . .

But she knew Karyn would be. This was just as great a chance for her as it was for Cilla.

Mindy called a few minutes later, and Cilla gave her daughter the exciting news.

"Mom . . . oh, Mom . . . that's super awesome!"

Cilla was close to crying with emotion. "Oh, Mindy! I'm going to be a CEO!"

"I knew you could do it, Mom. I'm so proud. I can't wait to tell my friends my mom's a CEO. They'll freak."

"Come home this weekend," Cilla begged. "Help me celebrate."

"You know I will, Mom. I'll even go out to dinner with you and Shane, just this once," Mindy specified, laughing a little. "See how grown-up I can be?"

"I love you just as you are," exulted Cilla.

Immediately on hanging up, Cilla called Shane, unable to stop bubbling over with joy and relief.

"Oh, Cilla, that's phenomenal. You are some woman." He seemed as pleased as she was. "Maybe you'll be a Don Carrara yourself someday."

"Wouldn't it be fantastic?" She laughed. "I could!" She wiped her eyes. "Oh, Shane, this is like finding the exit door of hell. There's a whole big world out there. And it's beautiful!"

"I love hearing you so happy," Shane murmured. "Just love it."

Her mood slid down a notch. "You know I'm testifying as Karyn's witness. It's going to be . . . rough. Some of the things I want to be private, Shane. It's not that I want to keep things from you but . . ."

"You don't have to say another word, darling. I'll never dig into your life and ferret out your secrets. I want you and love you just as you are—your past, present and future, no changes necessary."

Cilla smiled and couldn't stop.

* * *

Karyn dreaded the deposition the following morning, knowing that they were really going to rake her over the coals. She just knew it was going to be very unpleasant. Amber had a sleep-over that night, Roger was on a buying trip, and the apartment was going to seem very empty without her daughter.

When Raquel called, asking her to have dinner that night with her at Bennigan's, Karyn accepted with alacrity.

"So how's the trial going?" Raquel wanted to know when they'd each ordered strawberry margaritas.

"It's not a trial, it's depositions, and it's going horrible. It's really awful, Raquel," Karyn told her friend.

Raquel wanted to know all of the details, and Karyn told her what she could, keeping back some of the more private things in case Raquel gossiped later at work.

"The buttface. I'm glad he's getting what's coming to him," Raquel gloated. "His wife has dumped him, you know. Somebody told her about Lou and Cilla, and somehow the shit just hit the fan. Big, nasty, messy divorce. That woman isn't going to give him a quarter unless he washes her car windshield for it."

"I wonder who told his wife?" remarked Karyn.

Raquel stared at Karyn for a few seconds, her eyes wide. Then she burst into giggles. After a minute Karyn started giggling, too, and the two of them laughed so loudly that people sitting at nearby tables turned to see what they were laughing about. This only made them laugh harder.

"I never knew an anonymous call could be . . . so much fun," whooped Raquel, nearly choking on her drink.

It took them minutes to calm down, and finally Raquel told Karyn she had good news herself. "Yeah, I'm Sondra Zapernick's assistant now; Sondra asked for me special. She and her husband are going to retire to Arizona next year and she wants to train me! Money, money, perks, perks!" she exulted.

"Incredible!" cried Karyn, remembering how Raquel had always coveted Sondra's job.

"But it's way up there on the executive floor and I've gotta buy a complete new wardrobe. I have to dress like an executive, Sondra says. No more skirts and blouses, you know what I mean. Hey, maybe you and I can go shopping together. Your style—well, you could really class me up, Karyn."

"Sure, I'll shop with you," said Karyn, her heart warming Raquel was special. No matter where Karyn worked, she'd always want Raquel as a friend.

"And listen," added Raquel, her eyes glinting.

"What?"

"You know that guy I met at the health club that time? The one that gave me his business card I put in my sock?"

"Yeah?

"I saved the card. I called him last week. We're gonna have lunch tomorrow!"

"Really?" Karyn laughed with pleasure. "Oh, Raquel that's wonderful news."

"Now, don't get me engaged or anything. It isn't even a date-date, it's just lunch. But . . ." Raquel paused, then laughed again. "He still remembered me, and he sounded so cute over the phone."

Karyn looked down at her friend's left hand. "Are you going to take off Brett's ring when you have lunch with this guy?"

"I . . . I might put it in my pocket," Raquel admitted.

Maybe it was the dinner with Raquel, or just the fact that a human being couldn't go night after night without sleeping no matter how upset she was. For the first night in a long time, Karyn actually slept through the entire night, waking up feeling reasonably refreshed. She even managed to eat half a bagel for breakfast.

                    *   *   *

"Ms. Cristophe, did you find Lou Hechter an attractive man?" Wallin began, fixing Karyn with his sharp, alert eyes, a faint smile on his face.

She hesitated. "No."

"You mean you did *not* find him attractive?"

"That's what I said."

Wallin frowned, obviously displeased with the way this line of questioning was going. Had Lou convinced him otherwise; making him believe that Karyn found him good-looking, sexy? She stared back at the attorney, looking him in the eye.

"Do you like kinky sex, Ms. Cristophe?"

"What?" Karyn said, unable to believe she had heard him correctly.

"Role playing, S&M, pretending you're getting a little beating or a little rape?"

"No!" she snapped.

"You played a sex game with Mr. Hechter, isn't that true?"

"No!" Karyn was rigid with fear and disgust. "Never."

"Objection." Malia sighed. "These questions are salacious, insulting and repetitive."

But Wallin wasn't yet finished. "Don't you have a history of engaging in sexual behavior while on the job, Ms. Cristophe?"

"I . . . No. I don't."

"Isn't it true that you were caught in a compromising position with Mack Cristophe in 1989 in Atlanta, Georgia, at the Reynolds-Witter Ford dealership?"

Karyn shook her head, hating the man for twisting her life like this. "The man became my *husband*," she emphasized.

"Answer the question. Weren't you caught half nude in a spare office at the dealership, with your naked breasts plainly visible?"

Karyn swallowed, her skin covered in sweat. "I was

twenty years old and Mack was all over me. I didn't mean harm. We were in love. I later—"

"So you allowed him to take off your blouse and bra?"

"Yes," admitted Karyn, so tense that she felt as if she might fly out of her chair. She gazed pleadingly at Malia.

"Time for a much-needed break," announced Malia, getting up before anyone could object. They all walked out of the room, Lou eyeing Karyn with obvious gloating. It was obvious he was very pleased with the way Wallin had had her squirming.

In the small conference room, Karyn gulped down a Diet Pepsi, struggling not to cry. "Malia . . . I'm ruining everything."

"No, you're not, baby. In court the jurors are going to dislike Wallin if he treats you like that. They'll go over to your side, dear. This is all part of what you have to do to get the jury to hate Lou Hechter."

But Karyn still felt very shaken.

"Remember, keep your answers short. Don't volunteer anything," advised Malia, squeezing Karyn's hand.

The grilling began again.

"Isn't it true that you were willing to do almost anything to advance in your job?"

Karyn recoiled, hoping Malia would again object, but she did not.

"No, I was not!" she snapped.

"Oh, come now, Ms. Cristophe. Wasn't it true that Cybelle paid extremely excellent benefits to its employees?"

"Yes, it did."

"And didn't you receive a very nice raise when you were taken on as a full-time employee?"

"Yes."

"And didn't you yourself know something sexual might be going to happen when you agreed to go to the meeting at the Four Towers Hotel?"

"I was afraid—"

"So you took a mini-cassette tape recorder down to the hotel with you, right, Ms. Cristophe."

"Yes," she admitted anxiously, sweat starting to collect underneath her arms again.

"You did it because you *knew* he would make advances."

"I had no choice but to go there if I wanted to keep my job."

"The fact that you took the tape recorder signifies that you were aware something 'might' happen, isn't that true, Ms. Cristophe?"

"I knew he would sexually harass me."

"And you were intending to allow it, weren't you, Ms. Cristophe?"

She stared at the attorney, fear warring in her with a terrible, fierce anger. They were accusing her of being an office whore who slept with the boss to get ahead. Worse than that, a loose woman who regularly engaged in sexual activities in the workplace.

Then she looked at Lou and saw that he was grinning salaciously. His white teeth gleamed. He was enjoying every minute of her humiliation. He'd probably been looking forward to this moment for weeks.

Whoa.

Karyn placed both of her hands flat on the table top in front of her. To hell with Malia's instructions. This was her life, her reputation.

She spat out, "I was *not* intending to allow it. I loathed the man. I was terrified of him. I had made up my mind that I was going to file a lawsuit and I wanted to get some proof so he couldn't come back and say that I 'wanted' it or 'asked for it,' or that anything we did was 'consensual'!" Karyn's voice rose. "*It was not consensual. There was nothing consensual about it.* I never accepted his advances—not once. I would have slit my throat before I slept with that—that monster."

"Hey!" cried Lou.

"Objection!" shouted Wallin.

Malia was touching her arm, but Karyn shook her attorney free.

"I loved my job, yes. I needed my job. But I wanted this man stopped." She glared at Lou Hechter. "He was making my days there a living hell. I couldn't sleep. My stomach was hurting me every day, I had headaches every day, I couldn't sleep at night, I was getting to be a wreck. He had no right! He had absolutely no right! He used his position! He used his rank against me! He felt entitled because he made two hundred thousand dollars a year and I made only twenty-six thousand. He felt entitled because he was a man! He thought he could threaten me into—"

"Ms. Cristophe, you must wait for me to ask you questions," began Wallin in a severe tone.

Karyn lifted her chin defiantly. "I will not be a prostitute for my employer. He could *not* do that to me. I would not allow it; I *will* not allow it. That's why I filed this lawsuit. *I will not. I will never*—"

"Bitch!" Lou burst out from the other end of the table.

Heads swiveled as everyone turned to stare, the court reporter uttering a tiny, startled cry.

"You little bitch. You flirted with me. You waved your ass at me. You wanted it, you wanted everything you got." The Cybelle attorney was trying to hush him up, but Lou would not be stopped. "Oh, yes, Ms. Cristophe. You dangled it in front of me. What's a man supposed to do when that happens? When something is offered to me, I take it. Why shouldn't I? It's free. *It's one of the perks of my goddamned job.*"

"Keep on talking," Malia Roberts drawled. "This is all very, very interesting, Mr. Hechter, especially as it's going to appear in the transcript and be a part of the discovery evidence. We *will* use it in court."

"All right," snapped Wallin. "I'd say it's time to adjourn

for the evening. We'll convene again tomorrow morning to depose Cilla Westheim and Nancy Shertzen."

Chairs scraped as they all got to their feet. The opposition lawyers for Cybelle were huddling together, their expressions grim.

Karyn and Malia walked down the hall. Karyn felt unsteady on her feet, the adrenaline having drained out of her so rapidly her knees wobbled. She felt as if she'd been in a train wreck.

"I guess I really screwed it up," she said to Malia.

"Well, you certainly spoke your mind." But Malia was smiling. "But, hey, Lou the creep also spoke his, didn't he? And it's right there on videotape, audiotape and as part of the stenographic transcript. We have him nailed down three ways."

"I can't believe he'd do that," said Karyn, beginning to realize what this might mean.

"Some men think with their penis," said Malia. "It leads them right into hell and they don't even care. Look at Bill Clinton and Gary Hart and John F. Kennedy and about a thousand other politicians who put getting a little piece of nooky over their honor and their public position. Say," she added, "those jerk-offs are in a huddle right now, and I think they're going to come at us with an offer we can't refuse. Let's you and I go out and have a drink. I don't know about you but I could sure as hell use one. Then I'll phone Mr. Wallin and we'll see just what he has to say."

Karyn wasn't in the mood for a drink, but she forced herself to have a glass of wine. She listened to some of Malia's "war" stories, but her heart wasn't in it. She felt so tired, so dirtied from Lou's ugly outburst. She wanted to wash him off her skin again, heave up the breathed air he'd released in the conference room.

Malia told Karyn to go home and she'd call her as soon as she had any sort of news.

Karyn did as she was told. Her entire body kept flushing

hot and cold, and she felt sick to her stomach with tension.

Malia called about two hours later, as Karyn was preparing tacos for her and Amber's dinner.

"Karyn . . . I have good news or bad news, depending on how you want to look at it."

"Yes?" Karyn held on tightly to the phone, her fingers starting to perspire. "Oh, please, tell me and get it over with."

"Your deposition scared the pants off Lou's lawyers. Plus his ill-timed tirade was the final blow. They're taking us very seriously now, and they've given us a settlement offer."

Karyn could scarcely breathe. "Yes?"

"Seven million dollars."

"Seven?" Karyn repeated dumbly. The number could have been 76 or 776, she could barely get it to enter her mind.

"That's an excellent offer, and I'm advising you to take it. For one thing, if we refuse and go to trial, we're putting everything up for grabs again. Yes, the case looks good, and yes, we have great witnesses, but we'll also be going in front of a jury, and juries are notably capricious. That testimony from the woman at the car dealership in Atlanta can be used against you, and you saw how they went into the office whore song and dance. All they have to do is offend a juror or two, some old lady on Social Security who's jealous because you might get a big settlement, or maybe some old fart who's harassed the women at his own office, and it could swing things the wrong way."

"Oh—"

"Karyn, listen," said Malia. "We aimed at the stars and we're going to get the moon. That's not so bad, is it? By the time we split the fee and you pay off the woman from NOW, your share will be around four and a half million. You can invest that in variable annuities—mutual funds—whatever, and never have to worry about money again. I'l help you find a reputable financial planner if you don't have one."

Karyn knew this was one of the most important decisions she would ever have to make. It would affect her and Amber's lives forever.

"I need to think," she said nervously.

"Call me back tomorrow morning at nine o'clock, honey. I want to grab this offer while it's hot."

Karyn agreed and hung up.

She continued automatically to shred cheese, chop lettuce, fry hamburger, warm up the mild taco sauce that Amber liked.

Settling. It would be so easy. It would end all of this stress. Write her a check, and presto, it was all over. She could take the money and quit her job at Cybelle, never have to work again if she didn't want to.

Still, Lou's outburst in the attorney's office today reverberated in her mind.

You dangled it in front of me. What's a man supposed to do when that happens? . . . It's one of the perks of my goddamned job.

If she wimped out now, other men like Lou would not learn their lesson.

It would go on and on. . . .

She picked up the phone and dialed Malia. The attorney picked up so fast that the first ring wasn't even finished.

"Yes?"

"I'm not settling."

"You sure?"

"Yes. Even if we don't win twenty million I'll bet we still win more than seven million, a whole lot more. I want to do it," Karyn insisted. "I want to go for it. The big payoff."

Malia Roberts expelled her breath in a long, long sigh, as if she'd been holding it for weeks. "Now that's what I wanted to hear from you, girlfriend. But I wanted to give you every chance to play safe."

"I don't want to play it safe."

"I know you don't. Oh, girl. Oh, my. We are gonna take those people and run 'em through the shredder, yes, we are." Malia crowed jubilantly. "We're going all the way on this one."

EPILOGUE

FLOOR-TO-CEILING WINDOWS ON TWO WALLS OVER-looked Troy's multilaned Big Beaver Road, where criss-crossing traffic was blurred by onslaughts of falling snow.

Cilla Westheim had finally finished moving the last of her new furniture, bookshelves and filing cabinets into her new office at Girlrags. A beige leather couch and chair were being delivered tomorrow, and Cilla was bringing a wall hanging from home. On one wall she'd hung a U.S. map with pins stuck in it to denote locations of the Girlrags mall stores. Existing stores had blue pins. New ones would get red pins, so she could easily see just how far she was coming, and how fast. Later, Cilla planned, there would be Canadian and European maps. This was her chance and she was going to run with it.

But best of all, the brass sign outside the office read CILLA WESTHEIM, PRESIDENT.

A title she'd achieved at such great cost.

And she'd even been able to bring Karyn Cristophe along with her, offering Karyn a position as her personal assistant and right hand. Karyn wanted to come, even though she'd decided to go ahead with her suit against Cybelle and might win millions. And if she could convince Karyn to take college courses in merchandising . . . Who knew? If Karyn was smart and worked her tail off, and if Girlrags grew the way Cilla intended it to, in twenty more years Karyn might be a vice president herself.

Cilla sighed with pleasure. She felt relaxed for the first time in years . . . as hopeful and optimistic as she'd been when she first went into retailing, over twenty-five years ago.

"Cilla? May I come in?"

Startled out of her reverie, Cilla jumped. Shane Gancer entered Cilla's new office, wearing a white-on-white striped shirt and a blue paisley tie loosened at the neck. The shirt emphasized the wideness of his shoulders, the deep Lake Michigan blue of his eyes. Some people would call him a hunk, Cilla thought, for the first time without nervousness. Some might see only the superficial man, but Cilla knew that Shane was kind, humorous, loving, sexy—everything she'd ever wanted in a man.

He gazed around approvingly at the furniture. "Need help hanging a few pictures? I happen to be terrific at lining them up straight, and I also happen to have a hammer, picture hooks and some picture wire with me."

Cilla laughed joyously. "You're wonderful."

"Of course I am." His smile lit up his face. He walked toward Cilla, closing the office door behind him, and then scooped her into his arms. "Cilla, Cilla," he whispered into her neck. "I'm so proud of you. Your courage overwhelms me."

Cilla closed her eyes, nuzzling into his shoulder. "Standing up to Lou didn't feel courageous at the time. It felt miserable. And it's not over with. When the case goes to trial I'll have to testify again. Karyn is the one with the real courage, not me. I wish I had half of her strength."

"But you did it. I love you so much, darling. Will we be together tonight?"

"We certainly will."

"Your place or mine?"

A smile tugged at her lips. "For tonight, my place. But maybe in the future there could be an 'our place.'"

He pulled away to eye her sharply. "Are you sure? A commitment? It's not going to be a one- or two-year thing with me, a short-term fling, then I walk away. I'm not walking. You know that."

"I know it."

"I want it to be a lifetime deal. I won't move in with you unless it is."

She nodded solemnly.

He went on, "You know it's not going to be the easiest thing. . . . There'll be drawbacks, jealousies, definitely gossip."

"So?" Her smile widened. "If I can survive what went on around here in the last few months and come out as well as I have, I can survive anything, Shane. I love you . . . I love you. . . ."

They embraced again, their mouths seeking each other hungrily. Cilla felt hot, happy tears sting her eyes, but she blinked them away and grabbed him tighter.

Karyn Cristophe let herself into her apartment building, flakes of snow dotting her hair and the shoulders of her winter coat. Her hand shook a little as she inserted the key. What a long day it had been, getting her office squared away at Girlrags—a real office, not just an alcove!—and helping Cilla with a hundred and one things, most of them simultaneous, all of them urgent.

Karyn could already see that she was going to be just as much an executive as Cilla was. And she'd loved it.

She was back working at Girlrags, and had received a raise. And the way Cilla had talked to her . . . it seemed like the sky was the limit as far as her job might go.

Walking down the apartment building's hall, Karyn stopped short, staring at what lay on the floor in front of her own door.

Two huge floral arrangements swathed in green paper.

Uttering a little cry, Karyn knelt down and began peeling away the paper, eager to see who had sent her flowers.

"Your first day on the job. Go for it, girlfriend," said the card signed in Malia Roberts's splashy scrawl. "Let's make you a multimillionaire, okay?"

The other card was from Roger Canton. "Just thinking of

you today and so proud. You're the greatest. Love, Roger."

Karyn scooped up both arrangements, balancing them with her shoulder bag, and deposited them inside the doorway before continuing on upstairs to pick up Amber from Jinny. Her heart was pounding; her pulse beat loud in her ears.

A millionaire? It didn't really seem possible. And she just did not want to think that far ahead, for fear the money might not come. Still, there was a strange feeling of vindication inside her, and a vast, vast relief. It was over. The worst of it. She had come out ahead, with a wonderful job she knew she was going to love, with a dazzling future ahead of her.

That meant a lot more than a legal settlement.

"You look smiling happy today," Amber chirped as Karyn picked her up.

"I really am, Amber." They walked downstairs.

"Did your boss say good things?" the savvy little girl wanted to know as they walked into their own apartment, Missy prowling up to greet them. The cat meowed and rubbed both of their legs, until Amber reached down and scooped her up, dangling the animal on her right hip.

"Yes, cupcake, she did. She said great things. And . . . and we're really going to stay here a long time. A long, long time."

"I *knew* we were," said Amber, her eyes bright.

"How did you know that, sweetie?"

" 'Cause you got me my Missy kitty. That's how I knew," said the child in triumph.

Karyn laughed, pulling her daughter to her and ruffling her hair.